I0691824

the
echo
of
regret

JILLIAN LIOTA

This book is a work of fiction. While reference might be made to actual historical events or existing locations, the names, characters, places and incidents are either the product of the author's imagination or are used fictitiously, and any resemblance to any actual persons, living or dead, business establishments, events, or locales is entirely coincidental.

Copyright © 2024 by Jillian Liota

All rights reserved. In accordance with the U.S. Copyright Act of 1976, the scanning, uplo¬ading, and electronic sharing of any part of this book without the permission from the author is unlawful piracy and theft of the author's intellectual property. Thank you for your support of the author's rights.

Love Is A Verb Books

Book Cover Design and Layout by Blue Moon Creative Studio

Cover Photo by Regina Wamba

Editing by C. Marie

ISBN 978-1-952549-41-0 (paperback)
ISBN 978-1-952549-39-7 (eBook)
ISBN 978-1-952549-40-3 (kindle)

for Julie

<3

chapter one
bishop

"I have a half-caff latte and an americano for Bam!"

Stepping forward to the drink counter to grab my order, I nod at the barista, who I recognize from high school. Doesn't matter where I go in this town—that nickname has stuck to me like glue for as long as I can remember. When you hold a record at your smalltown high school for most home runs in a single baseball season and your initials are B.A.M., it's easy for a moniker like that to take hold and never let go.

I eye the two drinks then glance down at my left arm resting tightly against my chest in a sling. One of the many inconveniences I'm facing with this stupid cast is shit like this. All I want to do is carry two cups of coffee outside. Instead, I have to ask for help.

"Hey, would you mind grabbing me a tray?" I motion to my arm.

"Oh, sure. Gimme just a sec." She dips down behind the counter for a few seconds before her smiling face returns with a cardboard drink holder. "Sorry about that. Didn't even think about it."

I shrug, watching as she slips both drinks into the little slots. "No worries."

"How'd the surgery go? Is it true you won't be able to play anymore?"

I freeze for just a beat but manage to keep the easy smile. "Nah, everything went great. I'll be better than ever next season." I pick up the tray and raise it slightly in her direction. "Thanks again. See you around."

I turn, slipping quickly but carefully through the folks standing around the counter waiting for their own morning caffeine boost. I focus on the door, not wanting any more interactions like that one, before finally pushing out onto Main Street. The cool, early autumn morning is a balm on my soul, and I take a deep breath, inhaling the fresh, crisp air.

It doesn't surprise me that word has spread that I'm home... and home with an injury at that. Even so, I don't like knowing people are already speculating about whether I'll be able to play anymore. I've had surgery, and I have a rehabilitation plan I'll be following to the letter. What I need right now is relentless optimism, not people asking questions that lean toward the negative.

I drop into a seat at one of the open tables in front of Ugly Mug, set the tray down, then take a few seconds to adjust the straps of my sling that are starting to rub uncomfortably against my neck.

I'm no stranger to injuries. It's rare to be an athlete and never face a broken, pulled, or twisted *something*, but I've never had to have surgery before. Never had to wear a cast and try to keep my wrist as immobile as possible.

Yeah, can't say I'm a fan.

Slipping my cup from the tray, I raise it to my mouth and take a sip of the same caffeinated beverage I've ordered since I was barely a teenager. The piping hot liquid bursts onto my tongue, the warm melody of roasted beans and milk the perfect way to jumpstart the morning.

Sighing, I settle more into my chair and tilt my head back, closing my eyes and taking another deep breath. As much as being back in Cedar Point isn't ideal, the familiarity of a Monday morning on Main Street eases some of the anxiousness that's been a weight on my chest ever since I arrived home last week. I've been kind of tired and achy, holed up in my childhood home after my surgery, and it feels good to get outside.

"Hey, man. Sorry I'm late."

My head turns at the sound of Rush's voice, and I smile at the sight of him. I push to standing and we embrace briefly.

"No worries, man," I say, patting him on the back a few times with my good arm. "None at all. Just stoked to see you."

He pulls back, a grin on his face. Then his eyes fall to my sling-encased arm, and he shakes his head.

"Seriously, I can't believe your luck."

I scoff as we both take a seat. "It wasn't luck. Trust me." I push the tray his direction and motion to his americano.

"Thanks." Picking up his cup, he takes a sip, eyeing me over the lid as he does. "So, how've you been feeling?

"Ah, you know. It hurts a bit still. But surgery went well, and that's all I can hope for."

Rush rolls his eyes. "Cut the shit, Bam. I'm not some reporter."

I pick up my own drink, chuckling. "Not shitting you, Rush. Things are fine. I'm gonna be better than ever once this thing has healed up. It's just inconvenient, that's all."

Fine and inconvenient: two words I've been using far too much. But what else am I supposed to say?

That I'm scared?

That I fucked up?

That there is a part of me—however small it might be—that worries I've done lasting damage to the body I've worked so relentlessly to hone?

Those are things I barely allow myself to think. I'm definitely not voicing anything like that out loud. Besides, those are the thoughts of someone who doesn't believe they'll be back, and I know I will be.

It's all that optimism that winds its way through my veins, keeps me looking on the bright side, trusting that everything will work itself out. It's been my greatest strength, my greatest ally, for as long as I can remember. It's gotten me through a few smaller injuries. It's gotten me through my hard days, my tough moments, my breakups. It will get me through this, too, and then I'll be back.

I know it.

"Well, if it's just *inconvenient*," he says, stressing the last word with a smirk, "maybe I can talk you into helping out with Fall Ball." Rush pauses, assessing me for a moment. "The team could use a batting coach. If you're up for it."

My eyebrows rise, both surprised by the offer and unsure if I should take it.

Rush and I have been friends for years—ever since Little League when we were both scraggly versions of who we are today—so my default desire is, of course, to help him whenever he needs it. He's the PE teacher at the high school and was just promoted to head coach of the baseball team last year. Last time we talked, he mentioned the workload was a bitch and he needed extra help, but I never imagined I'd be the guy he asked.

"You paying?" I joke with a grin.

He barks out a laugh. "A big ball player like you? Wringing your alma mater dry for giving some batting pointers?"

I laugh, too. "Now who's full of shit?" I ask, my chest shaking.

Rush shrugs, a huge, stupid smile on his face.

"You know as well as I do that Triple-A guys make nothing."

"No cushy signing bonus to sit on for a while?"

I snort. "I wish."

The reality of playing professionally—in any sport, at any level—is that it's rare for someone fresh out of college to get a massive signing deal. Most newbies get a pretty small bonus. The big money goes to the big players at the top level, and I have some work to put in before I begin truly making a name for myself.

The first step was signing with a team and playing at the minor league level, which I did about a month ago. I signed with the Portland Flame and went up to Salem to play for their Triple-A affiliate, the Kings.

And then I got injured. In my very first game. Broke my wrist and several fingers.

Thankfully, the season was practically over so I just followed the team doc's orders to get surgery and begin rehabbing, get myself better for next season. I could have stayed in Salem for the winter. I was planning to sus out some side jobs with a few of my new teammates, but it was mostly physical labor, and that's pretty much out for me at this point.

I thought it would be easier to manage at home with some extra help from my parents, so as soon as I had the surgery, I packed my shit and booked a flight home. I'm sure most 22-year-olds don't want to move back in with their mom and dad, but I have a pretty awesome family that I actually like to be around. My baby sister, Busy, is still in Los Angeles, going to college, but my older sister, Briar, still lives in town, and my brother, Boyd, is visiting for a while to help open up his brewery. My twin sister, Bellamy, still lives at home, too.

While being back home isn't my dream scenario, it also isn't a hardship. Besides, maybe it'll do us Mitchell kids good to all be together for longer than a few days at a time for once.

Or maybe we'll annoy the hell out of each other. I guess only time will tell.

"I'm just teasing," Rush continues, rolling his cardboard coffee cup between his palms and drawing me back to our conversation. "I have a stipend for a part-time coach. I know the kids look up to you and would really benefit from your advice. I'd love to have you on board for the rest of Fall Ball if you have the time, maybe even the regular season if you're gonna be here in the spring."

I nod, my mind trying to digest the idea of coaching—even just for a little while—my old high school team.

"Let me think about it," I finally say, even though I know I'll probably say yes. "I can let you know in the next few days. But just to put it out there, I'm not sure how long I'll be in town."

Rush shrugs and gives me an easy smile. "Hey, if it works out, that's great. I'll take you for however long you're here."

We settle into other conversation points after that: family updates, childhood bullshit, the usual stuff we talk about when I come home. He doesn't ask any more about my arm, my recovery, or how long I'll be in town.

And I can't ignore the tiny thing inside me that breathes a sigh of relief.

Eventually, Rush heads off to work, and I leave Ugly Mug behind to begin a leisurely stroll down the length of Main Street, heading toward the lake stretched out in the distance.

Downtown Cedar Point is normally pretty calm this early on weekdays, even as we tip into the fall, our busiest tourist season. In an hour or so, there will be plenty of people littering the sidewalks, pushing their way into the shops that boast tchotchkes and "lake life" swag for people to lug home after they're done with their vacations.

But at 7:45am on a Monday morning, only a handful of stores are open, meaning it's mostly just locals dropping off dry cleaning or grabbing coffee before heading to work. It's not surprising that most of the people I see as I walk are faces I recognize: a few parents of old high school friends, one of our neighbors, a couple that hangs out with my mom and dad fairly regularly. I greet everyone with an easy smile, saying hello but continuing with my walk, not wanting to get stopped by anyone. I just want to enjoy the morning and the familiarity of being back in my hometown.

But then I see a face that *is* a surprise, so much so that I come to a halt in the middle of the sidewalk, old sensations rushing through me.

Gabriela Ventura.

She's standing in front of the hardware store, her arms crossed and an irritated expression on her face as she paces in front of the entrance.

A million memories rush through my mind, and a pang of…something hits me as I take her in. I've been on the receiving end of that look more times than I can count. I mean, I know Gabi's facial expressions better than I know baseball, and that's saying a lot.

Part of me wants to go to her and say hello, wrap her up in a hug and say how much I've missed her—a truth I've thought about more than a few times over the years. But I'm not sure how she'd respond, especially with the way things ended. Another part of me also knows seeing an ex for the first time in four years can be…awkward.

Before I get a chance to decide one way or another, her eyes connect with mine, and she stops moving. Her arms fall to her sides, her lips parting just slightly. She looks just as surprised to see me as I feel to see her, and for a long moment, we just stare at each other. A decade of memories races through me in an instant, the montage of our history playing like a silent movie in my mind.

Before I can move to say or do anything, the jingle of the bell on the hardware store's door rings as it opens behind her, startling us both out of whatever frozen moment we'd fallen into.

Gabi spins away, turning her glare on Roy Pulasky, the owner, as he steps outside.

"It's about time!" she barks, her voice bristling with the irritation that was evident on her body just a moment ago. "You were supposed to open at 7:30."

She blows past him and storms inside. She doesn't say a word to me, doesn't give me a wave or anything like that, just walks away, ignoring me entirely.

Part of me wants to laugh, because it's such a Gabi thing to do. She was always that way, quick to spin on her heel and dart away from…anything. Awkwardness. Conversations. Things she doesn't like.

She once told me she'd rather pretend a problem doesn't exist than face it head on because it means she doesn't have to deal with it as quickly. "It becomes a future Gabi problem," she told me, her eyes studiously focused on whatever she was working on in her sketchbook.

It felt funny back then. Maybe I'm reading way too much into our very brief non-interaction, but an uncomfortable feeling slices through me at the idea that *I'm* the future Gabi problem, one she'll deal with later. Or never.

Just as quickly as it arrived, that little part of me that wanted to laugh fades away completely, my heart feeling heavy in my chest. No matter what, Gabi was never that way with me. I was her safe place, the person she turned *to*, first as a friend, then as a boyfriend.

The realization that after all this time, after all our history, she'd rather flee than talk to me…

It hits me harder than I expect.

chapter two
gabi

The sound of the door slamming behind me announces my arrival before I do.

"I'm home!" I shout, marching through the house and into the kitchen then dumping my bags on the table.

My aunt glances over from where she sits on the couch in the living room, knitting next to the fireplace, and smiles. "Get what you need?"

"Yup."

The word comes out slightly more forcefully than I intend, and I can feel her eyes on me as I begin tugging my purchases out of the paper bags and placing them on the counter.

We don't have an art supply store in Cedar Point—a tragedy if you ask me and a missed opportunity, surely—but I'm able to get most of what I need online and a few items locally from the hardware store. My secret assumption is that Roy keeps some of the things I regularly need on hand just because he's hoping my Aunt Leah will come shopping with me.

Roy's a nice guy and all, but he should know better than to think he has a chance with my aunt. *Nobody* has a chance. Leah is a confirmed bachelorette with no intention of changing things up. It's been that way for as long as I can remember. She mostly just keeps to herself, does her own thing, and enjoys being an old cat lady with no cats—a label she bestowed upon herself.

"Everything go okay?"

I sigh, trying to keep my mind focused on putting away a few grocery items I picked up at One Stop after the hardware store. I needed an extra few minutes of wandering around aimlessly to clear my mind after my run-in with Bishop, but when I look at what I grabbed—a half gallon of milk, some tomatoes, and a bottle of shampoo—I realize my mind must have been quite distracted, because I'm pretty sure none of this was even on our grocery list.

"It was fine."

It was not fine.

What is he doing here?

I mean, realistically I've always known that I wouldn't be able to dodge him forever. That we would eventually bump into each other. His family lives here. He grew up here. He visits a few times a year.

But after nearly four years of studiously avoiding town whenever I know he's home, I was far more surprised by Bishop's appearance this morning than I expected. It would have been different if it was still summer, or even the holidays, when he normally returns to Cedar Point to visit his family. At least then I would have been somewhat prepared.

Instead, it was a random Monday at the end of September.

I bristle. It's so like him to just…show up like that.

"Yeah, you're really selling me on the whole *fine* thing."

I look up, finding Leah watching me with concern. Narrowing my eyes, I shove the milk into the fridge.

She's doing the thing, the thing she always does where she tries to be both motherly and sisterly in the same breath. She hovers like a mom but wants to sass me like a sister, and normally, I'm fine with it.

Not today though. Not when I feel so…on edge.

"I'll be in the shed." It's all I say before I stride out of the room, cutting through the garage and out the side door, away from the additional questions I know are imminent.

I shiver slightly as I tromp my way across the space between our house and the shed that sits about 20 yards away, the cool breeze of the early fall morning raising the hairs on my arms and leaving goose bumps in its wake.

The last day of summer was just a few days ago, and I've been holding out hope that the warm weather will linger a bit longer. Clearly, Mother Nature didn't receive all my desperate requests. I'll need to pull out the space heater soon, one of the irritating 'quirks' of working in a poorly constructed shack that barely has any electricity, let alone something useful like insulation.

Better electricity, insulation, and central air and heat are at the top of the list when it comes to things I want to change once I've finished saving to build a new workspace. Just a few more months and I should be able to actually confirm construction dates for the spring or summer, an exciting reality that even a year and a half ago I wouldn't have ever believed possible.

Shoving the door open, I step into the shed and flip on the lights. The halogen brightness floods the room, and I wince just slightly before blinking a few times, letting my eyes adjust.

The dusty old shed has been my escape and home to all my creative inspirations for the past two years. It does serve partially as storage for my aunt's thrifting addiction. Leah's goodies are all tucked away in the back half, stacked precariously on top of each other.

The front half, though, is all mine. Three rows of shelves, an old drafting desk, a pottery wheel, and an electric kiln. A sink and cleaning area in the corner and hooks to hang my aprons and lay things out to dry.

There's nothing fancy about the place, nothing on the walls or hanging from the ceiling. No big, beautiful windows that look out to nature, just tiny ones along the roofline that barely let in any natural light. But it has served me well and provided me a place to do the work I love so much, especially when I'm irritated and need to be alone, which is more often than I like to admit.

There have been many occasions when I've come in here and chucked a mound of clay on the wheel in anger, allowing the methodical work of throwing a plate or bowl or vase to level me out. It calms me in a way nothing else seems to.

It's what I wish I could do right now. I am tempted, but I have more than a few projects that need my attention, ones that are due to clients in the coming weeks. So I turn my eyes away from my wheel and instead head to the kiln.

I never expected to end up doing ceramics as a way to make a living. Hell, I never truly believed I'd *ever* make a living off my art, but especially not when I was focusing on dark watercolors and edgy oils and smudgy charcoals. My fingers were always stained, and I just assumed I'd be doing the artist's hustle for the rest of my life: working on my passion when I could but filling my bank account with a paycheck from a "real job".

Then I went to art school, which was two incredible years of stripping me of everything I ever thought I knew about art and who I wanted to be and what I wanted to create. I took a ceramics class first semester as an elective, and it became my new passion. I still love to paint and draw and many other creative pursuits, but sitting at a wheel and literally forming something that didn't exist before? Then bringing it to life with underglaze and oxides and special design elements I come up with in my own mind?

It's magical. I love everything about it, especially how it focuses my mind when it feels so scattered and angry.

I grab a cup and plate set out of the kiln and carry it over to my workstation to sit and examine the etchings and indents. I'll need to do a bit of light cleanup work and apply glaze before I fire them again to finish everything off. I like to sit with each piece for a minute or two after each step of the process to make sure I've thought through the entire thing. It's my way of reminding myself not to move faster than I can think. That's how mistakes get made.

I sigh internally when I hear the door open, but I don't move or look in that direction. Instead, I continue examining the cup I'm rotating in my hands.

"You forgot your bag in the kitchen. Just wanted to make sure you didn't need anything from it before you dive too deep into work."

I hear the crinkle of the paper bag as she sets it down behind me. That's not why she's here. If I hadn't forgotten that bag, she would have found some other reason to poke her head in and check up on me.

"I didn't need it yet."

I'm lying and she knows it. There's no reason I would be up this early to pick up supplies from the hardware store if I didn't need them this morning. I actually need something from that bag to work on the cup currently in my hand, but this is how we do things.

She pretends to have a reason to hover.

I studiously avoid her.

Eventually we find some sort of middle ground after she's done poking and prodding.

The last thing I want to talk to her about, though, is the man I saw downtown this morning.

Bishop Mitchell.

God, even just his *name* makes my heart begin to beat erratically. It's been four years since I've seen him in person, and as much as I hate to admit it, he looks good. Like…really good. The grown-up kind of good that only comes after that last bit of youthful roundness fades away. Well, that and an almost religious dedication to fitness and exercise and athletics.

Bishop always had that, though. He was always moving, always running somewhere, always playing some sort of ball—football, soccer, baseball, you name it—until eventually baseball became his life. It became his life and led him away from me… from here…and the last thing I want now is to still be bitter about it.

But I am.

So, Leah can prod and poke all she wants this time. I have no intention of sharing.

I glance her way before returning my eyes to the mug I'm still examining.

"Thanks for bringing me my stuff. I need to get to work."

It's a firm dismissal, and I watch her out of the corner of my eye as she crosses her arms and her hip pops out to the side.

"Fine, if you want to hide in here, that's your choice. Just know you're not fooling anyone. So why don't you just tell me what it is and save us from this back and forth."

I remain silent long enough that she sighs and finally leaves me in peace.

Leah's the best 'mom' a girl could ask for, especially considering the fact that she never actually intended to be one in the first place. Still, she has yet to accept the reality that I'm not a teenager anymore. I don't always want—or need—to talk everything out with her. Sometimes, I want to keep my thoughts to myself, and I wish, every once in a while, she'd let me.

Once I've finished adding in the gold leaf and glaze, I add my pieces back to the kiln and turn my attention to a different project. Technically, it's nothing I need to work on for at least a few more days, but I'm desperate to use my muscles and focus my energy on something creative. There's nothing that both consumes my energy and stokes it at the same time like throwing pottery.

I grab a block of clay and chuck it on the bat—a flat disc that sits in the center that allows me to swap out projects more quickly—then drop down into my seat and start the wheel. I add water and press my hands downward, putting the full weight of my body into centering the clay, until I've finally gotten it into a dome shape. Then I press two fingers into the center, pulling outward to open the mouth, before pulling up on the sides. It doesn't take long to get the shape right for the first of four bowls, each just slightly smaller than the last.

A version of this nested set is what first boomed my business online when one of the most popular food bloggers used my pottery to plate her food in a video that went viral. My website actually shut down because there was so much traffic, and I got close to 300 emails in just a few days asking if I had more of the bowls or other items for sale.

Needless to say, I jumped at the opportunity in front of me and took full advantage. I began posting 'in-progress' videos regularly on my socials, hired a friend in town to take professional photos of my work, leveled up my website with a shop, and updated my commission request form. I booked out for the rest of the year within just a few weeks, and I've never looked back.

I'm shocked at how lucrative it's been. I've been able to pay off my student loans, begin putting aside emergency savings every month, and actually start paying myself with the remaining profit. It's why I'm planning to build a new workspace, and I'm even thinking about hiring a part-time employee to handle some of the administrative stuff I'm not as good at. It's been a wild ride for the past two years as I've been figuring this business out, and I'm finally feeling truly settled into my life again, in my work as a creator, in my routine and my process.

Which is why it's so irritating that Bishop is here. I don't want him to disrupt the life I've finally gotten my footing in.

I might not be a big joiner, but I still hear town gossip. I knew he got injured during his first game, knew it was serious enough he needed surgery. I know far more than I should about his life, if I'm honest. Doesn't seem to matter if I'm studiously avoiding him when he's home or diligent about not snooping about his life online—which would be so easy to do and I've thought about more than once.

Smalltown rules are that you always hear about what your ex

is up to, whether you want to or not. For most people, it might just be a snippet of news here and there.

I'm not so lucky. I'm the girl who fell in love with and dated a Mitchell, and this town *loves* to talk about the Mitchells, so I get regular updates. His batting average each year. The fact that he waited on the draft until after he graduated because he wanted to get his degree. His grades suffering sophomore year to the point that he needed a tutor. News about his girlfriend. How things went with the combine and then the draft.

There's no way I would have *not* heard about his injury— half the town was watching his first game for the Kings on a TV Melvin Kinny brought into The Mitch and got set up with a streamed feed. Leah boycotted the townie bar that night, even though I told her she should go. She was adamant, though.

"No boy who breaks my Gabi's heart is going to get even a lick of my time."

I love when she says that—my Gabi—but it hurts a little bit, too. I was always Gabriela until Bishop. He was the only one who called me Gabi for years, until Leah started using it occasionally as well. Nobody else has picked it up, and for that, I'm thankful, because Gabi *did* have her heart broken. She was a moody, lovelorn sap for far longer than she'd like to admit.

I don't want to be Gabi, Bishop's ex-girlfriend.

I want to be Gabriela, the artist. Gabriela, the creator. Gabriela, the *insert badass thing here*.

And I can't be her if I'm just the heartbroken girl Bishop left behind.

chapter three
bishop

The sound of rain hitting my window should be enough to lull me to sleep. Normally, the gentle tapping is exactly what I need to quiet my ever-racing mind, and there have been more than a few occasions when I've popped on an ambient rain playlist on my phone to help me nod off.

Tonight, though, my mind won't quiet. Instead of creating a calming environment, those familiar little noises are like nails clattering angrily against the glass, an incessant annoyance I can't escape.

I shift out of bed, being careful not to put too much pressure on my left arm as I do. I glance at the sling resting on my desk—the one I'm supposed to wear whenever I'm not in bed—wishing I could just leave it there. I almost do, but the part of me that knows I need to follow the rules reaches forward and grabs it, and I grumble to myself the entire time I'm putting it on.

Quietly, I slip out of my childhood bedroom and make my way downstairs, hoping a midnight snack and some mindless television might lull me to sleep. After a snoop through the fridge, I collapse on the couch, wincing at how the action sends an unexpected ribbon of pain ricocheting through my arm. I sigh in frustration, rubbing my fingers over the bit of stubble growing along my jawline.

I feel off tonight, sour and bristly in a way I rarely experience, and there are only two reasons that come to mind as to why.

The first is the message that came through earlier today. Glancing down at my phone, I read it again.

Eliza: Heard about your arm. Just wanted to see how you're doing.

I haven't responded, because I don't know what to say. The fact that she's texting me at all feels like a joke in and of itself. I'm not a callous kind of guy, but my lack of sleep and poor attitude get the best of me, and I begin a text in response.

Me: You want to see how I'm doing? Or you want to assuage your guilt about cheating on me all summer by 'checking in' on poor, sad Bishop?

My non-dominant hand moves slowly as I type, and by the time I've written it all out, all the prickly irritation I've felt since she first contacted me has leaked out, leaving me feeling like a deflated balloon.

Lashing out like that isn't my style. I might get a rush of anger here and there—who doesn't?—but it usually dissipates almost as quickly as it arrives.

I delete the message and compose a new one.

Me: I'm fine. Thanks for checking in.

The truth is I don't hate Eliza for what she did. The two of us were more fuck-buddies than soulmates anyway, and it's probably better for both of us that things are over.

Still, I can't help the bruise to my ego over the fact that she started hooking up with Heath on her trip to Europe, especially since we'd have these FaceTime chats and he would pop on to say hi, knowing damn well he was taking her to bed after we got off the call.

I roll my eyes and click send, hoping this one text from her is the last time she reaches out, then I toss my phone to the coffee table. I power on the TV, intending to search for a show to watch that will distract me, maybe something mindless.

Instead, the bright light of baseball replays stream through the dark room, and I grit my teeth, watching a muted recap from last night's game between the Flame and the A's. It was the final game of the regular season, nothing particularly spectacular since neither team was heading to the playoffs.

It just smarts to know everyone else playing the sport I love is finishing up their season, and I'm "stuck on the bench", so to speak.

But I'm not even on the bench. I'm on the couch, with an injury that required fucking surgery.

I let out a long breath and stretch my neck from side to side, trying to mentally set Eliza and my injury aside...which only creates room in my mind for me to think about the second reason I feel off today.

Gabi.

I don't know why her bristly reaction to me this morning is sitting so poorly with me. We each left town to go to school—to follow our dreams—and when it got too difficult, we broke up. It makes sense that she wouldn't be rejoicing at the sight of me, but I guess…I don't know. I thought the split was a bit more amicable, thought we'd still be the 'wish the best for you' kind of exes.

I thought there was too much history, too much love, for us to ever hate each other.

Clearly I was wrong, at least on her end.

"You sure you should be watching that?"

The sound of my father's voice in the quiet of the room startles me just slightly, and I glance over my shoulder to find him in the kitchen, pulling a glass down from an overhead cabinet.

I turn back to the TV.

"Probably not."

There are some light sounds behind me, and then eventually, Dad drops down on the couch next to me, a glass of amber-colored liquid in each hand.

"I'm not supposed to drink right now," I tell him.

"You weren't supposed to drink while you were on your antibiotics. You took your last ones…" He glances at the clock on the wall that says it's 3am. "What…yesterday? I'm sure you'll be fine."

I chuckle, accepting the rocks glass from him, the two of us clinking them together before each taking a sip. The bitter alcohol touches every surface of my mouth, and I hold it there a tad longer than normal before finally swallowing it down, enjoying the way it warms my body. My dad's not a big drinker, so I don't doubt his midnight snack run becoming a whiskey break is entirely about me.

"How's your arm feeling?"

I shake my head and bring the glass to my lips again. "Like

shit," I say, more honestly than I've been with anyone so far. Taking another sip, I keep my eyes on the commentators on the TV. "But not too bad, all things considered."

He nods, and we sit in silence together for a long moment, the highlight reel moving on to teams heading to the playoffs.

"Rush asked me to be the batting coach for the Pirates," I eventually say.

My dad glances at me, a smile on his face. "Well that would be a fun way to spend your time at home."

I nod. "Maybe."

"Just maybe?"

Taking another sip, I think it over again, the idea of helping out with my old team. It could be fun, building up the players who are where I was not too long ago, not to mention it would be nice to spend more time with Rush. *And* get a paycheck to boot.

But for whatever reason, there's a part of me that doesn't want to do it, even though I can't figure out why.

"Well, I think you should consider it," my dad offers. "Those kids would be lucky to work with someone as talented as you."

I give him a tight smile. "Yeah. I guess you're right."

Though how lucky could they be to get stuck with some guy who can't even hack it in Triple-A? The thought is unusual, likely the result of the touch of whiskey in my blood, and I do my best to push it away so it doesn't take hold.

As if he can sense my thoughts, my dad wraps his arm around my shoulders.

"You'll overcome this challenge, Bishop. I know you will."

That uneasy feeling eases slightly at his encouragement. I always feel buoyed by my dad's support, and I'm particularly thankful for it in this moment when I feel so uncharacteristically down.

That's Mark Mitchell, though. He knows how to show up at just the right moment, to provide just that one gentle hand on your back that helps you feel a little more balanced, a little less alone. It was like that all growing up, and it doesn't surprise me that it's like that now.

"Thanks, Pop," I say. "Appreciate it."

We watch the replay on mute for a bit, the light from the TV glowing through the room, until we each finish our glass of whiskey. Then I push awkwardly off the couch, give my dad a hug, say good night, and head back up the stairs to my room.

It should be comforting, coming home, and on most occasions, it is. I return a few times a year, mostly for family stuff or holidays. It was easy enough, being only an hour and a half down the mountain at college, popping back for quick trips just to see the fam.

I loved growing up in Cedar Point, loved everything about it, but I always assumed if I came back someday, it would be on *my* terms, because *I* wanted to. Not because of…this. Not because of a foolish mistake, an injury that could have easily been avoided.

I sink back into my bed, gritting my teeth as a twinge of discomfort slices through my arm at the movement, though the pain doesn't linger long. The whiskey has lessened my inhibitions, and the alcohol lets through that tiny kernel of fear I can't eliminate entirely. My mind swirls, thinking over the things I don't dare to think during the daytime: what this injury might do to my career, to my future, to everything I've worked so hard for, for so long.

Hopefully, this is just a small setback, just a temporary delay, and not the end before anything has really even begun.

I sleep in the next morning, which is unusual for me but expected considering how late I was lying awake, staring at the ceiling. My eyes didn't close until I saw a faint hint of color beginning to lighten the sky, so I'm still kind of groggy when I rise, a delicious smell in the air.

Skipping the shower, I rinse my face and head downstairs, grinning when I spot my sister in the kitchen and what looks to be a grilled cheese on the stove.

"Making breakfast?"

Bellamy snorts and uses a spatula to flip the sandwich. "Try lunch. It's 12:30." She grabs an orange and glances back at me, her nose wrinkling at my disheveled state. "You look like you slept horribly."

I make a face at her then step up to where she's standing at the counter, watching as she begins peeling.

"Thanks for that. *Morning Bish, you look like shit,*" I mock on a laugh, snagging a piece of her orange and popping it in my mouth. "It's not like I'm recovering from a devastating injury or anything."

She rolls her eyes then slaps my hand when I reach out for another piece of fruit.

"This is my lunch. Get your own."

I point dramatically at my left arm, wrapped snugly against my chest in the ever-present sling. "You think I'm trying to peel an orange? I'm wearing a cast, Bells. I could have lost my arm."

That last part's not true and she knows it, but I can't help the theatrics. It's in my nature.

Bellamy's eyes narrow, but I see the playful spirit behind it. Without saying anything, she steps to the side, opens the fridge, and finds an apple.

"Oh look, a fruit you can eat with one hand," she says, tossing it my way.

Catching it with my right hand, I narrow my eyes right back. "Little brat."

"Little shit."

We stare at each other for a long minute before she returns to her place at the stove and I move to sit at the kitchen island.

"Any chance you wanna make me a grilled cheese?" I take a huge bite from the apple. "I'll be forever in your debt."

Bellamy looks at me like she can't believe I even asked, but when I wriggle my eyes up and down and give her the biggest grin I can manage, the corners of her mouth rise. She flips the finished sandwich onto her plate and turns toward me.

"You're already forever in my debt."

She slides the plate across the island between us.

I grin, snagging it. "Sweet."

My twin sister is my favorite human. As annoying as we can be to each other, we are also best friends, so this kind of poking is how we say I love you. Most of the time.

"How are you feeling, though?" Bellamy tugs out two new slices of bread and glances my way. "Really."

I shrug, wishing she'd stop asking. "My arm fucking hurts. Other than that, I'm fine."

"Still a definite no to taking the pain meds? Even just a little bit?"

"Nah. Too many guys get hooked on that shit," I tell her. "I'm not willing to risk it. Not when I can just suck it up and deal, you know?"

Bellamy gives me a look. "You should at least ask your doctor about other ways—"

"Other ways to minimize the pain? Yeah, I've already done that. I'm taking exactly as much Tylenol as I can without ruining my liver. Trust me."

She sighs then nods. "As long as you're not being an idiot." Her eyes flick my way for just a second before returning to where she's adding a sliver of butter to her pan. "I don't like when you're hurt."

I know the feeling, and I don't doubt that what she's *not* saying is that when I hurt, she hurts, too. It's one of those weird twin things that can't be explained by science. As much as Bellamy and I give each other shit, we also baby each other a lot when it comes to how we treat ourselves. When she's going through something, I am, too, and vice versa.

But she can't help with this apart from peeling my oranges. I have to deal with this on my own, and I'm just not willing to risk getting addicted to pain meds.

Setting my apple core on the plate, I pick up the grilled cheese and take a big bite.

"How are you *other* than your arm?"

"You already asked me that. I said I'm fine."

My answer comes out a bit brisk, but I can only handle so much of her prodding. She's been asking me a slightly different version of the same question every day since I've been home. *How are you? How're you doing? You doing okay?*

I know what she really wants. She wants to know how I'm *feeling*, how I'm doing *emotionally*, and I get it. Shit has kind of hit the fan in my life when it seemed to be going so well just a few weeks ago. My girlfriend cheated on me. I seriously injured my arm, had to have surgery. Now I'm living with my parents, a useless lump in my childhood home.

I want to go for a run. Or a swim. Or a bike ride. It's how I normally process things, but all of those are out for at least four weeks—three, now, until they take this stupid cast off. Even then, I'm facing physical therapy and limited use of my left hand and arm until I go through several months of rehabbing it to get the full range of motion back.

Sighing, I scrub at my face. I'm still exhausted, and it's harder to stay positive when all I want to do is crawl back into bed.

"How's Rusty?" I ask, diverting the conversation away from me.

My sister hops up onto a seat at the island, her face brightening at the mention of her boyfriend. "Really good. Cedar Cider is doing their soft opening this weekend, you know."

I nod at her reference to the brewery Rusty and Boyd are opening up downtown with another buddy of theirs, Jackson. "Shit, I knew it was coming up, but I didn't realize it was so soon."

She grins. "Yup. And everything is going so well. All the furniture was moved in last week, and all the glasses and stuff were delivered over the weekend. I'm going in after work today to help with setup." She pauses, and I don't miss the glow on her face. "I know Boyd and Jackson have definitely had a hand, but this is Rusty's baby and he is doing such an amazing job, you know?"

When Bellamy looks at me, her brows furrow at my expression.

"What?"

I shake my head, smiling. "Nothing, it's just…I've never seen you like this."

She makes a face. "Like what?"

"All..." I wave a hand at her. "In love and stuff."

She rolls her eyes. "You watched me moon over Connor for years."

"Meh, that guy was a chode, and you didn't love him. Not really." I pause. "It looks good on you, this kind of happiness. The real kind."

Bellamy doesn't say anything for a few minutes after that, but a small smile lingers on her face as we finish eating our sandwiches.

"Are you going to come on Saturday? To the opening?" she asks me a while later as we're putting our plates in the dishwasher. "Busy's driving up for the weekend to help out."

It's been a few months since I've seen my younger sister. I attended a baseball camp in LA over the summer to prep for the draft combine, and Busy—who attends college only twenty minutes from where I was staying—visited me a couple of times when it worked for our schedules. She's wildly independent. Maybe even more so than Briar and Boyd. And I loved getting to see her in her element.

But as much as I enjoy knowing I'll get to see her this weekend, I can't help but shrug in response to Bellamy's question. "We'll see. Depends how I feel."

My sister's smile dims, and she nods. "Okay, well...I hope you can make it. I know it would mean a lot to...everyone."

She leaves the kitchen, and only a few minutes later, I hear the front door open and close, Bellamy probably heading back to her office. As much as we've been able to play and tease since I've been home, there's been a thread of strain between us, and I'm not entirely sure why.

Part of me thinks it's because she's constantly pushing me to talk to her about how I *feel* when I don't want to. If I have to be honest about how I feel, I'll have to admit that the voice in my head telling me I fucked up is a lot louder than I want it to be.

chapter four

gabi

"A lot of you tend to move your wheel too slowly while you're getting your clay centered. You need to make sure it's moving at least medium-high. It will give you more control."

My eyes scan the room, watching as my students respond to my instructions, each resulting in completely different outcomes. Helene presses too hard on her foot pedal, and the lump of clay begins to wobble as she attempts to raise the edges to create a bowl. Mary's speed doesn't change at all—she just presses harder on her clay, trying to force it where she wants it. Johnny keeps pressing and releasing instead of finding a consistent speed, and the shape of his clay continues to change.

There are only seven students taking the Fundamentals of Ceramics class I teach on Tuesdays and Thursdays after school, and sometimes I wonder what the hell this place was thinking, hiring me to be a teacher.

Also, high schoolers are little weirdos, and my eyes narrow as Johnny flags down Peter two chairs away to point at the phallic shape of his clay. They laugh silently until they catch me watching them, and then they quickly return to their forming.

I step next to Mary and bend slightly, keeping my voice low.

"Let's try increasing your speed just a bit. Then you won't have to push so hard to get it centered," I tell her. "If you have to use a lot of muscle to get it going, you'll wear yourself out really quickly."

"I got it," she says, mostly ignoring me. "I'm probably a lot stronger than you are, so I'm not worried about getting too tired."

Rolling my eyes, I return to the front, retaking a seat at my wheel and stepping gently on the pedal. I can't get too irritated at kids like Mary, so certain she has all the answers and doesn't need any help from anyone. That's just part of being a teenager, I guess.

I have plenty of memories of receiving unwanted advice when I was young and ignoring it completely. Sometimes, only growing up a bit will provide the ability to take suggestions on board.

I cup some water into my hand and add it to my clay, gently molding it into the small bowl everyone is attempting to make. Well, except for Johnny. Who knows what that kid is making.

"You make it look so easy."

I glance up at Helene, who has come to the front to watch me, and I give her a small smile.

"It takes time. You'll get there. Just don't expect more from yourself than what you already know how to do, until you feel confident doing it."

Her nose scrunches up and her brows furrow. "Huh?"

I hide my smile at her response, pulling the clay gently upward and outward, forming the curved sides of the bowl.

"Pottery skills are layered. Practice the basics over and over until you feel like you have a really good handle on them. Then move on to something new. You've been at this for a few weeks now. Can you think of anything you need to work on?"

She pauses for a second, thinking it over. "I think I need to get better at centering."

I nod. "Great idea. Maybe try centering at a higher speed."

Helene watches me for another beat or two as I perfect the edges of the bowl, then she returns to her workstation. I can't help but smile to myself. She didn't really listen to me when I was suggesting that same bit of advice to the class before, but she finally heard it when I was gently nudging her toward figuring it out herself.

Like I said, little weirdos.

Once I'm finished with my bowl, I wire my piece off the bat and set it on a table in the middle of the room as an example. Then I return to my wheel and begin working on a vase. I continue glancing up, checking in on everyone over the course of the remaining 30 minutes of class to make sure they're working well with their clay, answering questions as they come.

When I was first approached about teaching a ceramics class for the summer school students, I rolled my eyes so hard they nearly fell out of my head.

The absolute *last* thing I would ever want to do with my time is teach, and teach *teenagers* at that. Teachers are supposed to be gentle and thoughtful and have an internal desire to build up the next generation of people.

Those are not my skill sets, but Principal Cohen basically begged me to do it—apparently Cedar Point High School needed another art class to offer during the summer or several students who were one art unit shy of what they needed for graduation wouldn't be able to collect their diplomas and go to college. It sounded like a made-up story to me, but I figured the three-hour class twice a week would basically be a chance for me to get paid and use free supplies to test out new stuff.

And it was. It was *also* a really cool way to spend some of my time over the summer. Sure, there were a few little shits who just wanted to mess around, but I met two very sweet girls who were interested in art, and I got to teach them how to do something new, something I love. It was a pass/fail art elective, so nobody needed to be graded and everyone just got to explore working with clay and water and a wheel. Watching them get better throughout our 6-week session was gratifying in a way I didn't know I could feel.

So when the principal asked if I was interested in transitioning the class into a 12-week elective during the fall semester—and promised I'd still only have to teach twice a week—I said yes. Now, we're a month into the semester, and I guess I'm technically a faculty member at my alma mater.

It's a wild thing to say considering all the trouble I got into when I was a student.

"Alright everyone, spend the last few minutes of class cleaning up your workstations. Most of you saw me up here making a vase. That's what *you're* going to be doing next week, so make sure you're here on time." I glance at Johnny as he passes by me, taking his phallic mound of clay to the clay heap. "I'm looking at you, mister. I'm not going to repeat the stuff I say at the start of class again. You need to be here at 2:30 with your butt in that chair. No more dawdling. Got it?"

I wince internally. Did I just say *no more dawdling*?

Johnny gives me a charming grin, oblivious to my internal critique. "I aim to please, Ms. Ventura."

I shake my head and begin cleaning up my own station, saying goodbye to the students as they wrap up and trickle out of the studio, eager to take off. I don't blame them; I remember being just as eager.

When the door shuts behind the last student, I let out a sigh and glance around at my classroom. The airy space is significantly larger than we need for such a small group of students, but it means everyone gets plenty of space, which is nice.

Cedar Point High School has an enrollment of around 500 students. The campus isn't that big, but it was designed to expand with anticipated city growth over the next 10 to 20 years. Even though ceramics was originally only supposed to be a temporary elective over the summer, I was given a full-size classroom in the annex alongside the other art classes.

It's where our current class is located as well, and I really love it. Unlike my own shed, it has huge windows and lets in lots of natural light. We get to prop the doors open and use outside space if we need it because we're at the back of campus adjacent to a long stretch of cement and grass. It's beginning to get a little too cold for that now, though, and the doors have stayed firmly closed over the past week. Even so, it's still such a bright, airy place to work.

Sometimes I wish I could bring my projects here, and on more than a few occasions, I've considered it. But it would be such an inconvenience to have to drive over here every day, and I can't be sure I'll be teaching this class again in the spring.

I'm locking up the studio when I hear my name.

"Heading home, Ms. Ventura?"

I smile at the sound of Sam Rush's voice, and I turn to look in his direction. "You know I hate when..." But my words die on my tongue when I see who he's walking with.

Son of a bitch. What the hell is *Bishop* doing here?

"...when you call me that," I finish, the playful lilt to my comment gone in a flash.

The two of them come to a stop a few steps away.

"Hey, Gabi."

The sound of Bishop's voice wraps around my chest, around my throat, making it impossible to breathe, let alone respond. It's exactly what happened earlier this week when he appeared out of nowhere in front of the hardware store.

"Good to see you," he continues. "It's been a while."

We stand there silently for longer than is comfortable before Sam finally speaks.

"Well that answers the question of whether you'll be happy to see each other," he says, chuckling awkwardly. "I'll let you two chat." He turns to Bishop. "See you tomorrow, *coach*," he says before giving me a nod and leaving us alone.

I feel like I should have been prepared for another bump-in, but again, I feel completely blindsided by his presence. It doesn't feel like there's any earthly reason why he would be at the high school at 4:30pm on a random Thursday. He should be...anywhere else. Anywhere else but here.

It's incredibly rude of Bishop to continue showing up in places where I don't expect him.

"How've you been?"

God, that voice. Like the rest of him, it has only gotten better with age. It's familiar, and yet new, somehow. A bit gruffer. A bit deeper.

"Good. Fine." I pause. "You?"

He chuckles and points a finger at his injured arm. "I've been better. Back in town for the off-season to rehab this thing."

I grit my teeth and nod. "Well...good luck with that."

Turning, I begin to walk away, headed in the direction of the parking lot, but I hear him speak again.

"Hey, I'll walk with you."

Then he's at my side, that infuriating smile on his face, the easygoing, friendly one I always envied. I've never had a smile like that, one that instantly puts people at ease. I'm more of a 'resting bitch face' type, though it's less 'resting' and more 'intentional'.

"I didn't realize you were doing stuff at the school," he says once we reach the top of the stairs and begin the walk across the quad, weaving our way through the handful of students still wandering around doing afterschool activities. "You teaching?"

"Yeah. Ceramics."

"That's awesome. You like it?"

I shrug. "It's alright."

We continue walking in silence, though eventually Bishop breaks it, much to my frustration.

"I'm helping Rush with Fall Ball," he offers. "Mostly just acting as a batting coach for a while. Keeping myself busy so I'm not just moping around waiting to get my cast off, you know?"

I just give him a pinched look and say nothing, hoping he'll take the hint and stay quiet. It's bad enough that he's walking with me. I don't need to also hear about anything to do with his plans while he's in town. It's easier to just pretend he's not here.

But then I sigh, realizing if he's helping with Fall Ball, he's not just visiting campus today. He'll be on campus *every* day. Which is when I remember what Sam said as he left the two of us behind. *See you tomorrow, coach.*

"I don't remember you being this quiet," Bishop says, chuckling slightly as we come up on the double doors that lead into the main building.

I come to a stop and let out a huff. "Maybe I just don't have anything to say to you."

He blinks in surprise then rubs his chest with his good hand. "Ouch."

Growling, I shove through the doors and down a long hallway, hoping he takes the hint and lets me go.

He doesn't.

"Woah, Gabi…hold up," Bishop says, catching up and then gently wrapping his hand around my wrist. "Just wait for a second."

Aware that there are at least a few students within eavesdropping distance, I keep a neutral expression on my face and my voice low.

"What, Bishop? What do you want?"

"I…" He pauses, shaking his head. "I don't know, but not this. I mean…I thought we were friends."

I laugh. I literally laugh, and his head jerks back in surprise.

Then I sigh, tilting my head back and looking at the ceiling before my eyes return to his, asking the gods why this problem is being returned to my plate. Haven't I dealt with enough?

"Look, I'm sorry I don't have it in me to be the girl who can be friendly with her ex," I tell him, my voice tight. "But I don't. I don't have it in me, and I don't *want* to have it in me. *You* dumped *me*, and in my book, that means I have no obligation to make nice, okay? So, no, Bishop, we are not friends. Unless you have something important to say to me, I just want to walk to my car and go home."

He blinks a few times then steps to the side. That's another thing that's so infuriating about Bishop—he fucking listens.

I walk past him and down the long hallway, the sound of my heart thumping loudly in my ears as I stride down the corridor until I push back out into the cool air.

Not once do I look back at him.

No matter how much I want to.

Nicole: I heard Bishop is working at CPHS

Groaning, I drop my phone back into my basket and continue browsing the shelves at One Stop Shop, Cedar Point's grocery store, not wanting to talk about it, not even with my closest friend. Knowing Nicole, she'll want to share everything she's heard—what he was doing on campus, who he was with, etc.—and I'm just not up for it, to be honest.

Instead, I refocus my attention on picking up the groceries we need. I'm getting the *actual* items from our grocery list, not like my blind shopping trip earlier this week, but even that gets shot to shit when I'm checking out.

"Hey, Gabriela. How's Leah doing?" Maryanne asks as she swipes my items through the check stand.

"Pretty good, thanks."

She nods. "I heard Bam's helping coach the team at the high school," she continues. "You're teaching there too, now, right?"

Gritting my teeth, I nod. "Yep."

"What are the odds of you two working there together, huh?" She chuckles. "Such a small world."

I just give her a tight smile, thinking it feels a little too small for my liking.

Maryanne continues to make small talk, but I barely hear it, mostly just nodding and then practically ripping my receipt from her hand as I bolt out the door. Then as I'm unloading the bags back at the house, my phone rings. When I see Nicole's name on the screen again, I know she's not going to give up until I answer.

After tapping the green button, I put it on speaker.

"Hey."

"Did you see my text?"

"I did."

"And you didn't call me immediately?"

"No."

"Why not? This is big news. I thought you'd want to know considering the fact that you *also* work there."

I snort, rising up on my tiptoes to shove a bag of flour onto one of the higher shelves in the pantry.

"I already knew."

There's silence for a second, and then I hear Nicole's voice again.

"Oh, no. Did you already see him?"

Chuckling, though there's no humor in my voice, I crumple up the empty brown paper bag and shove it into the trash can.

"You already saw him," she answers for me. "What happened?"

Sighing, I drop down into one of the kitchen chairs and stare blankly at the remaining two bags of groceries that need to be put away.

"He's going to be *Coach Mitchell*. He's helping Sam Rush with the team."

"So you talked to him? Tell me everything."

I shake my head, though I know she can't see me. "It was

only for a second. He just mentioned he'd be coaching while he's rehabbing his arm."

"That's it?"

"Pretty much."

I don't tell her the other part, about how I was so brittle, or the part where I told him not to talk to me. Both of those things mean I'm not over what happened between us, even though part of me hoped I'd moved on.

"Well if that's it...I mean, I know this is going to sound selfish, but...are you still coming with me on Saturday?"

At that, I actually laugh. Leave it to Nicole to make this about being at the biggest thing to happen in this town since the grocery store caught fire last year.

"I don't know, Nic," I tell her honestly. "I'm not sure I'm up for it. You know he'll be there."

"And? Show him what a mistake he made," she volleys back. "Dress up in something gorgeous and shake your ass every time he's behind you. You can't miss the biggest event this town has seen in years!"

I nibble on the inside of my cheek. There's no way in hell Bishop won't be at the Cedar Cider opening this weekend. His brother is one of the owners. His twin sister is dating one of the *other* owners. Plus, his parents go to every major event around here. If he's in town, he'll be there.

"I'll think about it," I tell her, not wanting to make any promises.

She grumbles about staying home with me if I decide not to go but then begs me not to make her miss it. We get off the phone, promising to see each other Saturday morning at yoga.

I sit there for a long moment, my mind skittering over every possibility of what could happen if I go to the brewery opening.

Seeing Bishop is a guarantee, but maybe I can avoid him. Maybe he'll avoid me. Maybe there will be so many people it'll just be a simple nod from across the room and then we'll both be too busy.

Ultimately, I set those thoughts aside and return to my task of putting away the groceries. I have too much to do today to think about this any longer, and I resign myself to making a game-time decision. Today, I don't want to deal with it.

It will just have to be a future Gabi problem.

When I arrive at Cedar Cider on Saturday night, I immediately realize past Gabi made a mistake.

I can make all the excuses I want about why I didn't want to come tonight. My busy schedule. My achy arms. The fact that I'm legitimately exhausted from the poor sleep I've been getting. All of those things might be true, but I know the real reason, and he's sitting in the corner, chatting with his parents and a few other people I recognize from around town.

Like magnets, our eyes lock across the space.

It's always been like that, for as long as I can remember, from the first minute I walked into homeroom in the seventh grade and saw him.

"You're new," he said, his eyes skimming over me.

He said it like it didn't happen that often. Eventually I learned it was because it really didn't. I was the first new student in his grade in several years, having just moved to Cedar Point to live with my aunt Leah.

"You're nosey," I replied, tugging my sketchbook closer when he tried to look at it.

He chuckled and just continued talking to me like we were already friends, and he did that every day in homeroom for the rest of the year. His eyes found mine as I walked through the door, and he grinned that grin I hate to love so much.

Like I said…magnets.

"Let's grab a beer and a table," Nicole says, leading me over to the bar. Her head tilts back and her eyes survey the room as we wait on one of the bartenders to take our order. "God, they did such a good job. Do you remember what this place used to look like?"

I nod, glancing around and taking it in myself for the first time, having been distracted when we first entered.

The Kelso Barn has sat empty at the very end of Main Street for as long as I've been alive, but I've seen a few photos at Town Hall of what it used to look like in the early 1900s. The work that has gone into making this place a brewery is astounding. From the beautiful way the old barn look is preserved to the mixture of modern finishes, all blending with warm, inviting furniture and the large brewing equipment against the wall… it's stunning.

"You gonna talk to him?" Nicole asks as we wait for our beers a few minutes later.

My eyes flick to Nicole's, and I see her watching me with a smirk.

"Who?"

"She says 'who' like I could mean anyone else." Nicole shakes her head, laughing.

Thankfully, the bartender drops a dark beer in front of me

at exactly that moment, and I dig into my purse and grab some cash.

"Thanks so much," I say, passing it over the counter. Then I look at Nicole. "I'll grab a table, and I suggest you find a new topic or find somewhere else to sit."

Nicole laughs again, knowing my bark is worse than my bite, and I leave her behind to put in her own order as I snake through the crowd looking for somewhere to rest my butt. I'm not surprised this place is so busy tonight. It's the first brewery to ever open in Cedar Point, and when you're a local in a small town with only so many places to visit on a night out, having a new option is life-changing.

I spot a couple getting up from a two-top in the corner and snag it as soon as they're gone, settling into one of the beautiful wooden chairs. Taking a sip of my beer, I wait for Nicole to join me and replay my conversation with Bishop for what feels like the thousandth time in two days.

He seemed so casual, talking to me outside the studio then babbling on about the baseball team as he walked alongside me through the campus. I know it's been four years and maybe I *should* be able to just shoot the shit, but it didn't feel that way when I saw him. Seeing Bishop again brought back all the pain of that autumn afternoon when he broke up with me over the phone.

"It just feels like it's not working," he said, like we were some sort of machine with broken parts and there wasn't a way to fix it.

I don't know…maybe the fact that we've never talked about what really happened back then has left everything feeling too raw and unresolved. Or maybe I just loved him far more than he loved me.

"Your man isn't the only handsome bachelor here tonight."

Nicole plops down in the seat across from me, a pale ale in hand.

I groan. "Don't call him *your man*. I don't want anyone to hear you and think *I'm* the one calling him that."

She just rolls her eyes. "Sam is here. That was my point."

Glancing over my shoulder, I spot him at the bar. He catches my eye and raises a hand in a friendly wave. I nod at him then look back to Nicole, a thought occurring to me.

"Bishop's not a bachelor."

Nicole pins me with a look. "*That's* what you took away from what I said? My point was Sam, not Bam. *Sam*, with an S. You told me to find a new topic and I did."

My lips turn up at the sides.

"But if *you're* going to bring it up," she continues, "Bam and his girlfriend broke up right before the draft. Apparently he wanted the freedom to bang whoever once he had a bit of fame."

My brow furrows. "Who told you that?"

"Danielle."

I roll my eyes. "Danielle likes to come up with the worst-case scenario for everything. If she can make it more dramatic, she will."

"I know. I'm not saying it's true, just repeating what I heard." She pauses, and we each take a sip of our drink. Then she speaks again. "Besides, isn't that what you assumed when you guys broke up? That he wanted the freedom to...play the field at college?"

I clench my jaw and roll my glass between my palms, staring down into the dark brown liquid.

"No. Bishop would never do that," I say. "He just... wouldn't."

It might have been my greatest fear, but I never really believed it was true. Bishop might be a charmer, but he's not a sleazeball. He wasn't ever the 'play the field' kind of guy when we were younger. We dated for two years and were friends for years before that. Not once did I worry that he wished he were free to screw around with other girls.

We were kids back then, though, and it's been four years since the last time we talked. A lot can happen over that much time.

"Besides…who knows what I assumed back then?" I finally say. "It's been so long, who can remember?"

It's a lie though. I do remember. I remember everything, the good *and* the bad, but mostly the good.

And that's the real reason why seeing him hurts so much.

chapter five
bishop

I take another sip of my beer and lean my hip against the railing, looking out along the length of Main Street from where Cedar Cider sits at the end of the road on an incline. It's a pretty dope view with all the shops stretched out and the lake in the background, and I don't doubt I'll be here on a regular basis.

Boyd and Rusty and their friend Jackson did an amazing job with this place. Part of me wishes I'd been around a bit more as it was being built, but I was busy all summer at a training camp prepping for the draft combine. I guess if I have to be back in town because of this stupid injury, I can be glad I'm at least here to see the opening and enjoy the fruits of my brother's labor: delicious beer on tap. Who knows? Maybe I can talk him into giving me a family discount or something.

I smile at the thought—Boyd would *never* go for that—then spin around, resting my butt against the rail and looking inside, through the windows, back into the crowd snuggled away from the late September air that's been a bit more chilly than normal.

Pretty much everyone in town is here tonight, enjoying beer, mingling inside or out here on the patio, chatting away.

They're also all asking a lot of questions about my arm, hence why I'm out here while most of the people I know are inside. Originally, I mustered up the energy to come because I wanted to be here to support Boyd. I love my brother, and Bellamy made a good point when she hinted that it would mean a lot to him for me to be here.

But the unwanted questions started almost immediately.

Are you moving back to town for good?

Did they release you from the team?

Will you still be able to play?

I grew tighter and tighter and tighter, until I could barely handle it anymore. Then Gabi walked in, and it felt like all the air had been vacuumed out of my lungs. She looked gorgeous, of course, like she always does. Long dark hair flowing down her back. Lips tinged with maroon, hazel eyes glowing.

She froze when she saw me then looked away quickly and moved to the bar with Nicole. I don't know what I pictured when I came home, but it definitely didn't include Gabi Ventura avoiding me like I have the plague.

Clearly I couldn't have been more wrong.

My mood, already sour, took an even more bitter dive after that, and now I just want to go home, but I promised my parents I'd stick around for a while. Also, it would feel shitty to bounce so quickly when I see my brother so rarely anymore.

Not that we're hanging out tonight. He's in there catching up with friends and helping problem solve, I'm sure. As he should be. As much as Boyd was ready to escape this town once he graduated, out of all the Mitchell children, he takes after my parents the most. He's a bit grumbly but knows how to converse with pretty much anyone. It helps that his fiancée, Ruby, is a bright, shining star as well.

Sure enough, when I shift around and scan the inside, I can see Boyd and Ruby chatting away with a handful of customers. If I want a chance to talk with my brother at all, I'm sure I'll be here for a while, waiting.

The door opens to my left and Rush walks out, beer in hand, smile on his face.

"This place is hoppin'," he says, crossing the patio and sidling up next to me where I'm still leaning back against the rail. "And *dang* it's getting cold. I am not ready for fall weather. Why are you out here freezing your ass off?"

I laugh. "I love the cold, man."

Rush takes a sip from his glass and nods. "I know, and I don't think I'll ever get it. Give me long summer days and hot, hot heat for as long as I live, and I'll be a happy man." He chuckles then glances at me. "You're seriously not cold?"

I shake my head. "Nah. I can't wait for it to snow."

Rush shakes his head again. "I guess it makes sense that it was *your* idea to start that polar plunge thing."

Grinning, I shrug. "What can I say? I'm a creative guy."

"Bullshit you're creative. You're a monster is what you are. Making us all freeze our nuts off in the lake in January."

Shrugging again, I take a drink from my own beer, a smirk on my face. "It was optional."

"Sure it was."

I wanted to make my mark freshman year with the team, and when we got into a kind of 'dare you to do this stupid thing' hazing situation during the winter between Fall Ball and the regular spring season, I had to go dunk in the brutally cold water of Cedar Lake. Instead of squealing and rushing out of the water, I just floated there, eyeing the upperclassmen with a smirk on my face as they all stood on the dock staring down at me.

"Anyone wanna join me? It's not so bad," I taunted.

Was I lying my ass off? Absolutely. Did I stay floating in the water for several minutes while the captain of the team got increasingly more anxious that I'd die of hypothermia and he'd get in trouble for hazing? You fucking bet, and it was worth every painful minute to watch him squirm.

The following year, we did it as a team and collectively agreed it was optional, officially putting the bullshit dares to rest. Even so, the polar plunge became a yearly tradition, and it stuck around after I left.

"Do the guys still do that shit?" I ask, double-checking that my legacy as the Polar King remains. A self-declared title, to be sure.

Rush pins me with a look. "Of course we do. *You* created the tradition and everyone knew you were going somewhere. Nobody wanted to risk ending something Bam created. Too much superstition."

I grin, finishing off the last of my beer and setting my glass on the railing next to me. Nothing is more a part of baseball than the superstition that comes along with almost every facet of the best sport on earth.

My junior year of college, I ate a ham and cheese sandwich before every single game for an entire season because we won the first game and I didn't want to ruin it for everyone. It's the one perfect season Whitney College has ever had. I can't officially take credit—we were a team, after all—but I definitely played a part in holding it together with those ham and cheese sammies.

"So...how was your chat with Gabriela?"

At Rush's question, I let out a sigh that ends in an awkward chuckle.

"It was…something." My eyes glance through the window and spot the woman in question as she crosses the room to head back to the bar.

"Seemed tense when I left you two alone."

"That's because it was."

We stand there for a while, not saying anything, before I finally speak again.

"She ever talk to you about our breakup?" I ask, glancing at Rush.

He shakes his head. "You two were off at college. I didn't see her again until she moved back, and at that point, two years had passed. I figured everyone had kind of moved on from it, you know?" He shrugs. "Besides, she and I weren't as close as you two were. If she wanted to talk to someone about you, it would have been Nicole, not me."

I nod, knowing he's right. Gabi isn't much for talking about the things going on in her mind. She tends to take her emotions and bottle them up pretty tight. So while Rush, Gabi, Nicole, and I did run in the same friend group, the idea that Gabi would confide in Rush about our breakup is a little far-fetched.

Still, would have been nice if he had some sort of insight.

"She said she has no obligation to make nice since I'm the one who dumped her," I share, having replayed that line over and over again in my mind since she said it two days ago.

Rush snorts. "Sounds like something she'd say." He takes a sip of his beer. "So what actually *did* happen between you two? The town talk made it seem like you dumped her because you wanted to sow your wild oats."

I look at him, a pinched expression on my face. "Who said that?"

"My dad."

My face falls and I rub a hand over my beard. The curse of living in a small town. Everyone thinks they know everything.

"Well, I can promise you that's not true. I'm not that kind of guy."

Rush nods. "Sure. That's fine. I'm just telling you what I heard. We never really talked about it, you know?"

Yeah, I know. I didn't talk about it with anyone. Just kept it to myself, this painful hole in my chest that made it hard to breathe. Eventually, I learned to deal with it, and it just became a part of me.

"I did break up with her," I tell him, "but it's a lot more complicated than that."

He sighs. "Isn't it always?" He tilts back his beer, finishing it off. "I'm gonna head back in. Want anything?"

"Nah, I'm good. Thanks, though. Just gonna stay out here for a while."

He nods then goes inside, leaving me alone with my thoughts. I keep thinking about the way she looked at me, both at the hardware store and in the hallway at school, and I can't get it out of my head.

There was a time when Gabi looked at me like I was the most important person in the world. I get that we're not together anymore, so it's unrealistic for me to think she'd still see me that way, but I didn't think she'd...*hate* me. I didn't think she wouldn't want to be in the same room as me. I assumed, at the very least, we could still be friends, but it seems like that's the absolute last thing she wants.

Once the chill starts to creep through my sweater a bit too deeply, I head back inside, crossing over to where Bellamy and my sister Busy are chatting near the bar.

"Amazing turnout, huh?" Bellamy says, linking her arm in my good one. "And all the Mitchell kids are together tonight. We should take a picture."

Busy snorts. "I came up to support Boyd, not to be a part of your scrapbook."

Bellamy grins and rolls her eyes. "I don't scrapbook."

The two of them return to the conversation they were in the middle of when I approached – talking about some guy Busy has been seeing at school – and I take that as a chance to look around the room.

I'm distracted by the fact that I don't see Gabi anywhere, and my shoulders fall when I realize she's probably gone home. I feel like I should go find her, talk to her, fix whatever thing has truly broken between us.

But at the same time, I know that brokenness is something I caused, and more importantly, she asked me to leave her alone. Even though I might want a chance to try to fix things, get things off my chest, I still want to respect what she's asked of me, no matter how shitty it feels.

"Hey, I'm gonna take off," I say, adjusting the sling at the back of my neck where it's rubbing against my skin too roughly. "I'm just not feeling it anymore."

Bellamy gives me a look I hate, one filled with pity.

"You sure? I think they're gonna do a speech soon."

Sighing, my shoulders fall. I'd feel guilty if I missed that, if I begged out early because...what? Because I'm feeling a bit sad about my ex not wanting to be besties? Pathetic, and worth every ounce of that pity look Bellamy gave me.

"I guess I can stay a little longer," I tell her, trying to force an easy smile.

It doesn't feel natural though. I still feel distracted, and I

can't help but look around the bar for Gabi one more time.
My heart dips when I realize she's really gone.

"We are excited to offer this in-service opportunity to our
new faculty members at CPHS every year," Principal Cohen begins, a wide smile on her face as she stands at the front of the
classroom.

A bright presentation is on the screen behind her reading
"New Employee In-Service Day". It matches the equally bright
folder on the desk in front of me containing a bunch of bullshit
on CPHS core foundations and some other stuff I scanned over
quickly. If I'd known staff development would be part of taking
on the job as a part-time baseball coach, I might not have agreed
to do it at all.

But even as I think it, I know that's not true. I've only been
helping out for a week so far, and I'm actually really enjoying
working with the kids. They seem enthusiastic about baseball,
and it fills me up inside, reminding me of the excitement I felt
during my own days on the team.

"Now that the school year has started and you've settled into
your new roles," Principal Cohen continues, drawing my attention back to this room, "we're going to spend some uninterrupt-
ed time together, focusing on professional development."

I can practically hear the collective groan in the room,
though there are only a handful of us present. The slide on the
screen changes, but before she says anything else, I hear the door

open behind me. When I glance back, I have to blink twice when I see Gabi entering the room, an apologetic smile on her face.

"Ms. Ventura. So glad you could join us."

By the sound of the principal's voice, I'd argue she is in fact *not* glad Gabi is here. *I*, on the other hand, am quite pleased to see her.

"I'm so sorry," she says, her eyes skimming the room briefly before stopping on me.

"Please take a seat. We're just getting started."

Gabi looks away and moves to the other side of the room, choosing a chair in the back corner. Realizing my opportunity to look at her is now gone, I spin back in my seat and face the front.

Everything Principal Cohen says after that is a bunch of gobbledygook. A few slides are displayed on the screen, something about the school's guiding principles, but all I can think about is the fact that Gabi is just a few feet away.

It feels like random luck that she's here, though I guess it's good luck for me and bad luck for her based on the way her nose wrinkled when she saw me.

Eventually, I drag my attention back to the screen.

"So, now that we've reviewed some of the information intrinsic to our educational approach here at CPHS, we're going to take a look at what the day ahead will bring."

She switches to a new slide.

"We've already started with reviewing our foundational ideas. Next we'll discuss some OSHA and legal updates that we just *have* to get out of the way. Sorry about that. Then we'll break for lunch before returning to do some teambuilding activities. We want to make sure you folks get to know each other and know you're not alone as our newest employees. Finally we'll wrap up by discussing the year and creating your professional development plans so you feel supported in pursuing the things that make you the most passionate about education."

I can't help but roll my eyes and glance back at Gabi, who is sitting with her arms crossed and about as much enthusiasm on her face as I'm sure is reflected on mine. This feels like a bunch of stuff that isn't going to apply to me as a part-time coach for just a few months. OSHA and legal are two things I couldn't care less about, and the professional development plan sounds like a nightmare.

I suppose the teambuilding doesn't seem so bad. We do a lot of those exercises at the start of each new year in baseball as a way to get to know the new guys and make them feel like part of the team.

We sit in silence for the next two hours, reviewing new regulations regarding workplace safety and discussing the impact of new laws on students working as TAs and blah blah blah. I find my eyes continuing to scan the room, straying back toward where Gabi sits, though I look away quickly as soon as I realize what I'm doing.

It truly is as boring as I assumed it would be, and when we finally stop for lunch, I'm practically crawling out of my skin. I've never been a good student. I don't mean I'm not smart, I mean I don't enjoy sitting silently in a room, staring at information on a screen for hours. It's boring as hell. Give me a lesson that's engaging and interactive and I'll be a vocal, active participant. Talk at me from a pulpit and you might as well be speaking a foreign language.

Once Principal Cohen leaves the room, letting us know she'll be back after lunch, the sense of relief is palpable.

"I hate these things," an elderly gentleman says as he grabs a sandwich and puts it on his plate. "I've been teaching for 20 years. I don't need to do any more teambuilding exercises."

"Tell me about it," says a blonde who looks a bit familiar. She's standing next to a window, scrolling on her phone. "I used to teach here. The fact that I have to go through this again is ridiculous."

"Ah, come on guys," I say as I head toward the lunch table along the back wall. "It's not that bad."

When I glance at Gabi, I find her just watching, having not moved out of her chair yet to grab any food.

"You're the kid helping with baseball, right?"

I look over to the older guy—Bill, according to his nametag—and nod. "Yeah."

"These aren't so bad the first few times. But after 20 years of these meetings, we'll see how bad you think they are."

My eyes widen and I can't help but chuckle. *Yeesh.* Wouldn't want this guy as a teacher, I can promise that.

"Thanks for the input, Bill," I say, giving him a salute. Then I make a bold decision to cross over to where Gabi is sitting and take the seat next to her. "If Cohen's not careful, she's gonna have a mutiny on her hands," I joke quietly before taking a big bite of my sandwich.

When Gabi doesn't say anything in response, just continues to sit there silently, I try something else.

"It's wild that she's still here, right? I mean, I know it's only been four years since we graduated, but it feels like forever."

"Yeah. Wild."

She pushes out of her seat and walks over to the table of food, leaving me behind.

My shoulders fall. Any hope I had that maybe today would be a chance for me to talk to her, even briefly, feels shot to shit.

When she finishes plating her food, she turns around and

glances at me for a long moment. A glimmer reappears...but then she walks to the other side of the room—the complete opposite from where she was sitting before, where I'm sitting now—and takes a seat, alone, before ripping open a bag of chips.

Suddenly, a mutiny doesn't sound so bad.

chapter six

gabi

When lunch is over and Principal Cohen returns, I'm almost grateful. The silence in the classroom was the worst, especially knowing Bishop was across the room, studiously looking at his phone.

But then she says three words that fill me with dread.

"Time for icebreakers!"

On any normal day, I hate these exercises. They feel like pointless excuses to get people to talk to each other who normally wouldn't. Not to mention the fact that icebreakers seem to be a time when the attention seekers dump all their emotional turmoil in the center of the room for everyone to stare at uncomfortably. I'm not interested in getting my own trauma from someone else's horror stories. Thanks, but no thanks.

But today isn't just a normal day. It's a day when I've had to work my ass off not to look at or talk to Bishop, and this exercise is basically going to chuck all that hard work right in the trash.

"Because there are only six of you today, we'll just start

out with a simple exercise of sharing a bit about ourselves and how we came to be working here at CPHS, okay? Then we'll do something a little more fun."

I gotta hand it to her. She was able to say all of that with a smile on her face, and I believed her excitement the entire time.

Wild.

Once we've moved our desks into a circle, the older guy starts first. Bill talks about how he just moved to Cedar Point a few months ago. He taught in Colorado for years but moved so he and his partner could be close to his in-laws.

Then the blonde—Gail—shares that she used to work at CPHS but retired a few years ago. I thought she looked familiar.

"I just didn't know what to do with all that free time, so…I've unretired," she says, drawing laughter from around the room.

Next it's Bishop's turn, and I can feel the way my body turns toward him as he speaks.

"Hey everyone, I'm Bishop. Some of you might know me because I used to be a student here at CPHS. Graduated about four years ago. I'm back in town for a few months, and Rush— he's the coach of the baseball team—asked for some extra help. So…that's me."

"Oh hey, I heard about you," Bill says. "Bishop Mitchell, right? Didn't you go play in the pros? I thought they were watching you on a TV at The Mitch just a little while ago."

I can see the discomfort in Bishop's face as he answers, though he hides it well behind that smile.

"Yeah, I was drafted to play for the Salem Kings. They're the affiliate team with the Portland Flame," he answers. Then he points to his arm, strapped tightly to his body in that sling he's always wearing. "But I got injured, so I'm just home for now while I rehab this thing. Then I'll be heading back to Oregon."

He pauses briefly. "Enjoying a break before *unretiring*, too," he jokes, his eyes sliding over to Gail.

Everyone chuckles, and then the introductions move on to the bearded guy sitting to Bishop's right, but I'm not listening when he speaks. Instead, I keep glancing discretely at Bishop.

There was something in the way he said that that stood out to me. When we were younger, I could always tell when Bishop was hiding something. It's not that he was inherently dishonest or anything like that. No, Bishop was always an almost overly truthful person. It's the reason we used to get in trouble so much—because he was so bad at lying.

But who knows? Maybe I didn't see anything. Maybe he's different now. Maybe I don't know Bishop anymore.

When he glances at me, I look quickly to Sheryl, a new administrative assistant who is talking about…well, I don't really know. But I still look her way, trying to refocus my attention on anyone else in the room.

Eventually it's my turn and I babble only slightly coherently about getting roped into summer school and then sticking around for the full semester. Though I can't remember exactly because I was too focused on the wall behind Principal Cohen's head.

Then we move on to other group exercises, which go quickly and aren't *too* painful. We work together to come up with a Mad Lib about a typical day at school. We move a marble across the room without touching it. We draw a classroom flag and then share what all the different elements mean. It's a bunch of nonsense, but it's not as shitty as some of the others I've done in the past.

Then we talk about professional development plans, which doesn't feel directly relevant to me since I doubt I'll be teaching for more than a semester or two at the most. I add things to my list of yearly goals like *attend an art seminar* and *enter my work in an art show*, which are things I already have planned for the next few months.

It's all pretty pointless, but at least we're getting paid to be here...I think. Actually, I never asked about that, and I make a mental note to check with Principal Cohen after we're done.

What *is* painful is when she announces the fact that we'll be in NSPs: new staff partnerships.

"The goal of an NSP is to provide resources to you as a new employee. You'll be paired with another new employee, someone you can turn to who is probably going through some of those same growing pains you are."

I know I'll be partnered with Bishop before she says it, and I can't help the little thing inside me that both groans and delights in the news. It's a very confusing reaction.

"Gabriela and Bishop. Normally we go by department, but since you're both part-time faculty with smaller workloads, this felt like the right call."

I want to stand up and shout *You're wrong!* It certainly doesn't feel like the right call to me.

"Go ahead and meet in your pairs and move through the NSP worksheet at the back of your folder. I'll be back in a half hour," she says before darting out of the room faster than I can think to beg her to change my partner.

I glance at Bishop, spotting the apprehension in his expression. Slowly, he pushes away from his desk, crosses over to where I am, and drops into a seat next to mine.

"We can ask her to switch. If you want to."

I'm not surprised he offers. Even though he might be misguided about the idea that we could be friends, he really is the kind of guy who won't push just to get what he wants. I don't doubt he'd be more than happy to be partners. I don't doubt he thinks we would find some sort of enjoyment in the process.

The hard part is, I agree with him. Given enough time together, Bishop and I probably *could* be friends again. I bet we *could* smile and laugh at memories from the past, from our years of friendship, all the inside jokes and happy moments.

But the part of me that's still hurt by the way things ended between us is standing tall, waving a giant warning flag.

I look over at the other two pairs, seeing them chatting animatedly, already making friends, then I look back at Bishop.

"We'll be fine," I say, giving him a tight smile, opting to just let it happen and not think too much about it. "I mean, how complicated can this NSP thing really be?"

"Weekly! Meetings!" I shout, pacing the length of the living room as Nicole sits on the couch.

She has a bowl of popcorn in her lap and watches me, her eyes tracking my path as I walk the same few feet of carpet over and over again.

"I've been assigned to weekly meetings with my ex-boyfriend as a part of my job. Why is this a thing?"

"Because you decided to teach a bunch of teenagers," she says, chuckling and tossing another piece of popcorn into her mouth.

I glare at her, and her expression becomes apologetic.

"Sorry," she says. "Not the point. Your luck in this situation is rotten. 100%. It is entirely unfair."

"*Entirely* unfair."

"You have every right to be irritated."

"So irritated."

"Have you thought about just...*not* meeting with him?"

Sighing, I stop my pacing and drop down on the couch next to her.

"I did think about that, but we have to email in each week sharing what we talked about and any concerns we have."

Reaching over, I grab a few pieces of popcorn from Nicole's bowl and pop one into my mouth.

"So lie."

"I'll just lie!" I snort, chucking a piece at her face. "I could probably do that," I tell her, "but Bishop couldn't."

Nicole slumps down, resting her bowl on her stomach and laying her feet across my lap.

"Well that sucks."

I've been thinking about it nonstop since Principal Cohen shared the expectations with us during the in-service earlier today, first wondering if I can get out of it and then imagining what it will be like.

"But what if it doesn't?" I say, speaking aloud the fear that has been pulsing in my chest from the moment I saw Bishop two weeks ago.

"What if what doesn't what?"

I look at Nicole. "What if it doesn't suck? What if I like spending time with him every week? What if I forget about how much it hurt when we broke up because I like what it feels like to spend time together again?"

She's silent for a while, and I'm not sure if it's because she doesn't know what to say or she doesn't know how to say it. Eventually, when she does speak, what she says isn't a surprise.

"The what-ifs don't matter because he's leaving again. Right?"

I let my head rest on the back of the couch and stare at the ceiling, knowing what she's saying is true. It's callous, sure, but true nonetheless.

"Bam's plan has always been to go chase his dream somewhere else. He's not staying, so you don't have to worry about all the what-ifs because eventually, he will leave. He will go back to his little farm team in suburban Oregon and keep focusing on *his* goals, and you'll still be here, focused on yours."

We're both silent as I ruminate on that thought, on this idea that I'll be spending regular time with Bishop Mitchell. Sure, it'll just be a brief meeting, twenty to thirty minutes at most, but it will still be there on my calendar every single week.

"And who knows, maybe it'll do you two some good," she continues. "You can hash out all that shit from four years ago, you know? Getting some closure does everyone at least a little good."

Also true, but not something I am interested in whatsoever. Bishop broke up with me, yes, but as devastated as I was, as much as it tore me apart, I've never been one to fault someone for doing what is right for them. For whatever reason—a reason I've never understood—Bishop thought it was better for us to end our relationship. There doesn't *need* to be some dramatic explanation. There doesn't *need* to be some…resolution to a pain from years ago.

Besides, talking about it means I'd have to share with him what it was like on *my* end, and that's the last thing I want to do.

Maybe it *is* better that we've been partnered together. We'll be forced to talk to each other in short spurts about meaningless bullshit.

I mean, he's a Mitchell. He's going to keep coming back here, year after year, and do I really want to continue having to avoid town every time I hear he's around?

Hopefully it will be just…simple, unemotional. And by being so simple and unemotional, maybe all the pain will leak out, just leaving behind two boring people talking about boring school stuff.

But then I think about the way my emotions overtook me when I saw him…just how *un*-unemotional it was…and I can't help but wonder if I'm hoping on a lark.

"You two will figure it out," she says. "But remember, if you ever need someone to hide a body, I will come along for emotional support but don't want to do any heavy lifting."

I laugh, and we move on.

Eventually, Nicole takes off—making me promise not to skip yoga ever again, even if it's for work—and I head into my shed. On top of completing work for clients who are waiting on commissioned pieces, I also have to finish some of the adjustments I'm making to a set of vases that are getting displayed in an art show in November.

It was Leah who encouraged me to submit my portfolio, which I never would have thought about doing on my own. She's had her macrame pieces featured in magazines and museums over the course of her life, and she told me those doors opened for her because of art shows she was featured in, times she networked and chatted with donors and other creators.

Just the idea of the whole thing makes my stomach turn over, but I'm trying to push myself harder when it comes to my art. I've been really fortunate so far to have a bit of luck take me a long way. If I want that to keep taking me places, I need to make sure I throw in a few challenges to prompt growth.

That's what this art show will be: a challenge. Not the art, but the networking. I'm not good at easy conversation. Never have been. Not like, say, Bishop, who could make a cement wall laugh.

I shake my head, not even sure where that thought came from, but before I can manage to shut him out completely, memories of what it was like to be on Bishop's arm—things I haven't thought about in years—come rushing back.

High school dances.

Dinner with his family.

Community gatherings.

Baseball events.

I always dragged my feet at first, complaining about all the people and all the talking and how I had homework or wanted to draw instead.

Secretly, though, I loved being at his side. My introverted nature was always exhausted when I got home, but there was a tiny well within me that was filled up any time we did something like that together.

Conversation always felt easier.

Laughter always hit harder.

Joy lasted longer.

That fear I shared with Nicole earlier still lingers in my spirit, whispering about the pain I felt all those years ago, but at this wave of good memories, those voices quiet.

Even if there are some awkward, uncomfortable moments with Bishop doing these meetings, surely there will be some positive ones, and maybe it *would* do me good to spend a few months dulling the rough edges of that bitterness that's still lodged in my chest.

Sighing, I tug out my phone, pull up Bishop's contact info, and give him a call. It rings three times before he answers, and I can hear the surprise in his voice when he does.

"Gabi. Hey."

"Hi, Bishop."

"How have the last few hours been?" he asks, his voice slightly teasing.

My lips curve. "Good. Hung out with Nicole for a bit. I was thinking about this whole…NSP thing."

"Yeah, I've been thinking about it, too. If you want to go to Principal Cohen and tell her we're not doing it, I'll support that. I'll say the same thing."

"I appreciate that. But…I've decided I'm okay with it. Maybe it'll be a good thing, us spending some time together while you're home."

There's a beat of silence on the other end, and I know I've surprised him again.

"Why do I feel like you're secretly plotting my murder?"

I can't help but smile.

"Look, a lot has happened between us over the years, but we were friends first, right? We…should be able to be friends again."

I'm not sure how convincing my words are, because there's a part of me that doesn't believe them myself. I do believe in their intention, to move on from the bitterness and into a place of peace, for both of us.

"I'd love that," he says, and I can hear the sincerity in his voice. It wraps tightly around my throat, and I swallow thickly, trying to shove it aside.

"Alright, well…I'll text you later to set up our first meeting."

"Sounds good. I'll talk to you later."

"Night, Bishop."

"Night, Gabs."

I end the call and stare at my phone for a long moment, a mixture of emotions swirling inside me. That wasn't so bad, right? And it should only get easier.

Turning back to my work, I try not to listen to the little thing inside me saying I'm kidding myself to think that could ever be true.

chapter seven
bishop

"Alright, Justin, this time I want you to turn your back foot a bit more. It's really important you turn your hips *all* the way out or you're not going to get a full rotation."

I demonstrate with my legs the movement I want him to make, and he just stares at me.

"The rotation starts when your front heel drops, right? You want your back hip to punch forward. Don't be afraid to let your toe drag." I smile and pat Justin on the shoulder. "Let's see you give it a try."

Stepping back, I motion for Tommy to drop a ball into the pitching machine. Justin sighs and gets into batting position, tapping the base twice with his bat then bringing it up behind his shoulders. The ball drops in, it shoots out at Justin…

…and he does the exact same swing he's been doing since I met him last week.

"That's okay, let's go over it again," I tell him, holding my good hand up to Tommy to indicate he should wait a minute.

"Was there something about how I explained this that didn't make sense?"

"Look, I get what you're doing and all," he replies, tucking his bat under his armpit and adjusting his gloves. "But my swing is fine. I don't know if you know, but I'm the number one hitter on the team this year."

I nod. "I know, Coach Rush has had amazing things to say about you. Says you have raw talent."

Justin smirks.

"But he also says you don't like to listen to advice, and if you don't learn to take in recommendations from coaches, your raw talent is going to peter out in comparison to people who put in the extra work."

At that, his arrogant expression falls, his eyes narrowing.

"I get where you're at. I was there, too," I continue. "You have a big swing. I had a big swing. You're a top player on your team. I was a top player on my team. I remember what it was like to think I knew it all. It's part of being young. You don't know what you don't know."

I rest my good hand on his shoulder and try to make sure I'm communicating this as clearly as possible.

"But if you want to play in college, you're going to have to learn to take on the critiques that come every time you level up. No coach wants a player who won't do what they're told."

Justin shakes off my hand, his expression souring.

"Says the guy who ignored *his* coach and fucked up his hand so bad he needed surgery."

I grit my teeth but let the irritation roll in one way and out the other.

"You're literally making my point for me, my guy." I chuckle, pointing at the stupid cast on my arm and wishing I wasn't

71

having to admit this out loud for the first time to a 16-year-old. "See what happens when you're only concerned with showing off? When you ignore the advice of the people who are literally being paid to help you get better? You can fucking hurt yourself, or someone else. Or cost your team a game."

He scoffs. "I've never cost my team a game." Justin looks around at the other players doing various exercises on the field. "You wanna help someone get better? Pick literally *anyone* else. I guarantee they need more work than me."

He chucks his bat on the ground and jogs off to where a handful of the guys are tossing the ball back and forth.

"I doubt anyone will get through to that kid," Rush says, coming up behind me, a clipboard in hand and a smile on his face. "Didn't you hear? He knows everything."

I roll my eyes. "Know-it-alls fuck me off so hard," I grumble, my eyes scanning the field. "Who's next?"

Rush glances down at his list, his finger tracing down the page. "Last one of the day," he tells me before shouting across the field at one of the players. "Ruben! You're up!"

A tall kid begins jogging over as Rush gives me a quick run-down of what his batting history has been like this year and last, and I mentally begin to frame up how I want to work with him.

We've been at these one-on-ones since the middle of last week. I spent the first week as the batting coach just observing the team as a whole, trying to get to know the guys. Then we moved into individual meetings. Rush said he wants me working individually with each player, helping them improve in my own area of expertise.

Which is, of course, batting. I make no bones about it: my shining feature is my big swing. My homerun record at this school was over 100 more than the second guy on the list. I averaged a homerun *per game.*

But in every other area, I'm just like everyone else. Sure, I can run fast, but other guys are faster. I'm a good fielder and I've done a few running dives for balls in the outfield, but I've had plenty hit the ground, and my arm is mid at best.

To make up for where I'm lacking, I condition harder. I practice more. I do research and watch tape of myself and take every piece of advice that will make me better.

In high school, though, I was more cocky than I am now. I mean, every athlete has at least a little bit of arrogance. You have to believe you're the best in order to put your body on the line like we do, day after day, practice after practice, game after game. Workouts and nutrition and on and on it goes.

But like I told Justin, when you're young, you don't know what you don't know. When I was a player here—a Cedar Point Pirate—I thought I knew it all. Then I had a meeting with Coach Graham where he kind of laid it out for me the way I just did for Justin, though Coach G was a lot more abrasive than I am. Hence why I tried a softer approach today.

Who knows? Maybe Justin *needs* the tough-as-nails coach in order to listen. I guess we'll have to wait and see.

"Alright, that's it for the day, guys!" Rush calls out once I've finished working with Ruben. "Clean up, round up!"

The players collect all the gear scattered across the field then make their way over, forming a half circle once they've put balls into buckets and cones in a pile.

"We only have a few weeks left of outdoor training before the temps start to really drop, and then we'll be relegated to indoor strength and conditioning. So make sure you're all bringing your A game, got it?"

A round of "*Yes, Coach*" rises from the guys, and then everyone is putting their hand in the middle.

"Pirates on three. One, two, three, Pirates!"

I catch Justin rolling his eyes, his mouth closed during the group cheer. When his gaze catches mine, he just stares at me blank-faced for a beat before jogging off the field to the locker rooms with everyone else.

Letting out a sigh, I glance at Rush. "You forgot to warn me about teenage attitudes when you offered me this job."

He laughs. "*Warn* you? If I remember correctly, you had just as much attitude when we were running around this place. Or did you forget about the time you gave Coach G the middle finger and stormed off the field after he benched you for that scrimmage with Spencer Creek?"

Wincing, I chuckle under my breath as I pick up a bucket of balls with my good hand. "Maybe not my finest moment. My dad lit into me about that one."

"Mark Mitchell? Mr. Calm? I don't believe it."

"Oh, yeah. He sat me down on the couch and let me know if he ever caught wind of me treating someone with disrespect like that again, there would be no more baseball. I was officially shaking in my boots at that threat."

Rush snorts. "I like how your idea of your dad 'lighting you up' is just him sitting you down to let you know there would be consequences."

I raise an eyebrow.

"You wanna know what being 'lit up' looks like, you should have seen my dad when I told him I wanted to be a high school baseball coach." He shakes his head, laughing.

"I can only imagine."

We step into his office, and I set down the bucket of balls.

"With Justin, though…his dad's not in the picture, you

know?" Rush continues. "He's got some anger he doesn't know how to deal with."

I nod, knowing from my relationship with Gabi what it looks like when parents let you down. Her mom up and left her when she was only a few years younger than Justin, and some of the armor she wears is a direct result of that.

"Well, hopefully he figures out how not to take it out on his teammates."

"Or his coaches," Rush volleys back with a smile."

I shake my head. "I'm gonna head out. See you tomorrow?"

He drops down into his desk chair. "Yep. You go ahead and have a nice evening while I sit here and grade papers."

"Grade papers?" I ask, laughing. "For a PE class?"

"We just started the health component," he grumbles. "It's scantrons, but still…"

Chuckling, I give him a wave. "Sounds lame. Glad I'm not you!" I joke.

Rush flips me off as I leave his office behind, still laughing while I stroll down the hallway toward the parking lot. When I come to the door leading outside, I see Gabi emerging from the main entrance, eyes on her phone as she makes her way to her car. For a minute, I just watch her, taking in the way her long hair whips behind her in the breeze.

Then I bring out my phone and open up a new text thread.

Me: So, when did you want to have our meeting?

I look up, watching her out the window. She slows to a stop, still looking at her phone, and stands there for a long minute before she begins texting. When I look at my phone, I see the gray bubbles pop up before a short message comes through.

Gabi: Thursday?

I respond quickly, trying to grab her before she drives away.

Me: Not today?
Gabi: I'm already on my way home.

I let out a long sigh then wait until she drives off before responding.

Me: No worries. Want me to just swing by your classroom?
Gabi: Sure. See you then.

It's not surprising that she wants to wait until Thursday. I'm sure in her mind, it's a future Gabi problem, but I wanted to at least try to see if we could chat today.

That conversation we had on Saturday night, where she told me she thinks we might be able to be friends again? I don't want her to forget that. I don't want her to change her mind and realize I still have that plague she was so sure I had when I first got to town.

The truth is that Gabi was just putting up a wall because I hurt her, something I swore I would never do. Any chance she'll give me to try to be her friend again, I'll take it. I just don't want to strike out before I even get to the plate.

I knock twice on Gabi's classroom door before I push it open, finding her sitting at a pottery wheel, a lump of clay spinning in front of her.

I'd heard she picked up pottery during art school from someone a few years ago, though I don't remember who. Watching her sit at that wheel, I can tell she enjoys it just from the way she's so focused on what's in front of her, not to mention the fact that she's teaching the class.

Somewhere in my head, I had just assumed if Gabi ever taught, it would have to do with drawing or sketching. When we were younger, she carried this sketchbook around with her everywhere. Seeing her now is a reminder of how much has changed over the years.

"Hey," I say, walking toward her, the thick door closing behind me with a loud thud.

"Hi," she replies, glancing up at me briefly but then returning her attention to whatever she's working on. "We can get started while I work on this, right?"

I nod, a little disappointed.

I imagined us sitting and chatting, not trying to cram this in while she's distracted by something else, but I shake it off. I said I wanted any chance to talk with her, to be a friend again, and this is it.

"Alright, I'll take notes on my phone and email them to Principal Cohen. Sound good?"

She nods. "Hit me with it."

I grin. "Okay. Share with your partner how you've been adjusting to your new position."

Gabi looks at me and rolls her eyes. "Is this seriously the type of shit we have to talk about every week?"

Shrugging, I scroll through the questions, looking at what

they ask of us.

"Adjusting to your new position…in need of any resources…best and worst part of your week," I say, listing them off one by one.

"Fine. No. The in-service," she says, looking at me with a sly smile. "Although I'm assuming that's not the type of answers she's looking for."

"Hey, we can try to get away with it if you want. Maybe it'll buy us a week or two."

Her grin remains, though she continues focusing on what she's making. Gabi's hands move gently, fluidly, like some sort of dance, as she pulls the clay upward and outward, into a large bowl.

"That's so cool. When did you get into ceramics?"

She licks her lips and puts one hand in the center then begins bringing the rims together.

Maybe it's not a bowl?

"I took a ceramics elective first semester at MSA. Fell head over heels for it. Changed my concentration and never looked back." Then she looks at me. "Have you ever thrown anything before?"

I raise an eyebrow. "Yeah. A baseball."

Gabi laughs, the sound familiar and beautiful as it blows open something inside me that I thought had closed.

"It's how we talk about pottery. You throw a vase, throw a mug. Right now, I'm throwing a pot."

"Ah, I thought it was a bowl."

She nods, continuing to gently edge the clay with her fingers.

"It looks that way when it starts, but then you bring it in and you get this really neat kind of rounded effect with the walls."

She narrows her eyes and leans forward, her wheel slowing down as she seemingly finishes off the rim. "And then you have a pot you can use for plants or…whatever."

Taking a wire, she scrapes it along the bottom, separating the clay from the wheel. Then she gently picks it up and puts it on a wooden board before crossing to the other side of the room and placing it on a rack next to a bunch of other pieces.

"Are those pieces your students have done?"

She nods. "They're doing a great job."

I watch her for a beat, noticing the hint of pride in her movements as she says that.

"Being a teacher suits you," I tell her.

Gabi looks surprised at my comment. "I'm not soft enough to be a teacher. You're supposed to want to like…change the world and stuff." She shakes her head. "But it's not the worst thing in the world."

"I bet you're better than you think. You're really good at pushing people to be better."

"Most people don't like to be pushed."

"Now *that*," I say, pointing at her, "is very true."

Gabi spends a few minutes washing her hands, and then she takes a seat at the computer sitting in the corner. Thankfully, she takes over trying to type up the notes because me pecking at my phone keyboard was not it.

"So let's type this thing up so we can get out of here?"

I nod, crossing over toward her. "Sure."

"How have you been adjusting to your new position?" she asks, wiggling her fingers above her keyboard.

"Good. It's been a lot of fun, very rewarding. The kids seem excited about baseball, which I like."

She records my answer, her fingers tapping the keys one at

a time. I grin, remembering watching her do that as she wrote her papers. Her typing skills aren't that much better than mine.

"Are you in need of any resources?"

"More baseballs and a better net to go in front of the pitching machine."

She types again.

"Best and worst part of your week."

I snort. "Well the worst part was getting talked to like I'm an idiot by a 16-year-old who thinks he knows how to play baseball better than everyone on the planet."

Gabi glances my way with raised eyebrows. "Tell me how you *really* feel."

I laugh. "Sorry. This kid is just a lot. Pushes all these buttons I didn't know I had."

She hums and returns her attention to the computer, typing up some version of my response.

"And the best part," I continue, deciding to be honest, "is right now, spending time with you."

Gabi's fingers freeze, whatever she was typing remaining unfinished.

She glances at me, her lips curved slightly, some amusement in her expression.

"I don't think that's the kind of answer she's looking for."

"Well it's the truth," I tell her. "I've been feeling off since I moved home, and sitting in here, talking to you...well, it's the happiest I've felt since being back."

She takes a deep breath and lets it out slowly.

"I'll just...put that you really like the kids' energy," she says, her fingers beginning to move again.

It's fine if she types up whatever, even if it's a lie. I don't care about this stupid NSP thing.

What I do care about is Gabi knowing how I feel, even if it surprises her, because it *is* the truth. I forgot what it was like to be around Gabi Ventura. The way my soul feels lighter. The way my smile is wider.

It's the best feeling in the world.

chapter eight
gabi

I'm sitting at my wheel, throwing the last piece of a matching set of four vases when my phone pings on Wednesday evening. Normally, I keep it on silent on the other side of the room while I'm working, but recently, I've been keeping it on and sitting on a white bucket next to me so I can see it when it lights up.

The reason for the change is something I don't want to think about too hard.

When the notification appears, my eyes dart to the screen, and my shoulders droop slightly when I see the text is from Nicole.

Nicole: Why are you always working? Don't you know your best friend is desperate for attention?

I huff out a laugh and return my focus to the clay in my hands, which is still in lump form and hasn't yet been molded into shape. I move slowly, adding water and pressing inward, bringing the clay up before pressing my fingers down in the center to open the middle.

The vases I'm working on are a new creation, long and narrow. So narrow that as I pull the clay upward, I have to use a wooden tool to even out the space at the bottom because my hand is too big to fit.

It requires a lot of focus, so when my phone chimes again ten minutes later and my eyes dart that way, I can tell instantly that I've made a mistake. I slow the wheel entirely so I don't risk damaging the piece and having to start fresh, then I use my elbow to wake my screen.

Bishop: You working?

I nibble on the inside of my cheek, warring with myself as I try to decide if I want to text him back. I'd have to wash my hands and pause my project for even longer and give in to the idea that I want to talk to him.

Ultimately, I let the screen go dark and begin spinning my wheel again.

It's been three weeks since Bishop and I had our first meeting, and it's been…surprisingly easy. We chat for a few minutes while I throw something on the wheel—a maneuver I drummed up so I didn't spend our first meeting together just staring at him—and then I type up some notes to send to Principal Cohen. It's been friendly and simple, and I don't mind them at all.

Which is maybe the problem. It's *nice* chatting with Bishop, sharing what's going on with my students and hearing about how things are going with his team. Listening to that deep voice of his is just…

I shake my head. I think it's a fair assessment to say I still

find Bishop attractive. I mean, I'm not blind, and he's still…
him. Kind and attentive and funny. God, he's funny. I'm not
one to laugh a lot, but the things he says always seem to hit me
in just the right spot.

I blush at that thought and try to return my attention to my
work, but Bishop is still there, hovering in the back of my mind.
And then two more texts pop up on my phone, back to back.

Bishop: I have an important request
Bishop: (image)

My curiosity finally gets the best of me, and I growl, letting
my wheel slow and crossing to the sink to wash my hands. This
better be good.

Grabbing the phone, I open my texts and pull up Bishop's
message. The picture is of him with a group of people I don't
recognize holding up a bunch of canvases that look very similar.
It looks like one of those wine and paint nights, and everyone
has some sort of yellow-orange sunset background with palm
tree silhouettes.

Except for Bishop, who clearly didn't follow directions. His
sunset is more brown than orange, and his trees look more like a
trunk with a scribble at the top than actual palm fronds.

He's never been particularly good at art—his words, not
mine—and he *barely* passed the art class we took together junior
year.

"Art requires a delicate, gentle approach," he said to Mrs.
Gardner, who stared at him, unimpressed. "I'm more of a bowling ball than a paper airplane."

I'd forgotten about that, and I grin to myself at the memory
as two more texts show up on my screen.

Bishop: I'm doing a paint thing Sunday night with Bellamy and a group of people, and I don't want to make a fool out of myself.
Bishop: Will you come and sit next to me and provide me with your secret art tips so I don't look like a complete neanderthal?

I shake my head, unable to keep the smile off my face.

Me: Isn't that the instructor's job?

Part of me thinks art classes like this are stupid. The people who organize them usually provide what is basically finger paint and then have everyone create the exact same image. It completely flies in the face of what makes art special—the unique quality.

But I also understand that it's more about socializing, and it makes art feel more accessible to people who don't have the tools in their home. Blah, blah, blah, I get it, though I'm not sure any of those reasons are enough to convince me one way or another. What *might* sway me is how I've felt about spending any more time with Bishop outside of our weekly meetings.

When I'm around him, I find myself beginning to forget about the past, and I don't want to forget about it. It needs to stand like a firmly rooted tree in the middle of the road between us as a reminder of something I *never* want to feel again in my life: discarded.

I felt it before as a child, when my dad left me and my mom. Then again in junior high, when my mom dropped me off at Leah's and never looked back. I thought that was it. No way could someone get hurt like that again, right?

Then Bishop dumped me, and I felt all those same pains anew. It affected my life, my relationships. I dated around quite a bit.

Okay, I slept around quite a bit.

I felt lost and alone and discarded *again*, and I didn't want to open myself up and get hurt. I tried to convince myself that sex could be an emotionless thing, just to get that physical release, to be wanted.

Eventually, I made it through that season and ended up in a relationship, though not an entirely appropriate one. Garrett was one of my professors, and what we were doing was a secret. Which is, I think, what made it so fun at first. It was an *affair*.

There was something enticing about it, sneaking around to have sex but not having to get too deep emotionally. Garrett essentially became my chance to get that physical release without having to trudge out to bars to find it.

I never felt the things I did with Bishop. Obviously. Garrett constantly commented on the fact that I wouldn't open up to him, and I made it clear that I didn't plan to. The last thing you want to do after you've felt such pain is open yourself up to it again.

I lick my lips and continue staring at my phone, trying to decide what to do. Ultimately, I hold off on responding and instead return to my workstation. There's no harm in giving it a few hours or a day to decide. It'll give me extra time to really think about it.

A little while later, I get another one.

Bishop: No pressure if it doesn't sound fun. Thought it might be a cool thing to do with friends but understand if you're not feeling it. Good luck with work tonight!

I sigh, wondering if I'm making a mistake by keeping him at a distance, or if the mistake is talking to him at all.

Immediately, I know that's not the case. I can just feel it in my bones. There is something relieving about knowing Bishop still seems like the same person in some ways, knowing he's still that kind and friendly and funny guy I knew. The last thing I would want is to realize I spent all those years with someone who wasn't anything like I remember him to be.

When I wrap up around 10, I head into the house and make a peanut butter sandwich before joining Leah at the dining room table where she's working on a large project.

"How's work coming?" she asks, her needles moving slowly and methodically. "You were starting those skinny vases tonight, right?"

Nodding, I finish my bite of sandwich before answering. "Yeah. It's going good. I finished forming, but now I'll still need to carve, put it in the fire, glaze, and then fire it again."

"Everything okay?"

I pause and glance at her. "Yeah, why?"

She shrugs, returning her eyes to her yarn. "You just never come in here and sit with me while I'm working. Thought maybe something was on your mind."

Taking another bite, I shake my head. "I'm good."

"So you said." Leah glances at me again. "But if you suddenly realize you're *not* good, you can talk to me about it."

At that, I snort. "Not about this," I mumble before I can stop myself.

She points at me. "I knew it. Spill."

"I'm *fine*."

"You're not, and someday, you'll finally learn that you feel better when you talk about things instead of letting them sit inside you forever."

I roll my eyes. "It's about Bishop," I share, uncharacteristically deciding I'd rather just tell her and get it over with than do our little dance.

When Leah doesn't say anything or even look at me, just goes back to her knitting, I spread my arms wide.

"See? Told you you wouldn't want to hear it."

"You're right, but go ahead, tell me," she replies.

"Not with *that* tone."

Leah growls. "Fine." She sets her knitting aside and gives me her full attention, a sweet smile on her face. "Tell me all the gory details."

I laugh. "God, you're the worst."

"I'm the best. Tell me."

Taking a deep breath, I push it out long and slow, and then I launch into sharing about Bishop's texts and this…paint party. She listens intently, though I can see just in the way she's staring at me that she already has an answer. It's clear she still holds on to every piece of resentment she's felt about him since we broke up.

"Part of me wants to go, part of me doesn't. I don't know what to do."

"Don't go."

Snorting, I take my last bite of sandwich and push up from the table. "Shocking."

"What?"

"You're just so…you about this. I'm not saying I want to *marry* the guy, but we were friends for years before we dated and, I don't know…sometimes I think maybe we can be friends again. What I *do* know is that you are absolutely zero help with this stuff."

"You mean with *the stuff* that has to do with you going to

hang out with the guy who shattered you?" she says, her voice rising. "*Excuse me* for having your best interests at heart."

"*My* best interests." I scoff, feeling slightly brittle at her 'shattered' comment. "If it were up to you, I'd never date again or get married or have a family. I'd be here with you until we're old and senile, though one of us is already well on her way."

Leah's eyes narrow.

"I have news for you, auntie dearest. This isn't *Grey Gardens*."

She laughs, and after a beat or two, I purse my lips, trying to hide my own smile. Eventually, she sighs, her laughter fading as she assesses me.

"You think I want you to stay here, lonely and alone?" she asks. "That's what you really think?"

Crossing my arms, I tip my chin up. "No."

"All I want is for you to be happy, Gabriela. I hope you know that."

My nostrils flare and I look away from her. "I do."

"The reason I said not to go hang out with Bishop is *not* because I want you to be alone forever. It's because he hurt you, and the last thing I want is for you to ever be hurt like that again."

I understand where she's coming from. I do, but I think she assumes he's playing some kind of game, because that's what she thinks all men do. Part of me gets why she feels that way. She had quite a few men string her along when she was younger, until she decided enough was enough and she was just going to live her life however she wanted without caring if she ended up with a partner.

She also doesn't know Bishop like I do.

That thought surprises me. Do I know Bishop anymore? Can I say that?

I think I can. After weeks of these meetings and the occasional interactions around campus, it *feels* like he's the same man I knew. The same kind heart. The same listening ear. The same tender soul.

As I think this, my decision feels made.

"Thanks for the chat," I finally say to Leah, setting my plate in the sink. "I think I'm good."

Her shoulders droop, but it's more out of resignation than disappointment. "You're gonna go, huh?"

I nod. "Yeah. He was my friend. My *best* friend," I tell her, shrugging a shoulder. "And even if it's imperfect and sometimes strained, I'd like us to be friends again."

She takes a deep breath then lets it out, long and dramatic. "So I guess I need to not chase him away if he comes by, then?"

I smirk at her. "If a little poking from Aunt Leah sends him running, he's not the man I think he is."

I spin on my heel and head to my room, leaving Leah cackling behind me.

I'm snuggled in bed when I finally pull out my phone and text Bishop.

Me: Sorry it took a while to respond. I was working and distracted. The paint thing is Sunday?

It only takes a few seconds before the bubbles pop up.

Bishop: Yeah. You in? *smile emoji*
Me: I'm in. Just as long as we aren't painting something stupid like a lake at sunset.
Bishop: Sweet.

Almost as soon as the text comes through, my phone buzzes with an incoming call.

"Is texting not good enough?" I ask, rolling onto my other side and holding the phone to my ear.

"I'd always rather hear the sound of your voice."

I close my eyes for just a second, the timbre of his voice rumbling through the speaker sending a familiar feeling skittering down my spine.

"But this is just a question that would be faster over the phone," he continues. "Any chance you have an idea for where we can host this paint night?"

"Seriously?" I ask, laughing quietly.

"Well, technically we have two options: Rusty's house or my parents' house. Bellamy said Rusty's living room is pretty small, and I know for a fact that as cool as my mom is about a lot of things, having people painting in her living room is *not* one of those things."

I flop onto my back, thinking it over.

"Um, my shed is smaller than Rusty's living room, so I can't offer that. But maybe we could do it in the annex on campus? I mean...nobody should be there on a Sunday night, right?"

Bishop chuckles. "Gabi Ventura. Look at you, breaking the rules."

I smirk. "I was always a rule breaker."

"Oh trust me, I remember you and Nicole sneaking little flasks into school dances. Don't act like I wasn't there for all that rule-breaking in real life."

"And *you* don't act like you weren't just as sneaky. There were plenty of times when we ditched class to go make out in your car."

"Was that really rule-breaking though?" he asks, the teasing lilt to his voice heavy. "I mean, making out at 17 isn't against the law."

I snort loudly. "But ditching class is against the rules. Don't pretend it's not."

"Alright, alright. We're both equal rule breakers. How about that?"

"I can accept that."

"Good."

"So, paint party—how many people?" I ask after doing some mental work on what I'd need to move around in my classroom in order to fit a group at a table with a bunch of easels.

"Eight of us. You and me, obviously. Rusty and Bellamy, Emily, Briar, Abby, and Jackson."

I nod, rolling through everyone he names. I know Emily from school—she and Bellamy and I were in the same grade with Bishop. Abby and Rusty I know from around town, but I've never met Abby's fiancé, Jackson. It'll be an interesting group, that's for sure.

"As long as the instructor is bringing all the supplies. I only have 4 easels myself, and I don't keep any in my classroom."

"Only four?" Bishop tsks . "Are you *really* an artist if you have less than a dozen?"

I roll my eyes. "How many bats do you have?"

"Almost 20."

"You do not."

"Hand to heaven, I have 18 and a half bats."

My lips curve. "Who has a half bat?"

"Someone who was very lucky and got to keep a broken bat after his walk-off grand slam at the D2 college baseball championships."

At that, I smile fully, unable to help myself at the visual. "You won a championship?"

"I did. Two of 'em."

"Hmm. Well look at you."

We're quiet for a beat, and I realize the silence between us is just as easy as it always was. Even so, there's an element of sadness in my soul at the fact that I didn't already know some of this stuff about him.

"I'll have Bellamy text you about the paint thing, okay?"

I nod, though I know he can't see me. "Sounds good."

"Night, Gabs."

"Night, Bishop."

I set my phone down on the nightstand next to me and tuck my hands under my pillow, shoving my face into the pale green fabric.

Then another text comes in, and I reach out to check it.

Bishop: I'm really looking forward to hanging out with you

My stomach dips, that old feeling swirling through me again. Letting out a long, slow breath, I start to worry I'm going to end up in over my head.

I can be friends with Bishop. I repeat it a few times to myself, trying to reaffirm that it's true. With the history we have, it makes sense that it might be a rocky road, trying to get back to a friendship, but something tells me I'll regret it if I don't try.

chapter nine
bishop

When I walk into Gabi's classroom on Sunday evening, I'm a lot more nervous than I expect to be. It's the first time we're spending casual, friendly time together since I moved back to town, and I don't want to fuck it up.

There's nothing casual about the way my heart thuds in my chest when I see her across the room. Her hair is pulled back from her face in a braid that trails long down her back, and she's wearing a long-sleeved cream sweater that makes me want to bring her in for a hug. Her jeans fit snugly and show off the thick curve of her ass.

I let out a long, slow breath, reminding myself that we are friends, and friends don't look at each other like that.

Her eyes find mine once I step fully inside, and she gives me a wave as the door shuts behind me.

"Only an accomplished artist would wear cream to a paint night."

She looks down at herself then back at me. "Makes sense

why you're wearing black, then."

Chuckling, I motion behind me. "Bellamy and Rusty and the instructor are bringing everything in. Do you need help moving anything around before they get here?"

Gabi shakes her head, glancing around the room. "No, I think everything's good. I moved all the pottery wheels to the side." She shrugs. "I wasn't sure what else to do. Bellamy just said to clear some space."

"This is perfect!"

We both turn at the sound of my sister's voice as she, Rusty, and Emily walk through the door, each holding a large box, followed by a middle-aged woman lugging two folding tables.

"I didn't know you were teaching at the high school," Bellamy continues, her eyes flicking around the room as she sets the box on a counter against the wall. "Gabriela, this is *so* cool."

Gabi nods. "Thanks."

"Where do we put the alcohol?"

I look at Rusty, who is carrying a box of what I'm assuming is the good stuff.

"Oh, um…probably by the sink," Gabi answers, pointing to the corner.

Rusty heads that way and begins unloading while Bellamy and the instructor start to get organized.

"Think there will be enough?" I joke to Rusty as he sets out several boxes of Cedar Cider beer on the counter.

He turns and looks at me, his eyes narrowed. "For a paint party? Not a chance in hell."

I laugh, and Gabi grins. Rusty is a great guy. I think he and my sister work well together. He's not much of a joiner, though, so I can only imagine what my sister did to get him to agree to this.

Okay, scratch that. That's the *last* thing I want to imagine.

Over the next fifteen minutes, I help with the setup as I'm physically able to, and we get the tables lined up and covered and the easels ready with a canvas on each one. The instructor sets out plates of paint at each station and cups filled with paint brushes, and then she puts up the image we're going to be painting tonight as a demonstration.

A lake in the mountains at sunset.

I twist my lips and glance at Gabi, trying to hold back my smile.

"Are you fucking serious," she grumbles, letting out a huff of laughter. Then she glares at me. "You think it's funny, but you can kiss my help goodbye."

Her threat has no heat, and I eat it up.

"You're going to refuse to help someone with an *injury?*" I gasp. "How insensitive of you, Gabi, really."

I can see that she wants to laugh. It's written all over her face, and no amount of glaring can convince me otherwise.

"Sorry we're late!" Abby calls out as she, Jackson, and my older sister Briar walk in. "*Someone* said we should stop to pick up more alcohol."

"Don't say *someone* like I did something wrong," Jackson replies, holding up two more six-packs. "I plan to drink heavily while we do this."

"Good man," Rusty calls out, taking one of the cardboard containers then shaking Jackson's hand. He glances at me. "*Now* there's enough alcohol."

"And then we got lost trying to find the annex. When did they build this?" Abby asks. "I don't remember it being here when I was in school."

"It was here," Bellamy and Gabi say at the same time.

"You just probably didn't come back here because it was only for the emo art kids," I say, pretending to hide the fact that I'm pointing at Gabi.

She swats me in the arm, but I can see the smile in her eyes.

It takes a few minutes to get everyone settled, then the instructor jumps in, giving us directions for our supplies and how we're going to go about the evening. I grab the large paint brush with my right hand and hold it awkwardly, watching Gabi next to me as she dips hers into the water, dabs it on her paper towel, and swipes it through the purple we're using for the sky. My first movements are clumsy, but eventually I figure out how to hold it with my non-dominant hand in a way that doesn't look completely ridiculous or make a mess.

"How am I doing?" I ask Gabi after we've been at it for a few minutes. Her eyes glance at my canvas. "Am I wowing you with my incredible talent? Or reminding you of all the reasons why you're unimpressed with me?"

"It actually looks pretty good. Especially considering you're using your right hand."

My chest puffs up a little bit.

"Any tips?"

Her head angles to the side, and she glances at the way I'm holding my brush.

"Try not to hold it so stiffly. Think about how you hold a pen or a fork. You don't grip it like a knife you want to stab into the canvas. You hold it loosely. Let it relax in your hand."

She reaches out and takes my hand, adjusting the brush so it *relaxes* more, but I can barely focus on what she's saying as she guides my hand back up to the canvas. All I can register is the warmth of her skin gently touching mine, the smell of her shampoo, and the subtle layer of perfume she's wearing. I breathe her in as she speaks, the scent of Gabi Ventura like a warm blanket wrapping around something I didn't realize had gone cold in my chest.

"Are you listening?" she asks, her eyebrow rising.

I grin, trying to downplay how lost I got for a second. "Sorry. Got distracted."

Gabi nibbles on the inside of her cheek, her eyes narrowing. "Did you hear anything I said?"

Not even trying to pretend, I shake my head.

"If you hold it like this," she says, making it clear that she's repeating herself, "you'll have a better distribution of your paint, and you won't end up with thick smears like on the bottom right."

"Got it."

She rolls her eyes then returns to her own canvas. I try to suppress the shiver that rolls down my spine, try to remind myself that the goal with Gabi is to be friends again.

Friends. I shake my head and pick up my drink, taking a long pull of the cool beer. We're going to be *friends*, and nothing more.

"You alright?"

I turn and look at Gabi, finding her gaze on me, one eyebrow lifted. Nodding, I set my drink down and pick up my brush.

"I'm good. You?"

She watches me for a long moment before she nods as well.

"I'd be better if you'd start holding your brush the way I told you to."

Smirking, I adjust my grip. "This better?"

"Yeah."

Then we get back to painting a lake in the mountains at sunset.

"Be honest. Was it way more fun than you expected?"

"Nope. It was just as lame as I thought it would be."

I bark out a laugh and hold up my canvas. "How can you say anything was lame when it ended with this masterpiece!?"

She leans her head to the side and gives me a placating look. "I'm so sorry. I hadn't considered your *masterpiece* in my assessment."

"Don't be glib. Would you like me to sign it for you so you can hang it in here somewhere?" I flip it over so I can look at it again then glance around the room, pretending to scout out the appropriate location to display it on the wall. "Your students can see it and admire the other incredible talent you've worked with."

"Glad to see your ego hasn't gotten any bigger over the years," she replies, raising an eyebrow. "You might not fit through the door."

"Ha-ha."

We make faces at each other then continue moving the pottery wheels back to where they were earlier, the easy playfulness between us both unsurprising and surprising in the best ways. Once we finished painting and all the supplies were cleaned up and the instructor had taken off, Bellamy offered to help Gabi put anything back that she wanted to rearrange. Being the 'I can do it myself' type, Gabi—predictably—declined the offer and shooed everyone out as quickly as possible.

Except for me. She didn't seem as eager to shove me out the

door, and when I offered to help with the rearranging, she accepted. Now that we're about to wrap up, I realize I'm not ready to let the night end.

I glance around, trying to come up with...something, knowing any suggestion will surely be pushing my luck. Then my eyes land on the single six-pack still sitting on the counter. Rusty said it was a thank you for hosting.

"Hey, wanna take the beers up to the roof of the gym?" I ask.

Gabi gives me a look like I'm an idiot.

"Oh, come on. You're already breaking rules tonight. Why not round out the evening with just a little bit more fun? Like we used to."

Her lips twist as she considers me.

"You know you want to."

Sighing, she narrows her eyes and crosses her arms. "Fine. But just one. I had a beer earlier and I still have to drive home."

On the inside, I give myself a fist bump. On the outside, I nod. "Sweet."

Ten minutes later, we emerge through the fire exit that opens up onto the roof of the gymnasium. Our feet crunch on the gravel as we cross over to the small ledge we sat on the handful of times we snuck up here when we were in high school.

"I'm surprised they haven't put a lock on that door," I say as Gabi pops the caps off two beers then hands one to me.

"They can't. It's a fire exit."

"Oh. That makes sense." I take a sip. "Although I'm not sure why someone would want to go up onto the roof of a burning building."

"My guess is that any direction is fine as long as it's not the one where the flames are."

I wink at her. "Touché, Professor Ventura."

She looks out in the distance, over the campus that stretches out below us. "One of my students called me that during the first week."

"Oh, yeah? How'd that feel."

"Weird. Being a teacher—even if it's just an afterschool thing—is *so* not something I ever assumed I would do."

"Don't say *just an afterschool thing* like that, like it's less than being a regular teacher." I bump my shoulder against hers. "If they let you make copies in the administrative offices, you're just as important of a faculty member as anyone else."

She smirks at me. "Is that an official identifier? Does it go on the name badge?"

"Obviously. You get a little X in the corner."

"And the X is for?"

"Xerox."

Gabi laughs. "I hope they're sponsoring the badges."

"They are. It's very official."

"Sounds like it."

We watch each other for a moment before we each take another sip of beer. *This.* This is what I missed the most. The easy banter. The back and forth. The teasing playfulness we've had since the first day we met…I do the math in my mind…ten years ago.

That number sounds so wild.

"Did you know we've known each other for more than a decade?"

Gabi rolls her eyes. "We haven't seen each other in four years, so saying we've *known each other* for a decade is kind of misleading."

"Fine. Did you know we *met* more than a decade ago?"

She pins me with a look. "And?"

"And? What do you mean *and*? It's a long-ass time, that's all. We were little babies going through puberty and we were talking about...I don't know...if we were going to get a phone for Christmas and how much we hated doing math homework."

Gabi's lips tilt up. "You were *definitely* talking about how much you hated math."

"I still can't believe Bellamy majored in that shit and share nearly identical DNA. Fucking nuts." Shaking my head, I take another sip of my beer.

"Ten years, huh?" she says, kind of to herself. "It does feel like a lifetime ago."

"You came into homeroom looking like you wanted to light everyone on fire, and you held that sketchbook close to your chest like someone was going to rob you at any minute."

"I *did* want to light everyone on fire."

I bob my head. I don't doubt it. If I'd been in her position, I probably would have felt the same, and the way she dealt with her emotions back then was sketching. Any time she was alone, she was drawing—landscapes, buildings, people—but drawing people was her specialty. Face close-ups and stark emotions. She held her sketchbook like it was her most prized possession—I think it might have been—and rarely let anyone see inside, including me.

I know I was one of the lucky few who got to see some of them. I even still have a few. They hung in my room freshman year and then got tucked into a drawer after we broke up. There's one I still keep with me. It's a small drawing that stays folded up inside my wallet.

"You still sketch like that?" I ask, setting that memory aside.

She glances at me then turns away. "Not so much. Most of my time has been consumed by my pottery work."

"You should make the time for it again," I say. "You loved it so much, and you were…god, you were *so* good at it. I remember this sketch you did of Leah one time. She was wearing a big coat or a blanket."

"It was a sweater I knit for her," Gabi says, her voice soft, and when I look her way, I see she's watching me with surprise. "You remember that? That was like…ninth grade."

"Oh, yeah. I remember a lot of the artwork you did back then. I have…" But my throat closes up, and I shake my head, deciding I'm not ready to admit to that. "I loved watching you draw. The way your hands moved, so fluid. It was beautiful. It's the same way they move when you're working with your clay."

Also, she didn't look like she wanted to burn everything to the ground when she was sketching. She seemed at ease, happy. Free.

She continues to watch me for a beat before looking away.

"Well, anyway," I continue, "you should start lugging a sketchbook around with you again. You never know when inspiration might strike."

"Maybe," she says, looking back at me.

We watch each other for a long moment, and I can't help it when my eyes dip to her lips, colored by that deep maroon lipstick she likes to wear. I haven't thought about what it would be like to kiss Gabi in quite some time, but I can't help the way the thoughts race through my mind. She was the first girl I ever kissed, and for a long time, I thought she'd be the last.

Suddenly, a ray of light smacks me in the face and I wince, holding up a hand to block it.

"Shit," Gabi whispers.

"Bishop?" a familiar voice calls from below us. "Is that Bishop Mitchell?"

I try to see who it is, but I can't tell with the light blasting me in the face.

"Who is that?" I ask Gabi, whispering.

"It's Sheriff Perry," she groans.

"Oh," I say, my shoulders relaxing.

Then I remember we're sitting on the roof of the school gymnasium, drinking beer, in the middle of the night.

"Oh," I say again, this time with a little less ease.

"Yeah—oh" is all Gabi says back to me.

"And Gabriela Ventura?"

"Hi, Sheriff," Gabi replies, her hand up, also trying to block the light from his flashlight.

"Don't 'Hi, Sheriff' me. You two get your butts down here right now."

I sigh, and then we're scooting off the ledge, collecting our beers, and heading down the stairs. Apparently, I did push my luck too far tonight. It has officially run out.

chapter ten
gabi

"Drinking on school property? Trespassing? Breaking and entering?" Sheriff Perry lists off our offenses as he drives us to the station, his voice gruff with irritation.

I wince. It didn't seem so bad when it was 'just a little rule-breaking.' Now it sounds like a whole lot of trouble.

"I had to get in my car and come out here on a Sunday night because you two were...what? Reliving your glory days?" he continues.

"I'm sorry, Sheriff," Bishop says. "I promise we had no intentions of causing any damage or doing anything illegal. And *technically*, we didn't break in. We had keys."

The sheriff glares at Bishop in the rearview mirror. "Did you not hear the list of *illegal things* I just rattled off to you? Just...sit back there and be quiet."

He mumbles to himself, something about it being the middle of the night and paperwork and keys, but I can't hear it all. We're only in the back of the cop car for about fifteen minutes, but it's still the back of a cop car. As much trouble as we got into when we were teens, we were kids and were given a bit more leeway, and we never did anything so bad that we got *arrested*.

Now we're adults. We should definitely know better. But when I glance over at Bishop, he has a tiny smile on his face. I glare at him then tug at where we each have one hand in a set of handcuffs.

"Stop smiling," I mouth.

"You first," he mouths back.

I can't help it when I start smiling as well. God, he's annoying.

A few minutes later, Sheriff Perry pulls up in front of the police station then lets us out of the back seat.

"Get your butts inside."

We move quickly, and Kelly Donahue smiles at us from behind the glass window as we walk in. Her expression falls quickly when she sees the sheriff behind us.

"I'm putting these two in cell one," he tells her, and the door to her right buzzes open.

Sheriff Perry leads us inside and back to an area with four desks, an office, and two jail cells. He keys one open and motions for us to get inside.

"Come on, Sheriff, do we really need to…"

"Shut it," he replies, and we step into the cell. He closes the door, locks it, and begins walking away.

"Don't we get a phone call?" I call after him.

Sheriff Perry spins around. "The way I see it, you two have two options. I can book you in right now for all your illegal activities tonight, and then you can have your phone call. Or, you can sit here and think about what you've done until Ned gets on shift in the morning, because you know he'll be a lot nicer to you than I will."

I lick my lips. "We'll sit here all night," I tell him. "Thank you, Sheriff."

He nods his head. "Let Kelly know if you need the bathroom," he grumbles.

As he turns again and leaves us alone, I groan and drop down onto the bench against the wall, and Bishop joins me. He doesn't really have a choice since we're handcuffed together.

Eventually, though, he starts chuckling next to me.

I whack him twice in the shoulder. "It's not funny."

"I know it's not. I'm sorry. I really get it. But also—we got arrested for drinking beers on top of the school gymnasium."

Rolling my eyes, I try not to smile, but the longer Bishop sits there chuckling next to me, the harder it is.

"God, how old are we?" I ask, shaking my head. "And how many times did we sneak around getting up to shit when we were younger and we never got caught? Clearly, our skills have drastically declined."

Bishop snorts. "Hey, at least it was just us and not everybody else."

"I hadn't even thought of that."

"Can you imagine? Sheriff Perry busting in on us painting? Like…how confused would he have been? Also, Bellamy has never gotten in trouble for anything in her life. I'm sure she would have been sobbing."

When I glance at the clock a few minutes later, I see it's almost 11.

"Do you know what time Ned starts working?"

Bishop shakes his head. "My guess is somewhere between 6 and 8?"

I groan and slump down on the bench. "Great."

We wait in silence for a while, each of us shifting every so often and trying to find a more comfortable position to sit in. At some point I realize Bishop keeps wincing and adjusting his uncuffed arm—the one with the cast and sling.

"You okay?"

He nods. "I'm fine. I just…my arm is hurting, and I normally take a few ibuprofen or something to manage it, you know?" He shakes his head and closes his eyes, leaning his head back against the concrete wall. "It'll be fine."

Licking my lips, I try to think of what I can do, only one idea eventually coming to mind.

"Turn to face me," I tell him, adjusting my position so I'm sitting sideways on the bench, one knee angled on top and one foot on the floor.

Huffing out a breath, he turns, mirroring my position, our handcuffed hands resting on our knees between us. Then I reach out with my free hand and begin gently massaging the muscles of his left bicep, above his cast.

Bishop groans, and I stop immediately.

"No, keep going. It feels so good," he says.

I return to what I was doing, applying gentle pressure on the muscles and ligaments that stretch along his bicep.

"I don't know if you remember, but I used to give *amazing* shoulder massages."

Bishop chuckles. "Oh, I remember. Part of the benefit of being an athlete is access to physical therapists and masseuses when you have an injury or are trying to prevent one." He shakes his head. "None of those people ever lived up to the ones you gave me after some of our harder practices."

I roll my eyes. "You're full of shit."

"I'm not. I'm being serious."

Pursing my lips and shaking my head, I continue what I'm doing, glancing at Bishop's face occasionally. It's a little difficult using just one hand, but it seems to be helping, and that's what matters.

"And you're even better at it now. Or maybe I'm just in more pain now, so it's making a bigger difference. I don't know. But seriously, Gabi. This is so helpful."

He closes his eyes and groans again, and I swallow thickly, diligently keeping my thoughts on his arm.

"I just have stronger hands than I used to, that's all."

Bishop opens one eye. "All that time on the wheel?" he asks.

I nod. "It's actually great exercise," I say as I slowly stroke down a particularly tight area, making him wince. "It works a lot of core muscles, and on more than one occasion I've woken up the next morning feeling like I did hundreds of crunches or something."

"You building up a six-pack?"

I shake my head. "Hardly. I like my croissants too much." I pause, debating sharing what's crossed my mind, eventually just saying it. "If either of us has a six-pack, it's definitely you. Look at all these muscles you've put on. They must have you in the gym every day."

I can feel Bishop's eyes on me, but I don't look at him. Instead I just focus on his arm.

"It feels like it," he offers, leaning slightly to the side against the concrete wall. "We had an intense training regimen during the off-season. Running, weights, HIIT workouts. You name it, we did it. And during the regular season, we were expected to be in the gym on any day we didn't have a game."

My brow furrows. "That sounds kind of extreme."

"It was, but my coach promised me I'd be ready for the draft combine. With the combination of the paces he put me through and a pre-draft training camp I went to over the summer, I was in the best shape of my life."

My lips tilt up. "I can tell."

I say it before I realize what I've said, and then my cheeks heat slightly. Thankfully, even though Bishop grins, he doesn't draw attention to my admiration of his body.

"How was it? The combine?"

"A lot harder than I was expecting." he says, his honesty surprising.

Bishop's never been one to point out when he's facing a particularly difficult challenge. He normally just puts his nose down and busts his ass then makes it look like it was easy all along.

"They do all these strength and conditioning tests to see where your baseline is. They take body measurements and check your range of motion. They watch you do squats and lunges and pushups. They test your balance and grip, make you do things like a 30-yard dash to see how fast you'd run bases." He shrugs. "It was only two hours, but it was nerve-racking."

That's another surprising statement.

"Since when does Bishop Mitchell get nervous when it comes to baseball?" I ask teasingly.

He chuckles. "Since I've seen what a small fish I really am in the big baseball pond."

"You're not a small fish."

He shakes his head. "I know my swing is good. I do. But the more elite you go, the more competitive it gets. Some of these guys can hit like me *and* run that 30-yard dash in under four seconds. They can hit like me *and* throw the ball to home plate from the outfield."

"Bishop Mitchell, you've always been someone who believes

in himself wholeheartedly. Don't tell me you're starting to doubt your dream."

He laughs. "Nah, nothing like that. It's just…you have this idea of what your future will look like when you're young, you know? What 'making it' looks like, how hard it will be and the kind of dedication you'll need." He shrugs a shoulder. "And you don't actually know what it will *really* look like until you get there. That's where I'm at right now. My life just looks a little different than I pictured it when I was first building that dream."

His eyes focus on mine as he says it, and I can't help but wonder if I factor into it at all, if any part of what he's said has to do with me. We used to talk about him being in the big time, playing for the MLB, and we were always an *us* in those conversations. There's a part of me that wants to know if he always pictured me at his side as he was reaching these milestones—the draft, the Triple-A team, etc. I want to know if he wished I was there when those happened.

"Alright, your turn," Bishop says, probably sensing the emotional turn of our conversation and rerouting us.

I take a deep breath and let it out slowly, thankful that we're moving on.

"My turn, what?"

"Tell me about art school."

"It was artsy."

He rolls his eyes. "Was it school-y too?"

I laugh under my breath. I did two years at Monterey School of Art a few hours away, and even though it was a rough transition, going from a small mountain town to a busy beach city, it was still an amazing experience.

"It was great. Only two years, I'm not sure if you remember. But I learned…so much. And I found my love for ceramics."

After a beat passes, he leans forward. "That's it? I shared all my secrets and you're giving me a few sentences?"

"There's no way you shared all of your secrets."

"All the good ones."

"Mhm. Fine, ask me my secrets. You want to know, I'm an open book."

Bishop purses his lips, assessing me for a long minute.

"Worst grade."

"Ugh…art history," I grumble. "I might love 'the arts', but the historical stuff is just a snooze-fest. Maybe I'm a bad artist for saying it, but it's the truth. I really struggled to finish the paper we had to write for our final. Fifteen pages on how Expressionism paved the way for later art movements. Literally the most difficult thing I've ever done in my life."

He smiles. "You did always hate having to explain art."

"I don't like having to verbalize what art means. Like…it's just supposed to be something you feel," I say, though I know without a doubt he's heard me say some version of that before.

"Alright, next secret. Best moment from the entire time you were there."

Twisting my lips, I think about it, trying to pull from everything that happened. Two years is a short time in the grand scheme of your life, but it felt really long while I was there. A lot happened.

"Probably when I got an A in my ceramics class first semester. I loved that class so much, and it opened up an entire world to me that I'd never considered before. Knowing my professor saw promise in my work meant so much."

Bishop grins. "You really love it, huh?"

I nod. "I do. I never thought I'd find anything I was *this* passionate about, you know? You always had baseball, you were always in it 100%. But me? I just knew I was an artist. I thought I'd do a little painting, probably wait tables or maybe work at one of the businesses in town. I never thought I'd be able to make a living off of work that I love to do."

"It's pretty magical, right?"

"It is."

Bishop pats my knee with his good hand. "You've been massaging me far longer than you needed to. Thank you so much."

"Oh, sorry," I say, drawing my hands back.

"No, you don't have to apologize. I'm just saying…my arm feels so much better."

I turn, glancing at the clock in the corner, seeing that only an hour has gone by since we were first locked in here. Sighing, I turn back to Bishop.

"It's going to be a long night, isn't it," I say, more like a statement than a question.

Bishop nods. "Looks like it."

Turning, I drop my leg so both feet are on the floor, and I rest my head on the wall behind me.

"I'm sorry I got us arrested," he tells me, taking my hand that's handcuffed to his and giving it a gentle squeeze. "But if I have to sit here with someone, I'm glad it's you."

I squeeze his hand as well, though I don't say anything back. I'm not ready to admit to him that I've enjoyed these chats we've been having tonight. I'm not ready to tell him I'm glad to be here with him, too.

At 7:55am, Lieutenant Ned Unger unlocks the jail cell and lets us out.

"I'll have Joey give you two a ride back to your cars," he says, waving over one of the deputies sitting at a conference table with a few others.

"Thanks, Ned," Bishop says. "We really appreciate it."

He smiles at us. "Heard you were caught on the roof of the gymnasium," he says, chuckling. "When I was in high school, we used to throw ragers on the old gym. Such bad luck that someone called in your cars in the parking lot."

Bishop lets out his own laugh. "Next time, we'll plan ahead and get dropped off."

I must be delirious from barely sleeping all night, because I actually laugh, too, even though I know there's not a chance in hell I'll ever be caught on that school campus without explicit permission ever again.

Joey loads us in the back of his car and drives us up to the school, where, thankfully, the students are already in class. The last thing I want is for them to see two of their teachers—though I'm not sure exactly what Bishop would be considered—getting dropped off in a patrol car looking worse for wear, though I don't doubt Principal Cohen is already well aware of our misdeeds.

"Thanks, Joey," I say as he unlocks the set of handcuffs we've been sharing all night.

"Have a good day, guys," he says, laughing.

"Do you get the feeling everyone in the police station thinks this is funny?" I ask Bishop as Joey drives off, leaving us standing next to my car.

He grins. "I don't doubt it in the slightest."

chapter eleven
bishop

"Your X-rays look perfect."

Dr. Ramos turns his computer screen to show me the imaging we just took of my wrist then uses his pinky to point to the spot where the break used to be.

"I think we should be good to take off that cast and get you into a removable brace."

My shoulders drop in relief, tension leaking out of them at his words, at the fact that I'll finally be able to use my damn hand again. My diligence in listening to his instructions about the first phase of my rehab plan has paid off.

"That's great. Thanks, doc."

He turns the computer screen back and clicks around a few times then begins typing as he continues speaking.

"You're going to need to start physical therapy to begin getting your range of motion back. Twice a week with a specialist, and daily exercises on your own as well. And for the next four weeks, I want you to do minimal weight-bearing on that wrist, okay? No more than five pounds."

I nod. "So I still have to take a leak with my good arm. Got it."

Dr. Ramos shakes his head, chuckling softly.

"And what are the limitations on exercise and baseball-related things that Bishop might want to start trying again?"

I turn, narrowing my eyes at my dad. I didn't ask that question because I didn't want to know.

"Exercise is fine as long as you're not using your wrist. Walking, running, a seated bike at the gym, but I'd hold off on any batting practice until after our next meeting. I want you to work with the physical therapist first, get at least a bit of your agility back before you start putting so much pressure on it."

My nose wrinkles, and my dad pats me on the shoulder.

"I know, it's not ideal," Dr. Ramos says, his smile understanding. "But you're doing great, Bishop. It's just one month, and then you *should* be able to get back out there and hit the ball to your heart's content."

Twenty minutes later, we've said goodbye to Dr. Ramos, collected a packet of information we're supposed to provide to my new PT, a guy my dad worked with in town when he had knee surgery a few years back, and begun our drive back to Cedar Point from Sacramento. I could have met with Dr. Neman in town, but my surgeon in Portland recommended Dr. Ramos and urged me to see an orthopedic surgeon throughout the length of my recovery for more specialized knowledge.

"Sorry to burst your bubble back there," Dad says as we hop on the freeway. "But I knew where your head was going to go the minute you got home, and it's always better to have more information than less."

I know he's right, but I'm still feeling a little sour about it.

When I had my surgery, I had a picture of what my recovery would look like. In my head, I'd be out of my cast in a month—which turned into six weeks—but then I'd mostly be free to do whatever as long as I was working with a PT. Clearly, that's not the case. Five pounds of weight is practically nothing—not even a gallon of milk—and I'm just feeling disappointed that I have another month of my wrist and hand being mostly useless.

I mess with the Velcro straps on my brand-new brace. At least I'll be able to take this off so I can shower. Wearing a plastic bag over my arm has been a pain in the ass.

"How has it been, helping Rush coach the Pirates?" Dad asks, drawing me out of my pity party as we blaze east along the freeway, toward the mountains. "I've been meaning to ask you."

"I'm not really sure yet," I say honestly. "The kids all really love baseball, which is great, and I think I'm doing a good job giving them advice and stuff. But...I don't know."

"What don't you know?" he prods.

"Well, there's this one kid—Justin—who is just...so filled with attitude. I've worked with him one on one a few times, and each time he's basically told me to take my advice and shove it up my ass."

At that, my dad chuckles, and I join him, the story funny in the moment even if the reality feels slightly less amusing.

"It's not funny," I say, even though it kind of is. "You don't know what it's like."

This time, my dad barks out a laugh. "I don't know what it's *like*?" He's incredulous. "I have five children, Bishop. *Five.* You think I don't know what it's like to have a teenager look at me like I have no fucking clue what I'm talking about?"

I try to hide my grin. "Okay, so maybe you do."

"Maybe," he grumbles, though he's still got a teasing lilt in his tone.

"Got any advice?"

He glances at me then, surprise on his face, before his eyes return to the road. "Well, tell me a bit more about him, about this…Justin kid."

I take the next ten minutes to tell my dad what I know, all about Justin's talent: his big swing, how fast he can run, the way I've seen him take angles for the ball. The kid could probably play any position he wanted if he would just put his nose down and focus.

I also share the attitude. The sour way he talks about his teammates. The anger I see boiling beneath his skin sometimes, when he'll chuck his bat because someone said something he doesn't like or he fouled a ball.

"I've been thinking about the way Coach G used to approach me. He was pretty stern. Maybe that's the way I should come at Justin?"

"Let me ask you something. Why do you think Coach G being really hard on you worked?"

I try to think back to the times when I was difficult or causing problems. "Probably because I never took anything seriously," I say, chuckling under my breath. "Like everything was a big joke."

"Exactly. He was trying to get you to be more serious, recognize your potential, focus yourself and your more…playful energy." He pauses. "This Justin kid sounds like he's got more of an angry edge. Do you think being intense with him will work?"

"I'm not sure," I answer honestly. "I'm kind of getting to a point where I'm out of options."

"You're never out of options," my dad corrects. "Just out of *ideas*."

"Okay fine. I'm out of ideas. What I'd really like to do is just kick him off the team."

Not that I necessarily have the authority to do so. I'm sure a decision like that rests with Rush, not with a part-time coach.

"And what do you think would happen then? To this kid who is already so angry."

"He'd...be angry somewhere else?"

"Probably, and he wouldn't have his one outlet—baseball—to help him."

I've never thought about it that way, like Justin is a kid I need to think about outside of just how he does at baseball. I mean, I've never assumed *any* of my coaches have thought about *me* that way.

Although, I guess that's not entirely true. Coach G might have ridden my ass, but he was always asking how school was going, how my girlfriend was, if everything was good at home. My assumption was that he didn't want those things fucking with baseball, that he was checking in to make sure I was keeping my nose clean. But maybe I was wrong. Maybe he *did* care about me on a personal level, and I just assumed he was a disconnected old guy with nothing important in his life besides coaching.

I wince. I know I was a good kid, but every so often, I'll think back on something from my youth and realize how self-centered I was. Or maybe...just how *young* I was.

It's what I've been telling Justin, isn't it? You don't know what you don't know, and when you're young, you think you know it all. You think you understand the way everyone sees the world because you only know one way to see it yourself. It takes some growing up to realize just how wrong you are.

"So then...what would you suggest?" I ask, deciding to take advantage of the man sitting next to me and his 59 years of life experience. "For how to approach Justin."

"Well, maybe try to look at Justin's anger as a ball of flames," he says, flicking on his blinker as we exit the freeway onto the road that will take us winding through the mountains. "What he needs is a good dunk in a pool, not fuel added on the fire. Someone to help him learn how to cool that anger. Which—to be fair—is not easy to do."

I nod, knowing he's right. When I consider what else Rush shared with me about Justin—that his dad's not around—it's easy to deduce that the only way he's learned to deal with his frustration is through anger.

"Hey, you don't happen to know Justin's mom, do you? Her last name is Chisholm."

Dad thinks about it for a second, probably running through a mental list of town residents, though it's likely he doesn't know *everyone*.

"I don't think so, but maybe your mother does. Why?"

I shrug. "Rush said Justin's dad bounced out on him when he was younger and I've been thinking a little bit about what his situation at home might be like. Just wondering if you knew anything about his mom."

Dad shakes his head. "Doesn't ring a bell, but you should definitely ask *your* mom. That woman's brain is like a rolodex."

I nod, my mind beginning to consider different ideas for how to approach Justin, or even Justin's mom. I consider how I might be able to metaphorically dunk Justin in a pool to help him cool some of that anger. I'm going to be in town at least through the holidays, and while three months working with a kid probably isn't enough to change them dramatically, maybe I can help nudge him in the right direction.

We drive for another hour, our conversation steering away

from the difficult topical points we've hit on so far and instead leading toward easier things. Just as we pull into town, something occurs to me, and I look at my dad.

"Hey, what's a rolodex?"

He just laughs.

"Nice hit, Ruben!" I shout, watching as the ball drops into Palmer's glove in right field.

This kid has been working hard on improving his swing over the past few weeks—extra time in the batting cages, listening intently to coach critique—and it's already starting to pay off. When we had our first conversation earlier this month, it was clear he had a lot of work to do. His timing was good, but his stance was off and his swing needed a lot of work. When I made some suggestions right then, he implemented them immediately, and it was actually pretty astounding how much of a change there was after just a few swings.

Now, a few weeks later, it feels like I'm looking at a completely different hitter. Some time working on his muscles to build up strength and the kid is going to be a big player during the spring season. I can just feel it.

Ruben grins at me, but the moment is shot to hell when Justin speaks from where he's standing off to the side, waiting for his turn.

"I don't know what you're celebrating. That would have been an out."

The grin on Ruben's face dims slightly, and I sigh, scratching at the stubble on my face.

"Justin, does the word *teammate* mean anything to you?" I look over at where he's standing with his bat on his shoulders and his arms looped over it.

So arrogant. So full of himself.

"Because when you're on a *team*, you encourage each other. Or have you forgotten all the lessons we learn in Little League?"

Justin rolls his eyes and releases his bat, swinging it down to tap against one foot before switching hands and tapping it against the other.

"Look, if you want me to baby these jokers because they're not very good, you're looking at the wrong guy. That's *your* job. Not mine."

Crossing my arms, I widen my stance, just watching him.

"It's going to be a long season if you're going to constantly give me this attitude, Justin."

"Long *season?*" Justin shakes his head. "Bro, you're here until what...February? Maybe? Then you're gone, and you won't have to deal with my attitude anymore."

"Well guess what. Until then, *bro*, you'll be running the field every time you give me shit. Out to the foul post, along the back wall to the other, and then home." I hitch my thumb in the direction of the outfield. "Get moving."

His face morphs into an expression filled with anger, and he chucks his bat against the chain link fence. Then he glares at me for a long beat before jogging off.

I let out a long sigh as I watch him for a minute. Clearly the conversation with my dad earlier went in one ear and out the other, my irritation with Justin's attitude getting the best of me. Hopefully a jog around the field or twelve will help the kid cool off a bit, though I'm surely just hoping.

"Alright, Ruben. Let's do it again."

I signal to Tommy to drop a ball into the machine, and a few seconds later, it's sailing toward Ruben, who gets another really decent hit. We stay at it for a few more minutes, and then I send Ruben over to the neighboring soccer field where Rush is working with players on throwing dynamics.

When I turn to motion for the next batter to come up to the plate, my eyes catch on a figure sitting in the bleachers, her long dark hair fluttering in the cool breeze. I grin but try not to call too much attention to where she sits. Instead, I step behind the mesh screen meant to protect me from rogue foul balls and return my attention to where Riley is getting into his stance. Observing his movements closely, I watch as he swings at the first ball, which sails right past him and into the catcher's mitt.

"One more," I say, holding up a single finger to Tommy.

Riley resets, and then a few seconds later he swings and misses again.

"Your timing is late," I tell him, making a note on my clipboard. "When you're making a mental judgment about when to swing, force yourself to swing just a little bit earlier. Okay?"

He nods, and then Tommy's dropping in another ball. This time, Riley swings and hits the ball, though it goes foul.

"Man," he groans, clicking his tongue at himself.

"Hey, don't get down on yourself. You're making adjustments, right? Nobody is perfect immediately. It takes a lot of tweaks and then a lot of repetition to make the new thing stick."

Riley sighs.

"Set up again."

We go through about 20 balls before we finish and move on to the next. He hits four of them foul before finally hitting one fair, and then on his last hit, he launches it into left field.

I never thought I would have it in me to coach. I enjoy playing too much and always assumed coaching was for people who didn't have the skill, but maybe I'm wrong on both accounts. Maybe I could coach one day, help kids the way my coaches have had an impact on me over the years.

The thought is surprising, but I don't dwell on it as we move through the rest of practice. My focus turns entirely to Gabi the minute we shout Pirates and send the kids off to the locker rooms, and I turn to look at where she's still sitting, wrapped up in a warm coat, her hands tucked into the pockets.

"To what do I owe this surprise," I say, coming up to the chain link fence.

"Well, I had some free time and wanted to come see…" She waves her hand in the direction of the field behind me. "What you do."

I chuckle. "What I do? You sat in the bleachers during enough of my practices and games to know what a coach does."

She stands then walks down the steps, approaching me from the other side of the fence.

"Yeah, but I've never seen *you* coach before."

Something warm works its way through my chest, a welcome reprieve from the cold air.

"And I also wanted to see if you'd like to grab a beer tonight."

That warm thing swirls and moves, and I set the bucket of balls down then grip the fence and lean forward.

"I'd love to."

She gives me a small smile, her eyes examining my face, and we just look at each other for a long moment. Then she clears her throat, her eyes glancing away briefly.

"Great. Nicole will be there. Feel free to invite whoever."

My excitement dips—not that it should. This is a good thing, a friendly thing, inviting me to get beers with a group, with her other friend. Technically *our* other friend, if I can still call Nicole that.

"Sounds great. I'll see if Rush wants to come. Maybe Bells."

Gabi nods. "Awesome. See you at eight."

She turns, walking off in the direction of the parking lot, and my eyes follow her until she disappears.

chapter twelve
gabi

"You *have* to come," I tell Nicole into the phone. "I told Bishop you would be there."

She snorts. "Why would you tell him that?"

Because when I asked him, it felt too much like a date. Not that I'm going to tell Nicole that.

"Because I assumed you'd be able to go," I say.

"Well, I hate to break it to you, but I'm busy tonight."

I groan. "Doing what?"

"I have a date."

"With who?" My voice can't hide my surprise.

"Just a guy I met at Lucky's while you were hosting an entire art party without me."

I roll my eyes. "I told you—it wasn't *my* paint party. It was Bellamy's."

"Even worse! I used to work with Bellamy. We're friends… kind of. And you know I love being a fly on the wall when it comes to the Mitchells. There were *three* of them there."

Laughing, I lean back against the wall and stretch my legs out in front of me along the length of my bed. Nicole acts like the Mitchell family is the Cedar Point equivalent of the Kennedys or the Vanderbilts. Sure, they're the town's founding family, but they're not *royalty* or anything. At least not to me.

But try telling that to Nicole. She loves to observe them, though she grew supremely unimpressed by Bishop after we broke up. After that mess, her only enjoyment when it came to him was *digging for dirt*, as she liked to call it.

"And I told you, literally nothing happened. We painted and then they left."

"Yeah, but that's because you were probably too busy mooning over Bishop to pay attention to what Bellamy and Briar were talking about."

I shake my head, a smile on my face.

"And don't say 'literally nothing happened' like it was a calm case of the Sundays. You got *arrested*."

I twist my lips, thankful she can't see me. "We didn't get arrested."

"You slept in a jail cell overnight, okay? Potato, potahto."

"My neck is still sore."

"You're lucky you don't have a felony."

"People don't get felonies for drinking beer on their high school campus, Nic. It would have been a misdemeanor at best. It's basically a ticket. And besides, I don't know why you're giving me the sass as if you haven't been arrested *for real*."

At my reference to her own antics, she pipes down.

"Yeah. Don't think I didn't hear about you smoking weed with Jennifer Sanders at Summerpalooza. I can't think of a better example of the pot calling the kettle black."

Nicole grumbles something about weed not being that big

of a deal, though I can't make it out entirely.

"So *anyway*," I say, dragging out the word and making it clear I'm moving us along and setting the conversation about my visit to the police station to the side. "Are you sure you can't come tonight? Maybe bring your guy?"

She chuckles. "Sorry, G. This man dragged me out of the drought the universe somehow thrust upon me. It was the first good orgasm I did not give myself in like…six months."

I grin. "Nicole Charles, did you have a one-night stand and not call me *immediately*? I thought you said there are no sex secrets between besties."

"It's not a secret. I've just been enjoying the haze of orgasms he's been giving me this week."

"This *week*!" I can't hide my shock. "You've seen him more than once? You *have* been holding out on me."

She makes a devious noise. "Trust me, I'll have plenty to share after he leaves to head back to Montana or wherever. I think he leaves Sunday, and I'm already crying about how lonely my vagina will be."

I snort. "You're ridiculous."

"Speaking of lonely vaginas," she continues, "how's yours?"

"Fine."

She hums. "Just fine? There haven't been any visits lately? From any…ex-boyfriends?"

I roll my eyes. "You think, what? We had sex in the jail cell? Come on, Nic."

"No, I wouldn't say you're *that* scandalous. Though who knows what you were getting up to on that rooftop."

"Not having sex, I can promise you that."

No. Instead we were taking a trip down memory lane, which—to me at least—feels even more intimate. My eyes drop to the sketchbook in my lap, the one I've been carrying around for the past few days. For whatever reason, Bishop's suggestion that I should start sketching again stuck.

I told him I didn't know why I stopped in the first place, but that's not the truth. I do know. A big part of it was the refocusing of my attention on ceramics during art school. I was in the studio all the time, and when I wasn't, I was handling things for other classes. Then I moved home and started this business and there just hasn't been the time.

That is true, but a small part of me knows it's also because of Bishop. Well...maybe not Bishop, exactly, but my thoughts about him. After we broke up, I sketched him relentlessly, from every angle and doing every activity. Hitting a baseball, studying at my kitchen table, lying next to me in bed. It felt like I was drawing every memory so I could purge him from my mind.

Then, one day, I didn't want to sketch him anymore, so I tucked that book onto my shelf and focused on something else. Now, just the act of holding it in my hand makes the desire to sketch build anew in my spirit, though I haven't taken the leap just yet. Maybe this weekend, if I have the time.

"Well, that doesn't mean you haven't had sex some other time." Nicole's comment jerks me back to our conversation. "You know, since you've been doing all these things without me recently."

I can hear the playful tease in her voice, but I also know Nicole well enough to hear the slight layer of sincerity behind her words.

"We haven't," I tell her. "And I have no plans to. Trust me."

It's true. I don't have plans to sleep with Bishop. It would be too messy, bringing the physical side of our relationship back into the mix when we're just now seeming to figure out how to be friends, though the thought has crossed my mind once or twice. How much might have changed in the years we've been apart...

"Hmm. I'm not buying it. Your words say one thing, but your voice says you might be considering it, so maybe take a few minutes before you go and rub one out," she says, and I gasp.

"Nicole," I say, flopping over onto my side and laughing into the phone. "Are you telling me to masturbate before I go out for beers with Bishop?"

"Absolutely," she replies, her voice unapologetic. "Just purge yourself of any sexual energy you might bring to the table when you go out tonight."

"I'm getting off the phone with you," I tell her, trying to infuse some strength and sass into my voice—and failing epically.

"It's because you want to, huh," she says, the smile clear in her voice. "You little minx."

Shaking my head, I let out a sighing laugh. "I love you, Nic. You're absolutely nuts, but I love you to absolute death."

"Yeah, yeah. Samesies."

"Call me later, okay? We can talk about your sexcapades."

"Sounds good. Have fun tonight."

We end the call and I drop my phone on the bed next to me then lie there for a while just looking at the ceiling. I can't help it when I start laughing again at Nicole's oh-so-casual suggestion.

Not that masturbation is funny. It's definitely something I enjoy when the need arises. It just felt like such a random thing for her to encourage tonight. I mean, we're just going out for beers. As *friends*. It's not like we're eyeing each other up and down with teenage lust.

I sigh.

Bishop is definitely not a teen anymore, and I wasn't lying

Sunday night as we sat in the jail cell when I told him I could tell he's in amazing shape. I've had to fight myself a few times when he's stopped by my classroom and I've found my eyes wandering over his physique.

Though I didn't stop myself from eyeing him all over as I sat in the bleachers earlier, drinking him in like I was starving. He was out there in a track jacket and a pair of black jogging pants that hugged his body in all the right places, and I couldn't help but notice…everything. His shoulders are broader, his biceps fuller, his chest more toned.

And then there's his ass. Full and round sitting on top of thick, muscular thighs.

I twist my legs together, feeling a pulse between my *own* thighs, and then I curse Nicole for putting any of this in my head in the first place.

Although, maybe there's some logic behind her suggestion. Maybe I *should* get an O under my belt for the evening, just to keep any potential desires at bay.

I glance at my closed bedroom door then reach over to my nightstand to pull out the vibe I use in moments like this one. It's slim, dark blue, and about six inches long, and I crawl under my covers and rest it over my clothes, turning it on and letting the lowest setting send gentle vibrations through the fabric.

That twist of desire inside me begins to build as I use my other hand to stroke gently against my nipples over my top. I sigh, enjoying the sensation, until the gentle pulsing doesn't feel like enough and I start to grow restless. Tugging down my leggings and panties, I slip my vibrator through my lower lips, unsurprised to find that it slides easily through the wetness that has collected.

The image of Bishop begins to form in my mind, the two of

us sitting on the roof of the gym, that mischievous smile crooked on his face, a bit of stubble across his cheeks. In this version of events, when his eyes dip to my lips, he leans forward and kisses me.

I circle my clit, whimpering quietly as pleasure zings its way through my hips.

I saw his eyes dip, wondered for a moment what it would be like to kiss him again, to wrap my arms around the man I knew, so similar and yet so different, to taste him on my tongue.

That adjusted memory fades, replaced by fantasy. Bishop and his large body hovering over me, kissing my neck then down my body. Licking my nipples. His face between my legs, then his fingers. Then his cock.

I slip the vibrator inside, tossing my head back and moaning softly as it rattles my pleasure points.

God, what it would be like to be underneath that big, strong body. How it would feel to have him sliding into me, stretching me, his dick hitting that place inside I can never seem to reach on my own. I lose myself in that vision, in us tangled together, a new version of what we once were, until I can't contain myself any longer. My orgasm rips through me, a series of waves that roll over my body one after the next, until I finally slump down, depleted.

After a few beats, I turn off my vibrator and set it on my nightstand to wash in a few minutes, once I've allowed the last of the endorphins to finish dancing in my veins. I can't remember the last time I came that hard on my own, and I snuggle into my pillow with a smile on my face. God, that felt so good. Exactly what I needed.

Until a thought occurs to me. Something Nicole didn't mention when she suggested this little dalliance before getting beers with Bishop. Something I hadn't considered at all.

The fact that I'll need to sit across from my ex, knowing just an hour earlier, I thought about him as I came.

I'm sure my cheeks are still slightly pink when I arrive at Cedar Cider an hour and ten minutes later, though I'm almost certain I can use the cold to explain it away. What I can't explain though is the disappointment that blows through me when I see Bishop sitting at a table with Bellamy, Rush, and Emily.

"Where's Nicole?" Bishop asks, standing as I approach them.

"Oh, she couldn't make it after all," I say. "Apparently she made last-minute plans with some guy."

Emily surprises me then, stepping over to give me a hug. I stand awkwardly as she embraces me, narrowing my eyes over her shoulder at Bishop, who is grinning at my obvious discomfort. Then she releases me and we take our seats.

"I hope it's the same guy she's been bringing into The Mitch this week," Emily says. "They look so adorable together."

Remembering Nicole's reference to this guy as someone she's basically banging until he leaves town, I decide to keep my mouth shut at Emily's insinuation that they're doing more than just having some fun.

"Heard you two had a little trip to the slammer after our paint party," Bellamy says, holding her beer in both hands and leaning back in her chair. She winces. "Sorry about that. I knew we were skirting some rules by being there, but I didn't think it would end in someone's arrest."

I laugh, shaking my head. "It's not your fault. Everything would have been fine if *someone* hadn't suggested we drink beer on the roof of the gym," I reply, eyeing Bishop. "Has Principal Cohen called you in to talk about it yet?"

Bishop nods his head, a wide smile on his face. "She did. We talked this morning, and it was just as intimidating as you would expect." Then he slices one hand across his neck and mouths, "Not at all."

"Well, *mine* was more intense. Can't say I have any intentions of getting in trouble like *that* again," I reply.

"Oh, come on. It wasn't worth it to you?"

I purse my lips but don't respond, just playing off my response as disbelief in Bishop's attitude. The truth, though, is that it was totally worth it. Do I want to get in trouble again? No. Would I do it the same if I could go back in time? Absolutely.

"I heard from Joey that you two were handcuffed together all night in that jail cell," Rush says before taking a sip of his beer. "That true?"

"You spent *all night* at the station?" Emily asks, incredulously. "Ick."

"It was definitely ick," I reply, aiming a thumb at Bishop. "Especially when this one fell asleep on the bench and started snoring uncontrollably." I look his way and find his mouth opened dramatically. "A lovely new quality you've picked up in the past few years, clearly."

"That is an outright lie. I do not snore," he says, chuckling.

"How would you know?" I cross my arms, narrowing my eyes. "Maybe you got hit with a ball and deviated your septum."

"I think I'd remember if I got hit in the face with a ball."

"I don't know, Bish. We share a wall, and I might have been

woken once or twice by you sawing logs since you've been back."

The entire table begins laughing at Bellamy's description, and when she glances at me and winks, Bishop stands dramatically.

"If all of you are finished poking fun at an injured man," he says, holding his hand up theatrically, "I'll be getting another beer at the bar. I had considered buying a round for everyone, but I've changed my mind."

He turns and storms off dramatically, leaving us all cackling in his wake.

"It's fun seeing you and Bam together again," Emily says. "You two always seemed like you had so much fun when we were in high school."

My face pinches. "We're not together," I say, my tone more curt than I intend. Clearing my throat, I ease back. "We're just…I guess we're friends. You know?"

Emily nods, though her smile is slightly less easy, and I wish I hadn't been so intense with my response.

"I never grabbed a drink when I got here. I'll be back," I tell everyone, pushing away from the table and heading over to the bar where Bishop is standing, tapping a coaster lightly against the wood grain as he waits.

"You don't really snore," I say, bumping his shoulder as I come up next to him. "Though your mouth does hang open a little bit, and there *might* have been some drool."

He grins.

"But that's no different than it used to be."

"Good to know," he replies.

We stand quietly side by side until the bartender sets a beer in front of Bishop. Then I order one as well.

"I'm glad we're doing this," I tell him. "Hanging out. Being…friends."

Bishop nods but doesn't say anything.

"It's nice, right?"

He turns to look at me, his eyes searching mine for a long beat. "It is. I missed being your friend." Tapping his coaster against the bar again, he angles his head in the direction of our table. "I'll see you over there?"

I nod. "Sure."

I don't watch him as he walks off toward our group, even though I want to. Emily's comment still rings through my mind on repeat. *It's fun seeing you and Bam together again.* Maybe that's why I felt the need to make some kind of declaration of our friendship to the group—to Bishop—so they all know that's all we are to each other.

Though another part of me thinks maybe who I really wanted to remind was myself.

chapter thirteen

bishop

"Thanks for helping me with this," Gabi says as we push open the door to The Vault on Wednesday morning, the warm air from inside a welcome reprieve. "I've been so wrapped up in work I completely forgot about Leah's birthday."

"No problem. You know I love looking at records, and it's been way too long since I've come in this place."

Four years, probably. I think the last time I remember visiting Cedar Point's vintage music shop was sometime during my senior year in high school, when I brought in all my dad's old CDs to exchange for store credit.

"The idea that these are vintage is laughable," he'd told me. "But if they'll take 'em, great."

Makes me wonder if I still have that credit.

We cross to the record section, which takes up the entire back half of the store, and we each start at opposite ends of the alphabet.

"Anything in particular you're looking for?"

Gabi nods. "She likes old folky stuff. Think like...Bob Dylan and Simon & Garfunkel."

"On it."

We spend a little while perusing, each of us selecting a few options to choose from, moving closer and closer to the center of the alphabet.

"Talk about a blast from the past."

I look over and find Gabi smiling, holding a record in her hand, and then her eyes fly to mine before she spins it around so I can see what it is.

"Nice," I say, crossing toward her and taking the *Best of Mumford and Sons* album from her hand. "God, I haven't listened to them in forever."

"Right? I mean, we have to get this."

I look up at her, finding Gabi watching me with one of the biggest smiles I've seen on her in a really long time. I'll agree with anything that puts that smile on her face, though buying a record certainly isn't a hardship.

"Absolutely."

We check out, using my remaining store credit to purchase our selections, including a Cat Stevens album for Leah's birthday, and then head back out to the street.

"Did you want to come over and listen to it?" Gabi asks as we come to a stop next to where her car is parked. "Mumford and Sons, I mean. I've never heard these songs on vinyl, and I feel like all the snobby music people I know say it sounds completely different."

"I actually have my first PT appointment in like, twenty minutes, and then I'll need to head to the school for practice," I tell her, wishing that wasn't the case. "But maybe we could do something this weekend? If you're not working. I don't want to get in the way of the creative process."

Gabi gives me a small grin. "Yeah, that could be fun," she tells me, holding the records tightly against her chest.

I nod. "Great. I'll text you about it soon?"

"Sounds good."

We stare at each other for a long beat before she hops into her car, and I continue walking down the street toward the doctor's office.

Gabi's been opening herself back up to me in these small pieces, these moments of togetherness that demonstrate we still have a closeness even time and pain from the past can't shatter entirely. It makes sense that she's been moving so slowly. Gabi doesn't let people in very easily. She's dealt with plenty of hurt in her life, and trust is a hard thing to come by. When we were younger, it was hard not to notice that she had built up a fortress around herself, a garrison with cannons and a moat and barbed wire, and a little army of words designed to protect her from being hurt again.

As someone who loved her, though, I wanted to be the person she let inside her heart, so I never gave up. I tried and I tried and I tried until she finally let me in. It was hard work, crawling through the barbed wire she surrounded herself with, but it was worth every single cut.

When we were talking at Cedar Cider last night, I was filled to the brim with this…memory, though I guess it's more of a feeling than anything super concrete. I've always known I missed her. I've always regretted how things ended between us, the fact that I lost my best friend and the love of my life in one fell swoop, but I didn't *get it* until we started spending more time together.

Now that I've had a hit of what it's like to be near her again,

I've been dealing with a rush of memories and emotions and reminders of who we used to be back when we didn't have such a chasm between us. That's what I'm facing now, trying to figure out how to bridge that gap, how to scale that moat and find my way back inside the space she protects so fiercely.

I just want her in my life again, however I can.

"Hey listen, I wanted to ask you a question."

I glance at Rush but look back to where I'm shoving cones into a bag, eager to get the equipment lugged inside and wrap up for the day. It was *another* afternoon of dealing with Justin's attitude. This time, I started with the jogs around the field early, not that it seemed to help. I sent him out six times, meaning he spent at least half of practice just running on his own. I doubt it's going to help him or make any real difference, but I still haven't figured out what to do.

Rush seems to be unconcerned with the way Justin acts, but I can see it leeching some of the joy out of the team and creating fissures between the players. Something needs to change. I just don't know what.

"Shoot," I say, swinging the bag of cones and gear over my shoulder.

"You and Gabriela." He lifts a bucket of balls and another bag of gear, and we start walking toward his office. "What's the deal?"

My stomach dips. "What do you mean?"

He chuckles. "Well, are you really just friends? Or is something else going on?"

Licking my lips, I shake my head, not really sure how to respond. There's a voice inside me saying there's still something there, still something between us, even after years apart. Sometimes, the way she looks at me reminds me of the way she looked at me back then, and it sends a warm feeling weaving its way through my veins.

Gabi doesn't laugh often for most people, but for me? She always did. Seeing her laugh and getting back to the playful way we tease each other has been...I don't even know how to describe it, but it makes me feel like that void that formed in my chest after we broke up is finally starting to fill back up.

But then there's the way she tells me we're friends, like she did last night at Cedar Cider. It was like she wanted to remind me that I need to keep up that boundary. It's confusing and hard to explain, so I don't really know how to answer Rush's question. Ultimately, I just default to what's easy.

"Yeah. We're friends, I guess. Or, trying to be."

"So if I told you I wanted to ask her out, you'd be cool with that?"

My throat tightens, and I know I don't mask the surprise on my face at his question.

"You want to go out with Gabi," I repeat.

He nods. "I mean...if you guys are just friends...yeah."

Everything within me revolts at this idea, at the idea of *my* Gabi dating Sam Rush. It just feels...wrong.

"I just figured, you know...I know you guys have a history. And you and me, we've been friends for years, and I don't want to fuck with that. But...she's gorgeous. So if nothing's going on between you two, I figured it couldn't hurt to at least ask."

But it does. It *does* hurt to have him ask, because it highlights to me the reality of what's going on between me and Gabi.

Nothing.

She's made it clear she just wants to be friends, right? Gabi deserves the world, a chance at every happiness any person could dream of, and Sam's a good guy. Kind and friendly and all that. Loyal, for sure.

It's just…I can't help but feel like if she and Rush start dating, it officially closes the door on us. Maybe I didn't realize until just this moment how much I want that door to still be open.

"I think I struck a nerve," he says after I've been silent for too long. "No worries, man. If it's a problem, I don't need to—"

"No, no. Sorry," I say, shaking my head and trying to push my own shit aside.

I don't have any claim on Gabi. I don't. Sometimes I think of her as *my* Gabi, but she belongs to herself. She's an adult who can do what she wants. I need to be thankful we're trying to be friends again and leave it at that.

Besides, after her reminder of the platonic nature of our relationship last night, it's clear that whatever romantic possibility there is between us, it has been firmly shut down on her end. Or maybe the door has been replaced by a wall of glass. We can see each other, wave, smile…but a boundary is in place. I have to respect that.

"Look, if you…want to ask Gabi out…if you think you guys would be a good match, I mean…I don't want to get in the way of that."

He eyes me for a beat. "Seriously?"

I let out a sigh then give him a smile, trying to convince myself as much as him.

"Seriously. You have my blessing."

He smiles. "Sweet. Thanks, man."

When I get home a while later, I shower, change, and stretch out on the couch, putting ESPN on then turning the volume low in the background. Rush's question is still throwing me for a loop, and I lay in a kind of daze for a while, trying to sort through it all in my mind. Maybe I didn't realize until he asked just how quickly all my feelings for Gabi have begun to return.

I grab my phone and bring up my personal social media account, the one I keep on private so I can have connections with just friends and family. Then I go into my photos and scroll through my albums from high school. It makes me smile, seeing the memories of what life was like back then. It wasn't that long ago, but it sure feels like it, like a lifetime has happened since I was a cocky teen with the world at his fingertips.

The photos of me and Gabi are few and far between. She was never much for wanting to be in front of the camera, but it doesn't take long for me to find the one I'm looking for.

It's a picture Nicole took of the two of us during the summer, right before we left for school. We'd been out on a boat enjoying the warm weather all day and were sitting on a dock at Miller's Landing. Our legs are crossed and we're facing each other, leaning forward. I have her face in my hands, and we're looking at each other like...

...like there's no one else in the entire world.

It's hard to look back on who we were and know the reason we're not together anymore is because, at some point, I decided to give up. Throw in the towel.

Why couldn't I have just told her how I really felt? Tell her something wasn't working, but I was willing to do whatever it took to figure out how to fix whatever felt broken?

But any excuse I have is a copout.

The fact that something broke between us is my fucking fault.

And I don't know if I'll ever be able to forgive myself.

Scrimmages at the high school level are primarily two things.

First, they're a low-stakes way to get those first-game jitters out before a real game. Even the most seasoned players get nervous before heading out onto the field for the first time in months, so it's only natural that kids feel the same.

Second, but more importantly from a coaching perspective, it's a chance to test the waters for things that are getting worked on in the off-season without risking a loss unnecessarily. Some players who are more superstitious might use it as a chance to try out new equipment. It might be a new hitting order or a chance for some of the players to test out different positions.

The Fall Ball scrimmage series the high school does each year with Spencer Creek and Belleview is a bit of a rivalry. To be honest, the kids care about it more than they do some of the regular season games. I certainly remember caring about it a whole lot, and with the first scrimmage right around the corner, I'm not surprised when Rush hands me a clipboard and a sheet of paper once we're done with practice.

"Batting order," he says. "Let me know what you think."

I scan the list quickly then hand it back only a few seconds later. "I think you should bump Justin down."

Rush leans back against his desk, setting the clipboard down then bracing himself with his hands against the edge. "Bump him down the list? Or bump him down a peg?"

I purse my lips. "Meaning?"

"Meaning…I don't make a habit of letting player attitudes dictate the way I coach."

"Well, maybe you should."

He grins, unperturbed by my comment. "We all have different opinions about the best way to lead people, Bam. I see a kid like Justin, with all that attitude, and you know what I think my job is? To help him get better then send him on his way. I don't need to be the person who fixes him."

"But you could be."

"Maybe, or maybe I just get into a pissing match with him like you are."

"That's not what I'm doing."

"Then what *are* you doing?"

Gritting my teeth, I cross my arms, my frustration about Rush's laidback approach and Justin's shitty attitude melding together and bubbling over.

"I'm trying to get him to drop the ego. If he doesn't learn how to do that, he's going to make the same mistakes I did."

Rush raises his eyebrows, clearly surprised at the direction this conversation has taken.

"I see a lot of me in Justin, alright? And think what you want about me believing he should be knocked down a peg, but I'm just trying to figure out how to get through to him."

"I'll be honest, Bam. I'm surprised you care so much."

I chuckle, the irritation leaking out of me just as fast as it came. "Yeah, well…so am I. Trust me."

"I think it's great that you want to help him." Rush pushes off of his desk and rounds to the other side. "But you're going to need to come up with something different that *doesn't* fuck with my lineup."

I snort. "Got it."

Clearly, I need to head back to the drawing board when it comes to this kid. Like my dad said, I'm out of *ideas*, not options.

I give Rush a wave and head out of his office then stroll slowly down the hallway toward the parking lot, letting my mind roll listlessly over some of the different things I might be able to do to reach Justin: talk to his mom...force him to coach a practice...but who really knows what might work?

When I hear my name called out from behind me, I stop, turning to find Gabi walking in my direction. All thoughts of Justin go right out the window.

"Heading home to get ready for tonight?" I ask with a grin, eyeing the box she has in her hands as she approaches me.

"Maybe."

"Do you have a costume?"

Her grin is wolfish. "Obviously."

I chuckle as we walk together toward the lot.

"Any hints? Or do you still keep it a secret until the final reveal?"

"Secret, of course. I don't want anyone copying my look."

Gabi loves Halloween. Makes sense considering her black cat energy.

"How was practice?" she asks as we push out into the parking lot.

"Apart from the kid that keeps driving me insane?" I grin. "Pretty good."

"Ah, your mini-Bishop still causing problems?"

I scoff, though I can see the bit of teasing flaring in her eyes.

"Come on, I might have been a little cocky, but I wasn't *that* bad."

Her eyes narrow a smidge. "I seem to remember someone stomping around my front yard because his coach got in his face." Her nose and cheeks scrunch up and her voice goes deep as she imitates Coach G. "*If you spent more time conditioning and less time making out with your new girlfriend, maybe you'd be able to keep up with the rest of the team during drills.*"

I wrinkle my nose, trying not to smile.

"And what did you say back to him?" she continues. "I can't remember, something about, if he spent more time coaching his team and less time…"

"Less time bitching, maybe he'd have a trophy to show for it. You know, I'm not a fan of everyone pointing out what a cocky little shit I was in high school."

Gabi pokes me in the chest. "We were all miniature know-it-alls. Remember when Mrs. Garland tried to get me to switch from exclusively working with charcoal pencils to using compressed charcoal? I told her not everyone needs to use every supply in the box to make their art look good."

My shoulders shake as I laugh, unsurprised at the reminder of Gabi's spitfire attitude. She used to say her life mascot was a house cat because they demand exactly what they want and are generally unimpressed by everyone, and she resonated with that.

"So I'll see you at Spooktacular?" I ask.

She nods then glances at her watch. "I'm starting to get worried about getting dressed and set up by 7."

"Hey, I have extra hands if you need them."

Gabi considers me for a long moment before she responds. "Actually, if you're willing, that would be amazing."

I smirk. "For you, I'm always willing."

Gabi rolls her eyes, her fingers drumming lightly on the box in her hands, but that smile is still there.

"I'll meet you there in an hour?" I ask as she pops the trunk of her car and slides her box inside.

"Sounds good."

Then she surprises me. Gabi steps forward and wraps her arms around my middle, embracing me. It's brief, but I tug her in close, enjoying the closeness of this moment.

When we let go, there's something in her expression that feels familiar, but just as quickly as I think I saw it, it disappears. Gabi slides into her car and gives me a small wave as she takes off, and I'm left there wondering if what I saw was really there.

chapter fourteen

gabi

Cedar Point's Halloween Spooktacular is one of a handful of staple events the town puts on every year, without fail. Main Street gets closed off to through traffic and all the businesses stay open late so kids can go from store to store for candy. There are booths set up by locals and businesses that are slightly off Main Street with a kind of farmers market vibe, and every year, there's a costume contest.

I've always wanted to enter, because I *love* Halloween and—in my opinion—dressing up in costume is one of the most fun things you can do, ever. But when I was in high school, the idea of getting up in front of a group of people and asking them to literally judge me sounded like a nightmare. As if they weren't judging me enough already.

This year, though, I've been putting together the most gorgeous, perfect costume, and I have every intention of entering that contest.

I look at myself in the mirror, assessing the final result, and

I feel immense pleasure at what I see.

Wednesday Addams.

Black tights under a long-sleeved black dress with a white collar and cuffs. A layer of pale foundation and a smoky eye. I even bought some clip-on bangs, and with my already long dark hair in two braids, it adds just the right final touch.

"You outdid yourself this year."

I turn, finding Leah standing in the doorway, watching me with a smile.

"You don't look so bad yourself," I volley back, eyeing her long black wig and the tight black dress that shows off just the right amount of cleavage.

She's going as Morticia, though surprisingly, we didn't plan to do this together. We decided on the outfits separately and then found out we were going to match. Clearly we both have cold, black hearts.

"Did you get all your stuff loaded in the car?"

I nod. "I'm not bringing a lot, so I won't take up too much space," I tell her as we head through the house and toward the garage.

"Hey, I'm thrilled to have you share my booth. Take up as much space as you need."

Grinning, we each tug on our coats and head outside. I was worried Spooktacular would be canceled because the temps are colder this year than last, but it looks like the weather is going to even out to a fairly normal evening for the end of October. Besides, I'm pretty sure kids would be willing to fight through a blizzard to get candy. If Halloween got canceled, the elementary school would riot.

My phone buzzes in my purse, and when I look at it, I can't help the grin that pops onto my face.

Bishop: On my way. See you in ten.

"What's that look for?"

"What look?"

Leah rolls her eyes at my feigned ignorance then starts the car.

Accepting Bishop's offer feels like a big step for me. Maybe that's stupid, and maybe most people don't struggle like I do to accept help from others, but having him come help set up our booth feels like I've finally accepted that I can rely on him again. Even if it's just in a small way.

"Bishop's gonna help us set up," I say to Leah as we're driving into town.

She eyes me briefly before looking back to the road. "You've been spending a bit of time together recently. Are you still…just friends?"

"Yup! Just friends."

My response is too quick, and I know it. She doesn't call me out though, just nods and continues driving, leaving me to my own thoughts. We *are* just friends. At least, that's what I keep telling myself. But I can't help the fact that recently I've been feeling the inkling of more, the stirring of feelings I'm not sure I want to feel.

I stare out the window, looking at the fall foliage that has finally taken a true hold of our forests. The oranges and browns and reds and yellows all blend together to create the magic of autumn in the mountains.

It's foolish. I know that. Anything that might happen with Bishop would need to end at some point. He's going to leave eventually, move back to Oregon and pursue his dream, like Nicole and I talked about. But…maybe that's what makes it feel slightly easier to manage emotionally. When things end—when he leaves—it won't be a surprise. I would be able to see it coming. Maybe we are just friends, but maybe…there's room for more, even if it's only temporary.

When we get to Main Street, Leah drops me off with all our stuff then tells me and Bishop to start setting up while she parks her truck.

As we start arranging everything, I can see Bishop struggling a bit while using his left hand, the frustration obvious in his face. He smiles when he sees me watching, so I don't make a big thing about it. Though it does highlight to me that we haven't really talked much about his injury since he's been home.

Once the tent is done, we pop up our table then begin to organize our goods. Leah's macrame wall art gets hung from the tent frame, the beautiful designs just a sample of my aunt's incredible talent. The pieces she brings to markets like this are small in comparison to the ones she sells to make a living, but they're just as beautiful. I like to think I got some of my artistic drive from her, though who knows if that's even a real thing.

I *have* learned plenty from her about selling the things I create, though. The only reason I know how important it is to charge what I'm worth when it comes to commissioned pieces is because of Leah. She's made some huge, incredibly intricate pieces for clients, and there have been plenty of times she's been told she's too expensive.

"I'm not for everyone," she used to tell me. "I'm not for every budget or every style or every vision. And that's okay. It doesn't mean you should value yourself and your talent any less."

It was a valuable lesson, in more ways than one.

"How was PT yesterday?" I ask once we've finished hanging Leah's items.

Bishop and I are standing side by side, trying to decide how to organize my pottery on the table. I've never sold my stuff at a market before, and I didn't fully think through how I want it set out. I should have brought wooden boxes or cute decorations... *something* to make it a bit more dynamic. Clearly I still have a lot to learn.

"Yeah...it sucked," he jokes, rounding to the other side of the table to eye how it looks to a customer. "Maybe move the big plate to the middle?"

I nod, taking his suggestion and centering the plate, moving the set of vases to the side instead.

"How often are you supposed to go?"

"Twice a week for a month."

"That's it?"

"Well, I also have to do exercises on my own."

"Every day?"

He sighs but keeps that same smile. "Every damn day."

"If you want help," I tell him, rounding the table to stand next to him so I can get the customer view as well, "I could probably find some exercises for you to do with your hands."

The minute I say it, my cheeks heat. I didn't mean it to come out like that. Or, maybe I just didn't mean to actually say it out loud. A big part of me hopes he'll think I'm just joking, but I can't deny the pleasure I get when I look at him and see the shock on his face. My lips tilt up at the sides, but I return my gaze to the table, moving to swap two other pieces.

"There." I step back again. "What do you think?"

"Looks perfect!"

I turn at the sound of Leah's voice, thankful she didn't over-hear my innuendo just a moment ago.

"You guys got it all set up without me. Great job."

She steps under the tent and reaches up, messing with one of her pieces, adjusting the way some of the loose strings hang from the bottom.

"I'll let you two enjoy yourselves," Bishop says, tucking his hands into the pockets of his sweatshirt. "Get out of your hair."

"You just want to go grab a beer from the beer tent," I joke, poking him in the stomach.

"Hey, I didn't claim otherwise," he replies, grinning. "But I also need to go help my parents. They're hosting the candy swap booth down the street, and I've been voluntold to take a shift."

I laugh. "See you later, then."

He nods then spins around and heads down the street to where his parents' booth is at the opposite end. Letting out a long sigh, I watch him until he disappears in the growing crowd then turn to begin helping Leah adjust her hangings.

Which is when I find *her* watching *me*.

"Still wanna tell me you guys are just friends?" she asks with a smirk.

Instead of responding, I just lift my chin and cross to the other side of the tent, focusing on a smaller piece that's hanging slightly on its side.

"Hey there, Leah. Gabriela."

I glance over, my eyes widening when I see Roy Pulasky approaching our table. My eyes track up and down, taking in his costume. He's dressed as Gomez Addams in a pinstripe suit and black tie, his mustache newly trimmed and his hair slicked back, and I don't doubt in the slightest he did it to match my aunt. Though I have no idea how he found out what she was dressing as.

"Hi, Roy. Is the hardware store not doing the event to-night?" I ask, glancing at Leah briefly and finding her standing as still as a statue.

"Oh, we always do the event. I have Jerry handling it right now. Just wanted to stop by and say hello."

"Well your costume looks awesome," I tell him, looking at Leah again.

I'm not sure why she's suddenly frozen, but I take that as a cue to leave her be for a few minutes. "Hey, I'm gonna pop over to Ugly Mug and get a coffee. Do you want one?"

Leah shakes her head, and I take off, heading across the street and down a few shops, occasionally turning back to see if she and Roy are talking. Ugly Mug has a table outside and they're passing out cups of drip coffee for free, so I ignore my aunt's decline and snag two cups then slowly make my way back to our booth. When I finally get there, Leah is alone again, fiddling with some of the items still in one of the boxes.

"Roy head back to his shop?" I ask, watching her closely as I pass over a cup. "Seemed like maybe he wanted to hang out for a bit."

She blows on the hot liquid for a beat. "Yeah, he needed to go finish getting set up."

"Bummer. We should have gotten a picture of us with our costumes."

Leah takes a sip, her eyes looking in the direction of the hardware store. Her expression is foggy, and I'm not sure why until she speaks again.

"He asked me out. On a date."

I blink, sure I misheard her. "And what did you say?"

"I think...I agreed?"

My head jerks back in surprise, but then a smile stretches across my face.

"That's great." I pause, taking in her awkward stance. "So

why do you look so constipated?"

At that, she narrows her eyes in my direction, and whatever daze she was in falls away. Leah swats at me, then moves over and distractedly begins rearranging things. I laugh quietly to myself and leave her be, tugging out the bags of candy we brought and dumping them into large bowls.

We work in relative silence for a few minutes, until the music begins to play from the big speakers set up at either end of the street. Then we completely move on, both of us focusing on the rush of families that swarm the block and begin approaching our booth.

But regardless of the crowd, my mind continues spinning a million miles an hour. I can't remember the last time Leah went on a date. It had to have been when I was in high school.

I know she's been asked plenty of times—usually by men who are just passing through town—but Leah has always turned them down. She's made it clear she has *zero* interest in fooling around with tourists who, for all she knows, could have a family wherever they live.

And then there's the fact she agreed to go out with *Roy*.

I have nothing against the guy. He's nice and friendly and always greets us with a smile whenever we come into the hardware store, even if he seems a bit nervous sometimes. I've assumed for a while that he's had a thing for my aunt, but I guess that's why it never felt like a match for me.

Roy gives off the appearance of a nice older guy with a crush, and Leah is…Leah. Sharp and wary and a bit jaded when it comes to men. Quick to avoid them or shut them down.

So the fact that he finally asked is wild in and of itself.

But the fact that she *agreed*?

It's a small-town miracle.

I shut the rear of Leah's truck, the items that didn't sell packed snugly back in their boxes next to our folded-up tent and table.

"Congrats on your win."

I glance at the small plastic trophy in my hand and shrug.

"It's just third place."

"Psht. You got robbed," Bishop tells me, eyeing my costume up and down. "They only gave the first two trophies to those kids because they're kids, you know?"

Snorting, I roll my eyes.

"But hey, I'm proud of you."

My gaze flicks to his, surprise rolling through me.

"You used to talk about this competition every year, how you were going to enter and blow everyone away...and then you always found some reason not to participate. But you did it this year. You're amazing."

I swallow thickly as I stare at the peeling paint on the back of Leah's truck, unsure how to process his praise. Eventually I just nod, knowing if I say anything, I'll just sound like an idiot. I don't handle stuff like that well.

"Thanks for your help today," I finally say, redirecting the conversation entirely.

Bishop grins, leaning his hip against the tailgate and crossing his arms. "Thanks for asking me."

"I didn't ask. You offered."

He narrows his eyes and hums. "Seems to me you said you

were worried about having enough time to set up after class *and* get into costume. All I did was say I had extra hands."

"Yes, you did. Thanks so much for *offering* those extra hands."

He gives me a wide smile. "Fine, if you want to play this game, you're welcome. Just remember that these *extra hands* are always available to you."

I blush at the reminder of my comment earlier. I worry I pushed too far with that, not because I don't think Bishop appreciated it—I've seen the heated way he's looked at me, on more than one occasion—but because I'm nervous. We're just starting to figure out this friend thing. I don't want to do something stupid and fuck it up.

"So, still wanna get together this weekend?"

Licking my lips, I nod. "Yeah. I need to work, but we should be able to figure something out."

He reaches out and tugs gently on my jacket, enough that I move forward just an inch. Nerves skitter down my spine as I gaze up at him, the world around us seemingly coming to a halt. I'm suddenly hyper aware of how close we are. I can feel the warmth from his large body, and I can't help when my eyes dip slightly, taking in the soft outline of his lips. The bit of stubble growing on his jaw.

Bishop licks his lips and then opens his mouth, like he's going to respond, and I wait with baited breath, wondering what it is.

But then he takes a step back, an uncertain expression flashing in his eyes just as Leah approaches us and chucks a large duffel bag into the bed of the truck.

"Good night, Bishop," she says, then hops in and closes the door.

I blink a few times, the moment evaporating quickly, and tilt my head toward the truck, indicating that I need to go. "I guess I'll...see you later?"

Bishop nods. "I'll see you this weekend."

I climb in next to Leah and shut the door, glancing at Bishop's retreating form in the side mirror.

"You two are *so* getting back together."

I turn, narrowing my eyes at her. "I don't want to hear it, *Mrs. Pulasky.*"

Leah smirks, and we both bust out in laughter. Eventually, she puts the car in drive and heads down the road, taking us back to the house.

I don't' know what that was back there, with Bishop. But I do know that it's becoming nearly impossible not to get lost in him.

And as much as that worries me, I can't help but admit...

...it excites me, too.

chapter fifteen
bishop

When I arrive at Gabi's house on Sunday evening, I pull to a stop at the end of the long dirt path that leads to the cabin she shares with her aunt. They're kind of tucked back into the wooded area on a large lot, which is great for privacy but shit during the winter when there's a heavy snow.

It suits them, though, Gabi and Leah, being so far out of the way and hidden from the world. It's the vibe they put out there, that they don't want to be disturbed. They like their space and their quiet.

As I get farther down the road, their house comes into view. It looks mostly the same as I remember, though I think they might have repainted the window shutters and planted some new bushes next to the driveway. Memories from the past assault me as I park, get out, and make my way toward the front door…

Lying on the grass in the yard on a blanket during the summer and staring up at the trees. All the times I'd drop Gabi off after school and we'd sit in the car making out until Leah had to rap on the window to get our attention. The first time I kissed her, right there in the doorway, after bringing her home from one of the summer bonfires before junior year started.

Before I even make it to the door, it opens, and Leah is standing in the doorway with her arms crossed.

"Never thought I'd see *you* walking up the drive again," she says, leaning against the jamb wearing a nice blue dress.

"Evening, Ms. Ventura. You look lovely this evening."

She snorts, then gives me a ghost of a smile. "You always were a kiss-ass."

I can't help grinning wide at her comment.

"She's in the shed working."

I nod. "Thanks."

"And Bishop?"

I look back at where Leah still stands at the entry, her expression much more serious.

"Don't break her heart again."

My smile dims at her words, and she nods once before stepping back inside and shutting the door. Clearing my throat, I turn and begin walking around the side of the house to the shed in the back, a detached garage Leah has always used for storage. Light from the three small windows just under the roof provides direction in the dimming evening light, and when I come to the shed, I stop at the door, listening intently for any indication of what Gabi's doing inside. All I can hear is the faint sound of Maggie Rogers playing, and I turn the handle, opening the door and peeking through. Then I open it wider in surprise.

"Wow," I say, stepping inside, taking it all in, my eyes tracking over all the art supplies and shelves filled with Gabi's work before finally landing on the woman herself. She smiles at me from where she sits at her wheel, working on a bowl, or possibly something else. Everything she makes seems to change shape so quickly.

"This place looks so different."

The last time I was in here, it was filled with old furniture and boxes. Now, it looks like Gabi has set up an art studio. There were a handful of times, back when we had just started dating, that we would sneak to the shed to make out, away from Leah's watchful eyes.

Gabi glances around, possibly remembering what it used to look like, maybe thinking about those stolen moments as well.

"I'm just finishing up. I'll only be a few minutes," she tells me.

I shake my head. "Take your time. This gives me a chance to snoop, see all this incredible work you've been doing."

"I don't know about incredible, but feel free," she replies, a smile still lingering in her voice.

I spent some time the other day looking at the stuff Gabi shares online, the videos and photos of her artwork. She has a huge following, with some of her videos racking up millions of views and thousands of comments.

I can see her talent in the items she's been working on in her classroom, and I've made a habit of observing it each week when we have our meetings. But seeing it up close like this—the items she's selling, not just creating as part of her class—makes it so clear why she's so sought after.

"Your stuff is really good," I say, staring at a tower of shelves in the corner, where Gabi's projects are all laid out in various stages of completion. Vases and mugs and plates and bowls, all with slightly different patterns, but each feeling like a part of the same collection.

"Thanks," she says, crossing the room behind me and moving to the sink.

"You really didn't do anything with ceramics before that first class at MSA?" I clarify.

"Do *you* remember me doing anything like that?" she replies, laughing.

I spin to look at her. "No, but that doesn't mean it couldn't have happened. We weren't together every second of every day."

She rolls her eyes as she rinses off some of her supplies in the sink. "But we talked about pretty much everything, so you would have known."

"True."

I find it hard to look away from her as she finishes at the sink, then pulls her long hair out of the loose ponytail that stretches down to the middle of her back. Her hair falls forward, and she runs her fingers through it. God, I always loved her hair.

"I don't know why, but I just had a knack for it, you know?" she continues, tucking her hair behind her ears and shrugging, oblivious to my perusal. "And after I finished those two years, I came home and started making stuff and posting it online to sell."

It doesn't surprise me at all. Gabi's plan was always to do two years at Monterey School of Art then return to Cedar Point and work somewhere in town while she did art on the side. She told me multiple times that this place was the only place she felt at home—with Leah, the most important person in her life—and she didn't want to lose it. The fact that she's here, creating and thriving, makes perfect sense.

"So you just…what, came home and started a business that took off? What a badass."

Gabi blushes slightly at my comment. "No. Some of my stuff went viral. It wasn't anything I did."

I scoff. "Bull*shit* it wasn't something you did. If you weren't so talented and if you hadn't created a product that was so amazing, there wouldn't have been anything *to* go viral. Don't brush it off like it's just luck, Gabi."

"It feels like luck." Her words are just a mumble, but I still hear them.

I hear the underlying fear behind what she's saying. It resonates with a truth Gabi has always struggled with her entire life: that people will see through the mask she wears so carefully. As confident as she is, as beautiful and smart and talented, there is something inside her that thinks she is undeserving.

"Was it luck that I was drafted?" I toss at her, intent on making a point. "Was I just lucky? After all my hard work and long practices and extra time in the gym and every single sacrifice I made...was it just luck?"

Gabi rolls her eyes and leans back against the sink, crossing her arms. "Of course not."

"Of course it wasn't. Sure, there was some luck in there, but that luck would have had nothing to stick to if I hadn't first done all the work."

"It's not the same."

"It *is* the same," I continue, crossing toward her. "You spent your entire life building yourself as an artist, someone with an eye for detail. And then you found a new way to bring that artistry to life. I don't doubt you were the first one spinning pottery each morning and the last one each night. Because that's the kind of effort you put into the things you care about."

"Throwing pottery," she says, her lips curving. "It's called *throwing* pottery."

I give her a look at says I'm unamused by her attempt to distract me. "Seriously?"

"I get it, okay? I do."

Even so, I'm certain the things I've said are already lost in the sea of Gabi's mind, swallowed up by the imposter syndrome and self-doubt she usually hides so well but has felt for as long as I've known her.

"If you can just take away from this conversation one thing that's true, can it be that I think you're amazing?" I say, taking one last shot at driving my message home. "Regardless of everything else, I'm supremely impressed by you and everything you've accomplished."

I can see some of the tension in her shoulders begin to leak out, and her eyes return to mine. She nods, and even though it's small, I take it as a win.

"You ready to head in? Give this record a listen?"

She sighs, her smile soft. "Yeah."

We shut off the lights in her shed and step outside, slipping into the cold evening air. Gabi starts giggling as we pick up the pace, jogging quickly across the property to the house. When we step into the blissful warmth of the kitchen, we find Leah standing at the counter, staring blankly out the window. I glance past her, spotting a red truck parked next to my SUV in the driveway.

"Is Roy here?" Gabi asks.

"Yeah. I guess it's time to go." She throws her purse over one shoulder then looks at Gabi. "Time to get this over with."

"Don't say that." Gabi glares at her. "You're going to have a great time."

"We'll see."

Leah gives Gabi a wave, nods her head at me, then heads out into the cool evening. We watch from the kitchen window as she almost jogs out to Roy's truck, meeting him in the drive. They talk for a beat or two, and even from here I can spot the excitement in Roy and the absolute terror in Leah.

"I feel like I'm watching something I shouldn't be," I say as Roy opens the passenger seat and Leah hops up into his truck, "but I don't want to look away."

Gabi laughs next to me, still watching them out the window as well. "It's weird, right? I mean…I've always hoped she'd find someone, but it's just an odd thing to see."

"You think Roy is the one?"

She snorts and rolls her eyes as the truck begins to pull out of the drive.

"Who knows?" she says as we turn and head into the living room. "Maybe it's all a ploy to help me get more art supplies in the hardware store, or at least get me some kind of discount."

Gabi grabs a blanket and wraps herself up snugly before collapsing on the couch, clearly leaving the music setup part to me.

"Alright, where's this record?"

A few moments later, there's a slight scratch as I set the needle on the vinyl, and then the familiar guitar stylings of Mumford and Sons come through the speakers, sucking me back to that summer we spent playing their music on repeat. After a few beats, I take a seat on the couch at the opposite end, and we sit listening together.

Mumford and Sons really took off when we were in junior high, but for whatever reason, we got hooked on one of the songs and it became the only thing we wanted to listen to during the summer before junior year. It was right before I asked Gabi to be my girlfriend, and I remember the many nights I spent listening to these lyrics, daydreaming about her, before I finally mustered up the courage to tell her how I felt.

Eventually, the record gets through the first side, and I return to the player, flipping it over and starting with the next song. When I drop back down on the couch, I land a little too roughly, and something twinges in my arm, the pain lancing through me.

"Fuck," I hiss, closing my eyes and gritting my teeth.

Before I can even fully focus on the dull ache that blooms, Gabi has launched out of her snuggly bubble and is next to me on her knees, her hands reaching out to gently touch my arm.

"Are you okay?"

"Yeah I'm okay. I just…jarred it a bit, that's all," I tell her, warming at her concern. "It's kind of tender from PT today, but I think I might…" I trail off, tugging on the Velcro of my brace until it's loose and I can pull my arm free. I gently roll my wrist, enjoying the freedom I'm allotted now that I can move it. "These PT sessions are a lot," I say, massaging my wrist slightly. "I didn't realize how achy it would be like…all day afterward."

"What do they have you do?"

"Just a bunch of tiny things over and over again, small movements to work out the joints and muscles."

I shake my head, just massaging gently.

"So, what really happened?" Gabi asks, dropping down slightly so she's sitting on her feet, her elbow resting on the back of the couch. "With your injury, I mean."

"You didn't see the video?"

She shakes her head, her lips pursed. "They had a viewing party at The Mitch, but…I didn't go."

I huff out an embarrassed laugh.

"I guess I shouldn't be surprised that everyone was watching as I made a complete fool of myself." Sighing, I shift slightly so I'm looking more at her. "What you missed was me sliding into third base wrong and breaking my wrist and three fingers."

Gabi winces. "That sounds like zero fun."

"You would be correct." I laugh then I point at the tiny scar on my wrist. "I had to have surgery, and then I spent about six weeks letting everything heal. Now I'm in this brace, which gives some more freedom, but I'm looking at probably two months of physical therapy to regain my full mobility." I shake my head and look down at my hand and forearm, the skin slightly paler than the rest from being concealed in the cast. "Such an idiot."

Her hand rests on top of mine, her thumb stroking gently along my skin, and I look back at her, finding her watching me with kind eyes.

"You might be an idiot, but we all do stupid things sometimes. It's how you come back from it that matters."

My lips tilt up. "You're not supposed to agree with me about the idiot thing. You're supposed to tell me I'm wrong."

"Bishop Mitchell, in what world have I ever coddled your emotions?" she asks, and I can see her smile in the brightness of her eyes, even in the dim lighting of the living room.

"Never."

"Never. And I don't plan to start anytime soon."

I just stare at her for a long moment, her long hair blocking out the light behind us like a curtain and trailing down her arm.

God, she's beautiful. I've never forgotten that as a finite truth, but it's different when I'm staring it in the face, staring at *her* face. Her wide eyes and button nose, the small bow at the top of her lips.

"I missed you," I tell her, not having planned to say the words out loud but feeling it so deeply that I'm practically compelled to. "God, Gabi…" Using my good hand, I caress the side of her face, stroking my thumb along the apple of her cheek. "I missed everything about you."

Something passes between us then, something deep and

emotional and charged with all the feelings that have been brought to the surface since I returned home six weeks ago.

And then, before I can react, before I can even think, Gabi leans in and presses her lips to mine.

chapter sixteen
gabi

I don't know what makes me kiss Bishop…except the fact that I can't *not*.

I can feel the surprise in his body, in his quick inhale of breath before our lips touch. Hell, I'm just as surprised, but then I can't be anything but wrapped up in him as our mouths open and his tongue dips and tangles with mine.

There's familiarity in the motion, but then his hand flexes where it was resting on my neck. Bishop grips me and guides our kiss with much more confidence than he did when we were younger. He nibbles gently at my lips, and I moan, feeling a pulsing low in my belly.

Almost on autopilot, I rise up to my knees and shift my weight, swinging one of my legs over where he sits then settling in on Bishop's lap. I can feel him, hard and thick beneath his jeans, and I grind down on top of him. Something in me has snapped and broken free, some small part of me that has wanted Bishop again from the moment I saw him on Main Street all those weeks ago.

I've missed him. He might have been the one to say it, but I feel it, too, feel it in my very depths, in the part of me that aches and longs for him, that has *always* longed for him. God, to feel the warmth of his arms around me when I've felt so cold for so long. His hands frame my face, and then he nibbles on my bottom lip, just like he used to.

That thought stops me cold, brings my movements to a halt, and Bishop's as well. He can feel that I've stopped, and he pulls back, eyeing me closely. Before he can say anything, I push off of him so I'm standing.

The movement bumps Bishop's wrist, and he winces, bringing his arm in tight against his chest.

"You should probably go," I tell him, ignoring the desire to check if he's okay. "I have to do some laundry for tomorrow."

A lie, but it's the only thing I can think to say that will usher him out the door and isn't a truth I'm not ready to speak. As much as I want Bishop, there's just too much hurt and confusion for me to get past, and it was stupid of me to lose sight of that.

He stands, eyeing me cautiously. "Gabi…"

"You can let yourself out, right?"

I ask the question but barely give him a chance to nod before I'm fleeing the room and heading down the short hallway to my bedroom. Once there, I shut the door and lean against it, my hand to my chest. My heart is pounding like I just ran a mile, and I sink down to the floor, my butt on the carpet and my arms wrapped around my knees.

I know I'm overreacting. I know it, but I can't help the fact that I suddenly needed to be anywhere but standing in front of the man who broke my heart.

"Gabi."

The sound of Bishop's voice on the other side of the door, quiet and steady, is just as much a burn as it is a balm. A few gentle taps, and he says my name again.

"Gabi, can I talk to you? Just for a second?"

I take a deep breath and let it out slowly, knowing if I don't bite the bullet and just talk to him, he'll be here even longer. Pushing to my feet, I shake out my hands and open the door, one eyebrow raised.

"What."

Bishop's head tilts to the side as he assesses me.

"Just didn't want to leave without knowing you're okay."

I cross my arms. "Why wouldn't I be?"

At my attitude, *he* raises his eyebrows. "You kissed me and then stormed out of the room," he says, being far more direct than I expect. "Don't try to bullshit me, Gabriela. You forget I know all your tells."

I narrow my eyes, my instincts kicking in.

"Well, I hate to break it to you, Bishop, but a lot has changed over the years. I'm a very different person now than I was when you knew me. So as much as you might have known me then, you *don't* anymore."

Then I shut the door in his face. I stand there, listening, making sure I know when he's gone. I hear him moving through the house, out to the living room, maybe gathering his stuff.

But then I hear the scratch of the record player, and I crack my door, my heart thudding when the music begins to play on low.

Our favorite song. *Believe.*

He switches off the lights and leaves through the front door, and not until I hear his tires rolling down the drive do I let my tears fall.

"This is looking really great, Helene," I say, crouching down to observe her movements as she carefully evens out her walls.

"Thanks," she says, her voice quiet and her eyes laser sharp on her project.

"It looks like you're pressing more with your outside hand. You want to keep that pressure really even, until you're ready to bubble outward. You'll have an easier time controlling your progress."

Helene nods, her eyes never moving away. I see the way she shifts her left hand just slightly where it rests against the outside of her vase, and she begins moving her inside hand upward again, stroking along the interior and slowly evening out the walls.

"Perfect. Great adjustments."

Standing, I look around the room, taking in the varying success levels of each student's vase. Alexa's is a little too short and wide but still looking fairly even. Nina's is a lot taller but looks like it's about to spin out at any second. And Johnny is still making things that look remarkably phallic to the point that I'm actually a little impressed.

We've finally tipped into November, which puts us more than halfway through the semester. The students are starting to look more confident and more capable than they did during those first few weeks.

It makes me proud to see how much they've improved. I might not be the most amazing instructor in the world, but I don't half-ass it, and I think it's made a difference.

When we end class for the day, I spend some time cleaning up, my mind lost in a fog of misshapen thoughts. I should be thinking about all the work things I need to get done when I get home, or about preparing for the art show that's looming around the corner.

Instead, all I can think about—all I've been able to think about since it happened this past weekend—is that kiss.

It has plagued my thoughts. Fucked with my work schedule. More than a few clay mugs have ended up in the bin over my lack of focus.

I wanted to kiss him. I wanted to remember what it felt like to be in his arms. I wanted to go back in time, at least for a while. Forget the pain.

It was everything I remembered and yet not the same at all.

The stubble on his face bit at my skin. The muscles under my hands were firmer and more defined. The control he wielded with a few simple movements set the blood in my veins on fire.

But then I came back to myself, and so did the heartache.

"Knock, knock."

My head flies up, and for a beat, I assume it's Bishop stopping by my classroom, but it's Sam at the door, and I give him a friendly smile, trying to ignore the disappointment I feel.

It's my own fault. Bishop asked me if I wanted to meet today to put together our notes for Principal Cohen, and I said no. He's not the kind of guy to just ignore me and show up anyway.

I usually appreciate that, but every once in a while, I wish he were.

"Hey there, Ms. Ventura," Sam says, grinning at me.

I shake my head. "You ever gonna call me Gabriela again?"

"Nah. Ms. Ventura suits you."

He steps fully into the classroom, letting the heavy door shut behind him. Then his eyes scan the room.

"So this is where you make all your little dishes, huh?"

My nose wrinkles at the way he says it. I know he doesn't mean anything by it, but it sure sounds like a complete write-off of what I do.

"No, I make all my pieces at my house," I say, collecting the last bricks of remaining unused clay and putting them into a plastic bin then sealing it closed. "You done with practice for the day?"

He nods. "Yep. Went short today. Weather's been pretty shit. Might need to finally give up on field work and move into the weight room."

"At least you'll be warm," I offer, grinning.

I hang up my apron on the rack in the corner then pick up my purse and head over to where he's standing near the door.

"You heading home for the night?"

"Yep. Have a bunch of work to get done."

He hums as I grab my coat from the hook by the door and shrug it on.

"Hey, listen, Gabriela…I've been thinking about it, and I was wondering if you'd like to grab dinner with me sometime."

I freeze, surprise rolling through my body.

"We could head into town—Dock 7, maybe—or we could go down the mountain and do something outside the typical Cedar Point wheelhouse, you know? Mix things up."

I blink a few times, trying to find the right words to say. There are a million reasons I could give him for why I need to say no, and at least half of them have to do with the fact that things between Bishop and me are far too complicated for me to be dating *anyone*.

Ultimately, though, I don't want to share that, so I just speak honestly.

"Look, Sam…I'm not sure it's such a good idea."

"Before you turn me down," he says, holding a finger up, a smile on his face, "you should know I already cleared it with Bam. He said it wasn't an issue, and he gave his blessing."

I'm so stunned I'm almost sure I misheard what Sam actually said.

"He…what?"

Sam's eyes search my face for a long beat, and then his face pinches slightly. "It's only now occurring to me that hearing that doesn't make things better for you, does it." He says it like a statement, not a question, because he already knows it to be true.

My nostrils flare, and a million things race through my head. Things I want to say to Sam. To Bishop. To men in general who somehow think women are still property to be passed along *with their blessing.*

Instead, I just grit my teeth. "No. Can't say that it does."

Before he can say anything else, I storm past him and outside, the sound of the door echoing loudly after I fling it wide and it slams into the wall.

The fucking *nerve.* The absolute *audacity.* Since when does Bishop have the fucking right to give other men his *blessing* to… to what? To take me out? Screw me? Marry me? Who knows? What I *do* know is that Bishop Andrew Mitchell is going to get a piece of my mind.

I peel out of the parking lot and head down the main highway, the drive to the Mitchell house taking less than ten minutes. He must have gotten home from school just a few minutes before me, because the garage is open and he looks to be unloading things from the back of his 4Runner. I throw my car in park and shove my door open, stepping out onto the driveway then slamming my door shut.

But before I can do anything, I hear my name.

"Is that Gabriela Ventura?"

I turn, spotting Patty Mitchell at the front door, a wide smile on her face.

Shit.

Bishop's mom is one of those women you can't help but wish was your *own* mom: kind and caring and always showing up for her kids, but firm and clear about what the rules are.

A sad biproduct of my breakup with Bishop is the awkwardness I've felt whenever I've bumped into Patty in public. *She's* a sweetheart, of course, always remembering little things and inquiring about my life. I mean, she was a maternal figure for me from the very first time I stepped through her front door when Bishop and I worked on a history project together in the seventh grade.

But when you go through a breakup, you break up with that person's family, too. Bellamy is the only Mitchell I've stayed on good speaking terms with, and that's just because we knew each other fairly well from going to school together, before Bishop and I ever started dating.

Now, as Patty crosses the drive toward me, pure joy stretching wide on her face, I wish I were the type who could have easy conversation with anyone, like Bishop does, or Bellamy. Or Patty, for that matter. Instead, I stand there like a damn statue as Patty flings her arms around my shoulders.

"Hi, Mrs. Mitchell."

"Hey there, sweetheart! It's so good to see you!" She leans back, keeping her hands on my biceps and not even batting an eyelash at my awkward body language and grumbled greeting.

"How've you been? Leah says your business is just booming."

Some of the tension leaks out of my body, and I try not to be a robot as I reply.

"I'm good. And yeah, business is going well."

"I'm so glad to hear that. You've always had such an incredible work ethic and so much talent in that tiny body of yours. It doesn't surprise me in the slightest to hear it's going well."

"Thank you so much."

"I'm assuming you're here to see Bishop?" she says, her eyes flicking behind me, toward where I know he's probably watching us from the garage.

I nod. "Yes, ma'am."

"Well, I'll get out of your hair, then. But I'd love for you to stay for dinner if you have the time. No pressure, of course."

"Thanks, Mrs. Mitchell. I'm not sure if…"

She holds her hands up, stopping me. "No excuses either. If it doesn't work out, that's totally fine."

I give her a tight smile, and she tugs me in for another hug.

"Good to see you, sweetie." She lets go and waves in the direction of the garage. "I'm heading to get some groceries for dinner. I'll be back in a bit," she calls, then she winks at me and heads over to where her SUV sits a few feet away from where I parked.

I don't watch her drive away. Instead, I spin around, looking at Bishop now walking toward me. Some of the anger I was feeling at hearing what Sam shared has now leaked out of me, but the reason I'm here still remains.

"Hey," he says, his smile uncertain as he takes me in.

"Can we talk please?"

He nods then tilts his head toward the house. "Wanna come in?"

As I follow reluctantly in Bishop's wake, we head through the front door then up the stairs to his bedroom. Memories flood my senses as I enter the room behind him, my eyes quickly roving over the dark blue bedding and the framed sports memorabilia on the walls. I've spent many afternoons in this room, many late evenings, studying and talking and making out.

But I can't think about that. Not right now.

"Is everything okay?" Bishop asks.

Instead of beating around the bush, I just ask exactly what I want to know. "Did you give Sam Rush your blessing to ask me out?"

I can tell it's the last thing he's expecting me to say by the way his head jerks back in surprise.

"What?"

"Did you tell Sam Rush," I repeat, my words firmer, my irritation from earlier beginning to resurface, "that he had your *blessing* to ask me out?"

Bishop blinks a few times then lifts both his hands. "I can explain."

"It's a yes-or-no question, Bishop."

"Yes, okay? I did."

I throw my hands in the air. "Are you fucking serious? I'm not your property. I'm not something you own that you can pass along to someone else."

His eyes fly wide. "Of course you're not."

"And yet you still felt the need to give Sam some sort of permission?"

Bishop's eyes narrow, and his voice comes out a growl. "It wasn't *permission*. It was...I don't know...relinquishing rights."

At that, I scoff, and he winces.

"That's not what I meant."

"There's no good way to explain it."

"Fine, there's no good way to explain it. But the full truth is that he wanted to ask you out, and for whatever reason—whether it's my history with you or my friendship with him—he wanted to make sure he wasn't stepping on toes. Okay?"

"No. It's *not* okay. It's misogynistic. And insulting. And... rude, on so many levels."

"Get off your high horse, Gabi. You know me and know I would never think I have any...rights to you." He pauses just briefly. "It would be no different than if Nicole asked you if it was okay to pursue me, okay? I didn't come up with the rules. It's just...social etiquette or something."

My nostrils flare, something inside me recoiling at the idea of Nicole and Bishop.

"Well that's a stupid example because that would never happen."

His eyes narrow. "Why?"

"Because."

"Because why?"

Clenching my hands in fists at my sides, I glare at him. "I don't want to do this with you."

"Well tough shit. You showed up here, wanting to talk. So we're gonna talk. We're sorting this out. Right here, right now."

"There's nothing to sort out, Bishop."

"There's plenty," he tosses back. "Why did you kiss me?"

I scoff, turning away from him and staring out the window.

"Tell me, Gabi."

Shaking my head, I just stand there, my arms crossed and my eyes beginning to sting with the tears that are surely soon to threaten to fall. I don't want to answer. Because if I do...

If I do, I'll have to be honest with him, and if I have to do that, I'll have to be honest with myself.

I startle when I feel his hands, gentle and strong, on my biceps. Somehow, that light touch as he stands behind me unravels a knot in my chest.

"Tell me," Bishop says again, his voice low, his words spoken gently against the crown of my head. "Why did you kiss me?"

"Because I wanted to," I whisper, the answer pouring from me unbidden. "Because I've missed you." I turn around and look up into that handsome face, those caring, honey eyes. "Because I couldn't not."

He licks his lips, his eyes searching my face. My body throbs. My chest aches. Everything within me is on high alert.

"But I'm scared if I let you in, I'm going to get hurt again," I finally say, giving voice to the fear that has been ever-present in my mind from the minute I saw him again on Main Street.

I'm scared I'll hand him my heart, already so battered and wounded, only for it to become a shattered mess again. I've worked hard to repair the damage that has been done to me over the course of my life, and I fear with one simple movement, Bishop might destroy it for good.

He takes a step toward me so we're just inches apart, then he takes my hand and places it on his chest so I can feel the steady beat of his heart under my palm.

"And the fact that you're so scared is entirely my fault." He pauses. "Let me show you that something good can come from all of this. Let me prove to you that I won't hurt you again."

We stare at each other for a long moment.

Then, like magnets, we come together. He dips and I press up on my toes and our mouths meet in the middle, each of us opening immediately, battling for control. I wrap my arms around Bishop's neck and he lifts me up, hands on my ass, my legs tightening snugly around his waist.

I'm still afraid I'm making a mistake. I doubt that fear will ever go away.

But as Bishop kicks his door closed then presses me up against it, I can't seem to find the will to care.

chapter seventeen
bishop

This wasn't what I planned when I brought Gabi up here. Far from it.

I hoped for us to talk about that kiss on Sunday night, but I assumed she would shut me down, push me away—not open her heart wide open for me to see the most vulnerable part of her. Now, I feel thrown for a loop in the best way.

Pressing Gabi back against the door alleviates some of the ache in my left hand, but I'll be honest, I've never cared less about my wrist. If it snaps again because I'm holding Gabi as close to me as possible, I'll wear the battle scar proudly.

Our mouths are at war, and I roll my hips against her, providing a brief moment of relief for where I ache.

"Bishop," she gasps, her head falling back against the door, her eyes closed.

I lean in and take advantage of her exposed neck, licking and sucking at the soft skin, nibbling gently. Her legs tighten around me, and I feel her grind down.

"Fuck," I groan, spinning us around, carrying her to the bed with one arm under her ass and the other wrapped around her waist.

When we were younger, I had a twin bed, which made fooling around particularly difficult, so I'm grateful I've upgraded to a queen. Once I set her feet on the floor, I reach for the button on my jeans, but Gabi takes control, slapping my hands out of the way and making quick work of tugging off my pants as I strip out of my sweater and undershirt. As soon as I'm down to my boxer briefs, my mouth is back on hers, my hands on her face and then in her hair, desperate to be near her, to be touching her, at every moment.

"Do you have anything?" she asks, stepping back and sliding her top over her head.

I'm so focused on her movements that it takes a second for me to register what she said, and then I nod. "Yeah."

I watch for another minute as she takes off her bra, revealing her gorgeous tits. Instead of reaching for the wallet in my jeans, I dip, pressing my face between her breasts, kissing and licking, my hands pressing them together and pinching at her nipples.

She moans, and I move, tugging one nipple into my mouth, watching her face as I do. Her eyes are focused on me just as intently, her hands stroking the back of my head as I tease first one, then the other.

Finally, I draw back, and Gabi shimmies out of her jeans and panties as I dig for my condom. Then I'm crawling into bed next to her, my hands roving and touching any part of her that I can reach. She's warm and soft and my entire body throbs with the need to be inside her, but I wait, not wanting it to be over too fast. It's been far too long since we've been together like this, and there's no way in hell I'm going to rush it.

I bring her snug against me, each of us on our side facing the other, and I hike one of her legs over my hip. Reaching around from the back, my fingers stroke gently through the wetness between her legs.

Gabi whimpers into my mouth and shifts her hips so she's slowly gyrating against my hand, and my heart begins to gallop in my chest. I'm using my non-dominant hand, and I don't doubt my movements as I slide my fingers through her wetness are just slightly stuttered. Changing tactics, I roll her on her back and spread her legs then shimmy down so my face is between her thighs.

Now *this* I can do completely hands-free.

Gabi's jaw drops, her hands caressing my hair as I give one long, slow lick through her lower lips then circle the little bud at the apex of her thighs. The taste of her is like fucking honey on my tongue, and I repeat the movement again. And again. And again. Until Gabi's head falls back, her chest heaving, her thighs twitching.

That's when I suck her clit into my mouth and flick it with my tongue. She cries out, her entire body convulsing as she flies over the precipice, and it's so beautiful to witness. I feel like a fucking warrior, like I want to pound my chest, knowing I was able to give her that kind of pleasure.

Gabi slumps into the mattress, spent, once her orgasm has crested. Her hairline is damp and a sheen of sweat covers her body. She's the fucking sexiest thing I've ever seen in my life.

"I want you inside me," she whispers, her hands sliding along my shoulders and caressing my skin.

I tug off my boxers then reach over to the condom I set on the nightstand, grabbing it and ripping the foil packet open. I rise onto my knees and slowly roll it on, but before I can take the lead, Gabi shoves me to my back and crawls on top of me, resting her pussy against my dick and rolling her hips.

I tilt my head back, gasping as she shifts so that I'm notched at her entrance, her eyes watching mine as she slowly takes me inside. Inch after inch I'm sheathed in her warmth, Gabi's hands braced on my chest. It's the most incredible pleasure I've ever felt in my entire life, being inside her, a truth I knew once but had somehow forgotten.

Once I'm in to the hilt, my hips flush against hers, I grit my teeth, my hands flexing and releasing where they rest on her waist. She looks like a fucking goddess sitting on top of me. Her eyes are closed, her mouth slightly open, her hair trailing down like a dark river around the peaks of her breasts.

And then she starts to move, rising and falling. The sound of our bodies colliding fills the room until all I can hear is a rhythmic slapping mixed in with her quiet pants and desperate moans.

"Fuck, Gabi," I say as she moves again so her feet are underneath her, and then she's bouncing on top of me.

Pleasure courses through my body, and I grip her waist tightly, shifting my hips up so I'm meeting her in the middle. She cries out, her movements stuttering, and that's when I know it's time to take back the control.

"Look how you take me," I growl, thrusting up into her. "How I fit inside you so perfectly."

Gabi's fingers dig into my chest, her eyes never leaving mine.

"You're like a fist around me, squeezing so tight. So perfect."

I move one hand so my thumb is grazing her clit, and she shouts out at the added stimulation. I keep at it, stroking her over and over as I spear up into her.

"Bishop, if you keep doing that I'm gonna—"

Her inner walls clamp down on me like a vise. The feeling shatters my resolve, and after a few more thrusts, I feel that twist in my spine, and then I'm coming, too. White heat licks its way through my body, and I fight to keep my eyes open, watching Gabi.

After a moment or two, we both start to come down, and she slumps over on top of me. I roll her to the side then make quick work of removing the condom and wrapping it in tissue that gets chucked in the trash can under my desk.

When I look back at her, looking thoroughly ravished and sprawled naked on her stomach, her gorgeous ass in the air, I can't help but admire the dips and curves of her body. Crawling into bed next to her, I kiss her ankle, then her calf, then her thigh. Gabi giggles quietly as I make my way up—her hip, her back, her shoulder—but it cuts off with a gasp when I roll her onto her back and spread her legs.

"One more," I whisper.

She watches me the entire time, her fingers stroking gently through my hair as I pulse my tongue against her already overstimulated clit, as I slip my fingers into her—first one, then two—and search for that deep, sensitive spot I know will tip her over the edge again. It takes a while, her body already depleted, but I don't give up. Not until I feel her thighs begin to twitch again and her hands in my hair begin to tug, her hips shifting with need. When she comes for the third time, it's with a soul-shaking cry, like something deep inside her has broken free.

We lie in bed together for a long time.

At some point, my mom comes home, and we can hear her moving around the house downstairs, though the noise is faint. It's interesting, having sex in this bedroom but being in my 20s. When we were younger, it was always a sneaky thing, so we never had the luxury of lazing around afterward, the idea of my parents catching us enough that we usually had our clothes back on within a minute or two of finishing, and we *never* had sex at Gabi's. She didn't have a lock on her door, and her fear of Leah walking in kept things strictly above the waist and fully clothed.

Today though, on a random Thursday evening, we get to lie here and hold each other, Gabi tucked snugly against me, her back flush to my chest, her ass cradled in my hips. She's running her fingers gently along the skin of my injured wrist, her eyes watching the movement.

"I never asked how it went, getting your cast off," she says, her voice low.

I press a kiss against her shoulder. "It went fine. It's nice to have the freedom to move a little bit, but the doctor was pretty intense with me about not overdoing it."

She glances over her shoulder, her eyebrows furrowed. "So you decided to lift me up and hold me against the door?"

I grin. "Worth it."

Gabi huffs and turns away, returning to her examination of my hand. It hurts like hell and I know I need to take some sort of pain reliever, but right now, the sensation is manageable, and I'd rather stay here, with Gabi wrapped in my arms.

"I've never broken a bone before. What does it feel like?"

I think back to that day, as I slid into third base, my arms stretched forward. I could feel the fact that I'd slid wrong, that I was at a weird angle and would have a hard time catching myself, but nothing in real life happens in slow motion, the thought barely through my mind before I was plowing into the bag.

"I actually didn't feel anything at first, but I heard it. It was a pop noise, and I'm not sure if it was something I heard in my mind or if someone else would have been able to hear it, too. And then there was this…rush of warmth, like I'd dipped my entire hand in warm water." I wiggle my fingers just a tiny bit in her hand. "It was when I stood up that I felt the pain, that I realized I'd hurt myself."

"What happened?"

"I finished the inning."

Gabi's head jerks as she looks back at me. "What?"

I laugh.

"What do you mean you finished the inning?"

"I mean, I stayed at third and ran home when the next batter hit a double."

She makes a noise of disbelief then turns around again.

"I got a triple and a run on my first at-bat. I'd call that pretty amazing."

"You broke your hand and risked injuring it further. I'd call that pretty idiotic."

Grinning, I bring her in closer. As much as Gabi gives attitude, she also cares deeply. I remember more than a few occasions when she got upset with me because I'd been so stupid and could have gotten hurt. Good to know that instinct is still there.

"So…your hand will be okay, though?" she asks after a few minutes have passed.

I nod. "Yeah. It'll be okay. The doc said the break was clean and I *should* regain full mobility. I just have to be really intentional about physical therapy if I want to be back to my full strength."

There's a long pause again, but unlike just a second ago when it felt like we were simply here together in the silence, this one feels heavy with something, like Gabi has disappeared into her mind. I don't understand where her thoughts have gone, but the easy quiet from before is absent. I can tell the lazy, post-sex haze has officially evaporated, at least for Gabi.

I could stay here for the rest of the afternoon, holding her, breathing in her scent, but I don't want to push too hard. Gabi isn't someone who likes to be rushed when it comes to anything. She moves slowly, needs time to think about things. Us falling into bed together today was probably not anything she was prepared for, so the best thing I can do is try to talk to her about it or give her the space to think it through.

That's what it's like with Gabi: one step forward, three steps back.

I press a kiss against her shoulder and then her neck, squeezing her tightly before releasing her and pushing out of bed to grab my clothes.

"Why don't we get dressed and go get a drink, huh?"

I tug on my boxers and reach for my jeans as Gabi rolls over and looks at me.

"Or we could get some dinner. Maybe a sandwich from the deli?"

She watches me for a long moment, and I know she's going to turn me down before she even says it.

"Bishop…" she starts, rising up onto one arm and tucking the sheet across her bare chest.

I sigh, giving her a resigned smile.

"Figured it couldn't hurt to ask," I tell her, buttoning my jeans then crouching down in front of her. "You take all the time you need to think about shit, Gabi. I'll always give you time, but we're going to talk about this, and I'd like it to be soon."

She nibbles on her cheek, assessing me for a beat before nodding her head.

I press a kiss to her lips. Then another one. And another one. Until she swats at me playfully, and I grab her hand. Her breath catches as I turn her arm so her wrist is exposed then press a gentle kiss to the soft skin there.

It's something I used to do all the time. I did it every time we said goodbye, whether it was between classes or after school or at the end of the night. It was a quiet 'I love you' until I was brave enough to say the words, so when I do it now, I hope she understands what I mean.

My lips pressed against her skin is a promise.

A promise that we'll get there again.

If she'll give me a chance to remind her just how good it can be.

chapter eighteen
gabi

"You *slept* with *Bishop*!?"

Nicole's shouted response is the exact reason why I didn't have this conversation in public. The girl can keep a secret like a steel trap, but doing so with others around would require that 'megaphone' not be her default setting. In a small town like this one, where everyone is listening and word spreads like wildfire, there was no chance in hell I was taking that risk.

"Are you fucking *serious*!?"

"Look, I would appreciate it if you could lower your voice." I rub at my right ear and then return my hand to the steering wheel. "I'd like to not go deaf today."

My best friend just stares at me, likely waiting for the full story. I know I'm right when, a beat later, she waves a hand between us and says, "Well? Are you going to spill or what?"

"Says the woman who *still* has not talked to me about this handsome stranger. I'd just like to point out that it has been almost *two* weeks and all I've gotten is 'Can't talk' texts."

When I look at Nicole, she has a wistful smile on her face, but then it disappears and she refocuses her attention on me.

"Look, we can talk about him another time. Right now, we are talking about the fact that you *swore* to me nothing was going on, and now I find out you've been spending all your time on his penis."

I roll my eyes. "Not *all* my time, Nic. It was *one time*. We got into an argument and one thing led to another and it just... happened. You know?"

Nicole makes a strangled noise. "Um, no, I definitely *don't* know. Especially because I thought we had vowed to hate him for all fucking time."

At that, I actually laugh. "We did not."

"Well *I* did, so this certainly throws a wrench in my plans."

Rolling my eyes, I use my blinker and turn into the parking lot at the community center then come to a stop in a parking space near the entrance. There are only a handful of cars in the lot right now, but in the next fifteen minutes, I don't doubt that many more will arrive.

"I've never hated Bishop. Even when I was the most...angry and devastated." I pause. "I could never hate Bishop."

Nicole is quiet next to me, and when I look at her, she's watching me with wide eyes.

"You're falling in love with him again."

I scoff. "I am not."

"You so are!"

"Nicole."

"Gabriela."

"I am *not* falling in love with Bishop *again*." Licking my lips, I decide to just be fucking honest for once. "Because the truth is...I never fell *out* of love with him."

Nicole sighs and slumps down in her seat, and I take the opening, giving her a brief rundown of everything that's happened since he's been home. The weekly meetings and all our little conversations. The kiss last weekend and then what happened at his house when I went by two days ago. By the time I'm finished, she's just staring at me, mouth agape.

"Are you getting back together?"

I pause, unsure how to answer.

"Because it sure sounds like you are."

"I don't know. Sometimes I think we're just...scratching an itch or something."

But even as I say it, I know that doesn't feel right. That's not what we're doing. If all we were doing was taking a romp down memory lane, all of this would have felt very different.

The problem, though, is that I don't know how to describe what we *are* doing.

"Besides, I don't know why you seem so flabbergasted," I say, crossing my arms. "You literally told me it was a good idea to spend time together, and *you're* the one who put the whole idea of sex with Bishop in my head in the first place."

Nicole's eyes narrow and she points a finger at me. "Don't pretend I'm at fault for this. I told you to talk to him and get closure, not have sex with him."

Pursing my lips, I turn the car off and grab my purse from the floor at Nicole's feet.

"We need to go inside."

She scoffs. "Only you would drop this...bomb in my face right before we're supposed to go do something to relax our bodies." She shoves her door open. "You think I'm gonna be able to center my chakras and recline into the donkey with all *this* on my mind?"

I shake my head, chuckling to myself as we emerge from the car and move quickly into the community center. The warmth envelops us as we step inside, and we head to the mud room to drop off our belongings and remove our shoes.

Nicole and I have been taking the Saturday morning yoga class at the Cedar Point Community Center since it began in the spring. I'm not particularly athletic or limber and I'm definitely not a joiner, but Nicole begged me to go with her—*just once*, she promised—because she wanted to try it out.

Now, we go almost every week. It's our ritual—first yoga, then we grab croissants and other goodies from Ruthie's to negate all the calories we just expended, then we go back to Nicole's apartment and watch an episode of whatever reality TV show has caught her attention. This month, it's a dating show where the contestants don't see each other before they get engaged. I don't know how people come up with this stuff.

I've been really enjoying the class. It stretches out all the muscles that get so tense from hovering over a wheel all the time, and there's something emotionally relieving about how I feel when the class is over. It feels like a form of therapy, but for my soul instead of my mind.

My *actual* therapist back in college recommended yoga to me as a way to manage some of my emotions that seem to burden me physically, but I wrote her off. Clearly, I was wrong.

"So you slept with him once, and then what? Are you going to *keep* sleeping with him?" Nicole asks as we toe off our shoes, her voice—thankfully—quiet enough that I think the other ladies can't hear her.

"I don't know, Nic. I haven't thought it all the way through yet." Though I've definitely thought about what might happen the *next* time we see each other.

I head into the main room, a large open space where several women are already laying out their mats and chatting quietly with each other. Once I've grabbed a mat from where a few dozen are rolled up and piled in the corner, I find a spot that works for me and get set up, taking a seat with my legs crossed.

Nicole drops her mat next to mine and sits as well, her voice hushed. "Well maybe you *should* think it through."

"What do you think I'm doing?" I ask her, bringing my feet together and bending forward, stretching gently. "I'm talking to you about it, aren't I? I'm trying to figure it out."

Thankfully, that seems to shut her up, at least for a few minutes, and we continue stretching in silence as the room fills with other yogis. Eventually, class begins, and we collectively move from child's pose to cat-cow, through puppy, and then into downward dog in silence.

During our three rounds of sun salutations, as we stop in sphinx pose, Nicole starts whispering to me.

"How was it?" she asks, and when I look at her, she wiggles her eyebrows up and down.

I grit my teeth, returning my attention to the front of the room and trying not to laugh.

"Did he get better?"

When I remain silent, trying to focus on my breaths, she gasps.

"Oh my god, did he get *worse?*"

I can't help but giggle, though I do my best to keep it quiet.

"Alright, moving into downward dog, now," our instructor says, and everyone begins moving. "Lengthen your back and let your head hang heavy. Then trace the shape with your breath. Imagine your breath entering your nose and then traveling through your body."

Sometimes, the things the instructor says don't make complete sense to me, but still, I try to focus on what she's saying instead of Nicole's question. Even so, I find myself remembering what it was like to go to bed with Bishop. The weight of him on my body. The strength of him under my hands.

He's not the boy he was when we were teens. His muscles have toned, his body has lengthened, his prowess grown. I could barely breathe as I came down on top of him, could barely think as he brought me to the brink, could barely move once we were done.

Unable to help myself, I *let my head hang heavy* between my arms and use the angle to glance at Nicole. Her eyes find mine.

"It was the best I've ever had," I whisper.

Her eyes widen. "Even better than the bar guy?"

I nod. "*Way* better."

Our instructor chooses that moment to walk by, and we both return to our positions, but again, my mind struggles to stay focused on what we're doing. 'The bar guy', as Nicole likes to refer to him, was a one-night stand from those early days when I was searching for a way to heal from the pain of my breakup. He's been the gold standard for the past few years when it comes to sexual ability, and in my mind, he's been officially bumped to silver.

Part of me just assumed maybe my memory was bad, or that, because I was young when we first met, my idea of who Bishop was might have been overinflated in my mind. Nothing could be *that* good, as good as I remember it being. Right?

Now, though...now I'm not so sure. Now that Bishop and I have had sex, I'm reminded of those very real things I felt before.

Feeling seen. Wanted. Consumed.

On its own, the sex was incredible, but part of what *makes* it so incredible is that it's more than just sex. It's all those other things, too.

But that makes it just as intimidating, too. Because when it's more than sex, and feelings are involved, people get hurt.

I get hurt.

And I don't want that to happen again.

"I think I might skip out on TV time," I say to Nicole as we push out of the bakery, croissants in hand. "I have a bunch of work to do."

She makes a face. "Oh, come on. I have a bunch of questions and couldn't ask them earlier because of stupid yoga."

"You'll have a chance to ask me—another time."

"But you know how impatient I am."

I laugh. "Do you want a ride home?"

Nicole waves a hand at me then hooks a thumb in the direction of her apartment. "Nah, I'll walk. Go ahead and be all committed to your clients or whatever."

I yank Nicole into a hug, a grin on my face. "I'll see you soon."

"You're the worst."

"Love you."

"Love you."

Forty minutes later, my croissant has been completely devoured and I've changed into work clothes and an apron. When I take a seat at my wheel, I end up just staring at it blankly. My conversation with Nicole swirls, unanswered questions about my relationship with Bishop weighing heavy in my mind.

I've been enjoying the time we've been sharing together, our weekly chats and the odd hangout, but now that things have become physical, that hard line I drew for myself of being *just friends* feels a little less firm. As much as I don't like to admit it, my feelings are involved again, though I guess it was foolish of me to ever think they wouldn't be.

Eventually, I get my new piece moving on the wheel, though I remain distracted as I wet the clay and begin centering. *Is* there a possibility that Bishop and I will get back together? Is that even something I want? Or that *he* wants? For all I know, maybe he really does want to be friends and this whole sex thing is just an enjoyable way to pass the time.

Though that sounds wrong. He wouldn't be so dedicated to talking to me about it, wouldn't be saying such big, emotional things to me like *Let me show you that something good can come from all of this.* I highly doubt he just meant a few orgasms.

A shiver races through me at the reminder of the fact that he brought me over the edge *three* times. Is it bad form for me to acknowledge that he's learned a few things in our time apart? I mean, it would be wrong for me not to admit that I have, too. I've always had a strong sexual appetite, but now I feel more confident in bed, a bit more adventurous, maybe. I don't doubt that played a role in how explosive things were.

Sighing, I realize my distraction has resulted in my bowl spinning out, and I turn the wheel off, accepting that right now might not be the best moment for work. I chuck the clay into the bucket in the corner and move to the sink to wash my hands, but the questions are still there, about who we were…who we are now…who we might become.

And then there is the unanswered question I still have from years ago, the one I try not to think about anymore.

Why did we really break up?

I've never felt like I received a truthful answer, never felt like I fully understood why. Maybe I was wrong all those weeks ago to assume getting closure wasn't something I needed. Maybe I do. Maybe I need to fully understand what happened between us in order to move on from some of these questions that still feel…so exhausting.

That said, now that Bishop and I feel like we're in somewhat of a good place, there's part of me that doesn't feel brave enough to ask.

Me: Do you have plans tonight?
Bishop: No. And if you're asking me to do something, the answer is yes.

My lips tilt up at his response. I've been waffling back and forth for the past few hours on whether I wanted to reach out to Bishop. I'm not even sure what I hope happens tonight, but I know I want to see him, and I'm trying to learn to trust my gut.

Me: You don't even know what I'm going to ask you.
Bishop: Doesn't matter.
Me: Really?
Bishop: Really.

Me: So if I asked you to come over and organize Leah's antiques?
Bishop: I can be there in an hour.
Me: Or if I asked you to come clean out our gutters?
Bishop: I can be there in an hour and ten minutes
Me: What's the extra ten minutes for?
Bishop: Gotta pick up a ladder.

I shake my head.

Me: How about if I ask you to dinner?
Bishop: Like a date?
Me: It's not NOT a date.
Bishop: Ooooh, that is quite a label.
Me: I'm reckless like that.
Bishop: Well, count me in for anything reckless. What did you have in mind?
Me: I've been craving a deli sandwich since you mentioned it the other day. I was thinking we could grab food and head to Hilltop?
Bishop: That sounds awesome. I'll pick you up in an hour?
Me: Sounds good.
Bishop: Can't wait.

Setting my phone down, I return to my wheel, shaking the nerves out of my hands as I do. Maybe it's the fact that I always feel so good after yoga, or maybe it's that my conversation with Nicole prompted me to really process some of what has happened between me and Bishop since he's been home.

Regardless, it feels like getting dinner and chatting about *us* might be the right call for today, even if I have no idea what it will result in. There's a voice inside me that says I just need to give in to how easy and natural it is between us, says I don't need to think too hard about it and I just need to go with the flow a little bit more. But going with the flow hasn't ever been my strong suit.

There's also another voice—a much louder one—trying to remind me of the fact that, eventually, Bishop is going to leave Cedar Point again. He's going to go back up to Oregon to continue pursuing his dream. I don't fault him for that. Nobody should feel restricted from going after their heart's desire. It's just a reality that Bishop's passion will always lead him away from me.

And if things between us are going to continue, at some point I have to decide if it will be worth it to face that truth again.

chapter nineteen
bishop

The sun is just beginning to set behind the treetops when Gabi and I pull up to the parking lot at Hilltop with sandwiches, a bottle of wine, and two big blankets. The picnic table overlooking the lake is a place we came together often to hang out when we were both high school students without any real money or anywhere private to go.

A lot of Cedar Point kids go up to the lookout behind the resort for a spot to make out—it's nicknamed Easy Street for a reason—but Gabi and I always came here, which is why I feel unsure about what's on her mind. This spot for us has a history that includes many things. Long, important chats. A few fights. Plenty of hot-and-heavy moments in the Ford Ranger I drove around back then.

Tonight could be anything.

The beautiful weather we had today is still barely hanging on, so we keep our blankets folded in a pile on one of the benches and sit side by side on the other, ripping open our sandwiches and twisting open the bottle of wine as we look out at the lake.

"I forgot cups," Gabi says. "So we'll be drinking straight from the bottle."

I chuckle and take a sip then pass it to her. "We've always been classy bitches."

She nods. "Don't I know it." Then she takes a sip herself.

We mostly sit in silence as we eat, just enjoying the setting sun and the view and passing the wine back and forth. It's the cheap stuff, grabbed from the bottom shelf at the grocery store as we were ordering sandwiches, and I don't doubt we'll both have hangovers tomorrow if we don't drink a gallon of water tonight.

"Thanks for inviting me to hang out," I say, finishing off the last of my sandwich. "I'll be honest, I was surprised to hear from you."

Gabi eyes me. "Why?"

I shrug. "I assumed I'd need to be the one to call you. After Thursday."

She nibbles on her cheek then bobs her head. "I guess I'm trying to face my problems more head on than I used to."

My stomach tightens at her words. "Is that what we are? A problem?"

"No." She pauses, but then her head tilts from side to side. "And yes. Maybe a little bit."

Well, that's not encouraging.

I'm starting to get a better idea of what tonight is going to look like, and while I didn't dare to hope we'd be fooling around in my car, I *did* think maybe it would be something on the more positive end of the spectrum.

"I think I'm just still trying to figure out how I feel about everything. The past and what's happening now..." She trails off, bunches up the wrapper from her sandwich, and rolls it into a ball. "We were friends for so long, it makes sense that things feel so easy to just…pick up again. You know?"

"It does."

"But just because it's easy doesn't mean it's right. Just because we have a lot of history doesn't mean we'll have a future."

I wince, her words hitting me square in the chest, and I think they hit so hard because they're true.

"Can I give you a different perspective?"

She nods, eyeing me briefly then looking back out to the lake in the distance.

"I feel like things between us *aren't* easy. They're natural, sure, but not easy. Yeah, we have so much history, but we also have…I don't know…old assumptions about each other and probably at least a few wounds to heal."

Licking my lips, I reach out and take her hand where she's fidgeting with the wrapper on the table. I draw it into my lap and hold it between both of my own.

"But the things I've told you are true. I've missed you. I've missed you and I don't know how I ever lost sight of how incredible we are together."

Gabi lets out a long sigh, and for a minute, I think what I've said hasn't made any difference. Then she finally speaks again, putting my fears to rest.

"I'm nervous, Bishop. I'm not going to pretend otherwise. But there's also a fear in me that if I shut this out—this idea that, maybe, we have a second chance—I'll regret it for the rest of my life."

I lift a hand and tuck some of her loose hair behind her ear then stroke gently down her jawline.

"*Is* this a second chance?"

Her eyes scan my face, over my hair and along my lips then

back up to my eyes before she nods.

"I think so."

I watch her for a long moment.

"You think? Or you know?"

"I know."

Lifting her hand, I kiss the inside of her wrist. I wish this were the time to tell her I love her, but I know we're already walking a delicate balance. We're already perching on the ledge, and I don't want to tip us over too quickly.

Gabi needs time to think everything through. I can't say something like that to her again until I know she already believes it. She has to feel it in her bones *first*, or else it's just lip service, just another thing someone says that they can't back up with anything else. With this woman who has spent most of her life dealing with important people letting her down—including me—I know I have quite a steep hill to climb before we get there.

Once we finish eating, we climb up onto the picnic table so our feet are resting on the bench and Gabi is sitting on the table between my legs. I wrap one of the blankets around us, snuggling her in close underneath, resting my chin against her shoulder. It's the happiest I've felt in years, like my heart was searching for what it lost and has now found it again.

The two of us sit at Hilltop for another thirty minutes or so, until the last bit of the sun has disappeared behind the trees, leaving the sky a beautiful purple reflected in the lake below.

When we pull up outside Gabi's later, I put my car in park.

"Do you want to come in?" she asks, gathering her things from the footwell.

I already knew what I would say if Gabi asked, but that doesn't mean turning her down is easy.

"Maybe another night."

I can tell by the rise of her eyebrows that she's surprised by my response, so I clarify.

"We might not be starting at the beginning, but that doesn't mean we should jump back into things too quickly, right?"

Gabi laughs. "Bishop, we had sex two days ago."

Grinning, I bite my lower lip. "I know, and it was amazing."

"So then…what? You want us to *not* have sex now that we're going to start dating again? That makes no sense."

"I'm not saying we shouldn't have sex. I'm just saying we have plenty of time, and I don't want us to miss the important things because we get too focused on the physical stuff too quickly."

Gabi doesn't like my answer, and it makes me laugh again. She's always had a strong sexual appetite. It was often *her* leading the charge when we were younger, even though I'm almost positive most people would have assumed I was the one doing the corrupting. They would not have been more wrong.

I take her hand in mine and press another kiss to the inside of her wrist. Then I lick it gently and suck lightly on the skin. Her lips part just slightly, and I see a shiver roll through her.

"Trust me, okay? I know that's not easy for you to do, but believe me when I say…" I lean forward so our mouths are inches apart. "It'll be worth it."

I kiss her, slow and sensual, my hand grazing the base of her throat before moving up into her hair and tugging gently. She moans as I kiss down her neck then lick my way back up. When I pull back, she has a glazed look in her eyes that I love to see.

"I'll talk to you soon," I tell her.

Gabi smirks at me. "You are such a fucking tease."

She hops out of my 4Runner and heads inside, turning to wave at me from the doorway before shutting the door behind her.

I'm sure there are plenty of men who would say I'm an idiot for what I just did, who would think the best way for Gabi and me to get back on the same page is to fuck constantly, bring back the physical intimacy, but I have some strong opinions myself. Physical intimacy can only help a relationship if the emotional intimacy is there first, and emotional intimacy only comes with trust—the thing that is the most difficult for Gabi to give.

I don't doubt that it would be so easy for us to jump into a heavily physical relationship, especially now that we aren't teenagers constantly trying to avoid getting caught. Gabi will give her body to me, but will she give me her heart? Her mind? Her soul?

That's what I want from her: everything.

I feel ready to jump back in with both feet, but Gabi is still wading in the shallows. I need to stay there with her until she feels safe, and until she does, I'm going to be moving a little more cautiously. In order for her to believe I'm going to protect her heart, she has to see me doing it.

Even if I'm protecting it from herself.

When I wander into the kitchen at 2am, craving a midnight snack, I'm surprised to find my dad seated at the counter with a glass of what I can only assume is whiskey.

"You're up late."

He grins. "Can't sleep."

"Same, old man. Same."

I grab a gallon of milk from the fridge—with my right hand, thanks a lot Dr. Ramos—a box of sugary cereal from the pantry, and an overly large bowl then join him at the island.

"Cheers," I say once I've got my snack set up, and I clink my spoon against my dad's glass before taking a large bite.

My dad chuckles. "Cheers."

We sit together for a while, my dad in silence and me crunching away noisily on my cereal, before I realize this is the third or fourth time since I've been home that I've found him in the kitchen in the middle of the night.

"Everything okay?" I ask, a sliver of unease threading its way through my veins.

What if something's seriously wrong? With him? Or with mom? My mind races, coming up with a million possibilities in an instant.

"Yeah, everything's good," he says, patting my hand. "Great, actually." And then he chuckles under his breath and takes another sip of his drink.

I raise an eyebrow. "Are you drunk?"

He glares at me. "No, Bishop. I'm not sitting out here drunk in the middle of the night. And nothing is wrong, either." He shakes his head. "I just… Did you know your mother and I are going to celebrate our 40th anniversary in March? Forty. Years. Of marriage."

I wait, knowing there's probably more.

A beat later, he speaks again.

"God, we're lucky."

"*That's* what you're sitting out here thinking about in the middle of the night? How *happy* you are?"

My dad chuckles again. "Yeah. I am. You know, we were your age when we got married. 22 seems so young to get married now, I'm sure, but forty years ago, we were actually on the older side in comparison to most of our friends."

I take another bite of my cereal. "Why's that?"

He hums. "Because your mother wasn't sure she wanted to marry me."

My mouth freezes mid-chew, my eyes returning to where my dad is now taking another sip of his drink. When it doesn't seem like he's planning to say anything else, I elbow him in the bicep.

"And?"

"Well…obviously she changed her mind."

Rolling my eyes, I swallow my bite then level him with a glare. "You know what I mean. How have I not ever known this? I thought you guys were like…high school sweethearts."

He nods. "We were. Until we weren't."

"You *broke up*!?" I ask, my voice getting louder as surprise rolls through me. "How am I just finding this out?"

"I'm actually not sure. I feel like your siblings all know this story."

My parents have always been the ideal couple, the people who have the relationship everybody wants. It's so wonderful it's nauseating, so the idea that there was a time when their relationship almost never became what it is today? It feels like it's just not possible.

"Well…what happened?"

"Your mom was upset because she thought I was choosing to stay with her *by default*. That's what she called it. Told me there might be other girls out there I'd love more if I wasn't stuck in a small town. And then..." He starts laughing. "She said she didn't want me to pick her just because she was the only option."

I watch him continue to chuckle, trying to understand why the hell he's laughing.

"And that's funny to you?"

He gives me a *No shit* look. "Of course it's funny, Bishop. It's funny because your mom *was* the only option, but not in the way she assumed. She was *it* for me because there couldn't be another person on this earth who fit me better than she did." He turns in his chair so he's facing me head on. "I could visit the farthest corners of the earth, and I'd never find someone who completes me like she does, who makes me the best version of me. Never."

I blink a few times, surprised, though not by what he's said; my dad has *always* been adamant that my mom is his dream girl. He never fails to tell her how much he loves her, in the moment, as he feels it. It's pretty amazing to watch considering all the train-wreck relationships that are out there.

I'm surprised because...I know how that feels. It's how I felt about Gabi. I was so sure we were it, forever.

And then when it got too hard, I gave up. I let Gabi's slow withdrawal be enough for me to throw in the towel when I should have done whatever my dad did and fought for her.

"So, what did you do?" I ask, curious. "How do you prove to someone they're the one for you if they're pushing you away?"

At my question, my dad's expression softens. I don't doubt he understands where my question is really coming from.

"You asking for the story or for the advice?"

Licking my lips, I reach over and take his glass. "That obvious, huh?"

He grins. "You wear your heart on your sleeve, Bishop. It's hard *not* to notice when something has caught your attention. Or someone."

"She hasn't just caught my attention though, Dad. She's always had it, and I don't know what I can do to prove to her that I never..." I shake my head. "I never want to hurt her again."

"There is no grand gesture that will *convince* someone you love them. It's a series of little things, small steps, tiny moments. It's the daily ritual of demonstrating that they're a priority—that they're *the* priority. That's all you can do."

"And if she can't forgive me? Can't move past the fact that I've hurt her?"

He watches me for a beat then rests his hand on my shoulder and gives it a squeeze.

"The hardest part about loving someone is giving them the freedom to make whatever decision they think is right for them, even if it's wrong for you."

My dad pats my back again and then pushes back from the counter, stepping off his stool and grabbing his empty glass before rounding to put it in the sink.

"You'll figure it out, Bishop. I know you will."

"Thanks, Pop."

He heads for the hallway that leads down to his room, but then something suddenly occurs to me. "Hey Dad?"

He stops, turns around.

"How *did* you get Mom to take you back, though?"

At that, he gives me a big smile. "I proposed to her in front of the entire elementary school during one of her assemblies," he says.

I laugh. "I thought you said no grand gesture would convince someone you love them."

"It doesn't. I spent years showing your mother how much I loved her before that day. I didn't need to convince her. She already knew."

Then he turns and heads down the hall.

When I eventually go back to bed a while later, his words are still on my mind. Love is a million little things. The paying attention. The listening. The caring. The effort.

As happy as I am about the direction Gabi and I are moving, I know my girl. I know she's going to pull back at some point like she did before, when I left for college. I'll know better this time. I'll know not to let her go too far.

But I can also start showing her all the ways I love her *now*. I can make sure if that day comes, I'll have already done everything I can to show her how important she is to me, show her she's *it* for me, and show her that will never change.

chapter twenty
gabi

When we walk into Cedar Cider hand in hand, I can feel the eyes on us almost instantly. I shouldn't be surprised, but it's been a long time since I've had the attention of almost everyone in town, and I forgot what it feels like. The biggest news to hit Cedar Point High School during the summer between sophomore year and junior year was the fact that Bishop Mitchell had asked Gabriela Ventura to be his girlfriend.

I've always had a secret belief that people watched us and secretly rooted for us to fail. How could the town's golden boy—the one who had all the promise to take the world by storm, the one who would make it big and put Cedar Point on the map—how could he fall for, as I heard one woman refer to me, "that emo girl with all the eyeliner"?

Granted, I've grown out of my sullen artist phase—for the most part. While that shouldn't be a deciding factor in whether or not one is *deserving* of a man's attention, there's a part of me, the girl who always felt like people saw us as a mismatched pair, that wants to parade around the room with our hands in the air. It wants to show off this shiny new relationship—or I guess, this recently dusted off and repolished relationship—and tell people to get fucked.

I definitely do *not* do that, though, instead walking with Bishop up to the bar to order a beer before we sit in two comfortable leather chairs in the corner.

"Getting excited for the scrimmage series?" I ask, taking a sip of my beer then setting it on a round, branded coaster on the wooden table between us.

Bishop grins. "Very excited. I'm really proud of how everyone's doing, and I think there's a good chance they'll actually surprise themselves."

I nod. "How are things going with that kid?"

"Which kid?"

I purse my lips and just stare at him. "I highly doubt there are *multiple* little shits you have complained about to me over the past few weeks," I reply. "You know who I'm talking about."

Bishop sighs, rubbing at the stubble that's been growing in on his face.

"He's still just as talented and just as stubborn as he's been since day one." He pauses. "He thinks he knows everything and doesn't want to listen to anyone."

Snorting, I shake my head. "A boy who thinks he knows everything and doesn't want to listen to anyone, huh? How is it looking in a mirror?"

He playfully tosses his coaster at me, and I catch it, giggling.

"You and Rush keep making that comparison—which I do not appreciate, by the way." He sighs again. "And say what you want about who I was as a cocky, young baseball player, but I was never angry. Even when I was mad."

I bob my head. "I guess something to think about is *why* someone becomes so angry. I mean, I wasn't very friendly when we first met. I was a teenager carrying a lot of hurt. My guess is your kid is dealing with hurt, too."

Bishop narrows his eyes at me. "Can't you just let me loathe him? Even for a little bit?"

Laughing, I pick up my beer and take another sip. "Nah. I did too much therapy to let moments like this pass me by. If I have advice, you're getting it."

His head tilts to the side, surprise on his face. "You finally went to therapy?"

I nod, twisting my beer on the coaster. "I did."

Bishop sits forward, resting his arms on the table. "That's so great, Gabi."

"It was great. I'm not like…*healed* or anything, but it helped to talk about my mom. A lot more than I realized it would."

He reaches forward and takes my hand in his. "I'm proud of you. I hope it doesn't sound condescending to say that."

I chuckle. "You know, there was a time in my life when I *would* have said it was condescending, but I don't feel that way now—because of therapy. So…thank you. It means a lot."

We sit quietly for a bit, sipping our beers and watching people as they come and go. As much as Bishop and I have always liked to talk, we also always found it very easy to sit in silence and watch people together.

After a while, we grab a deck of cards from the cabinet in the corner and deal out a round of Speed, a game his older brother Boyd taught us when we were in junior high. It's been close to a decade since I've played this game, junior high being probably the last occasion I did so, and Bishop absolutely destroys me to the point that he asks multiple times if I want to try a different game.

Eventually, I admit complete annihilation and we switch to the much calmer gin rummy, spending another hour or so playing and chatting before calling it quits for the night.

"You *sure* you don't want to come in?"

Bishop grins at me. "I'm sure. But I'll definitely walk you to your door."

I'm not much of a giggler, but this thing Bishop is doing makes me want to do just that. Part of me gets it. He's making a point that he's not just in this for the sex. It's sweet, though entirely unnecessary. That's where the other part of me lands: in the camp of *We've been apart for years, we have a lot of sex on the horizon to make up for what we've missed out on.*

But I don't say that. Instead, we walk to the front door and kiss like we're 16 again. It's filled with passion and anticipation and I can't help but moan when he pushes me up against the door and begins to lick down my neck.

Okay, he definitely didn't do *this* when we were 16. The stubble on his face tickles me, but I love it, and I tilt my head back, communicating with my body that I want him to continue doing just that.

"Be careful," I murmur as he sucks gently on my skin. "I can't show up to school with a hickey."

He chuckles then leans back slightly, one hand braced on the door behind me and the other resting gently on my hip.

"What a scandal that would be, Ms. Ventura." He kisses me again, this one more chaste. "You coming to the game on Wednesday night?"

I nod. "Wouldn't miss it."

One more kiss, and then he pushes away, takes my hand, and presses a kiss against my wrist. He told me once that kissing my wrist was how he told me he loved me back when we were too young to say the words. Now, years later, I wonder if that's still true.

As Bishop smiles and takes a few steps backward, his eyes watching me like I'm the most important, beautiful thing in the world, I worry that it is.

When I take a seat in the bleachers on Wednesday evening, I'm grateful I brought a thicker jacket and a blanket to sit on. Cedar Point normally doesn't get too cold until closer to Christmas, with most of the snow coming in the new year, but the weather report is showing that we're going to start dipping into even cooler temperatures by this weekend, and there's been plenty of talk around town about if we'll get snow earlier than normal. I'm hopeful it holds off just a bit longer, at least until after Thanksgiving. But maybe that's all it is: hope.

"I can't believe you're forcing me to come to a children's baseball game," Nicole says as she collapses next to me as if she's just climbed Mount Everest and not to the sixth bench on a high school bleacher.

"We used to come to these all the time," I reply, rolling my eyes and tugging a box of M&Ms out of my purse.

She snatches it from my hand. "Yeah, and it was just as much a waste of time then as it is now."

I roll my eyes. "You didn't think that when you were watching Christopher Hernandez."

She smirks. "Well, there *was* Christopher Hernandez." She rips open the box of chocolate and then glances at me. "Did I ever tell you about when we hooked up…"

"…after homecoming senior year? Yes. I've heard that story like, at least ten times."

Her smile remains, though, and she chucks a few colorful candies into her mouth. "He's my 'bar guy'."

My brow furrows. "What happened to Mr. Montana? I know he left, but I thought he like…blew open your curtains or whatever."

Nicole laughs hysterically at my comment, and I can't help but join her. "Blew open my curtains, oh my god. I'm using that for the rest of my life." She sighs. "He was fun, but that was more about getting a steady rain after a drought. Christopher Hernandez was a torrential downpour, you know?"

Shaking my head, I bring out a bag of Raisinets. "The shit you say."

The crowd starts cheering as both teams jog out onto the field, and my eyes search for Bishop, catching sight of him in a pair of those black jogging pants I love so much and a dark red Cedar Point High School Baseball jacket.

Enough people are here tonight that you'd think it was a regular season game. There is quite a rivalry between Cedar Point, Spencer Creek, and Belleview, and the scrimmage series is always a big draw. Such a weird part of smalltown life, and I can't help but love it just as much as everyone else.

Some of that is, of course, due to the man holding a clipboard and chatting with the umpire, the handsome son of a bitch I've watched play on this field more times than I can remember. It's a new experience, watching him coach instead of play, and there's something exciting about it. It's not because I want him to be a coach necessarily, but because it's new.

So much of our reconnection so far has been reliving things from the past, but at some point, that can't be the only thing we talk about or experience. Eventually, we need to push beyond the things that connected us when we were young and find the new things that connect us now. Although, that feels too much like I'm banking on this thing between us continuing once Bishop leaves to go back to Oregon, and I'm still struggling to see that happening.

Both teams finish their warmup, and the Pirates take to the field. Despite all her protesting, Nicole is just as focused as I am as each inning ticks by. I try to determine who the players are based on different things Bishop has said to me about them, and the one I can spot almost right away is Justin.

Everything I've been told about the kid is immediately apparent. His anger rolls off him in waves as he strolls up to the plate during his first at-bat, and when he swings at the first ball and hits a homerun, he chucks his bat then slowly removes his gloves before jogging around the bases at a leisurely pace.

He keeps that same cocky swagger through the entire game. After the final inning an hour and a half later, the Cedar Point Pirates having demolished the Belleview Bears 13-1, all the kids line up to 'Good game' each other, and my jaw drops as Justin walks through with his hands at his sides, refusing to high-five any of the players from the other team.

I do not envy Bishop figuring out what to do about that attitude. I remember being angry when I was younger, but I was never vicious like that. For not the first time in my life, I'm grateful for Leah, someone who helped me navigate some of my wounds and showed up for me on a regular basis. I complain about her plenty—the fact that she's always getting into

my business and can never let me just be alone with my emotions—but I'm also thankful for the very things that irritate me.
She doesn't let me push her away, and when you're an angry kid
dealing with a lot of hurt, that's all you want to do.

"Lemme guess: now that I've sat with you through this entire game, you're gonna go hang out with that guy just because
you like what his ass looks like in those joggers?" Nicole says as
we come to a stop at the bottom of the bleachers.

I roll my eyes. "Don't say 'that guy' like he's some guy," I tell
her. Then, in an entirely-off-brand-for-me moment, I bump her
with my hip. "But his ass *does* look amazing, right?"

Nicole's eyes widen, and then she bursts into laughter before
drawing me in for a hug.

"Good lord, lady. I was not expecting that." She pulls back
and looks at me. "Maybe I don't hate him so much if he makes
you smile like that."

I scoff, waving her comment away, but I don't actually say
anything else as she says goodbye and blends into the crowd
heading out to the parking lot. I stay quiet because there's part
of me that knows she's right.

There's a type of lightness in my soul that I can only attri-
bute to the fact that Bishop is back in my life. His silly jokes and
the way he plays with and teases me, the way he stays positive
and almost always wears a smile…it buoys something inside me
that I didn't realize had sunk so low until just now.

I spin and look over to where the team is collecting their gear
and filing out of the dugout, and I move back up the bleachers
and take a seat again. We have plans to go to The Mitch tonight
to grab a drink. Originally I was going to meet him there, but I
don't want to wait until later to see him again. I want to see him
now, so I wait.

When he finally emerges from the field, I head his way, reveling in the way he grins when he sees me.

"Hey. I thought I was going to meet you—"

I wrap my arms around him and yank him in for a kiss. It's brief, and far more chaste than I'd like it to be, but we're in the middle of a crowd after a high school baseball game. I can save the spice for later.

When I pull back, he grins at me. "Hey."

"Hey," I reply, keeping my arms around his neck. "Just wanted to do that. Hope it was okay."

His smile grows. "Consider this my official permission to do that at literally any moment."

Angling my head to the side, I slip my hand into his. "Ready to get out of here? Or do you have things you need to do?"

He glances over at Rush, who is hoisting some supplies over his shoulder. He waves us off, clearly having seen our public display.

"I think I'm good if you want to head out," Bishop says, returning his attention to me.

"Alright then…let's go."

"Good job today, Coach," I tell him, squeezing his hand as we approach where his car is parked in the corner of the lot.

He chuckles. "It's still weird when people call me that. But when *you* say it, it's kind of sexy."

"Good to know."

Bishop tugs the passenger door open, but before I can step inside, he yanks me toward him, bringing our mouths together in a kiss that tastes just as delicious as it feels. His tongue twists with mine, and for a moment I forget where I am. I am lost to him and this moment, to the way it feels to be consumed by Bishop Mitchell.

When he looks at me again, his eyes are glazed and filled with desire. He puts his hands on either side of my face and just stares at me for a long minute, his eyes scanning over my mouth and my cheeks and my nose until he reaches my eyes again. He licks his lips then chuckles, kissing me one more time before backing away completely.

"Let's get out of here or we're going to get in a lot more trouble than when we were just drinking beer on the roof."

I grin and hop into the front seat then Bishop closes the door behind me. That look was the same one he gave me the other night at my doorstep, the one that says he feels the very big feelings that come with a few very small words. As we drive out of the high school lot and onto the road, our hands intertwined, I'm finding I don't mind as much as I thought I did.

In fact, maybe I don't mind at all.

chapter twenty-one
bishop

"This was not what I had in mind."

"I'm sure it wasn't," she jokes. "But that doesn't mean it won't help."

Sighing, I take a seat at the wheel, resigned to my fate. At the very least, I'll learn a little more about pottery, the thing Gabi seems to love more than anything. That perks me up a bit, giving me a new perspective.

"And no," Gabi says before I can say anything as she takes a seat next to me, "this will not look anything like *Ghost*."

"Are you even old enough to have seen that movie?"

She scoffs. "Are you kidding? Every pottery nerd has seen that movie."

Over the next ten minutes, she teaches me a little bit about the wheel and the clay and the steps that go into getting it ready to be shaped. Then she hands me a lump of clay and tells me to chuck it down onto the center of the wheel. Eventually, I'm adding water and using my hands to make the material into a smooth round ball in the middle of the wheel.

"If you were trying to make a bowl or a vase, I'd tell you how to use your hands to make those different shapes," she says, leaning closer. "But right now, this is just giving you a bit of gentle exercise on your wrist and your fingers. So do whatever feels natural, or whatever you think imitates the exercises your PT uses."

Licking my lips, I think it over, watching the clay as it spins in a circle in front of me. Then I put my right hand on the side of the clay and bend my left wrist, pointing my fingers and pressing them into the center so I'm stretching the clay outward and bending each of my fingers.

After we were done with our NSP meeting this afternoon, Gabi invited me over, asking if I could give her some help with my *extra hands*. I had no idea she was actually planning to give me a PT session by putting me at the wheel. Sure, there was that sexual innuendo lacing her words, which made me laugh, but mostly I assumed she was finally taking me up on my very real offer to help with anything she needs. I meant it when she asked if I'd be available to organize antiques or clear gutters. Not only because I want to be someone Gabi can ask for help, but also because I will gladly take every moment I can get with her.

Now, as my hands move over the wet clay, my muscles and joints getting small movements and tiny bits of pressure that demonstrate what a workout this is, a spot within me thrills at the fact that she is using something she loves to help *me*. If I were doing this on my own, I'd end up with a useless slab of clay on the wheel. But Gabi's hands join me, and she takes a few moments to guide my movements so I'm using these simple shifts but still actually creating something, what looks to be a shallow, wide bowl.

"That's so cool," I say, grinning as the wheel comes to a stop.

"I know I basically didn't do anything, but it really is so amazing how things are created like this."

"All I did was shift your hands just a bit," she tells me. "You made that bowl, not me." She pauses, glancing at it then back at me. "Did you want to keep it?" she asks. "I can reclaim it to use later, but if you want to keep it, I can put it on the rack to dry."

My lips tick up at the idea that I could own a piece of pottery we created together. "Yeah, let's keep it."

Nodding, Gabi grabs a wire and scrapes it underneath the bowl then lifts it gently onto a board before carrying it over to a shelf in the corner.

"We can come back later and look at it. Once it's hardened somewhat, we can decorate it, if you want." She grins. "Maybe a hot pink polka dot look?"

"Very my style," I joke.

We spend another hour in the shed, making differently shaped items and gently working the muscles and ligaments in my left hand. In the end, we have a set of matching bowls and mugs that Gabi promises we will decorate tomorrow. *More wrist exercises.*

"Hey, listen, I've been meaning to ask you something," she says as we stand in the entryway a few hours later, after we've eaten some pizza and listened to that Mumford and Sons record again.

I put on my jacket and zip up the front then wrap my scarf around my neck, sensing a bit of nervousness from Gabi.

"Okay. Is it about where I got this scarf? Because this is a Patty Mitchell original." I pose then shift and pose again.

Gabi laughs and rolls her eyes, swatting at my chest, which I take as an opportunity to tug her in against me. "No. Although now I'm jealous and desperately want a Patty Mitchell scarf."

I hum and press a kiss to her lips. "Maybe I can talk her into making you one for Christma—"

"Will you be my date to an exhibit this weekend?"

She blurts it out, and I can't help but get the feeling she thinks there's a possibility I might say no.

"It's in San Francisco, and I have two pieces that will be on display, and originally I was just going to go alone but I think I'd really like for you to come. As my date." She pauses. "If you want."

I'm unable to hide my excitement, both at being asked to join her as her date *and* at this amazing professional step I know a younger Gabi wouldn't have taken. Not in a million years.

"Your stuff is going to be in an exhibit?" I ask, pride swelling in my chest. "Gabi, that's incredible." I bring her in closer, wrapping my arms around her waist so she's snug against me. "I would love to be your date. I would love nothing more than to be your sexy arm candy while you walk around, listening to everyone compliment you on how amazing you are."

Gabi giggles quietly against my chest, and I feel the tension inside her ease slightly.

"Really?" she asks, leaning back and looking up into my eyes. "You don't have other stuff going on?"

"Even if I did, I'd cancel it. This is a big deal, right?"

She licks her lips and nods.

"Then the only thing I want to be doing is whatever I can do to support you. Just tell me where to be, when we're leaving, and if I need to buy a new little black dress."

Gabi laughs, and then I tug her in again, pressing my lips to hers.

A night in San Francisco supporting the woman I love? I can't imagine anything sounding better.

When we arrive at the Sixth House Art Museum, I can feel Gabi still vibrating with nerves. She's been slightly distracted during our drive and as we checked into our hotel, but I'm used to that from the past. Gabi's responses become shorter when she's nervous, her mind floating out in the ether, sorting through things she doesn't want to put to words.

Even though we used to go on long drives together through the winding mountain roads and never be at a loss for something to talk about, our three-hour drive into San Francisco is mostly silent, with only Maggie Rogers playing over the speakers. Usually, I try to make Gabi laugh as a way to help ease some of her tension, but today, it felt like the wrong call.

Today, I let her take all the time she needed to process whatever she's going through in her mind so she can feel mentally ready for the event.

"Hey," I say as I shift into park in front of the valet.

Gabi looks at me and I reach over, squeezing her hand.

"It's going to be great. And I know you don't need me to tell you that, but I wanted to anyway. You're amazing, and everyone is going to be able to see it."

Her lips tilt up, and she squeezes my hand as well. But then she gets out of the car without saying anything and rounds to the back to begin unloading her stuff.

Once we've gotten everything and I've handed the keys over to the valet, we head inside. Almost immediately, someone calls out her name.

"Gabriela! Oh my gosh, I'm so excited you're here!" a blonde woman enthuses, her shoes clacking loudly on the hardwood floors as she crosses toward us.

I can literally hear Gabi take a deep breath and let it out long and slow just before the woman envelops Gabi in a hug. When she pulls back, she has a wide smile stretched across her face.

"I was so thrilled when I saw your name on the list of artists being showcased. I mean...it's been so long!"

Licking her lips, Gabi nods, shifting back slightly so she's stepping in closer to my side. I take her behavior at face value and wrap my arm around her shoulders, staying quiet but hopefully providing whatever support she needs.

"I know, since we finished with school," Gabi replies. "How have you been?"

"Good," the blonde says, her eyes flicking back and forth between us. "But I'm assuming you've been better? Who's this?"

"Oh, this is..." Gabi pauses, looking up at me briefly. "Bishop" is what she eventually settles on. "My date."

Smiling, I reach out my hand, which the blonde takes, her lips curving as she looks me up and down.

"Bishop, this is Marie. We were friends at MSA."

"Nice to meet you, Marie," I say, wrapping my arm back around Gabi again.

"You, too," she says, still perusing me, which feels like the only word I can use to describe what she's doing, her eyes continuing to trail a leisurely path along my chest and face.

"And don't say 'We were friends at MSA' as if we aren't friends anymore," Marie continues, her eyes finally returning to Gabi. "We should go out for drinks after this if you two are up for it. We need to catch up!"

"I'm not sure we'll have the time," I say, trying to give Marie a sympathetic look and hoping I'm not overstepping. "But thanks for the invitation." I turn to Gabi. "We better get you over to where you need to set up, right?" I ask.

She takes a deep breath and nods. "Yeah, we need to get moving. But it was good to see you, Marie."

"You, too, honey," she replies, waving before trotting off in the direction of where another group of people are standing.

"Why do I feel like I need to take a shower?" I mumble quietly to Gabi as we move through the room and over to where a woman with a clipboard stands in the corner, directing as a piece of art gets hung on a wall.

"That's just the magic of Marie," Gabi offers, chuckling uncomfortably. "I didn't click with a lot of my classmates during art school. I've never found talking to new people particularly easy."

"You don't say," I tease, and she pokes me in the side.

"Marie was one of the few people who actually seemed to make an effort." Gabi shrugs. "So even though she can be a lot, it was still nice to have a friend, someone to talk to."

"Is that how you feel about me sometimes?" I ask with a grin. "I'm a lot to handle, but you put up with me because you have someone to reenact your *Ghost* fantasies with?"

At that, she barks out a laugh and shoves me, and I can't help but laugh, too.

"Gabriela."

I turn, still chuckling to myself, spotting a guy in slacks and a button-up standing a few feet away, watching us with a curious expression on his face.

Then when I look at Gabi, I see that she's frozen, staring at him with surprise.

"Garrett."

All she says is his name, and everything inside me bristles.

I have no idea who this man is, but I know without a doubt he means something to Gabi.

"What are you doing here?" she asks, glancing at me then returning her eyes to him.

"A few of my students are showcasing tonight," he answers. "So I'm here to support them." He looks my way. "Apologies, I'm Garrett Hastings," he says, extending a hand.

I take it, shaking it briefly before letting go.

"Garrett was…one of my professors. At MSA," Gabi says, wearing an uncomfortable smile on her face.

"Interesting," I say, turning toward him. "What do you teach, Professor Hastings?"

He gives me an easy smile, so in contrast to Gabi's, and then tucks his hands into his pockets. "I teach a variety of classes, but Gabi took a drawing course from me during her first semester." He looks back at her, though he continues talking to me. "I'm not sure if you're aware, but she's an incredibly talented sketch artist. Even though she doesn't do it very much anymore."

"I still sketch," she says, raising her chin just slightly. "I just…used my time at MSA to focus primarily on pottery."

"And I've seen plenty of her sketches," I add in, jealousy seemingly getting the best of me.

The air feels heavy, far heavier than it did just a few minutes ago when we were talking with Marie. I don't know for sure what happened between these two, but I can guess, and I can't help the part of me that wants this *Garrett* guy to know who I am to Gabi.

"I'm sorry, what was your name?" he asks, his head tipping to the side as he assesses me.

Before I can say anything, Gabi speaks.

"This is my boyfriend, Bishop Mitchell."

A mixture of emotions rolls through me at the label she provides. It's a bit of surprise and a dash of happiness, though it's all coated in more than plenty of disbelief. It was clear to me that with her other friend, she didn't know what to call me. But now, with *this* guy, I'm her boyfriend?

Garrett's eyebrows rise as he takes me in. "Well, nice to meet you, Bishop." Then he glances at Gabi, his eyes drinking her in in a way that makes me want to blind him so he can't ever look at her again. "It's great to see you," he finally tells her.

He gives us both that same easy smile before heading off in whatever direction I'm assuming he came from. I watch him for a beat before turning my focus on Gabi, more than a few questions on the tip of my tongue, who he was to her being the primary one. Even an idiot would be able to observe the way the two of them interacted and see that they have some kind of history, one that didn't happen inside a classroom.

But before I can say anything to Gabi, she gives me a tight smile and turns, heading in the opposite direction toward where the woman with the clipboard is still examining the piece getting adjusted on the wall.

Something inside me feels shaken, rattled loose in a way I wasn't expecting. Definitely not tonight, at least. At some point, logically, I knew we'd need to talk about what happened during the years we were apart, the other people we've been with, the relationships we've had, but I didn't expect to be confronted by it tonight.

Letting out a long, slow breath, I tuck those feelings to the side and follow in Gabi's wake. Tonight is not about me or how suspecting that Gabi may have had a relationship with one of her professors makes me feel.

No. Tonight is about Gabi. It's about her career and this

exciting thing she's doing for the first time, and I came with her to support her and help with the conversational stuff that always makes her feel so awkward.

I can still do that. I can still be the guy she needs me to be.

chapter twenty-two
gabi

When we get back to our hotel room, all I want to do is take a long hot shower and curl up in bed, but I know after our run-in with Garrett, there's no way that's happening.

All things considered, the night actually went exceptionally well, better than I ever could have hoped for. I received plenty of praise for the vases I had on display, and Bishop was an absolute saint in how he made conversation feel so much easier than I ever seem to be able to make it. If not for running into a man I had an affair with, I would have been calling the night a complete success.

I would guess not a single person Bishop met tonight knew he had something else on his mind. As we discussed the influence nature has had on the way I mark my pots before they go into the kiln and how gold leafing has been regaining popularity in pottery, he was following along and chiming in, even though his mind was somewhere else. He does an amazing job of putting on this calm, friendly, easy-to-talk-to front even when he's upset, and he did that tonight. He showed up for me in a way I didn't even fully realize I needed.

But I know Bishop unlike I know anybody. Sometimes I think I know him better than I know myself, which is why I know that as we walk into our room and he takes a seat on the edge of the bed, he's not going to let this conversation slide. The man has always been good about balancing when he pushes and when he gives grace, and tonight will definitely be the former.

"We started seeing each other after my first semester," I say, just speaking into the quiet of our room, not waiting for him to ask. "We dated for about 8 months."

Bishop nods his head, his face remaining infuriatingly neutral.

"You dated a professor," he says, like he needs to say it out loud to reconfirm it for himself.

I nod. "Not one of my finer moments. But yes, I did."

"Why?"

Sighing, I tilt my head back, trying to figure out how to explain it.

"Because I found him attractive. He was so talented, and I admired that. The…nature of it…being against the rules…well, I found that attractive, too. At the time."

He licks his lips. "And why did you break up?"

"He wanted to become more serious, and I didn't. I'd been going to therapy and working through some things, and…I don't know…I guess I realized I was more attracted to the fact that we were having an affair that I believed would end than I was to the idea of staying together."

Bishop seems to roll that idea around in his mind, and I grit my teeth, suddenly feeling that it's unfair for him to be so clearly upset by this.

"What about you, huh?" I ask, crossing my arms. "I wasn't the *only* one to have a relationship while we weren't together. I heard all about *your* girlfriend."

He laughs, though there's no humor in it. "You think I'm upset because you slept with someone else? Because you dated someone else?" he asks, shaking his head. "Fine, yeah, there's a part of me that's...jealous. Okay? I don't like that there's been anyone else, but I get that it's unfair for me to feel that way."

"So then why are you so upset?" I demand. "I don't want to be made to feel bad over something that had nothing to do with you."

He scoffs. "Nothing to do with me? You had an affair with a college professor, and you don't think it had even a little bit to do with the guy who'd broken up with you a month or two before?"

"What are you talking about, Bishop? *You* broke up with *me*, remember? I was in love with you. I wanted to spend the rest of my life with you. And then you called me up on a random Wednesday and told me it wasn't working anymore."

"And you agreed!"

My head jerks back in surprise at his raised voice, but even more at what he's said.

"You echoed my words right back to me. 'Yeah, it doesn't seem like it's working.' That's what you said."

"Well what was I supposed to do?" I shout back. "Beg you not to break up with me?"

"Yes!"

I laugh, though it's filled with irritation. "You're an idiot if you think I'd ever stoop to begging a man to love me, Bishop Mitchell."

"I wasn't saying you needed to beg me to love you, Gabi. I loved you more than anything in the world. I'm saying you could have literally said *anything*." He pushes off the bed. "You could have cried or yelled or hung up on me in anger. But it didn't even seem like you cared."

I shake my head, anger roiling through me. All the feelings from back then flood my mind. They've been waiting there, for years, waiting for a chance to be purged, to demand answers, to understand...and he's going to say I didn't *care*?

"You're twisting this whole fucking thing," I growl. "*You* dumped *me*, Bishop. I *was* devastated. I've never felt pain like that in my *life*."

Bishop blinks a few times in shock, surely knowing what it means for me to say those words. Considering my past with my mother, for me to tell him the end of us eclipses that pain...well, I don't say it lightly.

"You're right, Gabi. I broke up with you. I'm the one who called it quits." He shakes his head, opening his arms wide. "I was young and didn't know what to do when my girlfriend started to pull away, so I gave up because I didn't know any better. I didn't know how to fight for someone the way I should have fought for you, and I will always take the blame for that. But you can't stand there and pretend you played no part. I might have broken up with you, but you had already started checking out, and I didn't know what else to do."

I'm furious.

I'm enraged.

I have this ball of shaking anger inside me and no place for it to go. I want to shout at him, tell him he's wrong, because there's no way what he's saying is true. There's no way I was the first to push away.

And yet...something in the back of my mind gasps at what he's said. I scramble through my memories, thinking back to that time, to when I was at art school in Monterey and he was hours away going to college.

I remember loving him more than I'd ever loved anyone. I remember worrying about the distance and what it would do to us. And I remember feeling this looming fear that he would get bored with me and move on, that I was just his hometown girlfriend and his life—on the fast track to success, the golden boy who was going to light the world on fire—was going to take him far away from me. I was scared he would leave me behind, felt like I'd already been left behind, so I...

It feels like all the air begins to leak out of my lungs. I... pushed him away? I...what? How have I never seen this before? How did I never realize?

We stand in silence for a long moment, the echo of regret reverberating around us with all the things we should have said, should have done. A different life might have played out for us if we'd just...talked. Been honest. Refused to let things fall apart.

The idea that all this pain we've been through, that it might be because we didn't trust each other as much as we thought we did...I don't even know how to process it.

"I'm gonna...go on a walk," he says, grabbing a room key and heading for the door. "Just get some air."

Before I can say anything in response, he's gone. I stand in the center of the room for long moments once the door shuts behind him, unsure of what to do with myself, my mind a mess.

Eventually, I climb into the shower, the hot water pounding down on my body, hoping it will relieve some of the tension lingering in my achy muscles, but the entire time, all I can think about is what Bishop said. No matter what I've said about our breakup, I've always believed he ended things because I wasn't enough, because he wanted more, something I couldn't give him.

Now I realize it's because he *did* want more…but from me. He just wanted…more of me, but because I was so sure he was going to leave me eventually, I began to pull back first.

Memories begin to trickle back in, times when he would call to talk and I would ignore him. Or if I did answer the phone, I'd say there wasn't much to share. He'd try to schedule plans for us to visit each other, and I'd be waffly about my schedule.

Tears track down my face, mixing with the water from the shower. I don't know where we go from here, if there's a road we take together or if this is it. Is this the culmination of what we're able to be to one another? Two people who love each other deeply, but can't seem to get over the pain from the past?

When I'm done soaking under the water, I dry off and get ready for bed, unable to let go of the nerves I feel about the fact that Bishop has yet to return. When we were younger, *I* was the one who would storm off, angry and upset. Bishop was always the calm one, the one who came after me, helped calm me down, leveled me out, showed me that whatever had upset me wasn't nearly as bad as I assumed it was.

Now, being on the other end of it and knowing Bishop needed some time to himself because he was upset…I don't like how it feels.

I turn the TV on, looking for anything to fill the silence, and I blindly watch some kind of reality show Nicole would surely love, though I don't remember a single thing that happens.

When the door beeps and then swings open about thirty minutes later, I'm relieved to see Bishop walk through, and I let out an exhale when I see the look on his face. Gone are the sad eyes and the furrowed brow and the clenched jaw. Instead, he looks like the Bishop I know and love, the man who can take any shitty moment and find a way to maintain an uplifted soul.

He toes off his shoes then crawls right onto the bed next to me, bringing me in tight against his chest. He feels cold from his walk outside, but I'm still warmed by his closeness.

"I'm sorry for being jealous of Garrett," he says, pressing a kiss against the crown of my head. "I've lived with what happened between us for so long, and it feels like we're finally starting to figure things out. And then I have to meet this…guy. Someone who was there for you when I wasn't. Someone who gave you what I didn't." His throat gets tight. "Someone who loved you when I let you go."

I can hear the pain in his voice, the truth in his words.

"We didn't love each other," I say, shaking my head. "We were…a distraction. That's all."

Bishop leans back and looks at me. "A distraction from what?"

I don't have to say anything for us to both know the answer. He gives me a sad smile then brings me back in again so I'm snug against him.

"Do you think we'll ever move on from the past?" I ask, finally voicing the question that's been plaguing me for the past few weeks.

I feel Bishop nod before he says anything. "I do," he tells me, his voice firm and sincere. He draws back again and takes my hand in his, holding it against his chest. "We were…like a broken bone, and when you reset it, there's going to be some hurt. It hurts and it's complicated and it isn't always pretty. There's work that goes into getting things set right, but it happens." Bishop rests his forehead against mine and closes his eyes. "It happens, and I know what we have is worth it."

He sounds so sure, and everything inside me wants to believe him. Things with Bishop are so good. So good and so right in so many ways. I can't help that I get scared, that the pain from my past sometimes dictates what I fear now, but I'm not the same person I was back then. I'm not the girl who pulls away anymore, and Bishop isn't the guy who gives up.

So we might not be able to control the fact that our old wounds will resurface—but we *can* help what we do when it happens.

We hold each other all night long, cocooned together in a big fancy bed with way too many pillows. We hold hands for almost the entire drive as we head home the following morning, but for some reason there's still an ache I feel in my chest when Bishop comes to a stop in front of my house and helps me unload all my stuff.

Our trip has left me unsettled. Even though we had a long, vulnerable chat, I can't help but feel like the honeymoon period we were in has finally ended. We were in a blissed-out state, just enjoying each other's company and trying to ignore the past. Now, we've reminded ourselves of the hard stuff, the big stuff, the emotional bullshit that comes along with relationships.

It isn't necessarily a bad thing, I don't think, but it still feels like we're standing at a precipice, on the verge of taking things a lot more seriously or completely falling apart.

The hard part is knowing which way it's gonna go.

chapter twenty-three
bishop

I love Thanksgiving. It's my favorite holiday, mostly because of the food. Sure, it's important to take time to be thankful, spend time with family, togetherness and whatnot. I get that.

But really? It's about the food. Turkey and mashed potatoes and gravy. Mac n cheese and homemade rolls and stuffing. Green bean casserole and butternut squash ravioli and of course, my favorite, pumpkin pie.

Every year I was away at college, I'd get invites from friends on the team, letting me know if I didn't have somewhere to go for the holidays, I could eat with them and their family. But I've never even considered going somewhere other than my parents' house for Turkey Day.

My dad starts cooking early and my mom runs around putting finishing touches on the decorations for her dinner table, which seems to get longer and longer every year because we're almost always hosting friends or other people around town. The house always smells incredible all day.

Before all the madness begins, bright and early on Thanksgiving morning, I meet up with a bunch of guys who used to play for the Cedar Point Pirates for a little game of baseball. It has been one of my favorite parts of coming home for the holidays each year and something I'm usually looking forward to.

Except for this year, because of my stupid fucking wrist.

"I can't believe you're not allowed to hit one ball," Rush says, his arm resting on a stack of black exercise mats tucked against the wall of the weight room. "That seems…almost criminal."

I snort. "It feels that way."

"I guess you'll just have to sit on the bench and watch me light everyone up," he jokes before hitting an imaginary ball then bringing one hand up to his forehead as if to shade his eyes from the sun so he can see how far that ball has gone.

"You're an idiot."

Rush just grins, proving my point.

I called Dr. Ramos' office yesterday, letting him know about the pickup game and asking if he thought it would be okay for me to play if I promised to have the ball pitched lightly. He made absolutely zero attempt at disguising his opinion.

"I want four solid weeks of PT before you start playing again, Bishop. You've been to, what? Four physical therapy sessions so far?"

"Five," I corrected him. "But it will be six before Thanksgiving."

He sighed. "Look, I can't control what you do, but my opinion is that you should get through the end of the month and then let us do one more X-ray."

And because I made a promise to myself that I was going to follow through on this rehab plan, I guess that means no baseball for Bam until December.

"Maybe I'll umpire," I offer. "But the last thing I want to do is just…sit on the bench."

"You hear that, guys?" Rush calls out, drawing the attention of our players from where they're focusing on various weight regimens. "Coach Mitchell's gonna be an umpire."

"Boo!" some of the guys call out, making me laugh.

"Kill the ump!" Tommy cackles, a phrase that's been used plenty throughout history to highlight how often players and fans are mad at the game officials.

"We don't joke about killing people here, Tommy," Rush replies, though he has a smile on his face as he says it.

I shake my head, unsurprised by the bit of ribbing.

"I promise not to cross over to the dark side for more than just this one game," I announce, pretending to take them seriously.

"Like anyone cares about your stupid game."

I glance at Justin where he's sitting in the hack squat machine, headphones in but clearly off if he's been listening to the conversation.

"I'll have you know that the CPPATDBG is one of the best games this town has ever seen," I say, crossing my arms.

Justin raises an eyebrow. "The CP-what?"

"Please don't ask him to repeat it," Rush jokes. "I can never keep all the letters straight."

At that, I grin. "The CPPATDBG," I say again. "Cedar Point Pirate Alumni Thanksgiving Day Ball Game."

Justin rolls his eyes. "Sounds lame."

"Well, it's not."

"What is it?" Ruben asks, coming to a stop next to where we're standing. "Like, graduated players or something?"

I nod. "That's exactly what it is. Anyone who has ever played for the Pirates is welcome, and we split into teams and play the game we love in the place we loved it."

"Can *we* play?"

I glance at Tommy and shake my head. "Alumni only. But you'll get invited once you graduate."

He grins. "Sweet. Then I can pitch to you and see if you can handle the heat."

A chorus of ooohs fills the room, followed by plenty of laughter. This is one of my favorite parts of being on a team, the friendly shit-talking and muscle-flexing that happens in the down time.

Sure, the game itself is my true joy. There is nothing like the feeling of walking up to home plate and staring down a pitcher, knowing I'm going to hit whatever he sends my way. But the comradery, the silly stuff that happens during practice and when things are a bit less serious—I love that, too. Sharing it with this bunch of high school guys has been…a lot better than I ever could have expected.

"A bunch of old losers who can't run around the bases anymore? Gimme a break," Justin grumbles.

I grit my teeth. I've been enjoying everything except for that. Can't say I'm a fan of the poison this kid seems to douse nearly every situation with. I wish he could just…see the bigger fucking picture.

Thankfully, I think I'm one of just a few people who hears him, his comment lost in the sea of adolescent male chatter and the clanking of weights.

"Alright, let's wrap it up," Rush calls out a few minutes later, bringing practice to an end.

The guys finish up at their machines or return their weights to the rack and create a half circle in the center of the room, looking at me and Rush.

"As you guys know, today was our last practice of the semester," Rush says, holding his clipboard against his chest. "Fall Ball is officially over."

There are a few hoots and some light applause before Rush continues.

"We'll reconvene in the spring. I'll be emailing you the practice and game schedule in the next week or two, so please watch for that." He shrugs. "And I think that's about it." Rush glances around. "Thanks for a great few months, guys." Then he looks at me. "Coach? You wanna say anything to close us out?"

I raise my eyebrows, surprised. I rack my brain for anything to say that might mean something after just two months together.

"I guess I just want to stress how impressed I am by so many of you, your willingness to take on board some of my feedback and welcome me in as part of the team. I'm not sure what the spring will look like, whether I'll still be here helping out or when I'll be heading back to Oregon, but I'll be following along with your season regardless. I'm excited to see what you guys do." I glance at Rush. "I think that's it."

He nods. "Alright, let's do Pirates on three. Pirates on three. One, two, three, Pirates!"

The guys all cheer together, and there're a few more hand claps before they begin to disperse, filing slowly out of the weight room and down the hallway toward the lockers. We make quick work of cleaning up the few things left out before flipping off the lights and heading down the hallway.

"So, I'll see you Thursday morning?"

"Yep. Bring a dish from your mom again this year, yeah?" He rubs his stomach. "Last year you brought that homemade cinnamon bun thing, and I've been thinking about it ever since."

Laughing, I nod. "I'll see what I can do. Did Leon give any idea of how many guys might show up?"

Leon Walker is an alum from '82 who has been the primary spearhead behind this game each year. The man is an icon, still hitting homeruns even though he's in his sixties. He might struggle a bit more to get around the bases, but he can still hit.

"He mentioned RSVPs were a little light this year, and it doesn't help that you're out of commission, either." He shrugs. "Who knows? Maybe it just becomes a homerun derby."

I nod, thinking a homerun derby would be even cooler than a game—if I wasn't injured.

Then an idea occurs to me, and I wish I'd thought of before, though I guess it wouldn't have been possible until now.

"Yeah, maybe. I'll see you later?"

Rush gives me a wave then heads into his office, and I turn back down the hallway we just came from.

Instead of heading to Gabi's classroom, I jog over toward the locker room, relieved when I see Justin adjusting his backpack over his shoulder and trudging down the hallway in the opposite direction.

"Hey, Justin!" I call out.

He turns, his eyes widening briefly when he sees me before narrowing. Then he stands there looking extremely put out until I come to a stop a few feet away.

"What?"

Ignoring the attitude, I ask him the question that came to mind when Rush told me we might be short a few players on Thursday.

"You have any plans Thursday morning?" I ask him.

His nose wrinkles. "Sleeping in."

I grin. "Well, instead of sleeping in, why don't you come out and play with us?"

Justin's head jerks back, his eyebrows rising high on his face. "What, in that stupid alumni game?" When I nod, he scoffs, glancing away and shaking his head. "Why the hell would I want to waste my time doing that?"

I shrug. "Why wouldn't you?"

He just stares at me, looking bewildered.

"You think you're so much better? Think all these guys are just a bunch of old hacks? Prove it. Come show everyone how you—a sixteen-year-old kid—can light them up."

Justin's eyes narrow, but that confusion is still there. "What are you playing at?"

"Not playing at anything, Justin. You talk more shit than anybody I know." I shrug. "Just thought maybe you'd like to do more than talk."

When he doesn't say yes or no, I take a step back.

"Look, think about it. At the very minimum, baseball is out until January, right? It's one more chance to play before everything shuts down for six weeks. We start at nine, and I hope you'll be there."

When I turn, Justin speaks again.

"I thought you said high schoolers can't play. Said you have to be an alum."

I glance back at him. "Maybe I'm willing to make an exception. You can play in my place."

I continue walking down the hall, finally heading toward Gabi's classroom and leaving Justin behind. I'm not sure if this idea will have any impact on the kid or if I'm grasping at straws, but my dad was right when he said you just have to keep trying.

And who knows? Maybe this will finally be the idea that

makes a difference. I can only hope I poked him just enough that he'll show. Maybe seeing the comradery, the togetherness, will show him that baseball is definitely about love of the game, but it's also about the friendships you make along the way.

"Welcome to the 35th Annual Cedar Point Pirate..."

Leon trails off and glances at me.

"Alumni Thanksgiving Day..." I whisper, helping with the rest of it.

"Alumni Thanksgiving Day..."

"Ball Game."

"Ball Game." Leon rolls his eyes and waves a hand in the air. "Someone needs to shorten that."

The group of men circled together around home plate chuckle, stamp their feet, and blow hot air on their hands in the cold weather of the late November morning.

"We're gonna split into two teams based on the year you were born. If it was an odd year, you're home. Even year, you're away."

Everyone begins shuffling around, moving toward the dugouts of their newly assigned teams, before Leon speaks again, rattling off a few rules. My attention is diverted as I spot movement on my left, and when I turn, I grin at the sight of Justin rounding the fence and heading toward us.

"What's Justin doing here?" Rush asks, keeping his voice low.

"I invited him."

Rush raises an eyebrow but returns his attention to Leon.

"And this year, due to an injury, we have Bam helping us out as umpire!" Leon adds, leading everyone in a round of applause. "Alright, let's play ball!"

As the home team jogs onto the field to warm up, I head toward Justin, who is standing off to the side, a duffle bag slung over his shoulder.

"Glad you could make it."

He raises his chin. "Figured it wouldn't be so bad to get in some more playing before wrapping up for the year," he says. Then he glances around. "Which team am I on?"

"Honestly, it doesn't really matter. I think the home team has less people, so head on over there."

He nods once then begins walking to the opposite dugout.

"And Justin?"

He stops and looks back at me.

"Make sure you introduce yourself."

He rolls his eyes and turns away. I chuckle and grab the mask and chest protector one of the guys brought for me before heading to home plate.

The game moves pretty quickly—it always does—and we're late in the second inning before Justin finally makes it up to bat. He looks a lot more cocky walking up to the plate than he did when he first arrived, but we have Gary Nilo on the mound. He graduated six or seven years ago—a few years before me—and went on to pitch in the D1 college championship with a top ten school. The guy is no joke, and a few years out from school, it doesn't seem like he's lost much, if any, of his speed.

Gary winds up then zings a ball right past Justin, into the catcher's mitt.

"Strike!"

Justin adjusts his stance, shifts his helmet, then gets back into position. When Gary throws one across the plate again, Justin swings.

And misses.

I call it again. "Strike!"

I can see his irritation bristling, and he whacks the bottom of each foot with his bat before setting up again, his jaw tight and his chin low. This time, when Gary throws, Justin makes contact, the ball sailing into an open spot in the outfield.

Justin chucks his bat and begins to run, but the guy at right field scoops it up and blazes it to second to get a runner out then second chucks it to first, who catches it right before Justin's foot hits the bag.

"Out! That's three," I call, and the away team begins jogging in.

I watch Justin, standing off to the side of first base, his hands on his hips, his chest heaving. I'm trying to remember what Rush said to me about the last time Justin hit a ball that resulted in him getting an out. It was something crazy like he went all of last season without ever getting out, just homeruns and base hits all the way through.

Eventually he returns to the dugout, grabs his mitt, and jogs out to left field. The game continues, and the away team begins to take off with run after run, resulting in them being up by three in the fifth inning.

"Go, Justin!" Rush shouts, the next time the kid heads to the plate. "You got this! Big swing!"

Before Justin sets up, I step forward. "Remember what I said about turning your hips more?" I ask, knowing I'm probably going to piss him off but deciding to take my chances.

He just glares at me.

"Make sure you punch them forward, alright? You'll get a more rounded swing. Just...try it." I pause. "Please."

Justin's nostrils flare, and then he looks toward his feet, stomping them into the dirt as he gets ready. Sighing, I tug my mask back on and move behind the catcher. Gary winds up, and when the ball crosses the plate, I blink in surprise at the fact that Justin...actually listened to me. He still got a strike, hitting the ball foul, but he listened!

Second ball, same thing. Gary throws, Justin opens his hips up a bit more, the ball goes foul. Justin growls, looking right at me for a beat before setting up again.

"One more time, Justin. Trust me."

I say it from behind the catcher, but I can tell he hears me by the way his body tenses just slightly.

Third ball comes flying over the plate...and Justin smacks it into space.

The guys all jump up from where they're sitting in the dugouts—on both sides—and cheer as the ball flies over the fence and into the trees behind the ballpark. Justin tosses his bat to the side, shouting with joy as he jogs around the bases, bringing another batter home as well. When he crosses the plate, a bunch of the guys are there, cheering for him and telling him what an amazing hit that was and clapping him on the back.

I can't hide my fucking smile the entire time. In fact, I can't hide my smile for the rest of the game.

The away team wins—edging out the home team by just one run—and my mom shows up with two huge trays of cinnamon roll croissants, still slightly warm from the oven, because that's the kind of badass Patty Mitchell is.

"Thanks for umping, Bam," Leon says, shaking my hand

as everyone begins to head out a little while later. "You heading back to Oregon soon?"

I nod, popping one more bite of croissant into my mouth. "That's the plan, if all goes well with this thing," I say, raising my wrist, still wrapped in the black brace.

"Well, we'll be rooting for you." He pats me on the shoulder then gives my mom a wave. "See you at the council meeting next week?"

My mom nods and gives him a wave. "See you, Leon!"

When I spot Justin shoving his shit in his bag, I head his direction.

"Hey you," I say, grinning when he looks up at me and hoists his bag over his shoulder. "That was a pretty big fucking swing."

"Yeah, I know." He tips his chin up and just stares at me.

I chuckle. "Jeez, Justin. Can you ever just say thanks? Why is everything a battle? Every single thing is a fight with you. Why?" Crossing my arms, I shake my head. "Like, I feel like I can't even be irritated about it anymore. It's just becoming funny at this point."

Justin purses his lips and looks to the side.

Sighing, I rest my hands on my hips. "Well, that was a great hit. And if you take anything away from being here today, I *hope* you realize that the people who are giving you advice—people like me and Rush, and whoever coaches you in the future—we're just trying to help. The only thing we care about is helping you be everything *you* want to be."

His body language shifts slightly, a layer of tension in his shoulders dissipating. I don't know what caused it, whether it was something I said or if I imagined it entirely, but there's a part of me that hopes he'll take at least *something* from today's game, even if it's small.

"Hey, sweetie," my mom says, coming up behind me, her eyes on Justin. "You have plans for Thanksgiving?"

Justin gives her a tight smile. "Hello, Mrs. Mitchell. Yeah, I'm...driving to my aunt's in Spencer Creek."

"Ah, well, if anything changes, you're always welcome at ours, okay? We're breaking bread at 2, if you wanna join."

He nods. "Thanks."

Mom turns to me. "Need a ride home?"

I shake my head. "I've got my car."

"Alright, see you in a bit. Love you." She rises up on her tip-toes and presses a kiss to my cheek then gives Justin a wave and heads toward the parking lot.

"How about you? Do you need a ride?" I ask Justin.

He glances off to the side, toward the parking lot, and my eyes follow his. It's mostly empty, almost all the guys having taken off already.

"Come on, dude. I'll drop you at home," I say, waving for him to follow me as I turn and head toward the bleachers to grab my bag. I don't glance back, but I hear a long sigh and then the sound of Justin's feet when he finally starts walking behind me.

"So you're heading to Spencer Creek, huh?" I ask once I've pulled out onto the main road a few minutes later.

Justin nods.

"You and your mom?"

"Mom's working today. I'm just...going by myself."

I blink a few times, saddened by that answer. I mean, I get it. Not every store closes for every holiday, but I guess I hadn't thought about how that results in some kids being left alone on a day that's supposed to be about togetherness.

Well, I guess Justin's not going to be *alone*, but he still won't be with his mom.

"What did you think of the game today?"

Justin sighs. "It was fine."

"Us old geezers know how to play, huh?" I tease, grinning at him.

His lips tilt up slightly, but just as quickly as the expression appeared, it's gone.

"I guess."

It might be the first time I've seen a smile from him that didn't come with a side of cocky attitude, and I'm nearly bowled over by it.

"And how'd I do as the ump?" I ask as I continue driving around the lake, toward town.

Justin glances at me, his eyes assessing. "I think you should make the change permanent."

I laugh. I laugh hard, and this time, Justin's smile is more pronounced and sticks around a bit longer.

"You're a regular comedian, you know that?"

He just shrugs, but his smile is still there. And I revel in it.

Justin guides me toward an apartment complex that abuts the elementary school a few blocks away from Main Street. When I come to a stop in the parking lot, he doesn't jump out of the car like his ass is on fire. Instead, he lets out a long sigh then turns to look at me.

"Thanks for inviting me today."

My eyebrows nearly fly off my face at his words, and I nod. "I'm glad you could make it."

He shoves the door open and steps outside, hoisting his bag over his shoulder.

"Happy Thanksgiving, Coach."

I smile, wondering who this kid is and hoping he plans to stick around for a while. "You too, Justin. See you around."

I wait for a minute, watching as he jogs over to a unit on the first floor, keys into it, and shuts the door behind him. Then I begin the fifteen-minute drive home.

I'm not sure what prompted Justin to relax some of his naturally bristly demeanor, but it feels like proof that he desperately needs someone in his life who will give him some attention—attention that doesn't have anything to do with how good he is with a bat.

The phone rings a few times before Busy picks up, and I smile when the familiar melody of my baby sister's voice comes through the speaker.

"I figured I'd hear from you at some point today," she grumbles.

Chuckling, I set the phone on my desk then tug open my dresser drawers, looking for my favorite pair of jeans.

"You figured right," I reply. "What's this about you not coming for Thanksgiving? I thought you were supposed to have landed a few hours ago."

When I returned from dropping Justin off, Mom told me Busy had some last-minute changes to her plans and wouldn't be coming. I can't remember a time when she wasn't here for a major holiday. Even though she's been enjoying her life in LA since she left for college, she still comes home for the important moments: holidays, big events—like the Cedar Cider opening—and the week over summer when we all return for a little vacay and togetherness.

"Is this about that guy you're dating?" I continue, the thought only just now occurring to me.

I tug my jeans on then begin digging through my closet for the green sweater I know Gabi loves. I didn't listen too closely when Busy and Bellamy were talking about this…Jay guy at Cedar Cider, but I *do* remember the way my younger sister's eyes glowed as she talked about him.

"No, this isn't about…*him*," she says before letting out a long sigh. "It just isn't a good time for me…to come home."

Something about that feels off. I know Busy, and this doesn't sound like her. The fact that she seems cagey about sharing whatever is really going on is surprising, especially with me, because I'm the sibling she talks to the most often.

"You know you can talk to me, right?"

There's a long pause, and I begin to think maybe she's going to spill, share whatever it is she's got on her mind or going on in her life that's important enough she'd skip out on time with her family. But even through the phone I can feel when she decides to shut me out.

"There's nothing to talk about, Bishop," she replies, her voice growing tight. "I just picked up an extra shift at work. That's all. I'm trying to…make some extra money."

Licking my lips, I nod. If that's how she wants to play it— flat-out lie about what she's doing in LA instead of coming home—then I guess that's just how it is.

"Well…we're going to miss you today. You know that, right?"

Busy sighs again, but this time it sounds more sad than irritated. "I know."

I think it over for a second, ultimately deciding to try again.

"Are you *sure*? There's *nothing* going on? I love you, Biz. Whatever it is—"

"God, Bishop. Will you just leave it?" she barks. "Everything is fine."

Now I believe it even less, but I have to respect that she doesn't want to talk about it. Whatever *it* is.

"Okay, okay. I'm sorry."

I tug my sweater over my head and slip my arms into the sleeves.

"You're fine. But, I need to go."

"Heading to work?"

"Yep."

She's lying, but I just need to let it go like she asked me to.

"Alright, well…like I said, I love you. Happy Thanksgiving."

"Love you, too."

Then the call ends. To anyone else, she might have sounded fine. Clearly, my mom wasn't worried about the fact that she's not coming home, but I can't help feeling like there's something going on with Busy.

Something big.

And a thread of worry remains in my chest for the rest of the morning.

chapter twenty-four

gabi

When the last few guests finally leave the Mitchell house at the end of the day, it's nearing ten, and I am exhausted. I don't know how Patty and Mark host such long events in their home without wanting to curl up into the fetal position. I wasn't even the host and I'm barely functional.

Originally, when Bishop invited Leah and me to join in on the holiday meal, I declined. I figured it might be awkward, having us back with the Mitchells for a holiday when we went several years after we broke up doing our own thing.

Not that we haven't been invited. Every year, Leah received a call from Patty, inviting her to both Thanksgiving *and* Christmas dinners. But during the two years I was at school, I went and celebrated with classmates, and for the past two years, Leah and I have done homemade lasagna and binge-watched episodes of some pottery competition in the UK.

After our trip to San Francisco last weekend, the idea of not spending the holiday with Bishop felt wrong. I thought our difficult conversation in the hotel would make things between us feel harder or more temporary, maybe even make us more distant again, like we may have handled things in the past.

But surprisingly, it's been the opposite.

Things feel more secure. Part of me thinks avoiding the conversation about what happened between us four years ago was threatening to tear us apart. It was something I hadn't realized, and now that we've talked about it, now that we've had the hard discussion and shifted through the honeymoon period…we've come out on the other side stronger.

Even so, I'm still trying to figure it all out in my mind. All I know for sure is spending the holiday meal with Bishop and his family felt like the right thing, and for that, I'm thankful.

"Think Principal Cohen wants an NSP update?" Bishop asks as we lie together on the couch.

I giggle. "Not the one *we* would send her."

We laugh together at that thought, about sending our boss an update on our relationship instead of on our students.

"Probably not the best idea. I'm not sure she's forgiven us for the rooftop beers."

I look up at him where he's lying beneath me, finding his eyes already looking in my direction, watching me.

"I doubt she'll *ever* forgive us for that."

We watch each other for a long moment, the fireplace dragging me into a lazy, post-holiday coma.

"Did you…want to stay?" he asks, almost like he can read my mind.

"Would your mom be okay with that?"

Bishop chuckles then tugs me closer, if that's even possible. "We're not sixteen anymore, Gabi. We can sleep together if we want."

I want nothing more than to stay here with him, but for a reason I can't name, I decide against it. Instead, I slide off his chest and place my feet on the floor. "I should probably head home."

He sighs and pushes himself up, first to sitting, then to standing next to me. "Or, hear me out..." He grins. "Don't."

I smile, shaking my head. Then I lean in and kiss him.

Bishop hums then pulls back, his eyes tracing my face. "I'll get my coat."

Twenty minutes later, we arrive at my house, dark except for the light over the front door, and I know Leah's already gone to bed. She left the Mitchells' house around six and told me to stay as long as I wanted, but she had to head home and get a good night of sleep before her trip.

Licking my lips, I glance at Bishop. "Hey, what do you think...about coming over tomorrow? Staying the night?"

He raises an eyebrow.

"Leah's heading down the mountain to do an art install tomorrow morning. Won't be back until sometime Sunday." I shrug. "If you wanted to hang out or listen to music or...whatever."

His lips tilt up at the sides.

"Unless, you know...you still want to keep ...drawing things out."

I hadn't planned that last part, but I couldn't help myself. Things between Bishop and me have been fairly PG since we got back together, which isn't bad by any means. We kiss a lot, and we hug and touch often. It's rare for us to go too long without holding hands or wrapping each other in a hug when we're in the same space.

But I can't deny that I've been craving the physical intimacy. I originally hoped for something to happen when we went to San Francisco, which clearly did not end up working out, though it was for the better. The fight and the time at the hotel brought us together in an emotional way, and inviting Bishop over while my aunt is out of town is my very obvious attempt at bringing us together in a more physical way.

"If you want me here, I'll be here," he says, that charming grin of his stretched wide on his face. "Just let me know what time to show up."

He tugs me across the center console and kisses me with all the same longing and passion and thirst I've been desperate for. He kisses me deeply, reverently, desperately, and as he shifts back, I can see in his eyes all the promise of what's to come.

When Bishop opens the box of pizza sitting on the living room coffee table, I groan.

"I haven't had a pizza from Reggie's in forever," he says, dragging a slice onto a plate and passing it to me before doing the same for himself. "The smell was taunting me in the car so much I almost pulled over and had some on the side of the road."

I laugh. "Eating without me?" I pop a piece of pepperoni into my mouth. "I would have never forgiven you."

"Hence the reason it remains in the box, untouched."

Grinning, I lift up my slice and take a big bite, groaning again.

"Literally the best in the world," Bishop says, nodding. "The absolute best."

We lapse into a brief silence as we each inhale a few quick bites, nothing but Mumford and Sons playing softly on the record player. The familiarity of this simple act—eating pizza with Bishop while sitting cross-legged on the floor of my living room—takes me briefly back to the days when we would spend hours hogging the room, watching TV while snacking or eating while studying.

It's different now, though. Bishop takes up more space, his large body dominates more of the couch, and the fact that we're here alone was *definitely* not anything Leah would have ever allowed back then.

It's nice. Familiar but still different, like most things with Bishop.

"So what's Leah working on?" he asks, picking a few olives off his slice. "You said she's installing some art?"

I nod. "Some woman in Sacramento commissioned a piece that reaches up to her 18-foot ceilings or something. It's wild."

"Sounds like it."

"It's going to require scaffolding in order to put up in this house. It's a whole ordeal. There are like 50 pieces. It's incredible, but it's going to take two whole days to install, so she's staying down there while she's doing it so she's not totally wiped from the drive both ways."

Bishop nods, listening intently.

"I didn't realize she'd started doing things like that. I mean, I knew she did macrame and wall art, but I thought it was on a smaller scale, like the stuff at your booth."

"It used to be," I reply, remembering what it was like back then. "But after I left for art school, she said she had more time on her hands and wanted more of a challenge. And she's killing it."

"Sounds like someone else I know," Bishop says, narrowing his eyes playfully in my direction.

I just roll my eyes, but I can't help the spark of joy I feel at his compliment.

We finish our first slices just as the record finishes, and Bishop makes quick work of plating more pizza while I flip the record over to the other side. Then we launch back into an easy conversation about friends from high school, from people still in town like Bellamy and Rush and Emily and Nicole to those who have moved away. We talk about art school and baseball. My ceramics class and the end of Fall Ball.

It feels easy. Simple. Wonderful.

Like all the conversations we had when we were younger, but with a new kind of honesty. The kind you can only find after you've been through something hard, together.

"Thanks again for picking up dinner," I say as Bishop rinses a plate in the sink. "I wish you hadn't eaten so many slices so there could be more for leftovers tomorrow."

"Who says you get to keep the leftovers?" he asks.

"Who says you won't be here to eat them with me?" I volley back.

Bishop glances at me, chuckling, then moves to set the plate in the dishwasher. But the movement is awkward and it slips from his hand, hitting the side before shattering on the ground.

"Fuck," he whispers, crouching down quickly to grab the handful of pieces. "I'm sorry."

I shake my head. "It's not a big deal. Let me get the vacuum."

We clean up the broken shards of the ceramic plate then do an extra vacuum over the entire kitchen floor to make sure we didn't miss anything.

"Sorry again," he says once everything's picked up and we're sure there are no little pieces left on the floor. "Most things aren't an issue, but every once in a while…" He trails off, massaging his left wrist and fingers with his other hand.

I shake my head and take his hand in mine. "*Not* a big deal," I promise, not wanting him to linger too long on it. "Now, let's get a glass of wine and go sit on the back porch."

Bishop grins. "It's pretty cold and rainy out there. I know you'd rather be in here, snuggled up next to the fire."

I shrug my shoulder as I retrieve two wine glasses. "But *you* love the cold." Then I smirk at him. "Besides, I'm sure you'll keep me warm."

A few minutes later, we're standing together on the covered back porch, listening to the rain as it falls behind our house, though we can't see it because it's well past sunset and the moon is only barely breaking through the dense covering of trees. I'm standing against the railing, and Bishop is behind me, my back to his front, his arm around my waist while the other holds his glass steady where it sits.

"I'm glad you're here tonight," I say, tilting back against his chest, enjoying how it feels as he presses a kiss to the top of my head.

"Me, too," he replies, nestling his chin into the crook of my neck. "I love being wherever you are."

We stay like that for a while, just enjoying the quiet together, listening to the sounds of nature and the rain falling softly. When I finish my glass of wine, I set it on a small table next to the bench tucked against the wall, then slip back to where I was snuggled against Bishop's front, but this time, facing him. I wrap my arms around his waist and press my face into his chest, breathing him in.

His hands rub at my back, a gentle rhythm, warming me even as we stand out in the cold. There's a pressure in my chest, a desire to tell him a few small words I'm not sure I'm ready to say, no matter how clearly I feel it.

Pulling back, I look up into his face, into those beautiful eyes that always hold me captive. I open my mouth, wanting to tell him how I feel, but something inside me freezes. Bishop looks back at me, surely wondering what I was going to say, but I come up empty.

Except the feeling, the knowledge that I love him, that I've always loved him…it builds within me. On instinct, I drag one of his arms away from where it's wrapped around me and bring his hand against my chest, where my heart thuds, unsteady in so many ways but beating strong for him. Then I raise his hand and press a kiss to the inside of his wrist, hoping he understands where my heart is at, where my mind is at, even if my words don't follow.

Bishop watches me for a long moment before he dips down and presses his lips to mine. The taste of him—wine mixed with something that is purely Bishop—explodes on my tongue, and I moan, slipping my hands up his chest and then wrapping them around his neck.

God, I love this man.

We kiss like that for long moments, for forever, until my lips become swollen, until a warm pulsing begins to wind its way through my center. Bishop's hands track down my back and over my ass, gripping me roughly, and I mirror the motion, bringing my hands down and grabbing the meatiness of his backside. His ass fills my palms, and when he leans back, he's grinning at me.

"Since when do you like to grab my ass?" he asks, his voice

husky but amused.

"Since when do you complain?" I reply, slipping my hands into his jeans and under his boxer briefs, grabbing him again.

He bites his lip then shifts his hips, the hardness in the *front* of his jeans just as eager for attention as the firmness in the back.

"Trust me, I'm not complaining," he replies, watching as I bring one hand around and stroke against his dick then groaning at the pleasure. "You feel free to grab anything of mine that you want."

I push up on my toes and nip his lips as I unbutton his jeans.

"My ass," he says as I tug the material to the side. "My arms."

I slowly draw his boxers down, watching hungrily as his dick springs free.

"My cock…" he finishes, his mouth falling open as I grip him, hot and hard in my hand, the cold clearly not having any kind of effect.

Bishop groans, and I keep my eyes on his as I drop to my knees, stroking him.

"Can I put anything I want inside my mouth?" I ask, leaning forward and licking him gently, my tongue swirling around his tip.

"Fuck yes," he says, licking his lips as I begin to slide his cock into my mouth, the salty tang of him filling my senses. "Shit, Gabi."

I take him all the way in, until his head bumps the back of my throat and he curses again. Bishop's hands move, sliding into my hair as I suck on him. Then he begins to guide my movements, the gentle pressure of his grasp moving my head and his hips beginning to thrust. I love seeing that expression on his face, like he's totally lost in this moment, like he's never felt a pleasure like this.

When we had sex that night at Bishop's, he spent so much time focused on me, on my pleasure and bringing me to the brink. I don't doubt in the slightest that he was trying to show me how he felt with his body, with his sweat and his effort and his dedication to making me come. I want a chance to do that for Bishop. I want to be whatever I can for him, to show him what he means to me, to show that bringing him pleasure is something that brings me joy.

Bishop continues to thrust into my mouth, and I suck him hard, wanting to wring him dry, wanting to draw him out of his skin. But then he slows, yanking himself out of my mouth and yanking me to my feet, kissing me deeply, roughly, desperately. And god, do I kiss him right back, with just as much desperation and need.

His hands begin to tug at my leggings. "I have a condom in my wallet," he says, his hands grabbing at my hips and my ass then returning to trying to pull my pants down, almost like he doesn't know what he wants to do first.

"I'm clean."

Bishop freezes then moves back, looking me in the eyes. Even in the dark, I can see uncertainty there.

"And I'm on birth control. I haven't been with anyone in like, a year."

He brings me in, kissing me briefly. "I'm clean, too, and it's been a while. But, are you sure?"

I nod. "I'm sure. I want you inside me. Nothing else."

He groans then yanks me in for one more kiss before he returns to removing my leggings. "Why are these so hard to get off?" he grumbles.

I giggle, aiding his efforts, until my leggings are finally down to my knees. He yanks off his sweatshirt and lays it on the railing behind me before spinning me around so I'm facing out into the forest and the dark of the night.

I've never had sex outside before, but as Bishop slides one finger between my lower lips and then into my core, I can't help but feel supremely thankful that we don't have any neighbors. I moan at the sensation, my legs already shaking slightly as he strokes that finger inside me. And then he adds another.

"You're so wet," he growls. "Is this for me?"

"Yes," I pant in response. "God, I get so turned on by you. By everything you do." I pause. "Sometimes I get turned on just thinking about you."

Bishop hums, his fingers pulsing again before he slides them out. The heat of his body envelops me as he presses up against my back, his hands wrapping around my front and reaching up to grab my breasts.

"When was the last time?" he asks, his dick hard and warm pressed against my ass, his hands slipping under the flimsy cotton bralette beneath my shirt.

I whimper as he pinches my nipples.

"When was the last time?" he asks again, one hand traveling low and returning to my pussy, a single finger zeroing in on the little bud between my thighs.

"For what?" I reply, struggling to understand him when I can only think about the way his fingers are bringing me so much pleasure. This was supposed to be about him, and now I feel like I might fall apart at any minute and he's not even inside me yet.

"When was the last time you got turned on thinking about me?" he asks.

His body shifts slightly, and then I feel the fat head of his dick pressing up against me, tucked against my opening.

I squirm, trying to push back against him, wanting him inside me.

"When, Gabi?" he asks, his voice gravelly and filled with desire.

"Last night," I whisper.

We both moan as he begins to slide into me from behind.

"I touched myself thinking about you, wishing I'd stayed, wishing we could have been doing this."

I hiss out the last word as Bishop's dick bottoms out, his hips flush with mine.

"Fuck, Gabi," he says. "Do you have any idea how crazy I am about you?" He pulls all the way out then slides back in, this time faster. "How hearing something like that makes me feel?"

Out and then in again, the clap of our joining bodies echoing against the wall of trees.

"Knowing you think about me when you're alone." Clap. "About me inside you." Clap. "Making you come."

I cry out into the darkness as Bishop begins to thrust into me earnestly, struggling to stand as the flickering of an orgasm begins to lick at the edges of my body.

"God, you're everything," he tells me, his voice hoarse, thick with emotion. "Everything, Gabi."

He thrusts a few more times, his hand sliding back down between my legs and rubbing at my clit again, and that does it. I splinter, shattering into a million pieces that scatter about on the ground below where we stand as my orgasm rips through me. It hits every nerve, tightens every muscle, from my nose to my toes and then back again.

I sob at how beautiful and wonderful it is, my body feeling flayed wide open. And then I hear Bishop shout, feel the way his hands grip me more roughly, the way his body freezes behind me as he tumbles over as well.

We stand there for a long minute, each of us catching our breath, the sound of the rain and nature around us rushing back in to fill the silence. But with the quiet and the calm also comes the reality that we're standing outside in various stages of nakedness, in nearly freezing weather. We make quick work of yanking our clothes back on, giggling as we rush inside to where it's warm and the fire is still blazing.

Bishop collapses on the couch, dragging me down with him and nestling me in tight between his body and the back of the sofa. We just lie there for a while, holding each other, kissing occasionally.

That desire is still there. To tell him that I love him. To communicate not just with my body, but with words, what he means to me. What I see for our future. The fact that I'm all in for whatever is to come.

But for whatever reason, even in the face of the raw intimacy we just shared, I can't seem to say it. I can't make the words come out.

So instead, I stay quiet, just enjoying the closeness and knowing it will come eventually, knowing at some point, I'll feel brave enough to tell him how I feel.

chapter twenty-five

bishop

...six weeks later...

Watching Gabi sleep might be my new favorite hobby.

When you're a teenager, sneaking around trying to find a place and time to have sex doesn't typically result in too much down time after it's all said and done. Once you're both finished, it's about getting dressed as quickly as possible so you don't get caught by anyone's parents.

So, getting the luxury of holding my girlfriend next to me until we each begin to stir, our naked bodies pressed together, is a new wonder, and watching her sleep is something special. I get to look at that beautiful face, completely at rest, her long eyelashes fluttering every so often. I take in the finer details I don't always notice, like the little freckles that dust her temples or the barely visible scar on her chin.

Because I'm the early riser, my body often waking me around 5:30, I get to just lie here next to her, reveling in what it means to get to hold her close again.

Things between us have been incredible. Better than ever. There's a new level of openness I don't think we ever had when we were younger, a new ability to communicate what we think and how we feel and what we want. It's still a new phenomenon, but it's one I'm enjoying.

Like last week, when Gabi was talking about the new workshop she's hoping to build in a few months, and she got mad because she thought I wasn't listening. In the past, she would have stormed out of the room and it would have taken me a while to figure out what was wrong and how to fix it.

But instead, she just let me know she was saying something important and she'd really like if I could stop glancing at my phone. Which I did, and then we moved on, and it was amazing. It's like I'm getting the chance to be back with the Gabi I've always known and loved, but I *also* get to learn some really cool new things about her, things that make me love her even more.

She breathes in deeply as she begins to wake next to me, and then her eyes peek open. She grins and then closes her eyes again before pressing her face into my chest.

"Good morning, sunshine," I say, kissing the top of her head. "How'd you sleep?"

Gabi nods and mumbles something, and I work my arms around her so she's tucked snugly against me.

"Do you still want me to go with you to yoga today?" I ask, secretly excited about it.

I've done yoga a few times, and it's a surprisingly good workout. Plus, with how well my wrist is doing, I'm looking forward to doing some stress-testing.

But Gabi shakes her head and begins kissing my chest. "No, let's skip."

I lick my lips, enjoying her attention. "You said you didn't want to miss just because Nicole is out of town and literally begged me to go," I tell her, chuckling when she nips at my skin. "You wanted to start the new year off by following through more often, remember? Get in regular workouts?"

She looks up at me, mischief in every line of her face. "But what if I want us to stay here?" Gabi licks my nipple, sending a light shiver through my body. "Get a different kind of workout."

Another thing I'm enjoying about this second chance with Gabi: sex whenever we want.

Well, within reason.

I groan quietly when I feel her small hand stroke down my abs and then wrap around my cock, which has been hard since before I even began to wake a little while ago.

"You make a very convincing argument," I tell her, my hips beginning to shift as she jacks me. "Maybe we can work something out."

I feel the huff of her laugh as she kisses my neck and sucks gently at my skin, the wet slide of her tongue against my pulse a delicious tease. She continues to stroke me, and I mimic her movements with my fingers as I glide them between her pussy lips then slip them inside her. I groan when I find her already soaked.

"Bishop," she whispers, her voice a quiet whimper as I begin to circle her clit. "Bishop, I need you."

God, nothing feels as incredible as hearing her say that.

Though being inside of her is a close second.

Gabi rolls onto her back and drags me on top, her hands caressing my flanks as she spreads her thighs and hooks them over my legs. Then I'm pressing into her, my cock sheathed in the warmth of her depths, and we both moan, our voices hushed.

I pump into her gently, at a steady pace, relishing our joining. There's an ecstasy in being wrapped up under the blankets in our own private cocoon.

Drawing back just slightly, I watch as her tits bounce with every thrust, using one hand to pinch at her nipples and the other to hold one of her legs wide. I feel the flutter of her internal walls and I drop down again so our faces are just inches apart, so we can hear the quiet pants of each other's pleasure.

"Touch me," she whispers, and I move my hand to her clit, rubbing a small circle over the tiny button. Gabi's eyes close, her mouth opening, and then she whispers again. "I'm coming."

Her pussy clamps down on me over and over again as she flies over the edge, and I moan, the sensation exactly what I needed. A few more pumps and I'm right there with her, the heat of my orgasm licking up my spine and shooting down through my muscles. I tuck my face into the crook of her neck, groaning through my release.

We lie there for a few minutes, our hands caressing as we gently bring each other down. Once it feels like both of our hearts have finally calmed, I lean back and look at Gabi in the face. She smiles softly at me, and then I kiss her on the lips.

"Alright," I say, pressing a kiss to her nose before I tug the covers off of us completely, exposing our naked bodies to the cold of her bedroom.

Gabi yelps, trying to reach for the blankets, but I pull them off the bed. "What are you doing?" she asks.

"Time for yoga."

"What?" she cries out.

"Come on, lady, move that sexy ass. You said this was important to you, and I'm going to be here, reminding you, as often as I can."

She glares at me like I've kicked a cat or something, but then she pushes out of bed, mumbling incoherently under her breath and surely plotting my demise.

I've only heard from my agent twice since I got out of surgery back in September: once to make sure everything went well, and then once last month via text to ask how the recovery was going.

He's not a man of many words, so when I spot the missed call from Richard after I get home from yoga with Gabi, a sense of foreboding skitters down my spine, and I just know he's going to tell me something I don't want to hear. I've had some questions about the upcoming season and the timing for when I'll be heading back to Oregon, but I've been living in a state of uninformed bliss, just enjoying my relationship with Gabi and spending time with my family.

Somehow, I can just tell the little bubble I've been living in is about to pop.

I give him a call once I've taken a seat on the edge of my bed, shaking my hands out and taking a few deep breaths as the phone rings.

"Hey, Bishop. Happy New Year. How're you doing, bud?"

I hate when he calls me bud.

"Good, thanks. How about you? Did you have a good holiday?"

"I did, I did. Took my wife to New York for the ball drop

this year. She's always wanted to do that, you know?"

I nod. "Yeah, that sounds awesome."

"Well, hey, I don't want to beat around the bush too much before I just get into it," he says, and I can hear the shift in his tone of voice before he even says the words. "The Kings are releasing you."

My entire body freezes as my brain tries to process those words.

Releasing you.

"The whole organization has been doing some moving around of their coaching staff, and the new guys, unfortunately, don't think there's a place for you on their roster."

I blink a few times, staring down at my left hand where it rests on my knee, wondering if it's about my injury, if bringing me back is too much of a risk because of this fucking...mistake.

Or maybe it's just that I don't have the talent. Or the skill. Or the drive.

"But hey, that doesn't mean anything super horrible just yet," Richard continues, though the rest of what he says sounds like a voice in the distance. Something about me being a free agent and how I could get signed at any time with a new team. It all goes in one ear and out the other.

I'm being released.

After one game.

After getting to play one game.

"You keep enjoying your time with your family, and I'll reach out if I have any news, alright?"

If, not when. *If* he has any news, the loud unspoken part being that he might not.

"Alright, Richard, well...thanks."

"Have a good one, okay?"

We say our goodbyes then get off the phone. I sit there for a long while, just staring at the wall across from my bed. Shelves of baseball trophies and MVP plaques and signed memorabilia from a few players I've admired my entire life.

The people who went on to be the greats.

Who definitely *didn't* get released from their teams.

I've spent my entire life working toward a future that seems suddenly gone in a blink, over before it ever really began, and that was my big fear, wasn't it? The thing that lurked in the back of my mind? That I'd made it to that next level and then fucked it up because I got cocky.

Since the second I broke my wrist, I tried to play it off in my mind. The choice to run through second and go for third. The foolish mistake my ego pushed me to make, because who hits a triple on their first at-bat in the minors?

Me. I wanted to say it was *me*. I'm the guy who does that, who shows up and blows everyone out of the water.

But now, I couldn't care less about that triple. Who fucking cares about a triple when it's the only thing you've ever done? When you only ever get a chance to play in one game? When all your effort and energy and talent get shot to shit with one fucking selfish choice?

"Alright, everybody—ready, set, go!"

Rush and I watch from the back of his truck, chuckling as Justin, Ruben, Tommy, and the rest of the Pirates book it down the dock at Miller's Landing. The sound of their bare feet hitting the wood makes them sound like a herd of buffalo as they speed through the cool air in nothing but swim trunks and then leap into the water. Some of them jump, some of them flip, some of them cannonball, but every single one of them launches their body into the freezing cold of Cedar Lake in 29-degree weather.

"Glad I don't have to do that anymore," Rush mumbles, taking another sip of his coffee. "I'll take my blanket and my coffee and my seat right here any day over *that*."

I snort. "You never *had* to do it. It was a choice."

"You keep saying that." He chuckles. "But I remember it differently. *The* Bam made that a tradition. You don't break a tradition, especially one by a Cedar Point icon."

Any other time, I'd hear his words and laugh, rib him a little, feel a bit of flattery. Today, less than 24 hours after getting released from my team, I feel...I don't know. Definitely something else. Shame, maybe. Embarrassment, obviously.

But the thing that surprises me the most is the relief. I'm kind of relieved that I'm no longer facing a reality where I'm leaving at an undetermined time in the next two months. There's no stress about needing to get settled back into that apartment I got with a few other players, no worry about what the next step is or whether I'll recover fully from my injury.

Instead, I get to just...let it all go. Let it go and stay here.

I mean, I love Cedar Point. I've always thought I'd come back. Sure, this might be earlier than I ever imagined, but that doesn't mean I can't make the best of it, can't find happiness here, enjoy a life with Gabi and my family and the familiarity of a town I love. Not everyone gets to live their dream, and getting a single game in Triple-A is more than some people ever get.

The guys are shouting out at the cold and scrambling up

from the water back onto the dock after only a few seconds, and Rush and I laugh.

"Hey, any idea how long you'll be helping out with the team?" he asks me then, almost like he can hear my thoughts. "I gotta sort out the stipend with HR, and it helps if I have an end date."

Licking my lips, I nod. "How would you feel if I helped the whole season?"

I can feel Rush looking at me, so when I turn his way, I'm not surprised to find his eyes watching me with confusion. His brow's furrowed and his nose is wrinkled.

"Don't you have to head back to Oregon?"

Lifting my coffee to my lips, I shake my head then take a sip. "I got released. So..." I shrug. "I'll be sticking around town. For good."

The silence is heavy, but the sound of the team still shouting and clamoring as they dry off in the parking lot and pull their clothes back on is enough to cut through it.

"That was fucking freezing!"

My eyes scan the group as they jog toward us.

"Hey, language," I call out, not sure who said it but reprimanding them just the same.

The guys swarm the truck, and Rush and I jump off the dropped tailgate, bringing forward the carafe of hot chocolate and cups, as well as the no-longer-warm muffins, courtesy of Patty Mitchell. They ravage the goods, most of them fairly quiet and still shivering a bit, their skin still not fully dry after the polar plunge.

"Alright, guys, get home safe. Make sure you take a warm shower or sit by a fire," Rush says a few minutes later. "I'll see you tomorrow in the weight room. 2:30 sharp."

A few groans and a few whoops sound out, some very different reactions to the start of the new semester. Then the group begins to disperse, heading toward waiting parents or hopping into vehicles with the older teammates who can drive.

Rush and I clean up the mess in the bed of his truck then load into the cab, each of us blowing hot air on our fingers and holding them up to the vents once he's cranked the heat. We head out of the lot, heading toward my parents' house.

Well...I guess it's my house again, too.

"So what's this about getting released?" Rush asks, almost the minute we're on the road. "You just got signed. Isn't that a little fast?"

Shaking my head, I let out a long sigh.

"Yeah, it's fast, but...who knows what the deal is. The team just decided they don't have room for me on their roster," I say, looking out the window at the light dusting of snow we got a few days ago that's still stuck to the ground. "So...my career is probably over."

It's unlike me to be so sour, and I think Rush can feel that, because he immediately scoffs.

"What? Nah, man. You'll find another team, I'm sure."

I shake my head, still looking out at the passing scenery, the negative voice inside me becoming uncharacteristically vocal. "I think I'm done, man. I think I got my one shot, my one game. That's it."

We're both quiet after that, the drive to my parents' house a short one. We've stopped in the drive when I speak again, trying to be the optimist everyone knows me to be.

"It's for the best, though, you know? I get to stay here, be with Gabi." I shake my head. "I don't want us to fall apart again, and maybe...maybe this is how we make it work."

There's a voice inside of me saying I'm not giving us enough credit. Reminding me that we've grown, that we're different people now than we were when we were young and unsure.

Rush lets out a sigh, and I shove open the cab door and hop to the ground.

"I'll see you at practice tomorrow?"

He looks at me for a long minute and then nods. "See you tomorrow."

I turn, but he calls my name.

"And hey, Bishop?"

I look back at him.

"I'm sorry, man. I really am."

I nod, giving him a tight smile, then shut the door and head inside. I don't doubt he has more questions, has more to say, and part of me knows I'll hear it from him at some point over the next few weeks as more time passes and he realizes I really am staying.

But today, I don't want to hear it, so I'm thankful he keeps his thoughts to himself.

When I get inside, I head through the house and straight out onto the back deck, looking at the long grassy knoll behind the house and the dock that stretches into the lake.

I love Cedar Point. I always have.

The woman I love is here. So is my family.

That should be more than enough.

chapter twenty-six
gabi

When Sam Rush walks into my classroom about thirty minutes before my first class of the new semester, I can't help the bit of surprise I feel. We haven't been alone together since I stormed away from him when he asked me out a few months ago, and I've always meant to apologize for that.

But when I see the pinched, concerned look on his face, I think maybe my apology will have to wait for another time.

"Hey, I know you're probably getting ready for class, but… do you have a minute?" he asks, crossing toward where I'm rearranging some of the supplies on a shelf along the wall.

I nod. "Sure. What's up?"

He lets out a long sigh. "Did Bishop talk to you already about getting released from his team?"

The hairs along the back of my neck stand up, shock rolling its way through my body. I turn toward Sam.

"What?" I ask, my question more of a gasp than a word.

Sam nods. "He mentioned it to me on Sunday. He hasn't

talked to you about it?"

I shake my head. "No. I didn't even... God, he must be devastated." I pause. "Why wouldn't he tell me?" I say out loud, more to myself than to Sam.

I thought we told each other everything. I thought we'd gotten back into a place where we would share big things like this, the good *and* the bad. The idea that he would get released from his team—his *dream*—and not say anything to me? I can barely believe it.

"Look, I just wanted to let you know because..." Sam pauses, his jaw shifting slightly, almost like he doesn't want to say whatever he was planning to. "Because he said he's planning to stay in town. Permanently."

My head jerks back.

"Said he's actually a little relieved and wants to stay here and coach, be here with his family. And you."

I blink a few times, feeling like I keep getting hit over the head with new information.

"I only wanted to tell you because I know you care about him and, well, I'd wanna know. You know?"

I nod. "Thanks, Sam. I really appreciate you telling me."

He gives me a tight smile and then a wave before heading back outside, probably over to the weight room where the guys will be spending the first month or so of the semester.

I just stand there, glancing around, trying to remember what it was I was doing. All I can think about is the fact that Bishop got cut from his team and is now suddenly staying in Cedar Point. Like, forever?

Shaking my head, I return to my shelves, glancing at my supplies and trying to force my head to go back to teacher mode. It takes great effort, but eventually the arrival of my first student clicks things back into place. I spend the class time getting the students familiar with clay and the wheel and the terminology we'll be using, and the time passes quickly.

Almost the *second* the last student is gone once class is over, I grab my phone and shoot Bishop a text.

Me: Can you come by my class when you're done with practice?

Nearly immediately, a text bubble pops up.

Bishop: I was already on my way over there *wink emoji*
See you in a few

I lick my lips, pacing the room, glancing around and knowing I need to clean up but unable to force myself to do so.

I know we have to talk about this, even though I'm not sure what I'm going to say when he gets here. But when Bishop finally pushes through the door a few minutes later with a smile on his face, part of me wants to keep what I know to myself, at least for a while. Let it be a future Gabi problem.

I love that smile. I love the way he looks at me. I love every goddamn thing about this man. But I also know shelving this conversation isn't something we can do. I love him too much to do that.

"Hey," he says, the door shutting loudly behind him.

"Did you get released from your team?"

I blurt it out. Maybe it's not the most eloquent way to ask, but I know if I don't just say it, I might not, because I knew his smile would fall just like it is right now. It only dips for a moment, and then in true Bishop style, it returns quickly.

"I did."

"And you didn't tell me?"

He chuckles and shakes his head. "I wanted it to be a surprise," he says, reaching out for my hands and taking them in his own. "I wanted everything to be set up first before I told you."

"You wanted *what* to be a surprise?"

"Me staying in town. Me not going anywhere."

I blink, that same surprise rolling through me even though Sam already told me this exact thing. Hearing it from Bishop's mouth is completely different.

"We haven't talked a lot about it, you know? Me leaving. It's like, the one thing we avoid, and now it's a non-issue."

I shake my head and tug my hands from his. "Why are you talking about this like it's a good thing?"

Bishop's head jerks back. "Why would it be a bad thing?"

"Because you don't *want* to be here, Bishop!" I shout. "Because you've been dreaming of playing baseball your entire life. Because it's your *dream!*" I shake my head. "Why would you give that up?"

"I'm not…" He shakes his head then rests his hands on his hips. "I'm not *giving it up*, Gabi. I got released from my team. The dream is over."

I scoff. "You're an idiot."

"Excuse me?"

"Even I know enough about baseball to tell you nobody in their right mind would assume your dream is over because you got cut from *one* team. You have an entire career ahead of you. Who knows what's going to happen?"

"I know what's going to happen, okay? Some part of me has always known."

He takes a breath and spins around, staring out the window

before turning to look at me again.

"When I hurt my hand, it was because I ignored my instincts *and* my coach. I should have stopped at second. There was a base coach telling me to stop, but I ran through to third because I wanted people to see me. I wanted to be great. Not just good—great." He licks his lips and then huffs. "And I knew. I just...knew I'd fucked it all up."

"Lots of people get injured, Bishop. This is just fear talking. Rejection is hard, but that doesn't mean your dream is over. You can't just...*stay* here. You can't give up."

He shakes his head. "Why not? Why can't I just accept that it's over? Instead of drawing it out and getting my hopes up and then watching as it still falls apart."

"Because you giving up on your dream is no different than when you gave up on *me*." I don't plan to say it so harshly, but it still comes out that way.

He recoils, as if I've hit him in the chest. And maybe I did.

"We talked through this. I know we did. I know I played my part, but you have to see it, right? You have to see the similarities. The truth that you can't just...give up on something you love. Any more than you can give up on some*one* you love."

Bishop's mouth opens, like he's going to respond. But then it shuts. He glances around the room for a moment, surely collecting his thoughts, before he speaks again.

"I will *never* give up on you, Gabi. Ever."

"So prove it. Show me you're the man I know you are. The one who has more commitment and dedication in his little finger than anyone else I know."

"I thought you'd be happy about this," he finally says. "Happy I'd still be here, with you."

"Well I'm not." I cross my arms. "And the fact that you

think I would be is actually infuriating."

Bishop grits his teeth, his hands fisting at his sides. "Why? Why doesn't this make you happy?"

"Because if I were happy that you were giving up your dream to stay here with me, I think that would be a pretty clear indicator that I don't love you as much as I fucking do."

I don't realize I'm going to say the words until I say them, don't realize exactly how much I mean them until they're out.

There may have been a day back when we were younger when the idea of Bishop staying in town would have been exactly what I wanted, would have been something that would make me happy because being together would have been the only thing that mattered.

But now, with some more age and wisdom, I can see that's not true.

As important as it is that we love each other, as important as it is that we prioritize each other, that can't be it.

We can't be it.

There has to be freedom to pursue our passions and our dreams and the things that make us happy. Even if that takes us away from each other, even if it means we have to put in all the extra effort to keep our relationship strong.

When we were younger, we didn't understand that. We didn't fully grasp what would be required of us, so when it became too hard, we gave up, pulled away, shut down. We made assumptions, threw in the towel.

Now though? Now we should know better.

It seems like maybe, for the first time, I can be the one who reminds Bishop of the bigger picture. Maybe, instead of him being the one to chase after me and fix things, I can be the one who helps us figure out what comes next.

"You are the most important person on this earth to me, Bishop Mitchell," I tell him, stepping over to where he's still watching me with an unreadable expression. "I love you. I've always loved you. And I don't think I've ever stopped."

Licking my lips, I take his hands in mine.

"But this is not the solution to your problem. This dream of yours is a part of what makes you so special. Your dedication and commitment, how you push yourself and never give up—those are part of what make you, you." I shake my head and take his face in my hands. "I believe in you. Don't give up because of whatever this setback is. Please. You have worked too hard and sacrificed too much to let it all go now."

He blinks, watching me for a long moment. For a few beats, I don't know how he'll respond. I wonder if he'll shut down and leave, something I used to do all the time.

But then his shoulders fall, and he draws me in for a kiss. His strong hands brace against my back and hold me close as his lips fuse with mine.

I breathe him in, this man I've loved since I was barely old enough to understand what it meant, and I know without a doubt he will never let me go again.

After a few moments—and a kiss that gets a little more heated than is entirely appropriate on school grounds—we pull back.

Bishop's eyes search mine, his lips tilting up at the sides. "You love me, huh?"

I smirk then shake my head. "Yeah. So?"

"Well, I love you, too," he tells me, his voice gruff, thick with emotion. "I love you more than I knew it was possible to love someone. I hope you know that."

I nod. "I do know that. I can feel it. In everything you do."

He yanks me back in, this time for a hug. It's a long embrace where we just hold each other and enjoy the beauty of this moment, of knowing how we feel about each other, of having the freedom to speak it out loud.

"So…I guess I'm *not* staying in Cedar Point, then," he says, chuckling slightly, his chest rumbling against mine.

I shake my head. "No. You're not." I step back and look at him again. "I hope you know if I thought, for even a second, it was what you really wanted, I would support you."

Bishop nods. "Yeah. I know." He lets out a long sigh. "But you're right. It's not what I want. Not right now, at least."

"So…what *do* you want?"

"You."

I grin. "Well, that's a given. But what *else* do you want?"

He thinks it over for a second, glancing around the room. "I honestly haven't thought about it. I mean, my goal was always to make it to the draft, but…I don't think I ever thought about what would happen next."

"Well, then why don't we sit down and talk about it."

He laughs. "You wanna sit down and talk about baseball with me?"

I shrug. "It's important to you. I want to hear everything you want to share. Besides, it's not just about baseball. We're going to talk about the future, and I have every intention of being there for that."

At that, Bishop smiles, and I know everything is going to be okay.

We spend the next few days talking about what Bishop wants going forward. At Cedar Cider. At The Mitch. On his couch. In bed.

I remember us talking very lightly about his future when we were in high school, and it was always vague, broad, sweeping statements about college ball and the draft. When you're a kid trying to figure out what's to come, it makes sense that you don't have a lot of specifics. You don't know all the possibilities. You don't know enough to know what to dream about.

Now, a few years later, Bishop and I have sufficient life experience to be more specific. This also has the unintended but surprisingly lovely effect of prompting us to talk about *us* in the future as well: the fact that we see ourselves being together forever, our willingness to do whatever it takes to make things work.

But the most surprising part—which isn't at all surprising, actually—is when Bishop flips the conversation, forcing me to talk about my future, too.

"Your dreams are just as important," he says as we sit side by side at The Mitch, sipping beers. "If this is a future plan, it can't just be mine. It needs to be ours."

I've never swooned so hard.

"How long could it take for Richard to find you a new team?"

We're lying in bed, staring up at the ceiling in my bedroom in a post-coital haze. After his declaration about my dreams at

The Mitch, I got the check and dragged him right home to show him my appreciation. With how appreciative I was, let's just say I'm glad Leah is out tonight on another date with Roy.

Earlier today, Bishop called his agent and talked for about an hour, letting him know exactly what he wanted and what he was willing to do to get it. It was sexy, listening to that conversation.

Now, having finally talked everything through, he's just playing the waiting game until a spot opens up on a roster, until a team wants him, or until there's an open tryout somewhere that fits his criteria.

"I mean, it could be tomorrow, or it could never happen," he says, squeezing my hand. "That's the thing with chasing this dream. You never know when a break might come."

I turn on my side, propping my head up on one hand and using my other to stroke gently along his abs. The muscles bunch and shift as I touch him, and I smile softly.

"I meant what I said yesterday," I tell him, turning to look him in the eye. "I'm with you, no matter what. And I promise never to pull away again."

Bishop surprises me then, shaking his head. "You can't promise that, Gabi."

My brow furrows. "Why not?"

"Because we can't promise we won't ever revert to old habits, you know?" He turns on his side as well and rests a hand on my hip. "Sometimes you'll pull away. That's just part of who you are. But I can promise I'll do what I know I'm good at, which is chasing you down until we figure things out."

I chuckle and roll my eyes. "You make it sound like you're always fixing things and I'm always screwing it up."

Bishop shakes his head again. "No way. I have plenty of my

own shit. Like…" He pauses for a second. "You're really good about thinking things all the way through, and I'm too quick to make rash decisions. You know?"

"So…I'm the one who will get us to think about things, and you'll be the one who gets us to talk about them?"

He grins. "Sounds like a match made in heaven."

I hum, liking the way it sounds. Bishop leans in and kisses me, his tongue dipping into my mouth and tangling with mine in a way that sends shivers down to my toes. It feels wild, knowing this is the man I'll be kissing for the rest of my life. We might not be married, or even engaged, but I have that much faith in us.

In what we want.

In where we're going.

In who we will become.

And that feeling—that knowing—settles something restless in my heart.

chapter twenty-seven
bishop

I stomp the snow off my feet as I enter Ugly Mug, the wet liquid dropping to the mats resting on the ground just inside the door.

The storm that hit Cedar Point a few days ago knocked out some powerlines and kept people at home for three full days. Thankfully, most of the main road finally got plowed yesterday, meaning I can grab a much-needed cup of coffee in town instead of drinking the dark muck my parents have been making since, if I had to guess based on the age of the can it comes in, probably the 1800s.

Unfortunately, it looks like everyone else had the exact same idea, because there are at least fifteen people in line ahead of me, and when I finally make it to the counter, I find out they're out of pretty much everything I like except for drip coffee, so I order a large one of those. Once I've added cream and sugar, I pop the lid back on and head over to an empty table, knowing I want to take my time after the harrowing drive from the house.

Almost as soon as I sit down, I spot a familiar face seated at the table across from me.

"Hey, Coach G!" I say, pushing out of my chair and crossing over to where he sits. "Mind if I sit with you?"

My old baseball coach gives me a surly nod as I take a seat. "Good to see you, Bishop. Heard you've been in town because of an injury."

Chuckling, I nod, rolling up my sleeve to show him the tiny scar left over from surgery.

"Wrist and three fingers. But I'm mostly feeling back to normal now."

He hums. "You're lucky."

I nod again, glancing back at my wrist as I rotate it around. "That I am. I had an amazing surgeon, and I followed the rehab plan to the letter."

Coach G barks a laugh. "Color me shocked," he says. "You always struggled to follow directions when you were younger."

"Well, we all grow up at some point, I guess."

"You've also been helping Rush out with the team, huh?"

I lean back in my chair, grinning at how much he seems to be paying attention to what I'm doing these days.

"Those kids giving you a hard time?"

"Most of them are pretty great," I reply, holding my coffee between both hands. "But there's one who might give me more shit than I'd like."

Coach G smirks. "You have a little Bishop, then?"

Shaking my head, I narrow my eyes playfully. "Was I really that difficult? I know I wasn't *easy*, but…I always thought I was at least fun, even if I did get on your bad side now and again."

He waves a hand at me. "You weren't so bad, and you were never 'on my bad side'. But sometimes you want a kid to take things seriously when they just want to joke around." He shrugs. "I'm sure you've seen how that can be, helping out."

I twist my lips, knowing he's right. "Well, now that I know all the shit you had to deal with, I guess I'll take this chance to say...I appreciate you and all you taught me back then. Even if I made teaching me more difficult than it needed to be."

At my words, he gives me a full smile. "You know, most coaches wait their entire lives to hear that from their favorite player, if they ever get to hear it at all." He reaches out and pats my hand. "Thank you, son."

Surprise hits me square in the chest at his words. Part of me thinks I misheard him, considering how exasperated he always seemed with me back in the day. "I was your favorite?"

His eyes narrow. "Don't you tell a single soul I said that. I don't want my other players to feel bad."

"Ah, so *that's* the gig. You tell all the players they're your favorite and then swear them to secrecy."

He grins. "That's actually a great idea."

I take another sip of my coffee then wrap my hands around my cup again. "Did you ever wonder if I was worth helping? I mean, did you ever think...man, this kid is just too much to deal with?"

Coach G shakes his head. "Never. I always knew you had it in you, knew you could do great things." He shrugs, his eyes assessing. "It's never 'not worth it' to give someone your time and effort, Bishop. So if you're thinking about this...boy, the one giving you a hard time? Let me be the first to tell you: it will make a difference, I guarantee it."

When I leave Ugly Mug a little while later—after Coach G and I do a true catching up about life and all things baseball—I find myself turning in the opposite direction of where I parked my car. I walk a few blocks over and then down the stretch of road that leads to Justin's apartment complex.

Things between us have been less tense over the past few weeks as spring training has begun. He seems to loathe me less and listen to me more, and I appreciate that. Apparently, something I did or said on Thanksgiving actually stuck and made a difference. What it was, I can't be sure. What I *do* know, I learned from Gabi back when she was dealing with the darkest of her own demons. Sometimes, it's not about doing or saying the right thing in the right moment. It's just about showing up, day after day, proving you care enough to be there.

I approach the first-floor unit I saw Justin enter back in November and knock a few times then tuck my hands into my pockets. Only a few beats pass before the door swings open, Justin looking at me suspiciously from inside the apartment.

"What are you doing here?" he asks.

I grin. "Just wanted to stop by, make sure you guys were okay with the storm and everything."

Before Justin can answer, I hear a woman's voice call out, "Shut the door. It's freezing."

Surprisingly, instead of telling me to go away and shutting the door in my face, Justin slips his feet into a pair of boots and steps out, closing the door behind him.

"Thanks for checking in," he tells me. "Really. I appreciate it. But we're okay. Most of the houses on this end of the lake didn't get hit by the power outage, so we were good."

I nod. "Glad to hear that." Pausing, I consider my words for a beat—the ones I planned out on my walk over—wanting to make sure I say them right. "Look, Justin...I'm not sure how long I'll be in town for. Helping with the team, I mean, and I just wanted to let you know I have really enjoyed getting to know you a little bit."

Justin grins. "You're full of shit."

I laugh, my head falling back as I do. When I look at Justin again, he's still smiling.

"I'm not."

"You are. You *so* are. I've annoyed the hell out of you since day one." His smile dims slightly. "Even if it wasn't intentional."

Laughing again, I poke him in the chest. "*Now* who's full of shit."

"I mean it," he tells me, his lips twisting to the side. "I wasn't trying to be a jerk, I just...I don't know."

I shake my head. "You're not a jerk, Justin. You're young and you're figuring things out. Life is hard sometimes; I don't doubt you know that. But as you get older, you have to decide how you want to deal with your anger and your disappointment, whether you want to lash out at the people around you or let them help you."

Justin crosses his arms and stares out at the recently-plowed parking lot behind me, the white of the snow bright enough that his eyes are narrowed.

"And I'm not just talking about baseball, either. College is around the corner, and you're going to have at least one asshole teacher and you'll probably date and make new friends. Decide *now* who you want to be then. The guy who throws his bat when he's angry, the one who thinks he's better than everyone else...or someone who can roll with the punches."

He takes a deep breath and lets it out, long and slow, then nods. "Yeah."

It's all he says in response, but I'll take it.

Justin shakes his arms out then returns his eyes to mine. "Look, I'm sure you came over to like...pep-talk me or whatever.

But do you wanna come in and play FIFA or something?"

I blink, surprised by his offer. "You into soccer?"

He shrugs. "Kind of."

"Get ready to get your ass kicked, kid."

At that, Justin laughs, pushing his front door open and leading me inside. "Sure, old man."

By the time I make it home a few hours later, I'm just as exhausted by the drive back as I was driving *in*to town, and I collapse on the couch. After lying there for a few minutes, I dig my phone out of my pocket and call Gabi.

"If you're calling for more phone sex, the answer is yes."

I laugh. "Well, that is quite the hello."

We were each in our own homes when the snow began to fall, so we were snowed in separately. Let me just say that watching Gabi strip for me over the phone was quite the experience and one I hope to repeat sometime in the future.

"But no, that's not why I called. I'm pretty sure my family wouldn't appreciate me talking dirty to you in the living room."

"You would be correct!"

I take a deep breath in surprise, glancing over the couch and catching my sister's retreating form as she heads into the kitchen.

"Was that Bellamy?"

I chuckle. "That was Bellamy."

Gabi groans, but I can hear her smile through the phone when she speaks again. "How was coffee?"

"It was good. Ran into Coach G."

"Really? How's he doing? I feel like I haven't seen him around lately."

"He's good. Still living over off Pineview, just doesn't go into town much anymore."

Gabi hums. "It was a good chat, though?"

"It was, yeah. It was good catching up. He told me I was his favorite player."

She scoffs. "I bet he says that to everyone."

"That's what I said!"

We both laugh, and I settle back into the couch, loving the sound of her giggling into the phone.

"I stopped by Justin's house on my way home."

I can practically hear her eyebrows rising through the phone. "And how did that go?"

I tell her about our conversation, how he invited me in to play FIFA, meeting his mom. It was a surprisingly chill way to spend part of my day, and that tenseness that is always present in Justin was absent by the time I left.

"Sounds like you might be getting through to him?" she asks.

"Maybe," I say, wondering the same thing myself.

We're silent for a beat before I change direction, wanting to hear how things are on her end.

"How are things over at Casa de Ventura? How are things going with the plans for the new workshop?"

Gabi sighs. "I don't know. Good, I guess."

"That was the least convincing response I've ever heard."

"Okay, well…it's average. It's fine. I think I've just been so excited that now it being a reality feels weird. Like I'm not sure what I actually want."

I set my phone on my chest and switch it to speaker.

"What does Nick say?" I ask, referring to the guy she's using for the project.

Nick did all the major construction on Cedar Cider and handled the rebuild of the grocery store when it caught on fire. I heard from Rusty that he's the best guy in town to trust with an important project, so I'm glad Gabi's decided to work with him.

She sighs again. "He says I can do whatever I want."

Chuckling, I shake my head. "You say that like it's a bad thing."

"Well, it's not bad, but it's also not helpful at all."

"You don't need that Nick guy. If you're looking for help, I'll do anything you ask," I tease.

"Oh *will* you?" she teases right back.

"You doubt me?"

Gabi laughs. "Not in the slightest."

We talk a bit longer before getting off the phone, promising to connect again later this evening when we have a bit more privacy. When I head into the kitchen looking for a snack, I find a concerned-looking Bellamy sitting at the island, staring at her phone.

"Everything okay?" I ask, resting my arms on the counter.

She opens her mouth then closes it again. Then she shakes her head. "Have you talked to Busy lately?"

A sense of foreboding hits me at her question. I haven't spoken with Busy since Thanksgiving, since that conversation that felt so weird and unlike my sister. She didn't come home for Christmas either, letting us all know she'd made plans with some friends to go to Mexico and enjoy warmer weather. My mom was crushed.

"We've texted a few times," I reply. "But she hasn't been answering my calls. She always seems to have some excuse. Why?"

Bellamy glances at her phone again and types out another message, sending it before returning her attention to me.

"I was supposed to go visit her next weekend, and she canceled. Said she has too much going on with school and work to have any visitors."

I shake my head. "What is going on with her? I'm starting to get really worried that something's wrong."

Bellamy rests her chin on her hand and looks out the window, out at the snowy expanse stretching along the back yard and down to the water.

"I am too."

I bring up my worries about Busy to Gabi the next day as we're lounging at her place, listening to a new record we got from The Vault last week.

"I mean, what could be going on that would make her want to avoid us?" I ask, voicing the question out loud for the first time even though I've thought it to myself more than once. "We are the people who love her the most."

"Maybe that's why," Gabi says.

I raise an eyebrow at where she sits on the other end of the couch, her body stretched long, her feet pressed against my hip.

"Maybe what's why?"

"You're the people who love her the most," she says, repeating my words. "Maybe whatever is wrong, she's afraid she'll let you all down."

Sighing, I tilt my head back and stare at the ceiling, my chest heavy with the weight of the unknowns. It's unlike my sister to hide from her family. Boyd and Briar are the more quiet, reclusive types, and Bellamy is the people pleaser. Busy and I are bowling balls—bright and loud and unapologetically ourselves—so to have her withdraw feels...wrong.

I lift my phone and quickly shoot off a text.

Bishop: Hey. Just missing you.

Then I drop the phone onto my chest and return to staring at the ceiling. It's the only thing I say, because it feels like the only thing that matters. I guess I just have to hope whatever is going on, Busy will remember we're here for her. All of us, no matter what.

An incoming call has me raising my phone again quickly, hope filling my chest that my sister is calling me after nearly two months of not talking. I'm pretty sure my heart stops when I see who it is.

"It's my agent."

Gabi sits up. "What?"

I blink a few times. "My agent's calling me."

She scrambles up so she's on her knees, and she takes my face between her hands. "I love you, and you're amazing. No matter what he says."

Then she presses her lips to mine quickly before pulling back and watching as I accept Richard's call, putting it on speaker. "Hey."

"Bishop! How are you, bud?"

I roll my eyes. "Doing good. We've been snowed in for a few

303

days, so…just keeping warm."

"Well, I have some news for you that will hopefully warm you up quite a bit."

I glance at Gabi, her eyes wide and her lips tilted up in a smile.

"Yeah, just…gimme a sec, okay?"

I put the call on mute and then push up off the couch. I pace the length of her living room a few times and stretch my back before I take a seat again, resting my elbows on my knees and holding the phone in front of me. Waiting…waiting with bated breath and a little bit of nausea.

This is good, right? This has to be good.

I exhale heavily, take Gabi's hand in mine, and unmute myself.

"Alright, hit me."

chapter twenty-eight
gabi

The next two weeks fly by faster than I could ever expect, faster than I would ever want. And then, suddenly, it's the night before Bishop leaves Cedar Point to join his new Triple-A team, the Carolina Blues.

His family had a going-away party for him this evening at Cedar Cider, and just about everyone in town showed up to wish him well and give him a proper sendoff. Now, it's the middle of the night, and we're tucked away in his bed, snuggled together under the covers. A small part of me wishes we could stay here forever, just the two of us, wishes he didn't have such big dreams that will always result in him leaving.

But my heart knows the truth. The Bishop I love wouldn't be the same without those big dreams, the ones that give him purpose and joy. So rather than focusing on the sadness of him leaving, I decide to put my attention on all the excitement to come.

Bishop kisses the back of my neck, his breath warm. I sigh,

shifting my head to the side, wanting him to continue. Instead, he rolls me onto my back and comes over me, his strong body hovering over mine as he kisses me.

It's a slow, lazy kiss, as if we have all the time in the world, as if he's not leaving in just a few hours to fly to the other side of the country. My emotions begin to bubble up, and I wrap my arms around him, pulling him as close as I can, my tongue tangling wildly with his.

I can feel him intentionally keeping this moment slow. Refusing to hurry. Not giving in to the suddenly frantic way I need him. No, Bishop stays strong and slow and steadfast, in the way he kisses my lips, the way he touches my body, how he moves as he slides inside of me. He still hits all those spots only he can seem to reach, but he seems unconcerned with the way the clock is quickly running out. His hips thrust in a slow, measured rhythm, his cock stroking between my walls and gliding into my depths over and over and over.

Until I can hardly breathe.

Until I am bursting at the seams.

But then he just keeps me there, his eyes on mine, refusing to send us over.

"Bishop," I whisper, my chest heaving, my entire body throbbing with need. "Bishop, please." I claw at his back, my desperation and desire leaking out of me unbidden.

But still, he stays steady. Still, he fucks into me like he never plans to stop.

"I don't want to leave you," he finally whispers.

That's when I notice his eyes are glassy, his jaw tense.

"I don't ever want to be apart from you," he continues, thrusting into me again and then halting his movements. "I love you more than anything, Gabi. *Anything.*"

I know what he's telling me, what he's saying even though he might not be using the exact words. If it came down to a choice between me and baseball, he would choose me.

It's something I already believed in my heart, but still, there's scar tissue in my chest that heals over at hearing it from his mouth. When you've lived your entire life feeling like the people who were supposed to love you saw you as second best, it's hard to believe you could ever be the most important priority to anyone. That fear creates a scar that twists and pulls, an ever-present reminder of just how little you were loved.

So Bishop's words…they mean far more than I was expecting them to.

"You're everything to me," I say, turning my head and pressing my lips to his wrist.

He begins to move again, his hips withdrawing and then snapping forward again, this time with more roughness than before.

"You're mine, Gabi," he tells me, his voice a growl.

"And you're mine," I respond.

"Forever. There's no going back."

"Never," I pant.

His pace picks up, our hips colliding, his dick crashing into that spot deep within me, bringing me right back to the precipice in an instant.

"My Gabi," he says, his thumb stroking my lips.

"Your Gabi," I repeat back.

I've always been his. Always. There might have been a time when we were apart, but we were fools to ever believe we didn't belong together, to think we weren't made for each other, molded out of the same clay.

The tightness in my spine becomes too much, and I splinter,

my entire soul breaking into bits, the pleasure spiraling through me until I can barely handle it. I collapse beneath him, a puddle of nothing. Bishop kisses my neck as he follows me over, sucking at my skin and groaning, pulsing hot inside me, and then he collapses as well.

We lie like that for long moments, long hours, who knows. All I know for sure is nothing feels like being in his arms, and nothing ever will.

"I'll see you in six weeks," I say, my head tilted back as I look up into Bishop's eyes.

"Six weeks. For the first game of the season."

I nod. "It's going to be amazing, and I can't wait."

"I can't either."

Bishop presses his lips to mine, one hand stroking through my hair, the other holding me close. I don't want him to go. Don't want to be without him. Don't want us to ever be apart again. Reminding myself of all the important reasons he needs to leave is becoming harder now that his SUV is loaded and we're standing in his driveway, saying goodbye.

He leans back, his hand coming to stroke my cheek then down my jaw to my chin.

"I…have something…for you," he says, licking his lips then taking a step back as he tugs out his wallet.

My eyes narrow as he retrieves a small square of lined notebook paper then unfolds it twice. It's no bigger than a post card, but when I see it, my heart flies into my throat, robbing me of words.

"How do you have that?" I ask.

I take the tattered slip of paper from his hand, the edges worn and slightly discolored, sure I must be misunderstanding what I'm seeing.

"It was sitting on your desk one day, and I took it. I wanted it and thought you'd be embarrassed if you knew I saw it."

He's right. Back then, when I drew this, I would have died rather than let him see it. But seeing it now…knowing he's had it all these years, knowing he kept it? Even when we weren't together? I'm having a hard time putting into words what it means to me.

It's a drawing of our hands, which is fairly innocuous. The embarrassing part is the infinity symbol I drew on my wrist, right in the spot Bishop always kisses, and the words "Gabi and Bishop Forever" written in a loopy scrawl at the bottom.

It's a simple sketch—far from my best—but I felt it so deeply when I drew it, when I scribbled those words so many years ago. And now, knowing what we've been through, having found each other again…well, it's even more profound.

"I could never bring myself to get rid of it," he tells me, shaking his head. "Something inside me just…knew I would regret it. Knew it was too important to just chuck in the trash."

"So it's been in your wallet this whole time?" I ask, still in disbelief.

He nods. "Yeah."

I fold the little drawing back up carefully then wrap my arms around his shoulders, pulling his big, strong body against mine.

"I love you," I whisper. "I've always loved you, and you've

been holding on to proof this whole time?" I laugh as I lean back and place my hands on either side of his face. "What am I going to do with you?"

He smirks and rests his forehead against mine. "That's easy. You're going to love me forever, and I'm going to do the same."

I mope around for a few days after Bishop leaves Cedar Point, though I eventually get my ass back into my workshop and return my attention to the projects still waiting on me. They prove to be exactly the distraction I need, and I spend the next two weeks nose down, only taking breaks for food, sleep, and phone calls with Bishop.

He spent a few nights at a hotel before moving into a one-bedroom apartment, thanks to the nicer salary the Carolina Blues offered him, and then used the week remaining before spring training to get some furniture and explore the area. Bishop also met up with some of the guys from his new team and has had nothing but great things to say about them and his new coaches.

I can tell by the sound of his voice that he's happy, and I love that for him, but I miss him, too. More than I ever thought was possible. I spend time with Nicole, and I teach my pottery class, and I work in my workshop. I hang out with Leah and listen to music.

And I daydream, about what it might be like to leave Cedar Point.

For years, I believed this would be the only place I'd ever live apart from college. I believed I was destined to be here forever, to raise a family here, grow old here, but maybe I was wrong. Maybe there's a different life I hadn't ever pictured for myself that brings just as much happiness. Just as much joy. Just as much love.

Or I guess…even more love, because I would be with Bishop. And maybe that's the place I want to be. Maybe that means more than living in the place I always thought would be my home for the rest of my life.

"Why did you move to Cedar Point?" I ask Leah one day, about three weeks after Bishop moves away.

We're sitting side by side on the couch as she works on a small project and I flip mindlessly through a trashy magazine Nicole left behind yesterday. Leah glances at me, her hands pausing their movements, and then her forehead crinkles as she returns to her work.

"I wanted to live in a small town, near water, in the mountains." She shrugs, her eyes on where her hands make quick knots. "And…there was a guy."

My eyebrows rise. "You followed a guy to Cedar Point?" I ask, unable to hide my shock. "Ms. I Would Never Compromise What I Want for a Man?"

Her lips purse, and she narrows her gaze at me only briefly before looking back at her own hands. "I did not *follow* a guy here. Vick and I picked Cedar Point together." Then she shakes her head. "But when things didn't work out, he left and I stayed. He wasn't ever really happy here. Vick liked the *idea* of small-town life, but not the reality."

"And you stayed because…"

"Because I *was* happy. I had almost everything I wanted.

311

A home, my work, a social life, the breathtaking nature at my doorstep." She pauses. "And then you came along, and I truly had everything."

My throat grows tight at her words.

I've always wondered if I screwed up Leah's life, if me being dropped on her doorstep meant all her plans had been ruined, though she never said anything like that or even implied it. My aunt has been an incredible mother, an incredible sister, an incredible friend.

But hearing her say that…it makes the reality of what I'm considering that much harder.

Leah turns then, giving me a watery smile. "You're leaving, aren't you."

Her words are a statement because she already knows, and when I nod, she nods too, tears spilling forth from her eyes.

I abandon the magazine and scoot over, wrapping my arms around the woman who raised me, who sacrificed everything to be everything for me. We just hold each other for a while, enjoying the closeness and the love we share, the love we'll *always* share.

Leah pats me on the arm then turns her head to look at me, her eyes examining my face.

"All I know is he better treat you like a fucking queen."

At that, I smile.

"He will."

Leah nods. "I know."

312

I spend the next few weeks making my plans in secret, deciding I want to surprise Bishop rather than tell him what I'm doing. In the past, younger Gabi would have done the same thing, but she would have done so because she didn't want to have the conversation. Now, it's because I don't want Bishop to tell me no.

I know him. I know him better than anyone, and if I tell him I'm planning to leave Cedar Point to 'follow him', he'll tell me not to. He doesn't want me to have to sacrifice what *I* want for what *he* wants, but that's not what I'm doing. Not at all. And I know I'll need to tell him in person for him to believe me.

So, I make my plans. I find a ceramic studio that rents workspaces a few miles away from Bishop's apartment. I begin to pack. I wrap up my projects and notify my clients that I'm taking a temporary break from work.

Yesterday, Leah and I filled a moving van, and she began her drive. This morning, I got on a plane and flew across the country, intending to move to a small town I've never been to before.

I can't remember ever being so nervous and so excited at the same time.

I glance down at my phone as I pull to a stop in the parking lot outside Bishop's.

Nicole: Miss you already. His dick better be worth it.

Laughing, I chuck my phone into my purse. Leave it to my best friend to make it about sex.

I enter the lobby and head up to the fourth floor then walk down a long hallway toward the end, until I reach unit 42. Bishop told me it felt lucky because it was Jackie Robinson's number, and I smile at that thought as I knock on the door.

"Just a second!" I hear from the other side.

Nerves race through me, and I let out a long, slow breath.

When the door opens, Bishop blinks in surprise. I barely give him a moment to try to figure out what's going on before I'm launching myself at him, pressing my lips to his.

"What are you doing here?" he asks, holding me tightly against his chest. "When we talked this morning, you said you were getting coffee with Nicole."

I pull back, unable to hide the smile stretching wide across my face. "It was a complete lie. I was hiding in the shitty coffee place at the airport trying to make sure you couldn't hear the airline announcements."

He chuckles then presses his lips against mine again, backing us into the apartment and kicking the door closed.

"God, I'm so glad to see you," he says. "I've missed you."

"I've missed you too."

"I'm sorry I've been so busy."

I pull back, grinning mischievously. "I know how you can make it up to me."

Twenty minutes later, we collapse on the couch, each of us panting. I feel like I could float away on a cloud, but Bishop looks only mildly satiated. Jacking in the shower almost every morning and trying to fit in the odd phone sex session here and there has been rough on him, I'm sure.

He leans over and kisses me then hops up, tugs on his shorts, and disappears into what I'm assuming is a bedroom, returning a beat later with a blanket that he wraps me in snugly before tucking me in against his side.

"I can't believe you're here," he says, pressing his lips against my forehead. "I thought you weren't coming for another two weeks."

We originally decided I'd come out to visit for the first few games of the season, before Bishop and his team start traveling nearly every other week. Apparently spring training is pretty grueling, so we agreed it would be better for me to wait until the official season had begun so we could enjoy that first week. He'd be playing, sure, but we'd still get time together here.

Now, though, Bishop is about to find out things are going to be completely different than we planned.

"Well, that was what we talked about...originally," I tell him, a bit of nervousness beginning to filter in.

"So what's the plan now?" He smiles at me. "How long are you staying?"

I lick my lips. "Well...technically...that's up to your coach."

His brow furrows. "What do you mean?"

"I mean...I'm staying here until you leave, until you get traded or called up or..." I trail off and shrug a shoulder.

Bishop sits up straight, surprise evident in every line of his face. "You mean..."

"I *mean*..." I continue, sitting up as well and wrapping my arms around his neck. "I'm moving. Here. So I hope you have a king size bed."

He blinks, almost like he's waiting for the rest of the information.

"What about work?" he asks. "And your studio? I thought you were moving forward with Nick on plans to break ground in like...a month?"

I shake my head. "Nothing about that ever felt right," I tell him. "I love doing pottery, but I can set up shop anywhere. I've already rented a space at a studio that's about twenty minutes away, and I can keep doing my commissioned work and selling pieces. All my stuff is in a truck Leah's driving out here as we speak."

His eyes widen. "I can't let you do this, Gabi. What about that whole conversation we had in your classroom? About not giving up your dream for the other person?"

"I'm *not* giving up my dream, Bishop. I wouldn't let you give up on baseball just to stay in town with me, but this is different."

"How?"

"Because this isn't me giving up on what *I* want," I tell him. "It's me finding a way for us to both have what we want, without being thousands of miles apart."

I watch him as he watches me right back, almost like he can't believe I'm here, can't believe it's true. But it is.

"I love you, Bishop," I say. "And when I think about my future, it's you. It's us. It's forever, and I want that forever to begin now."

He pulls me in and presses his lips to mine again.

"I can't believe you're here," he whispers, his hands on my face, our foreheads touching.

"I can," I reply, bumping my nose gently against his. "I only wanted to stay in Cedar Point because it was the only place I ever felt at home. But then I realized the truth."

"What truth?"

I grin. "The place I really feel at home is with you."

Bishop watches me for a long moment, his smile growing wider. Then he kisses me again, briefly, before tugging us both to our feet and beginning to walk me around the apartment, showing me our new home.

It feels magical. Wonderful. Special in a way I can't describe.

And for the first time in my entire life, the voice inside me that wondered if I'd ever find somewhere to truly belong finally quiets.

epilogue
bishop

I come to a stop in a parking stall near the entrance, and we sit together in silence, just staring at the stadium where it looms before us.

"Are you ready?" Gabi asks.

I snort. "Is anyone ever truly ready for something like this?"

The nerves are stronger than I was expecting, but I've heard that's normal. I assumed I'd be coming into this with the kind of confidence I normally bring to anything I take on. Instead, I'm drawing in long breaths, trying to steady my racing heart.

It's my first game playing for the Raleigh Rush. It's been three long years of busting my ass at the Triple-A level, giving everything I have and more to the Carolina Blues. Then, earlier this week, I got the call. They had a permanent space on their 40-man roster, and they wanted me. Cue excitement and freaking out and telling all my family and friends and packing to travel. Gabi and I grabbed all the essentials and flew in yesterday, and the team will be arranging for a moving company to relocate us once we find a place in town.

It all happened faster than I thought it would, faster than I ever thought it *could*, and now I'm here, sitting outside the park, gearing up for my major league debut.

It's really happening.

"Of course it's really happening," Gabi says.

I look at her, realizing I said it out loud.

"It's happening because of all the work you put in to get here. Because you never, ever gave up, even when it got hard." She squeezes my hand, a smile stretching across her face. "And because you're fucking *Bam*, and all these guys are going to know who Bam is after tonight."

My eyes search hers, soaking in her confidence and making it my own. Nobody has believed in me more than my Gabi. For the past three years, she has been almost relentless in her support of me and this dream. Coming to games, cheering me on, talking shop. When we were kids, she listened when I talked about baseball, but I don't think she really got the sport. Now, it feels like she knows more than some of the guys who were on my team. It's been amazing.

"What time is everyone showing up?" I ask, glancing at my watch.

"I told your mom I'd be leading the caravan from the hotel at 5:30."

I nod. My entire family flew in for the game. I planned to just grab them whatever seats were available, but apparently there's a guy whose entire job is to provide concierge service to players' guests. The whole group of them—my parents, all my siblings and their partners, my niece, Junie Bee, and a few friends from Cedar Point—will be sitting in a section that comes with food and drinks and a great view of home plate.

"And she also told me to tell you she flew out a surprise as well."

Grinning, I shake my head. "What does that mean?"

She shrugs. "Who knows? But Patty's always a little sneaky like that, isn't she?"

I laugh. "I guess she is."

It's funny hearing Gabi call my mom by her first name. All growing up, she always used Mrs. Mitchell, but about six months after we started dating again, Mom decided to try her hand at a pottery class at the community center and called Gabi to ask about it. Mom really took a liking to it, and now the two of them talk on a regular basis. They're friends, which is both funny and amazing.

Mentoring my mom from afar was helpful to Gabi as she transitioned to her new studio space once she moved out to North Carolina. She enjoyed the new place—it had huge windows overlooking a park and it was great for her to network with other artists in the area—but she missed teaching ceramics a lot more than she expected to, so my mom became her new student.

Not that she would have the time for teaching these days. Working in a space with other creators stoked a new fire in Gabi, and her business really took off. She's had her work featured in magazines and was approached recently about starting a line to feature in a major retailer. It's incredible to see how far she has come. I couldn't be more proud. It'll be exciting to see how she transitions again now that we're going to be in the Raleigh area, a much larger city with so many more resources and opportunities.

"I probably need to head in soon," I finally say, letting out another long breath then taking Gabi's hand in mine, both of them resting against the center console. "But I'll see you in a little bit?"

She smiles. "I wouldn't miss it for the world."

My thumb strokes against the ring on her fourth finger, the one I slipped onto her hand as we got married in a small ceremony back in Cedar Point last spring. It had snowed the night before, layering the ground with a beautiful white sheet that didn't melt away until several hours after we exchanged our vows. It was a beautiful day, and it still floors me knowing the most incredible woman in the world agreed to marry me.

We hop out of the car and embrace briefly, then Gabi slides into the driver's seat as I head toward the player's entrance.

"Bishop!" she shouts.

I turn, laughing when I find her holding up her phone, taking my picture.

"Just don't want you to forget this feeling," she calls. "Good luck! I love you!"

Taking a deep breath, I head inside, and then everything is a whirlwind. Somehow, five hours pass in a flash, filled with stretching, batting practice, and other muscle warmups then hanging out with the other guys before we head out onto the field.

I barely hear the announcer as he says his spiel, my ears overwhelmed by the sound of the crowd. When I step out of the dugout, I turn, scanning the section I was told everyone would be sitting in. Sure enough, there they are. My eyes track over each person, over smiling face after smiling face—including Leah and Roy, who stand and wave with far more enthusiasm than I'm expecting—until I see someone I'm not expecting.

Justin. This must be Mom's surprise.

He puts his hands on either side of his face and cheers then claps his hands.

We've grown close over the past few years, even though I moved away. We talk a few times a month and text regularly, and he keeps me updated on how things are going at school. He got a full ride to Whitney College to play for the baseball team, like I did. I'm incredibly proud.

More than that, some of his rougher edges seem to have lost a bit of their sharpness. He's still cocky as hell—he wouldn't be Justin if he wasn't—but he's turning into an amazing, thoughtful young man, and I feel proud to know him.

I wave at my family and friends then wait as Gabi gets out of her seat and jogs down to me.

"Just wanted to say one more time: I love you so much," she tells me from the other side of the net that divides the field from the seats behind home plate. "*So* much."

"Love you, too."

She blows me a kiss, and my eyes fall to the little tattoo on her wrist. The same one I have on mine.

The infinity symbol is a representation of our love, which has made it through everything and come out stronger and deeper on the other side.

Gabi heads back up to her seat, and I wave at everyone again before going back into the dugout, unable to hide my smile. I feel more at peace than I ever realized I could be. I never knew I could feel a love like this, never knew something we felt when we were so young could grow roots this deep.

When I used to imagine my future, the only thing I could see was baseball, that dream of making it to the big time. Nothing could have prepared me for the shift I'd feel once I realized there is so much more to life than just that.

Sure, having that dream is important. It gives a sense of purpose and drive, a challenge. But when I think about what makes me happy, what brings me joy, what fills my life…it's not hitting a ball or running the bases or hearing the roar of the crowd.

It's being with the woman I love. It's holding her tight, hearing her laugh, watching her smile.

As I step out onto the field a while later, walking toward the plate for my first major league at-bat, I turn, gazing into the crowd. When I find Gabi, I kiss my wrist then hold it up over my head, wanting to show her, wanting to show everyone…

…this moment might be amazing, but when I think about my dreams for the future, what I think about is her.

For more stories from Cedar Point and the Mitchell family,
visit my website:

www.jillianliota.com/cedar-point

jillian liota

acknowledgments
from the author

Bishop's story was one I have had swirling in my mind since I first created his character in early 2022, as I wrote *The Trouble with Wanting*. I always knew what his challenge would be, but the journey was created as I wrote. And that journey would not have been as beautiful had it not been for some amazing people:

To the love of my life, my husband, **Danny**. Thank you for supporting me as I tuned out the world to complete this project. Thank you for beta reading, for providing your incredible insight into the human spirit and the art of storytelling (and baseball), and - as always - for inspiring the heart of every hero I write.

To **Julie**. This book is dedicated to you for a reason, girl. You know what I went through to get this completed, and without our writing sprints and our constant check-ins, I'm not sure the book would have come to fruition. I love you, and I'm so thankful we are friends.

To **"What's the Buzz"**, for believing in me and understanding when I disappear for weeks on end.

To **C. Marie** - every book is an opportunity for me to sing your praises, and this one is no different. You're amazing, and I apologize for my incessantly repetitive words :)

To **Kristina**, for looking over all of my pottery notes and making sure I'm not totally getting things wrong. Love you so much!

To **The Jillybeans**, for always rallying behind each project and getting so excited whenever I share news.

To **Grey's Promotions** and **Jen** for helping me get the word out about Bishop and Gabi.

And to every reader who picks this book up: thank you for giving me a chance.

I love you all, and I can't wait to be back in Cedar Point again very soon.

<3 always,
Jillian

If you've loved Cedar Point, make sure you take a trip to Sandalwood! Continue reading for the first two chapters of my steamy single dad, boss/employee romance:

Solo

chapter one

- SOREN -

"Need anything else from me before I take off, boss?"

I turn to look at Ozzy where she leans against the edge of the doorway to my office then return my attention to the liquor order I need to get sent out today.

"You should be letting Jon know you're leaving, not me. He's in charge of the front tonight."

There's a pause before she responds.

"Will do."

When another ten or so seconds go by and she's still standing there, I look at her again, struggling to hide the irritation in my voice.

"What?"

She clears her throat, takes a deep breath, and shakes her head.

"Never mind."

Then she disappears, heading off down the hallway toward the front, likely to tell Jon she's heading home for the evening. I can't help but let out a little sigh of relief.

Ozzy is my newest employee, having only been here about a month, and I've been questioning Jon's decision to hire her since the day she started.

She has no bartending experience, no waitressing experience, no restaurant experience...it's like the guy thought it would be a good idea to hire the least qualified person from the stack of applicants I handed to him.

She's friendly enough and seems to do okay with customers, but just...seems to always be in the way.

I also can't help but notice the way she watches me, her hazel eyes following my movements from across the room—though in all fairness, I only started picking up on it when one of my other waitresses, Tessa, told me Ozzy has a 'crush' on me.

Fuck, what are we, teenagers?

Part of me was flattered, of course, when Tessa shared the conversation the two of them had on Ozzy's first day. I mean, who wouldn't want the attention of a knockout like Ozzy? But she's still struggling to keep up, and I can't help but wonder if maybe she would have fewer issues if she watched me less and listened to directions more.

Besides, I might enjoy the charcuterie board of beautiful women who come through my bar, but I promised myself when I bought the place that crossing the lines with my employees was a nonstarter. Ozzy is...well, I don't know exactly what she is, but she feels like a massive headache and a lot of temptation wrapped into one.

Eventually, I submit my online order to our distributor then head up to the front to relieve Jon so he can take a break.

"Hey there, Solo."

My lips tilt up at the sound of the nickname bar patrons know me by, and I flick my eyes to the blonde sitting halfway down the bar, a smirk hanging on the edge of her lips.

Tossing a hand towel over my shoulder, I head in her direction then brace myself against the bar top and give her a charming smile.

"Back so soon?"

She shrugs a shoulder but eyes me with a coy look that makes it clear she's interested.

"You make a mean vodka cranberry."

I nod my head.

"That what you're hoping for tonight?"

She props her chin on one of her hands then lets her eyes rove up and down my body.

"Among other things."

Biting my lip, I nod again.

"One vodka cran, coming up."

I get started making her drink, tugging out a tall glass and filling it with ice then grabbing the vodka and pouring in two shots. The cranberry is next, and I fill the rest of the glass before garnishing it with a lime.

"Here you go," I say, popping in a straw then setting it on a napkin in front of her. "Anything else?"

She takes a sip then gives me another smile.

"This is all for now."

I bob my head. "I'm gonna make a few more drinks, but I'll be back," I tell her, and I see the way her eyes brighten.

As I stroll to the other end of the bar to fulfill drink orders for a table in the corner, I try to remember her name. McKenna? McKayla? Something like that. She told me yesterday when she came in with a big group of friends who are in town for some sort of trip.

Those friends are nowhere to be seen today, though. She's returned alone, and the way her eyes are devouring me gives off the vibe that she wants to have a little fun with the tattooed bartender while she's on vacation.

I pop the tops off a few Coronas and shove limes into each of the necks, then I place them on a round serving tray at the end of the bar. I flag Tessa to pick up the tray that's heading to table six then turn to head back to where the blonde is still eyeing me.

"So what does a guy like you get up to when he's not working behind the bar?" she asks as her hand absentmindedly stirs her drink.

I shrug and lean back against the counter along the back wall.

"Trouble."

I know I've said the right thing when she bites her lip. That action says she wants me to tease her and take her to bed, then tease her some more.

"Oh yeah? What kind of trouble?"

I step forward then reach out to brace myself against the bar and lean closer to her, close enough that I can smell the faint scent of her fading sunscreen.

"If you wanna find *that* out, you gotta give me your number first."

At that, McKenna leans to her right and snags the black billfold from where another customer paid for their tab. Dragging the pen out, she jots her digits on the little white napkin I gave her with her drink then slides it toward me.

I glance at it on the bar.

McKenzie. That's her name.

"I'm here for two more nights," she tells me. "My guess is they'd be a lot more fun spent with you than my sisters."

My eyebrows rise, remembering the group of ten or so women she came in with yesterday.

"You have a big family," I joke.

She giggles again. "*Sorority* sisters," she clarifies, lifting her hands in what looks remarkably like a gang sign. "Kappa Kappa Gamma! We're on spring break, visiting from Phoenix."

I bob my head, my plans for the evening deflating at the realization that this chick is probably barely old enough to be ordering that drink she has in front of her. It's been a long time since I've forgotten to card someone.

My mind scrambles as I try to come up with an excuse, something that doesn't hurt the girl's feelings but frees me from using the number on that napkin.

Before anything comes to mind, the entry door flies open, the fading sunlight from outside streaming in as a tiny blur races across the room and around the bar with a brilliant smile on her face.

"I found it! I found it! I found it!" her voice repeats over and over until she's just a foot away from me, her eyes bright, the excitement clear in just about every part of her face.

I return her smile, unable to help myself.

"And just what, exactly, did you find?" I ask.

She thrusts a photo in my direction, and as excited as Millie is, I can't help the way my smile dims just slightly at the sight of it.

"The picture of you and mommy," she says, bouncing on her toes and clapping her hands as I appraise her findings.

The aged picture I'm holding is of me and Toni, back when we first met here in the bar, almost ten years ago.

Before I bought the place.

Before she got pregnant with Millie.

Before she left us for the dreams she decided were more important than being a family.

It feels like a time capsule, looking at this thing, allowing myself a moment to remember the way we were together as my fingers touch the faded edges softly.

I clear my throat and try to keep a smile on my face as my daughter rambles on about needing the picture for some sort of family book they're creating at school after they return from spring break.

"…thought I was going to have to draw a picture of mom, but now I have this picture and it's going to be so much better!" she shrieks, her words tumbling one over the other in that way overly excited seven-year-olds do when they have something important to talk about.

"It's going to be *so* much better," I reassure her, handing the photo back and watching as she examines it again, her small fingers holding it like a delicate treasure.

"Can I get a baggie from the kitchen to make sure it stays safe?" she asks, and I nod, watching after her for a long moment as she barrels through the swinging door and through the kitchen, her little voice shouting, "Hi, Marco!" to one of my kitchen staff before she disappears into the pantry on the right where we keep supplies like foil and napkins and, apparently, plastic baggies.

Though, how my kid knows that is beyond me.

I shake my head and turn around, preparing to let *McKenzie* know I won't be calling her since I will most likely have a project to help my daughter with—a lie, but one that probably won't hurt her feelings—only to freeze when I see she's gone.

Glancing around, I wonder if maybe she went to use the bathroom or something, but then I spot two things that confirm she's not coming back.

One is the damp ten-dollar bill under her half-empty drink, and two is the fact that the napkin with her name and number is nowhere to be seen.

I chuckle to myself then collect the cash and dump the drink before wiping down where the condensation left a pool of water. I guess that was a bullet dodged, even if there is a tiny wound to my ego at the fact she bounced without a word.

I'm not sure if it was the revelation that I'm a father that scared her off or Millie shouting about a picture of me and her mother that drove her away, but ultimately, it doesn't matter.

There will be other nights and other women, hopefully ones who are much older than *McKenzie* and her gaggle of sisters from Kappa Mocha Frappa or whatever it was called.

* * *

"I just didn't think it would be a big deal."

I cross my arms, then think better of it and drop them to my sides, not wanting to be *too* intimidating when I speak to my daughter's babysitter.

"I understand that, Kasey, but I'm clarifying with you now why it *is* a big deal. Millie is only seven. I don't have a problem with you bringing her to see me at the bar when I'm working, but she shouldn't be walking all the way down the street by herself."

And, though I don't add this part out loud, the fact that Kasey *isn't* worried about it makes me concerned about how much attention she's giving Millie during the time the two of them are together.

Sandalwood is a safe little beach town, without question, but she's still a child.

"I'm sorry, Mr. Lock. It won't happen again."

I stare at Kasey for a long minute before I nod, deciding to accept her apology and take her at her word. I mean, I hate to admit it, but I don't have a lot of options when it comes to making sure Millie is taken care of while I'm working. Sure, I'm the owner and I *could* set her up in the back—or hell, even in the front—if I wanted to while I'm working, but I promised myself before I even bought the place that a life of being raised in a bar wasn't going to be what I exposed Millie to.

"Also, just a reminder, I'm taking this whole week off for Millie's spring break, so I won't need you to babysit next weekend."

Kasey bobs her head. "Yeah, I remember." Then she gives me kind of a sheepish look. "And I know it's last minute, but I actually can't babysit tomorrow night. I have a paper due Monday and I'm way behind."

Inwardly, I bristle in irritation. She couldn't have mentioned this earlier?

But I've dealt with babysitters cancelling late before, so I take it in stride. Because, really, it's the only thing I *can* do.

So instead, I just give her a thin smile.

"Okay, I'll figure it out. Good luck with your paper."

"Thanks. Have a good night, Mr. Lock," she tells me, giving a friendly wave before grabbing her backpack and heading out the front door.

I take a deep breath then let out a long sigh as her feet thud softly down the stairs from our second-floor apartment, thankful for a few moments of silence. Crossing the small living room to the kitchen, I snag a bottle of beer from the fridge.

I'm proud of the way I handled that, knowing how angry I was earlier when I realized Millie had come to the bar without Kasey, meaning she walked all the way there from our apartment alone. She could have been snatched off the street. Or hit by a car. Or wandered off to the ocean a block from the bar and drowned.

Thank God she's a levelheaded kid. More levelheaded than Kasey, apparently.

I shake my head and sink down into the leather chair that used to belong to my grandfather, the familiar feel of the cool material and the comforting way it fits my body shape as I settle and lean my head back giving me a moment of reprieve.

Clearly, I need to make some changes when it comes to Millie's daycare situation.

Thankfully, my mom helps by watching her on weekdays after school until I get home just before Millie's bedtime, but I'm still struggling to find someone for the weekend nights, like tonight, when I work until after midnight. Kasey has been okay since she started babysitting a few months ago, but if she's letting Millie wander off, especially on Friday and Saturday nights when Sandalwood is a little more chaotic, I'm not sure whether she's the right person for the job.

I sigh and take a swig of my beer. It's definitely something I'll need to think about this week, but thankfully not for a few days at least.

Millie's mom is coming to town for the week our daughter is out of school. Even though Toni is almost entirely focused on her tour, she's not doing a *completely* horrible job at making time here and there for Millie. This will be the third spring break in a row that she has cleared away completely, so I need to at least give her that much credit.

Almost as if my thoughts conjured her into being, my phone pings with a message from Toni, reminding me she'll be here on Sunday afternoon.

I frown. It's unlike her to be so…specific.

I don't doubt that she's coming to town. She's not *that* negligent that she just no-shows her own kid, but she's never been punctual, preferring to be vague so as not to disappoint anyone when she's inevitably late or delayed because of something *super important*.

I flick a message back, letting her know we'll be at the house all day Sunday and to just let me know once she's an hour out.

It's easier that way. If I try to get a specific time from her and then I tell Millie, she'll be waiting by the window, her forehead creased with a worry wrinkle that shouldn't already be on the face of a seven-year-old.

Looking forward to seeing you, Toni responds.

I chew on the inside of my cheek and stare at those words for a long moment before taking another sip from my beer.

She always sends me stuff like that. 'Can't wait to see you' or 'Looking forward to being together again'…and then she gets here and shows me just how much she means it.

It's unspoken that she'll be staying here, at my apartment with Millie. It always is. She'll offer to take the couch, but we both know the blankets and pillow I pull out for her are just a formality. I can't be within a hundred yards of Antonina Crawford and not be sucked in, like a gravitational pull.

I mean, it makes sense considering the history we have between us. The connection we have. The *daughter* we share.

Which is why her visits are always complicated.

I spend months and months putting Toni out of my mind, enjoying life as a bachelor. Well, a bachelor-father. I don't really *date* per se because I'm certain my life with Millie is easier just the two of us than if I tried to introduce any other complications besides her own mother.

I don't ask what she's been up to while she was gone and she doesn't tell me. Neither of us share the things we do while we're apart—another unspoken rule, another way we tiptoe around things instead of addressing them head on.

But then she comes back to town and, like I said...gravity. That familiar pull of how good we are together. The heat between us. The way she feels in my arms.

We both know it's only while she's here, because after a few days or a few weeks, she's gone again, off on her next tour or booking gigs with her band somewhere on the other side of the country as she chases her dream.

A dream that takes her away from us.

From her daughter.

Keeping her on the road almost 50 weeks out of the year.

It's when she leaves that I see the same familiar heartbreaking expression of disappointment on Millie's face that I see on my own when I look in the mirror.

Each time Toni comes to town, I can't help but let my mind wonder if this is it. The sticking point. The time she'll tell me she's done and ready to come back to be with us. To be a mom. A partner. A family.

I wonder if this will be the time when she realizes all the happiness she's looking for has been here, in Sandalwood, all along.

chapter two

- SOREN -

Saturdays at The Lighthouse are always slammed, regardless of the time of year. During the low season, the locals pack in, enjoying the freedom, and during summer or spring break, it's overflowing with visitors and unfamiliar faces.

Part of me loves when I get to see people I know from around town, the conversations a bit more drawn out and friendly, but the baser part of me enjoys the busy season as it means a constant stream of tourists looking to have some fun.

Like the sisters from yesterday, but *after* they've graduated and lived in the real world for a while.

Tonight, though, with my mind clouded by Toni's impending arrival and exhausted by the amount of work I pushed to get done today, finding a hookup is the last thing on my mind. Instead, I'm putting together drinks with only half my normal focus, the rest of my brain imagining what this next week might look like for the three of us.

"I'll have a gin and tonic, neat, and four shots of vodka."

I nod at the brunette on the other side of the bar. "Well or something specific?"

"Well, please," she says, and I spin to grab the right glass-ware.

But when I turn back to the bar, I collide hard with another body, and everything falls out of my hands and to the floor.

"Oh, shit."

My shoulders drop at the sound of Ozzy's voice, and I have to refrain from rolling my eyes as she lowers herself to the ground, trying to collect the broken glass.

"Fuck," I hear her whisper. "I'm so sorry, boss. I didn't mean—"

"Leave it or else you'll—"

Ozzy hisses and yanks her hand back, but not before I spot the long red mark on her palm.

"...cut yourself," I finish, dipping down to grab her under the arm and help her to stand. "Come with me to the back. Jon, can you get someone to clean up this glass, please?"

I don't even wait to see if he's heard me, instead tugging Ozzy with me quickly through the kitchen and to the break room in the back where we keep the first aid kit.

"I'm sorry," Ozzy says. "It was an accident."

I don't say anything, instead focusing on finding the kit that's tucked somewhere in the metal cabinets I've been meaning to reorganize for the past few months.

"Why were you behind the bar in the first place?" I ask her, unable to hide the irritation in my voice.

Finally, I spot the familiar red and white box behind a stack of white dish towels.

"I was trying to help restock."

"But you're a waitress," I say, yanking the box down and turning to find her leaning against the table and holding her hand in a paper towel she must have grabbed at some point. "Not a barback. It's not your job to stock the back of the bar, and things are busy enough tonight that you should have been running drinks or clearing tables. Hell, I'd rather have you helping Marco *wash* the dishes."

She doesn't say anything in response, just holds her injured hand in her other and watches me with an uncomfortable expression, so I let it go for a minute and instead focus on her cut.

It doesn't look particularly deep, even though there's a fair amount of blood pooling in her hand, so I motion for her to join me at the sink. Once she's rinsed it clean, I examine it a little bit closer to confirm it's shallow and won't need stitches, then I clean it with sanitizing wipes and place a piece of gauze over it before wrapping her hand with athletic tape to hold it in place.

"I don't think you'll need stitches," I tell her, "but I'm not a doctor."

"But you're an EMT!"

The sound of Millie's voice has me spinning around to find my daughter standing in the doorway holding a brown paper bag from The Burger Bar in one hand and a small cup that's probably a chocolate shake in the other.

"An EMT isn't a doctor. Besides, I'm not an EMT *anymore*, so I can't give medical advice. And the fact that you're standing here right now means you walked here by yourself. You were supposed to call me."

She shrugs and takes a sip of her shake then walks past me to sit at the table. "I did. You didn't answer."

I blink and dig my phone out of my back pocket, finding a missed call from The Burger Bar.

"Besides, Uncle Rudy knows you're a weirdo about me walking alone, so he stood outside and watched me walk the *two whole blocks* to make sure I didn't get *kidnapped* or *abducted by aliens*."

She says this to me with the kind of exasperation only a child can seem to muster, all while she's digging her burger and fries out of the bag and setting them out on the table for consumption.

"Rudy's your uncle? The guy who owns the burger place?"

My head turns and I look at Ozzy, who I forgot was in the room for a second.

"Not really, but I've known him my whole life, and family isn't just based on blood."

Hearing the enthusiasm behind the way Millie says it has me hiding a smile. I've been telling her that for her entire life, never wanting her to feel like she doesn't have enough family just because her mom isn't around very often. Instead, all the people we love are family.

Uncle Rudy, the elderly owner of The Burger Bar, and his wife, Auntie Marie, are two of Millie's favorite 'family members.'

"I love that," Ozzy says, a sweet smile on her face. "Choosing your family. My family is like that, too."

Millie beams at her, little streaks of ketchup marking the edges of her mouth from where she tried to take too big of a bite into her burger.

"Really?"

Ozzy nods. "Yup."

But just as quickly as Millie delights in finding someone who understands her, the sweet, tender heart she has tugs her expression into something filled with concern.

"So where's your real family?"

Ozzy takes a deep breath, and for the briefest moment, I see something flash across her face that hints at an undeniable pain. Just as quickly, though, the look is gone, and that sweet expression is back on Ozzy's face.

"You don't have to answer that," I tell her before she can say anything. My tone is gruffer than I intend, but I don't like the soft spot that seemed to suddenly arrive out of nowhere. When it comes to Ozzy, no tenderness allowed. "Millie, you have to be careful when you ask people personal questions. Not everyone wants to talk about things like that."

Millie looks at me in surprise, and it makes sense. Rarely does she hear this voice from me, and when she does, it's because she's in trouble. How am I supposed to explain to her that she's *not* in trouble and instead I'm trying not to feel all sappy for one of my employees? Especially Ozzy.

"It's alright," Ozzy says, looking slightly uncomfortable but still speaking to Millie with a calm, gentle voice. "People's lives are complicated, but it's a wonderful thing to care enough to ask."

I blink a few times, feeling something unfamiliar worming its way underneath my rib cage and scraping at the scar tissue that has been there for years.

Clearing my throat, I glance at my watch, realizing we've been back here for far too long during the busiest part of the night.

"I need to get back behind the bar. Ozzy, are you well enough to keep working, or do you need to go home for the night?"

I watch as she flexes her hand a few times, then her blue eyes look up and connect with mine.

"Might be a little sensitive, but I've got a high pain tolerance, so…" She bobs her head. "As long as you don't want me to juggle glasses on the bar, I should be good."

Millie giggles and I blink a few times, Ozzy's joke catching me off guard.

"Okay, then head back out there, please. I'll follow behind you."

Instead of rushing off to follow my directions, she turns and looks at my daughter.

"I'm Ozzy, by the way. You're Millie, right?"

She nods as she chews some of her burger.

"Well, Millie, it was nice to meet you. Did you draw this?"

Her head bobs aggressively and she wipes her mouth with the back of her hand before declaring, "I *love* to draw."

Ozzy laughs, a sweet sound that threads through my chest in an unfamiliar way I don't like.

"Well, so do I. And I just wanted to say…" Her hand reaches across the table and taps on the sketchbook Millie was doodling in before she ran off to pick up her dinner. "This picture of the beach is really, really good."

Millie's smile looks like it could stretch right off the edges of her face as Ozzy stands.

"Keep at it," she says, giving my daughter a wave.

For whatever reason, I can't help but watch her go, my eyes following her as she crosses the room and heads down the hallway.

"She's pretty."

I blank my expression immediately and turn to look at my daughter, unsurprised by her description of Ozzy.

A part of me wants to correct her, though, tell her Ozzy isn't *pretty*, she's…well…the only word that comes to mind is *exquisite*, but I doubt she even knows what that means, so there's no reason to say it.

Hell, I shouldn't even be *thinking* it.

She's not exquisite; she's a nuisance, and she clearly shouldn't be working here if she can't get through a shift without injuring herself.

I ignore the little voice that tells me I'm being entirely unfair and return my attention to Millie, dismissing her comment about Ozzy completely.

Besides, I have something fun to talk to her about.

"I know being stuck back here all evening isn't your favorite, *but* it's going to all pay off in the end. Wanna know why?"

Millie nods then tugs the lid off her shake and begins spooning it into her mouth like a savage.

Good lord.

"Because I'm going to take this week off."

She stops her unladylike slurping and looks at me with a furrowed brow.

"I've been coming in early all week to make sure I'm ahead of everything, and Uncle Jon is going to be the manager during spring break. That way, I'll be able to have lots of fun with you and your mom."

Millie practically shoots out of her chair and launches herself at me, the chocolate smeared around her mouth getting dangerously close to my work shirt when she wraps her arms around my stomach and leans her head back to look at me.

"Are you *serious*, serious?"

I nod, smiling.

"Like, you're not pretending and making a joke?"

Chuckling, I rest a hand on her head. "Why would I pretend about this?"

Her big smile returns and she jumps up and down while she hugs me, squealing in that little kid way I know I won't get to hear too many more times from her.

Every time Toni comes to town, Millie asks why we can't do something all three of us, *as a family*, and every year, Toni asks if I can take time off work to join them on their adventures. Normally, I just don't think about it ahead of time, and it's hard to cover all your shifts when you're the owner. Some things just need to be done by me.

Which is why I planned ahead this year. Cleared my entire schedule. Covered all my shifts. Completed all my inventory and admin early. Taught Jon how to manage the things only I know how to do.

It's all worth it to see this look right here on Millie's face.

And it'll be just as great to see Toni's expression tomorrow.

* * *

"I'm sorry, again, about earlier."

I sigh as I hoist two heavy black trash bags down the hallway toward where Ozzy is holding open the door out to the back.

"You don't need to apologize for cutting yourself, Ozzy," I tell her as I step by, my muscles straining as I lift the bags off the ground and down the couple of steps to the gravel lot.

"No, I know that. I mean for being behind the bar. It felt like there was a lull and I was just trying to be helpful."

I step up to the green dumpster and heave one bag up and over then the other before rounding the back to close the plastic lid.

"Well, maybe don't worry about being helpful and instead focus on doing the very simple job you were hired to do."

My words come out blunt and maybe a bit rude. Part of me regrets the way I just spoke to her, because I can see almost immediately how her face shifts and her eyebrows dip.

We step back inside, the fire door slamming behind us as I make my way down the hallway and to the front so I can turn off the lights.

That's when I realize Ozzy has followed me, and when I stop to look at her, she crosses her arms and glares at me.

"Did I do something to upset you? Or offend you?"

Her question surprises me, and the fact that she keeps talking tells me she can see it on my face as my brows furrow in confusion.

"I've thought about asking a few times, even though I keep trying to convince myself I'm overthinking it, but you seemed to dislike me from almost day one. I mean, I know I had a lot to learn when I started, but I work my ass off trying to make up for where I might have some shortcomings. I feel like you're friendly enough with everyone else, and I don't understand what I did to..."

Her words trail off, and I can tell that brief bout of confidence and bravery has run its course. Even though her head is tilted back, her chin high and her arms crossed, she still looks kind of worried.

Like I might fire her right here and now.

I reach up and rub at the back of my neck, trying to decide what to say in response.

Because…she's right. I *am* a lot more blunt and curt with her than with the rest of my dozen or so employees. And even though she might not be an exceptional waitress, she *does* work her ass off more than pretty much anyone else on my payroll.

The real reason I'm so short with her all the time, something I'd rather not have to admit to Ozzy, or even to myself, is because of what Tessa told me.

"I mean, if you just tell me what I can do," she starts again, but I hold up a hand to silence her, trying to decide the best way to say this without sounding like an asshole.

Though I'm not sure there really *is* a way to do that.

"I think I just feel the need to be a little more…direct and formal with you to…establish boundaries."

Ozzy's head tilts to the side for a second, confusion evident on her face.

"It's important to me that my employees never misunderstand me or assume I'm being more friendly than I should be. As their boss."

Almost like a stone plunking into a still pond and rippling outward, I can see the moment my words make sense to her. She gasps, her hands coming to her mouth and her eyes widening.

"Ohmygod," she whispers to herself, her words barely even loud enough for me to hear.

"Look, I've had plenty of my own crushes at places I've worked over the years, alright?" I take a step closer and lower my voice, trying to make this less uncomfortable—for both of us.

"But as the owner, I have to set the standard, and when Tessa told me about your conversation, I felt like…"

Ozzy's hands come up, her eyes closed in a wince, and I fall silent.

"You don't have to…keep explaining," she tells me, her eyes laser focused on the ground. "I get it."

We both stand there in silence for a long, extremely uncomfortable moment.

"As long as you understand…"

"I do."

Her words come out quick and sharp, and there's a part of me that wishes I'd kept what Tessa told me to myself, wishes I hadn't caused Ozzy this kind of discomfort. At the same time, I don't want to risk things between us getting…misconstrued.

I nod. "Alright. Well, let's get you clocked out and you can take off for the night."

Ozzy grits her teeth and heads over to the register behind the bar, punching a few buttons before spinning around and walking quickly past me and down the hallway to the break room.

Just a few seconds later she's heading out the back door carrying a jacket and a backpack.

"Have a good night," I call after her, though she gives me nothing more than a little wave over her shoulder before the door slams behind her.

I let out a long sigh.

Well, that could almost certainly have gone better.

I flick off the lights in the main bar front and then the kitchen and office before heading down to the break room. My eyes fall on where Millie is passed out on the couch, a book still open in her hands and a light snoring sound falling from her lips.

Why couldn't I have just told Ozzy she'd been misunderstanding me? Why did I have to be so damn…honest about it?

When I bought this place six years ago, I was a bartender who had no problems hooking up with coworkers. Hell, that's how Toni and I first got together. I mean, she wasn't technically staff, but she was a paid performer, setting up in the corner with her mic and guitar to perform on Friday and Saturday nights.

I knew my transition from bartender to owner meant I had to change my boundaries when it came to hooking up, and I made a point to never start something with an employee. Sure, there have been a few employees that have made their interest known over the years. A part-time summer bartender last year comes to mind, but I don't remember giving *her* any attitude—nothing like the intensity with which I speak to Ozzy.

For some reason, though, after Tessa told me about Ozzy's comments when they were doing her training, I knew I needed to put up some sort of wall.

"God, I haven't seen a bona fide *crush* since high school," Tessa told me in my office after Ozzy clocked out from her first shift.

"What are you talking about?"

At my confusion, Tessa launched into a horrible imitation of Ozzy.

"*He has such gorgeous eyes,*" she said first. "And...*damn, he's the kind of man that makes me wish I had time to date.*" She laughed again. "And my favorite...*that ass, though.*"

Tessa isn't mean by nature, so I knew she was only telling me because she thought I would get a kick out of it.

And I did.

Looking back on the way I felt when Tessa told me about the things Ozzy said about me, I have to admit to myself that I *liked* it. I liked how it made me feel, the way it buoyed something in my chest that had felt kind of, I don't know, deflated.

Which is stupid. I get plenty of attention from women.

Getting it from *Ozzy* shouldn't matter.

As I softly wake Millie and help her collect her things so we can head home, and even later as I get Millie settled into bed, my mind stays focused on Ozzy and our conversation.

Why did I need so badly to make sure I set some kind of boundary with her?

As I crawl into my own bed that night, I have a startling thought just before my tired mind fades off into darkness.

Do I need to set boundaries with her because I'm concerned about *her* actions...or *mine*?

SOREN AND OZZY'S LOVE STORY CONTINUES IN

AVAILABLE NOW!

jillian liota

about the author
jillian liota

Jillian Liota is a Southern California native currently living in Suwanee, Georgia. She is married to her best friend, has a three-legged pup with endless energy, and acts as a servant to a very temperamental cat.

Jillian writes contemporary and new adult romance, and has had her writing praised for depth of character, strong female friendships, deliciously steamy scenes, and positive portrayal of mental health.

To connect with Jillian:

Join her **Reader Group**
Sign up for her **Newsletter**
Rate her on **Goodreads**
Visit her on **Facebook**

Check out her **Website**
Send her an **Email**
Stalk her on **Instagram**
Add her on **Amazon**

jillian liota

additional titles
from jillian

For an up-to-date list of titles, visit:
www.jillianliota.com/books

For bonus content, visit:
www.jillianliota.com/bonus